ALONE WITH THE DEAD

Donal is new to working the beat in London, trying his best to forget *that* night. Not many police officers can say they have a convicted murderer for an ex-girlfriend. So when a woman is murdered on his patch, Donal throws himself into the case. As the first person on the scene, he can't forget the horrific sight that faced him. But how do you solve a case with no lead suspect and no evidence? As his past catches up with him, Donal is forced to confront his demons. But what will crack first, the case or Donal?

ALONE WITH THE DEAD

ALONE WITH THE DEAD

by

James Nally

Magna Large Print Books
Long Preston, North Yorkshire,
BD23 4ND, England.

British Library Cataloguing in Publication Data.

A catalogue record of this book is
available from the British Library

ISBN   978-0-7505-4386-6

First published in Great Britain 2015 by Avon,
a division of HarperCollins*Publishers*

Copyright © James Nally 2015

Cover illustration © Stephen Burrows by arrangement with
Alamy Stock Photo

James Nally asserts the moral right to be identified as the author of
this work

Published in Large Print 2017 by arrangement with
HarperCollins Publishers

Magna Large Print is an imprint of Library Magna Books Ltd.

Printed and bound in Great Britain by
T.J. (International) Ltd., Cornwall, PL28 8RW

Acknowledgements

Thanks Ben Mason, literary agent and lover of the long-shot who took an enormous punt on me. Without you Ben, there'd be no book. I'm truly blessed by your wisdom and patience.

Thanks Katy Loftus, former Avon editor, for seeing something in this and painstakingly coaxing it out with your unique combo of guile and chutzpah.

Thanks to the immensely talented and supportive team at Avon: Senior Commissioning Editor, Helen Huthwaite, Editor Kate Ellis and Digital Executive Parastou Khiaban. Jem Carter: you didn't so much design the cover as bottle the essence of the book. Wow. Thanks Ed Wilson and Anna Power from Johnson and Alcock for taking it forward with such verve and passion and to the ingenious team from LightBrigade PR.

On a more personal note: -

Thanks Pat Hogan, Ireland's finest English teacher, for giving me the itch to scribble. I hope you've aged disgracefully into that pipe!

Thanks to the class of Harlesden '91: Davey Hayes, the Bracken brothers Donal, Seamus and Frankie, Barty Kennedy, Tom Larkin, David Burke. We made it, somehow.

Thanks Margaret Grennan for giving me that all-important first break into reporting. Thanks Frank Roche from Moate for mentoring me through those early years, and always being there. Thanks National News Press Agency in London – especially former editors Richard Leifer, Mike Doran and Mike McCarthy – for recognising that, somehow, crime reporting suited me.

Thanks Fleet Street legends Ian Gallagher, Dennis Rice, Ian Sparks, Oonagh Blackman for the memories or, at least, the bits I can remember.

My crime contacts and experience soon led me into a far murkier world – that of TV production. Thanks to my comrades in documentary: Paul Crompton, Jeremy Hall, Kathryn Johnson, Emma Shaw, Dan Reeves, Jo Cantello, Andy Wells, David G Hill, Peter Roemmele, Laura Jones, Andy Mason, Max Williams, Hugh Williams, Alastair Cook and Paul Williams.

Thanks to my friends in Brighton for their tireless encouragement: Alun and Hayley Price, Dom Peers and Zoe Fawcett, Rob and Linda Laurens, Gavin and Vicky Shepherd, Charlie and Karen Harrison.

Thanks to my in-laws, the incomparable Mc-

Graths; racing legend Jim 'the Croc', Anita, Rebecca, Mike, Brian. To the Viels, Philippe and Raphael, Laura Giles and Meagan Jamieson.

Special thanks to my family: parents Jim and Bunny, sisters Helen, Jacqui and Claire; brother-in-law Greg Woods, nephews Lee Ryan, Joe Woods and Lucas Nally and niece Amelie Woods.

Thanks Alison Clements for the friendship. Thanks to my son James Nally the fifth for all the brilliant ideas when I've been stuck. Thanks to my new daughter Emma Nally for waiting to pop out literally eight hours after I completed the manuscript.

Thanks Bridget Kathleen McGrath for always believing in this book and encouraging me to chase my dream. That to me represents true love.

For Bridget, James and Emma

Who looks outside, dreams;
Who looks inside, awakes.

CARL JUNG

Prologue

Occasionally, we experience things that make no sense.

You hum an old song, only to hear it moments later on the radio. You think of someone out of the blue and they call. You get the feeling you're being watched, turn and meet the stare you'd somehow felt.

Sometimes, it's life changing. A driver swerves to avoid a pedestrian. He doesn't remember reacting. A firefighter pulls his team out of a burning building. Seconds later, it collapses. Two strangers' eyes meet over a crowded room. Somehow, right away, both know the other is THE ONE.

Some credit these experiences to extra-sensory perception – our so-called sixth sense. Others put it down to gut instinct, animal intuition. The point is, we know things but we don't know *why* we know them.

I don't know *why* the recent dead come to me, or if the things they show me are clues as to how they died. I don't know *why* it happens, but it must be the reason I became a murder detective. That – and what happened to Eve.

It's my unconscious mind, of course, piecing together fragments of information and presenting answers to me in a novel way. Isn't it?

'I See Dead People,' says the creepy little boy in *The Sixth Sense*. Cole Sear he's called. Cole

Queer, my brother calls me. That and 'Hormonal Donal'.

I don't care. I've got more important things to worry about, now I'm the go-to guy for the recently murdered.

Chapter 1

Clapham Junction, London
Monday, July 1, 1991; 21:14

'It's a bit like taking a shit, when you think about it,' said Clive, his mouth grinding away on a Wimpy quarter pounder.

Flanked by over-lit pastel walls and screwed-down metal seats, we could have been in the canteen of a children's correctional centre. Welcome to the Wimpy burger bar – the British McDonald's but with a unique selling point: table service.

'Thank you garçon,' I said, as I watched my order slide from stained tray to half-wiped melamine.

'Bon appetit,' he grunted and I silently congratulated acne for turning his face to pizza.

A quick glance at my chicken burger revealed it to be simply that: no sauce, no salad – just cartoon-flattened white meat clamped between two constipating white buns.

'Hard to imagine that pecking in the yard,' I said, 'landing on this table is probably the furthest it ever flew.'

'Isn't it though, Donal?' said PC Clive Hunt, my forty-something beat partner who came from one of those Northern English towns that begins with either B or W and all sound alike.

Incredibly – at least to me – we'd walked past a McDonald's to get here. Clive's nostalgic bond to Wimpy once again had proved unshakeable. This was one of the countless things I failed to understand about the English – they get nostalgic about things that were crap in their time: TV shows with shaky sets like *Dr Who* and *Crossroads;* British-made cars that always broke down; the Second World War, for Christ's sake.

McDonald's might have been wiping Wimpy off the face of the earth, but it would never get Clive's custom. You see, no one lamented London's lack of chips-based meals more than Clive. How many times had I heard how, up North, you can get gravy with your chips, curry with your chips, mushy peas with your chips.

The moment a McDonald's worker cheerfully informed Clive that they didn't stock vinegar, his Golden Arches crumbled and fell. After several wordless seconds, he calmly placed his tray back on the counter, turned and marched out, never to return.

I relented. 'What's like taking a shit?'

'Eating burger and chips,' he said, chewing, his mouth a toothy cement mixer.

Clive swallowed hard, burped urgently into his hand, desperate to enlighten: 'You eat some chips, then you eat *all* of the burger, then you finish off yer chips.'

He could see I wasn't getting it.

19

'It's like you piss a bit, then you take your dump, then you piss again to finish.' He beamed in satisfaction.

My radio scrambled, its frenzied fuzz cutting short Clive's scatological musings.

It was a T call demanding immediate response to an accident on Sangora Road, just round the corner. I almost had to beat the burger out of Clive's hand.

We were the first uniforms on the scene. A young woman with dark curly hair was going bonkers in the street. A crowd had gathered, some panicking, some nosy, some trying to comfort Ms Hysteria. When she saw us, she pointed at a house and gasped in a nasal South East London accent: 'My friend Marion's inside. I think she's dead.'

A surge of adrenaline slowed the world down to a hi-definition dream. The front door to number 21 hung open, but there were no signs of a forced entry. I noticed two buzzers: the property had been divided into flats. Inside the communal hallway, a chiselled, red-haired man in his twenties looked ashen. 'I don't know what happened,' he said in a remarkably high-pitched Irish accent, pointing to a door.

'I don't know what happened,' he squeaked again.

'Well you'll know soon enough,' mumbled Clive.

The door was on the latch. I pulled it open. The door fought back, forcing me to use both hands. I planted an elbow against its over-sprung resistance so Clive could follow me in.

'Try not to touch anything,' hissed Clive, and I

thought about letting the door slam into his thick head.

I floated up the stairs towards the first floor flat, adrenaline numbing my feet to the carpet beneath.

She lay on the landing, on her side, an untamed red mane of hair sprawled almost ceremonially across the carpet. Her moon-white face lay awkwardly on her outstretched arm; her bloodshot blue eyes staring into nothingness. She looked no more than twenty-five, probably younger.

Her sad mouth had cried blood. One trail made it all the way down to her slender white throat. Her flowery summer dress was laddered with stab wounds – still fresh. My head swooned. I leaned back against the wall of the landing, exhaled hard.

Clive bent down and placed a reluctant finger to her porcelain neck.

'She put up a hell of a fight,' he said flatly, 'but she's dead.'

He backed away apologetically. My eyes fastened upon her limp hand, focusing upon the nail hanging from her little finger which had almost been completely ripped off. Sadness flooded me. My stinging eyes blinked and shifted to the floor next to her: a set of keys, a handbag, her jacket, some post.

'She must have let her killer in,' I squeaked, sounding every bit as shocked as I felt.

'Looks like it,' said Clive, reassuringly unmoved.

'Right,' he added brightly, 'best get back downstairs. We don't want to contaminate the crime scene.'

A cold breath chilled the right side of my face.

21

I turned to see a small window on the landing, slightly open. 'Fuck,' I said. All this time, I'd been standing between her newly dead body and an open window. Where I came from, this spelt doom. I shivered, then snapped myself out of it. There was work to be done.

I'd never understood officers who said that, in really stressful situations, 'your training kicks in'. I did now. Clive started questioning Chiselled Ginge and taking notes. His name was Peter Ryan. He was twenty-eight. The dead woman was his wife of thirteen months, Marion, aged twenty-three. She usually got home before six. He and Karen – a colleague from work – got back just after nine and found her like that on the landing. Police officers and forensics were wandering in, so I went outside to find Karen.

In the darkening, humming summer night, Sangora Road flashed blue and red, a grotesque carnival of morbid curiosity. Neighbours who'd never shared a word before chatted intently: lots of 'apparently' and 'oh my God'. The petite, curly-haired brunette I assumed to be Karen was being comforted by a group of middle-aged men. One edgy-looking sleaze ball in a wife-beater vest and school-shooter combats rubbed her upper arm vigorously. He looked like a man who spent his life hunting down any kind of a leg-over whatsoever.

'Karen?' I asked. She looked up sharply, surprised by the sound of her own name. 'PC Donal Lynch. Sorry, but I'm going to have to ask you a few questions.' Her arm rubber – a Poster Boy for Families Need Fathers – glared at me, ready to back up his potential new squeeze against the filth.

Karen took a long deep breath and nodded. Instead of structured questions, I let her ramble. In a quivering, childlike, barely audible voice, she told me the following: her name was Karen Foster, twenty-five, from Lee in South East London, a colleague of Pete's at the Pines old people's home in Lambeth. She told me Pete was the gardener there. She'd given him a lift back to his flat tonight to pick up some heavy pots to take back to the home, where she lived in staff accommodation. They'd got here just after nine. He had unlocked the front door, then the door to their flat and went in first. Pete had stopped suddenly on the stairs and screamed, 'Marion, Marion!' He went to her. Karen had followed and saw Marion lying there. She checked for signs of life.

She shivered. Arm Rubber gave me a look that said: 'C'mon mate, I think she's had enough', but I hadn't. I may have been new to murder, but I understood the value of first-hand, untainted, lawyer-free testimony.

'Go on,' I demanded.

'I got her blood on my hands, so I washed them. Then I had to get out of there.'

A shiver rattled her entire frame.

'Did Pete definitely unlock both doors?' I asked. She nodded and bowed her head. Her centre parting wobbled and so did I.

'Look, Karen, I'm sorry, I have to ask ... we need to find whoever did this.'

She sniffed hard at the pavement, and I lamented yet another failure to channel my inner bad cop. I fought the urge to place a comforting hand on her quivering shoulder and walked away.

I joined Clive inside the front door just as three hotshot detectives swaggered in. The senior of the trio wore the hangdog expression of a man put out by life. 'Detective Superintendent Glenn,' he barked. Clive unloaded the basic detail while DS Glenn nodded impatiently. As I took up the slack, he fixed me with a scowl. Clearly, I was way too excited for his deadpan taste.

They made what seemed to me a cursory inspection of the crime scene: skirting around it as you might a dead bird on the pavement, or a splatter of puke. Then DS Glenn stomped off outside.

'Is that it?' I asked Clive.

'It's not *Magnum P.I.,*' he laughed, 'they'll wait for forensics and statements, then they'll decide what lines of enquiry to take.'

One of Hangdog Glenn's bitches stopped by on his way out to treat us to a condescending glare: 'What time do you go off duty, lads?'

'We finished almost an hour ago at nine,' said Clive, all chipper, just so he'd know we didn't mind the inconvenience one bit.

'Okay, call Clapham. Get them to send an officer to guard the door overnight and an unmarked car to take the husband and woman in to make a statement.'

'Right now?' I asked.

'Of course right now,' he spat, 'and we'll need statements from you two before you start your shifts tomorrow.' He scuttled off down the garden steps, his gumshoe mac flapping in the summer breeze. At the gate, he turned. 'Make sure you get the front door keys off the husband,' he shouted, not realising that said husband was stood right there.

As Peter fished around for his keys, Clive and I descended the steps towards him. A sickening dread tugged at my guts.

What could I possibly say to him now? I thought back to all those funerals in Ireland, how we always spouted the same stock phrases to mourners. 'Doesn't he look peaceful?' was a classic. I mean what did we expect? Signs of a struggle? Fingernail scratch marks down the side of the coffin?

Then I remembered the one cover-all stock phrase, used by everyone when coming face-to-face with the principal mourners: 'I'm sorry for your trouble.' That line always seemed so anodyne, so emotionally detached, so generic. My brother Fintan and I used to dream up equivalents. 'Oh dear,' was his favourite. I liked: 'Sure, it could be worse.'

Clive took Peter's keys and spoke first. 'Who else has a set?'

'Just me and ... Marion,' said Peter, his voice cracking at the mention of her name.

'We're fetching a car for you and your colleague. I'm afraid we need statements from both of you tonight.'

Peter just stared into space.

'Where can you go after the police station?' asked Clive. 'Have you got family near here?'

Peter shook his pale face mournfully. 'The only place I can go is to Marion's mum and dad up in Enfield.'

Clive and I exchanged frowns.

'Do you think that's wise, son?' asked Clive.

25

Peter looked at him blankly.

'Okay,' said Clive, 'first I've got to get officers round there to tell them the news.'

'Oh Jesus,' Peter gasped and we all baulked. Every parent's worst nightmare: the death knock. Peter walked slowly away from us but I could hear every word. 'Oh Jesus, Jesus,' he muttered, over and over.

A sudden deafening bellow made us jump. Peter's wails were primeval, from the very core of his being. My mind flashed back to the time the Dalys' prize-winning cow died howling in their shed. I'm sure their mother said she'd developed gangrenous teats. I couldn't drink milk for a month after.

I turned to Clive: 'If he did it, he surely wouldn't go and stay with her family.'

'He's either innocent or one hell of an actor,' said Clive, 'I mean look at him, he's shivering like a shitting dog.'

'Maybe he's racked with guilt. She must have known her killer. She let him in.'

'And it must have been a man,' said Clive, 'I mean, just from the point of view of strength. It's always the man, isn't it?'

'They were only married thirteen months,' I said, 'I just don't see it.'

'Neither did she,' deadpanned Clive, chuckling as he set off across the road. I wondered if that's what happened to all cops, in the end.

I couldn't just leave Peter like that, bent double, bawling at the pavement. I walked over and put a hand on his heaving shoulders. He calmed almost instantly. I couldn't think of a thing to say, so I said: 'I'm sorry for your trouble.'

He breathed in deeply.

'Thank you, Officer,' he blurted, and I could tell he meant it, before the spasms of grief swept him away once more.

As the car taking Peter and Karen to Clapham police station moved off, a flash of streetlight illuminated the interior. Freeze-framed in the back seat, Peter's ghostly white face stared straight ahead, as if into an abyss. How I longed for a glimpse inside that mind. On the far side of him, two large teary eyes gazed into his. Then, for a nanosecond, the eyes of Karen Foster locked onto mine, glinting wounded confusion.

The murder scene buzz snapped off like a light. A sense of helplessness gnawed away at my red-raw nerves.

'Go home, son, you look shattered,' said Clive, and I lacked the will to argue.

It was less than a mile to the flat I shared with Aidan, an old friend from back home.

Aidan was a psychiatric nurse at the Maudsley hospital, and on 'earlies' that week. But I guessed he'd still be up, chain-smoking his Marlboro Reds, noodling on his guitar, crafting a ballad to the latest random woman he'd fallen in love with at the bus stop or in some supermarket queue, the soft eejit.

Like so many gifted musicians I'd known, Aidan existed in a perpetual emotional state of either unrequited love or rejection. It was as if he'd absorbed the lyrics of all the epic love songs he'd ever learned so that they became his doomed emotional landscape. Any girl he got off with instantly became 'the one' – cue a week of Van Morrison (early era), Stone Roses, The Sugarcubes. Then his intensity would scare her off, making her 'the one who got away' – cue a week of Van Morrison (late era), Nick Cave and Tom Waits in his locked smoky bedroom. If music be the food of love, Aidan ate only sweet 'n sour.

His self-inflicted lovelorn existence, coupled with the fact he didn't drink or take an interest in sport, outcast Aidan from the rest of our circle. But his tendency to get depressed worried me, so I'd always kept in touch. When the cash-in-hand, hard-drinking madness of the North London Irish scene became too much, I 'retired' to South London and Aidan's calm exile. 'Be good training for when you move in with a woman,' the lads joked.

Aidan's emotional pogo would be too much for me tonight. I elected to walk home, nice and steady, so he'd be asleep by the time I got there.

The lightest of rain filled the air, cool and gentle, as if a weary cloud had sunk upon the road. 'Soft rain, thank God,' the old boys back home would say. The streets went slick. Car wheels sizzled like frying pans. The night buses groaned and closing time laughs rang hollow.

A lonely phone box cast piss-green light upon the wet pavement. I stared through the scratched glass at the grubby phone inside. I wanted to call her right now, badly. But how could I, at this time of night, after two long years?

I walked on, unable to fathom why seeing Marion's body had affected me so much. God knows, like any young Irish adult, I'd seen more dead bodies than Ted Bundy's chest freezer. It's nothing sinister – at least not to us. It comes down to one stubbornly lingering Irish tradition: the Wake.

I remembered comedian Dave Allen's line: In Ireland, death is a way of life. Whenever someone dies, we lay them out in their coffin and look at them for a few days. Tradition demands that the body is accompanied at all times until its 'removal' to the church. Cue an endless stream of relatives and neighbours through the house, a reservoir of tea, a landfill of sandwiches. From the age of seven or eight, every time a relative croaked it – and my extended clan was massive – you were hauled along to the Wake to say goodbye to someone you didn't know who was already dead.

Before the corpse is displayed to all and sundry – usually in a bedroom or the sitting room of their home – some poor soul has to wrestle them into their Sunday best, wrench their eyes and mouth shut, apply make-up, and discreetly stuff cotton wool up their nostrils so that they don't cave in. You never seemed to meet an embalmer socially.

In some homes, clocks are stopped at the time of death and all mirrors turned to the wall. Once the coffin is hauled into its display position, the family opens the window, to allow the deceased person's spirit to leave. After two hours, they close the window, to ensure that the spirit doesn't return. If you stand between the window and the body during this time, then God help you.

I shuddered at the memory of that open landing window tonight. Did Marion's spirit pass through me?

I scolded myself for entertaining such superstitious nonsense. My thoughts turned instead to Marion. I knew that every square inch of her body would be poked and prodded, then photographed, scraped, swabbed or cut open. Body fluids, fingernail dirt and pubic hair would be sealed in plastic or glass and then passed, hand to hand, along the evidential chain; from pathologist to the laboratory, to the prosecution, to the court and to the jury. When you become the central piece of evidence in your own murder, there's no dignity. Poor Marion – probably worrying about what to make for tea when she got to her front door. I tried to block out how she must have felt the moment she saw the knife. How could someone she knew do this to her?

Then I thought about Eve. Another blazing redhead ambushed by evil.

I rubbed my eyes. The soft rain had made my face all wet.

Eve Daly was more Irish-looking than any woman has a right to be: mischievous green eyes; a pale, sculpted face with just enough freckles; wild hair as red as the flesh of a blood orange. Sexy, curvy, five foot five in heels, her nose crinkled when she laughed, she smelled of pine needles and, when she came, her lips felt as cold and soft as fresh snow. And she was mine.

Eve's daddy, Philandering Frank, had fled to London with his secretary three years earlier in a scandal that had seemed to delight everyone except his family.

Before his midnight flit, Frank had painstakingly stashed his fortune into a myriad of untraceable off-shore accounts, leaving the family penniless and saddled with a sprawling, heavily mortgaged bungalow. In an effort to save their home – and face – Eve's mum, Mad Mo, and her two older brothers moved to New York. Once her clan had split, Eve felt like she was in Ireland on borrowed time, which is exactly how I felt. She was going to New York; I was bound for London – neither of us really belonged anymore. And so we became an island. Our romance flourished on a shared musical snobbery and a mutual disdain for pretty much everything and everyone around us.

On Saturday nights, we cemented our superiority at Rocky's in Tullamore – 'the Midlands' hottest nightspot' – where we perfected our disaffection and snorted with laughter and contempt at the music, the dancing and the fashion.

The girls sat on one side of the empty dance floor, dressed to repel adverse weather and stray hands. The DJ never warned them of 'a slow set' in case they scattered to the toilets. We'd watch in horrified fascination as local men walked the line in vain, seemingly immune to serial rejection.

On the other side of the dance floor, we identified two clear tribes of men: the Posers and the Poodles. The motto of the Posers seemed to be: if a piece of clothing rolls, then roll it. They wore *Miami Vice*-style pastel suit jackets (sleeves rolled up to the elbow), pink or blue t-shirts (arm sleeves rolled up to the pit), pegged jeans (scrunched up at the bottom, then rolled up: always twice), slip-on shoes (Oxblood moccasins with the natty little tassels), no socks (inexplicably spurning two glorious rolling opportunities)

31

and mullet hair-dos.

On the other end of the scale: the heavy rocker types known as the 'hard chaws' who rode Honda 50s, head-banged (even during slow sets) and preferred to end the evening with a brawl. The Chaws had wholeheartedly embraced American Poodle Rock, which involved wearing your hair big and your denim bleached. The jeans were so tight they required zips in the lower leg to get on, or off, while the denim jackets were oversized, with obligatory rolled-up sleeves and US band badges on the back: Van Halen, Bon Jovi, Guns N' Roses.

At the end of the night, we'd dare each other to order curry chips from Mrs Maguire's rancid van: baulking at the peeled spuds in the rusty sink, her crusted black fingernails and the ringworm on her grease-creased forehead. But at two, a.m., nothing in the world tasted better and, as exhaustive research had taught me, no one ever hits you when you're holding a punnet of chips.

We'd walk back to hers, singing 'Stand By Me' and 'I Just Died in Your Arms Tonight' while checking out the big sky for shooting stars. I didn't know if I loved Eve, or if she loved me. But I loved life with her in it.

Before it all went so horribly wrong.

I got home just after eleven p.m, registered Aidan's closed bedroom door with a silent fist pump and uncorked a bottle of red.

I flopped onto the couch without even switching on a lamp. My mood deserved the streetlight's soothing amber gloom. I knew I'd have to ration my Shiraz and my irrational emotions for

32

a longer stretch than usual tonight.

The worst part about insomnia is all the empty time you have to fill. I'm awake four or five hours longer than you each day – up to thirty-five hours every week: that's twenty-three soccer matches, twelve *The Godfathers,* an entire French working week. Each year, I've got seventy-six extra days to kill when hardly anyone else is awake and nothing is open. These stats alone prove that I've far too much time on my hands.

When an inability to 'drop off' first struck me three years ago, I was scorching through three books a week. I read everything I could lay my hands on about sleep, dreams, insomnia. All I learned was how little we know about any of it: the scientific world has yet to even figure out why we dream.

Just because you can't sleep doesn't mean you don't *need* sleep and little by little my ability to concentrate ebbed away, leaving me with just the one trusty sedative. Someone clever once said: 'Time, Motion and Wine Cause Sleep.' I could rely only on the latter. I opted for Shiraz – that charred fruit flavour making it the hardest to drink fast – and I tried to limit my intake to two bottles a night. That might sound excessive but, spread normally over eight hours – eight p.m. until four a.m. – it's less than a glass an hour. Trust me, it felt moderate. More often than not, I dropped off somewhere between three and four a.m., congratulating myself on the quarter of a bottle left.

Some nights, regardless of grape intake, I knew sleep wouldn't take me. This would be one of those nights.

'Well, Van Winkle, how are they hanging?' Aidan's voice startled me.

'Before you display the deep personal concern typical of you,' he added, sitting beside me on the couch, 'you didn't wake me up. I just can't seem to nod off tonight. It must be catching.'

After a while, he spoke again. 'Why don't you watch telly? That'd help pass the time.'

'Have you seen late-night TV? Their target audience must be Travis Bickle. You have to like your rock soft and your porn hard.'

'And your university open. Speaking of which, what happened to that home course you were doing?'

'I'm still dipping in and out of it,' I lied, 'struggling a bit to concentrate at the moment.'

'Criminology eh? But you just can't do the time.'

'Ha, yeah. Very good.'

'Of course you could try history, but there's no future in it.' He did one of those comedy drum flourishes while racking his brain for more.

'Theology's another option, but I suspect you lack the belief.'

'We got called to a house tonight.'

'I'd recommend French but, to be frank, I'd say you lack that certain – oh how can I say it – *je ne sais quoi?*'

'A girl stabbed to death, twenty-three.'

'Oh Christ,' said Aidan.

'Nothing taken, so it must have been domestic, her husband, or a spurned ex. God knows.'

'Or maybe a random nutter. Some of the loons on my ward are capable of anything.'

'She let whoever it was in. She knew him.'

34

'Jesus. And he stabbed her?'

'Loads of times, multiple wounds. It looked frenzied.'

'He must have been in a rage. Why would someone who knew her be so ... angry?'

I shrugged.

Aidan was obviously bursting to know more, but had the good grace to park it for now.

'I'll leave you to it so,' he said, skulking back to his room.

The wine slipped down like water. Halfway through the second bottle, I panicked that I'd run out early. I was pondering a trip to the all-night off-licence in Clapham Junction when a slither of cold air wormed its way around my neck, causing me to shudder.

Unease twanged at my gut. I squinted hard into the other side of the room, beyond the amber gloom, and sensed someone there. I shuffled in my seat: 'Aid?'

The air crackled with intent.

'Who's there?' I called out.

I squinted harder, then stiffened. A figure stood just inside the sitting room door, head bowed.

'Aidan?' I shouted, my heart revving like a getaway car.

Somehow, soundlessly, this fucker had got into the flat. Now he just stood there, still but poised. He'd come to hurt me. I knew it.

'What the fuck...' I said, trying to rouse myself. But I couldn't move a muscle. My body had frozen to ice, but my heart thrashed inside my chest like a trapped bird.

Head still bowed, the figure started inching towards me. I sat there paralysed, powerless, as he got closer and closer; steady, unflinching, fearless. He grew bigger, until his black frame filled my vision. I realised that it had to be him. After all these years, Meehan had found me. Now he was going to finish the job.

Inches from my face, he raised his head. Fuck, no. I recognised those staring bloodshot blue eyes, that bleeding mouth. Marion Ryan glared at me with murderous rage.

Unblinking, deranged, Marion pushed her grotesquely distorted, milk-white face into mine. I screamed, but nothing came out. She smiled a malevolent smile that said: 'You're mine now.'

A loud bang made me jump. Suddenly she stood by the door, violently slamming it shut, over and over. Boom. Boom. Boom. I put my hands over my ringing ears and screamed.

In a flash, everything turned yellow. My squinting eyes finally made out Aidan's horrified face in the house lights. 'What the fuck?' he cried, surveying me in undisguised disgust. I could smell and feel warm puke on my chest.

'It's wine, just red wine,' I gasped.

'Jesus, I thought you'd been stabbed or something. What the fuck was all that about?'

I turned to the flat door: it was closed.

'Just a nightmare.'

'Jesus,' he said again, and headed to the kitchen. I heard water pouring out of the tap. I took the glass of water and tea towel from him and wiped my mouth. I realised how grotesque I must have looked and smiled. It was the sheer relief of being alive.

'It's no fucking laughing matter,' he snapped, 'you've got to see someone about this shit. Oh Christ, the smell, get that shirt off, for fuck's sake.'

As I unbuttoned I tried to convince myself that it really had been a nightmare. But I felt sure I'd been awake the whole time. Sitting here on the couch, everything around Marion in that street-light orange glow – the lamp, the posters, the table, my jacket on the back of the chair. It had been *real*.

Aidan returned to the kitchen door, where he stood in judgement for fully three minutes.

'You have to see someone, Donal. Not sleeping is one thing, but this...'

'It was Marion, the girl from tonight.'

'What?'

'She appeared to me. I thought she was going to kill me. She seemed so angry. Did you hear the door slamming?'

'All I heard was you howling at the fucking moon.'

'I thought it was Meehan.'

'What?'

'I thought it was Tony Meehan, coming to finish me off.'

'You're raving now, Donal. Jesus. That guy's long gone.'

'I've been expecting him for three fucking years. Every night.'

'What are you talking about? Why would he be wanting to finish you off?'

'It's why I can't sleep.'

Aidan couldn't have looked more bewildered.

'Something weird happened that night, Aidan. Honestly, I don't think I'll ever get over it. I've never told anyone. You'll think I'm insane.'

'What with some of the people I deal with? I doubt it,' Aidan laughed, but kindly. 'Try me.'

Chapter 2

**The Irish Midlands
Thursday, August 18, 1988**

I last clapped eyes on Tony Meehan three years ago at Tullamore General Hospital in rural Ireland.

He'd put me there.

We, the class of '88, had completed the Leaving Cert exams. It was late summer and tomorrow I'd be flying to London, with Eve. Before the exams, I'd asked her to change her plans and come to England with me. After a few days, she had agreed. She told me that her dad, Frank, would put down a deposit on a flat for her in Camden, where we could both live. She'd work for his construction company and, hopefully, so would I. She was waiting for the right time to tell her mum, Mad Mo.

I would have jumped on the next flight out after the exams. But for Eve, this felt too sudden; too final.

'We have the rest of our lives to work and pay bills,' she reasoned, 'let's spend one last carefree summer at home, with our friends.' *One last care-free summer.* How that statement haunts me still.

I had conceded to her demands, as usual, but on the condition that we draw a line at the Leaving Cert results.

And now, finally, we were nearly there. There was just one last hurdle before our flight tomorrow. Never one to knowingly shun a pun, Eve had arranged 'The Eve of Results Fancy Dress Party', to be hosted at her sprawling family bungalow.

Eve loved fancy dress as much as I loathed it. Whoever said that sarcasm is the lowest form of wit hadn't seen people over the age of ten dressed up as Disney characters, pop stars or zombies.

This party's theme: heroes. I could hear myself now: *'Hang on a minute, you're a woman dressed as a male singer. You're blowing my mind. Tell me you don't have a lightning bolt on the other side of your face? Oh you do! Holy shit, you're David Bowie – and you're mad and funny and not remotely tragic.'*

I appealed to Eve: 'Don't you trust us to get drunk and have fun in normal clothes?'

She was having none of it: 'Would you not just dress up and have a laugh? What's wrong with you?'

'I'm just saying it's a big occasion. We don't need props.'

Her response stunned me: 'Jesus, Donal, for once in your life can you stop being so ... aloof? You think you're so above it all, don't you? Just put in some effort and have some fun and don't be so fucking up yourself.'

She gave the door a Force 10 slam that caused the lights to flicker.

Charitably, I put it down to insecurity. Fancy dress would *force* people to have fun, thereby *guaranteeing* a night to remember. And saying a final farewell to lifelong friends would surely be less upsetting when we were all dressed up like eejits.

The day came and, after thirty seconds of deliberation, I opted for Hunter S. Thompson. For one thing, the Doc is easy: all you need are shades, a pork pie hat and a Hawaiian shirt. Like most men, I'd been storing a Hawaiian shirt in my closet for years, unable to offer a single good reason why until that very moment. Mum dug out the rest, somehow even exhuming a plastic cigarette holder.

Hunter got the nod, for another reason. It was thanks to the Doc that I first struck up a conversation with Eve Daly.

Having lusted after her for two years, I'd all but given up hope of ever uttering a single word to Eve Daly. Then, in the school library one day, I heard her faux-Dublin accent say: 'A bit of cult reading then?'

I turned to see her nodding towards the book, already slippery in my quivering hand.

I'd only read about twenty pages of *Fear and Loathing in Las Vegas* because it scared me and I hated it. But I wasn't about to tell her that. So I just stood there, reddening, while failing to think of a single thing to say, until I wanted to die of awkwardness.

'You must be Fintan's little brother,' she purred, eyeing me playfully, as a cat might a wounded mouse.

My face was toast now but, somehow, I managed to nod nonchalantly.

'Yeah, not so little actually.'

For months after, she never missed an opportunity to mock me mercilessly over that line. It became our secret catch-phrase. I hoped that my homage to Hunter tonight would propel her back to those giddy early days of illicit cider and snogging; the first sweet breaths of our awakening love. In fact, I was counting on it: things had grown strained between us lately. Waiting didn't agree with me.

Before I set off, Mum felt compelled to issue those classic Irish maternal warnings.

'Don't drink too much now,' was self-explanatory. 'No messing,' she said, which meant no fighting. 'And no carrying on,' she added, which meant no shagging.

She cupped my chin: 'Think once, think twice, then think M-A-M-M-Y.'

I nodded and smiled. I couldn't believe I was hearing this for the last time.

'Be good now, and be careful,' she concluded.

'Oh I'll be good, Mammy,' I quipped, setting off on the bike, 'it's up to her to be careful.'

Where the bungalows ceased between Clara and Tullamore, a blood-red sun sank behind the cooling fields, turning sleepy cows into steaming silhouettes. Chirpy birds made their racket on the crooked black power lines, distant African heat urging them onwards. I felt strangely gloomy, unsettled.

Discontented air nibbled at my skin; that damp heavy Midlands air that slides inside your clothes and your bed sheets and chills your bones. I

41

squinted at the winking downtown lights in the distance, trying to picture where Eve's bungalow sat in the Tullamore ground mist. But the drifting white steam kept deceiving me.

As I dumped the bike behind the tree in her front garden, I assumed she was still waiting for the right opportunity to break the news to her mum. This, surely, could be the only remaining obstacle to our new life together.

Eve answered her front door, a knockout in a Viking helmet, tiny animal-skin mini dress, fishnets, a leather hip holster sporting a shiny little prop dagger and a whale bone on a string around her neck.

'We can't stop here, this is bat country,' I said, in my best American accent.

The Viking heroine looked me up and down, her face crumpling in disdain.

'You know who I am, right?' I pleaded.

'James Joyce?' she ventured, her top lip curled in disgust.

'James Joyce? What, on a Caribbean cruise?'

She looked set to burst into tears.

'Hunter S. Thompson,' I announced, OD'ing on indignation.

'Jesus, Donal, you could've made a bit more effort,' she said, shaking her head, then stomping back into the house.

I hauled myself through the front door, wincing at the Dire Straits track booming out of the sitting room to my right. Someone must have commandeered the hi-fi. 'Twisting by the Pool'? Twisting by the fucking neck would be preferable. I couldn't resist a smirk of superiority, watching

42

these musically illiterate morons bouncing around the room to this shite. I walked on into the hallway, soothingly dark save for some randomly-draped strings of white fairy lights, giving it a grotto vibe.

'Good,' I thought; easier to hide.

The dressing down I'd just received for not dressing up had stripped me of party spirit.

But guilt soon burrowed its way to my frazzled nerve endings: Eve was right, I should have made more of an effort. I thought about going to find her, to say sorry. But, recently, her hair-trigger outbursts were taking longer to pass. I decided to beg for forgiveness later, when the party would be jumping and she'd be less stressed.

I headed to the refuge of the kitchen at the back of the house. To my horror, it was packed too, everyone yelling at the same time. The smug Unibound crowd were enjoying one last gleeful blast of 'points', 'grades', 'retakes', and 'grants' before tomorrow's life-defining results. A bottle of gin grinned at me from the top of the fridge. I snaffled it all for myself and headed to the little utility room, tucked away next to the back door. I kept the light off and poured a kamikaze measure. 'Make it better, Beefeater,' I demanded, downing it in one.

Sometime later, with Beefy half-empty and me half-cut, a pair of disconnected white eyes suddenly sprang through the doorway. I recoiled. My eyes adjusted to take in a trilby, a checked dickie-bow and pristine white gloves. My brain finally made sense of it: Choker, the mad bastard, being so politically incorrect that it surely constituted a hate crime.

Tony 'Choker' Meehan, blacked up as a minstrel. Or was it Al Jolson? Either way, he'd somehow transcended gloriously offensive. As he wallowed in near-the-knuckle notoriety, I pulled a mug off the shelf and poured him a large one. Better to appease him, a fact I knew only too well...

Choker had been brought up by the Jesuit Brothers in the town's orphanage – as it was still called. Legend has it that, aged four, he saw his dad murder his mum with his bare hands. That'd certainly explain his penchant for strangulation. In primary school, he used to sneak up behind kids and wordlessly throttle them. Some of his victims actually passed out. He even got hold of a pair of black leather gloves, which he touchingly christened his 'stranglers' – a development that spread mild alarm through the entire town.

Unchecked, his levels of violence spiralled. A few months ago, he jumped off a stage at the local community hall disco and scissor-kicked a complete stranger in the head. The victim spent three months in hospital, two of them on a liquid diet. Meehan's solicitor played the 'poor orphan' card in court and the judge acquitted him of GBH.

We should have universally ostracised him after that, but we didn't. We couldn't. Any group of Irish male teens needed a psycho to call on occasionally, either on the Gaelic football pitch or outside the chippie.

Even the Gardai seemed wary of him, and turned a blind eye to his pot dealing. Some put this down to Choker's close relationship with

Father Devlin, a senior Jesuit who trained the college football team and, reputedly, liked a fiddle with teenage boys. Acutely aware of this, none of his players ever went down injured.

Eve, a true crime nut, was obsessed with the murder of Meehan's mother. She asked my brother Fintan – a newspaper reporter in Dublin – to get cuttings on the case. I refused to read them. It was difficult enough facing Choker without knowing about his homicidal genetic disposition.

'Mr Aaaal Jolson,' he sang, to the tune of 'Mr Bojangles' while jazz-wafting his enormous white hands. I stared speechlessly, trying to decide if it would be safer to join in or just carry on feigning delight.

'Who are you supposed to be?' he demanded accusingly.

'James Joyce,' I said, wanting to keep it simple.

He shook his head mournfully: 'Jeez, you could have made some effort.'

Then, seemingly out of nowhere, he produced a bottle with no label.

'I was gonna save this for later,' said Choker, 'but I bet you'd like some right now.' His tone suggested that I *should* like some, right now.

As the Incredible Hulk-hued green liquid glugged into my glass for way too long, I heard myself warble: 'What is it?'

'Absinthe makes the heart grow fonder,' smiled Choker, sounding like Shank would, if he'd been brought up in a bog.

I took a sip and fought back tears. Choker nodded, so I took another.

'The really fit birds love fancy dress, don't

45

they?' declared Choker. 'Gives them a chance to strut their stuff. Put those swotty heifer lumps back in their hay boxes, what?'

He could tell I didn't follow.

'All those chubby bitches banging on about their As and Bs and which Uni they're going to? When they see a woman like Eve in an outfit like that, puts them right back in their place, doesn't it?'

He grimaced at my confused face, strutted towards the door, then turned.

'You need to keep an eye on that one.' Choker smiled to reveal his blinding white teeth, then jazz-wafted his huge white hands again, lingering just a bit too long, like a baddie in a B-movie.

I gulped hard: so hard I could hear it. In my mind flashed Choker's big white hands, closing in on Eve's pale and oh-so-thin and snappable neck. My heart felt too big for my chest. My temples throbbed sweat.

I should definitely go and find Eve.

As I turned into the hallway, Dinosaur Jr.'s 'Freak Scene' skidded into life. Eve had clearly re-appropriated the hi-fi. I was halfway to the sitting room pondering what, if anything, I could do if the orphan got frisky with the Viking, when my legs started to lose their feeling. With every step, they got heavier and heavier. This rattled me. I'd been pissed before, often enough. This felt different, like my legs were dying.

'So fucked I can't believe it,' drawled J Mascis and he wasn't wrong. I felt dead-legged, sweat-soaked and zoned-out, as if life itself was leaking out of my feet. Vanity prevented me raising the

46

alarm. I needed Eve not to see me like this. I needed Tullamore's teen population not to see me like this; not on my final public appearance. I had to get outside. My only hope was the back door.

It took some sort of indefinable judo throw to uproot my dead legs and hoist them around, so that they now faced the rear of the house. I set off in a straight-legged goose-step towards the back door, holding my arms ahead of me in case I fell.

I couldn't feel my feet or legs now at all. I actually wondered if I was dying. I couldn't help thinking how gloriously rock 'n' roll it would be if I dropped dead, right here and now, Eve cradling my head, kissing me one last time, Yoko to my John Lennon.

Suddenly one of the closed bedroom doors creaked open. Out of it came a meek-looking Tara Molloy. In the dark behind her, some fella was struggling to get his trousers back on. She stood and stared but said nothing of my dead-legged, metronomic stomp. What did she think I was doing? My own *Thriller* tribute?

I goose-stepped on like a Nazi on acid. I only had to make it past the kitchen now and the back door was right there.

As the kitchen clatter came into range, I kept my eyes fixed straight ahead. It seemed to take an age. *Please don't anyone look. Please don't anyone see.* I got past. Then – dread – footsteps sounded behind me. I stopped, waited, breathing hard. The footsteps went away. Thank Christ. I leaned my raging forehead against the back door's cold glass. Relief.

47

I slipped the door open. The damp cold jolted me, injecting fresh will into my knotted veins. I dragged the two leaden hunks of meat, formerly known as legs, outside and closed the door quietly. I performed my paralytic can-can across the well-lit crazy paving, towards the lonely black shed, now looking a long thirty feet away. If I could just get to the shed, then round the corner into the black, no one would be able to see me. I could talk myself through this. Get my head together.

I made it to the middle of the crazy paving, then I couldn't move my legs another inch. The paralysis had crept up to my hips. I was stuck, stranded under the hottest part of the outside security light, lucid but unable to walk. I felt real fear now. What was wrong with me? But I had to keep going. I couldn't let anyone see me. Whatever was going on inside my head and body would pass. If I could just make it to that dark shed.

There was only one thing for it. I went all Sergeant Elias out of *Platoon* and dropped melodramatically to my knees, then frontwards onto my arms. Somehow, elbow after concrete-grinding elbow, I wormed my way across the dewy patio. I hoped to Christ no one was seeing this. I'd never, ever live it down.

I got to the shed and dragged myself to sitting, my elbows burning.

I bum-shuffled sideways into the shadows and sat there for I don't know how long, frozen to the spot, crazy scenes unfolding in my mind. At one stage, I was running away from my own home, where I'd just stabbed someone. I felt myself run. I heard people coming after me, shouting, scream-

48

ing, a flashing blue light, a police siren. Then, relief when I saw myself still rooted to the same spot, my hands planted against the shed wall.

I don't know how long I'd been there when a blinding light criss-crossed my vision, scoring my sight. Next thing I knew, I was floating through a drifting starscape, arse-first like a breeched baby, slowly and in total silence. I found myself inside Eve's bedroom, but somehow I was hovering a foot off the floor. I saw clearly the details of the room I knew so well. Across from me, illuminated light from the hallway lit the cracks around the closed bedroom door. Beside it, Eve's clothes sat in a heap on the chair. I could see the top she wore that morning; the bank of photos of Philandering Frank on the wall; the headboard; the garish scarlet duvet cover; the bedside tables. On my side, the ashtray from Majorca, next to the lamp that refused to break no matter how many times we knocked it to the floor. On the far side of the bed blinked the clock radio. It read 01.09. My God, had I been outside for three hours?

The hallway door opened. Something glinted. It was Eve in her Viking outfit. 'This is live!' I thought. She pushed the door shut, placed her helmet and sword on the bedside table next to the clock radio and collapsed dramatically onto the bed. I realised all this was happening in total silence, yet I could tell she was crying.

I felt this overwhelming urge to go to her, to touch her, to put my arm around her shoulder. To say sorry. *Are you okay, Eve?* I said, but nothing came out. I knew it was hopeless, that I was trapped in some sort of sensory vacuum, there

49

but not there. Here, but only in spirit.

The door to the hallway opened very slowly. First came yellow light, then a silhouetted head. I couldn't make out who it belonged to.

Eve sat up on the bed with a start. I could tell she was asking who was there. She was telling the person to get out, leave her alone. I couldn't hear her speak, but I could clearly read her body language.

The unidentified person didn't leave, but shut the door carefully behind him and walked to the bed. I knew that strut, that side profile, that trilby hat. It was Choker Meehan.

Eve sat bolt upright on the bed, as still as a statue.

Choker gently took hold of her hands, sliding his right knee, then his left, onto the bed, so that they were planted between her pale, outstretched legs. He whipped off his hat, tossing it away like a frisbee towards the window. I was bursting to do something, but it was hopeless. Eve pushed back against the headboard defensively. Choker leaned forward, so he was nose to nose with Eve, his hands smothering hers.

He was saying something. Eve remained still, poised, defiant.

He placed his right hand on her left shoulder. 'Eve,' my shout was swallowed by black. I tried to lunge, but I was a fly trapped in an invisible web.

Now his right hand moved from her shoulder to the base of her skull, then to her pale neck. His other hand moved in under her cheek. His fingers spread round the back of her neck so that his thumbs sat twitching on her windpipe. 'Eve, Eve, for fuck's sake, Eve,' I cried, but only my guts thrashed about.

Look after Eve for me, Mo had pleaded into my eyes before she left.

Eve tried to turn her head away. He wouldn't let her. She wriggled hard. He easily pushed her back on the bed underneath him, his left hand now moving up to cover her mouth, dwarfing her face.

I'm counting on you, Donal.

I went apeshit; screaming, thrashing, fighting with all my might. But no one could hear me. She had lost her fight and just lay there, her skirt above her waist, her white panties yanked to one side. He fiddled furiously with his trousers while I just hovered, in hell.

Of course, Mrs Daly.

He pounded now, rhythmically. His downward motion revealed the clock radio on the far side of the bed, its luminous green digits flipping casually to 01.13.

Except all our lives stopped dead right then, never to be the same again.

I woke to my own screaming voice, loud, desperate, primeval. I saw blood glistening on the pebbledash, the skin on my hands, minced. I was breathing hard but I still couldn't lift my feet. Slowly, sounds formed. The nearby church bells clanged twelve times.

But it's after one a.m. right? Why are they chiming midnight?

Trapped birds flapped and flailed inside my skull. A ball of nausea in my chest. I still had time to get back inside, to save Eve. I went to move but my legs stuck to the earth. I refused to believe I was gravity's prisoner. I lurched forward;

51

determined, incensed, but went into free fall through cold, streaking lights into dark, darker black.

I woke up in darkness, to an unfamiliar bed, my guts clanking like an out-of-tune bass.

Flash-frame images of Meehan forcing himself upon Eve flipped through my mind, a rolodex of horrors. I fought an aching neck to sit up. All hopes that it had been some sort of horrific nightmare fled when I saw my bandaged hands, remembering how I'd minced them against the shed's pebbledash wall.

Far away, I could hear the click-clack of retreating footsteps and a swinging door. Shapes formed in the gloom. Weird patterns became curtains, closed around beds opposite. I hadn't spent a night in hospital since I was a kid.

They'd left the curtains around my bed open, presumably to keep me under observation. I sensed someone watching me. Sure enough, a silhouette stood beyond the end of my metal bed, in the middle of the ward, as still as a corpse. I strained to see the face, but it was too dark.

'Who are you?' I said. The person didn't move a muscle. A current of unease zapped through me.

'What do you want?' I called.

The figure started moving towards me, slowly, silently, with intent.

I backed up against the metal frame of the bed, the cold steel reminding me I was awake. Still he came, steady, unflinching, unstoppable.

'What do you want?' I shouted.

The head tilted up to reveal coal-black pupils glistening inside caked white spots. Meehan's bloodshot eyes glared hate.

I scrambled to get up, to fight. But I was frozen, helpless.

Those unblinking murderous eyes kept coming, closer, closer, until we were nose to nose. I felt his gloved hands on my throat, his putrid breath on my face.

He leaned all his weight on my neck until my chest caved in and my eyes bulged. My head pounded as dots bounced off the edges of my fading vision. My head drifted, I was floating off.

I knew this was it. I wanted the end. *Sorry, Eve.*

Then screaming white light gored at my clenched eyelids. I thought: 'Christ no, don't tell me all that shit about God and heaven is true.'

Something made me defy the hot white needles and haul my eyelids open. Shapes formed. A face swooned and flickered, eventually settling to reveal Mum's fretting smile. It was morning and I was alive. Relief overwhelmed me. Someone must have caught him, stopped him, in the nick of time.

'Meehan tried to kill me,' I croaked.

She tiptoed slowly to my left side, warily, uncertain. She squeezed my shoulder so hard it hurt.

'Shhh, don't get yourself upset now, Donal. Try to relax,' she said.

I defied her Vulcan death grip to sit up. I didn't know who the man was to my right, but his snow-white, side-parted hair, fuzzy eyebrows, formal grey suit and hooked nose screamed cop, doc, lawyer; professional busybody.

My neck hurt and my throat burned when I swallowed. I wondered how close Meehan had come to finishing me off.

'Eve?' I gasped at Mum, desperate to know if she was okay; desperate to hear that what I'd seen last night wasn't real, but some sort of absinthe-induced hallucination.

'Take it easy,' said Mum, shoulder-crushing again, 'everything's okay, love.' I pulled away before she snapped my collarbone.

'Everything's far from okay.' I jumped at the man's guttural, knowing voice. I turned to him, confused.

His piercing blue eyes seemed to be searching inside my face: a cop, for sure. 'We found you unconscious, having imbibed some sort of substance, no doubt illicit,' he snapped. 'I trust you won't object to answering a few questions.'

'Substance?' I rasped. 'What are you on about?'

As I spoke, the pieces clicked together. Absinthe alone couldn't have done that to me. Choker, the fucker, had spiked me.

I told the cop about the weird green drink, the dead legs, the shed.

I sensed Mum shaking her head sadly. I couldn't bear to look her way. Instead, my eyes met the nurse's disgusted glare. What was her problem? Unwelcome, my eyes drifted back to the cop's piercing blue sparklers.

I asked again: 'Eve, is she okay?'

I sensed he was holding something back. I vowed there and then that if Meehan *had* attacked her, I'd kill him myself.

'Well,' said the cop, 'you were out of it, so I guess that rules you out as a potential suspect, or indeed as a witness.'

Suspect? Witness? Christ, no. Say it didn't happen. Say what I saw wasn't real...

The cop carried on, measured, enjoying his moment, even producing one of those black flip notebooks you see only in cop shows.

'We are investigating a very serious crime,' he began.

'What the fuck happened?' I felt like screaming.

'Someone dialled 999 from the house phone, but refused to give their name. Medics removed you from the garden of the house at 01.52 a.m.'

'Removed...?' I couldn't help picturing the scene; a bloodied and half-frozen Hunter S. Thompson, flat out on a stretcher, hands covered in blood, the glasses skewwhiff on my face. I was sure to hear every last detail soon, if I could ever face them again.

The cop went on, impassively: 'You were unconscious. An officer at the scene found the bottle of absinthe. It's gone to Dublin for tests but my bet is it'd been mixed with some sort of tranquilliser or cannabis, possibly both.'

He stopped for effect. I nodded gravely, because I felt that's what he wanted me to do. Finally, he continued.

'Whatever substance was in that drink caused a rapid drop in your blood pressure, which explains why you felt paralysed. The good news is, there's no long-term damage.'

Good news, but not the news I most wanted to hear, so I nodded rapidly.

He got to his feet and started pacing about the room, Poirot-style. The gobshite. Then his throaty 'ahem', and my mother's averted gaze confirmed my worst fear: what I'd heard so far was merely the preamble to this morning's Main Story. I swallowed hard. God, it hurt.

'Look,' said the cop, 'I might as well tell you. Your girlfriend, Eve Daly...'

I shivered, froze.

'She's under arrest.'

I couldn't speak, couldn't think.

'For stabbing Anthony Meehan to death.'

From somewhere deep, deep inside me spewed a hideous, cackling, panto-laugh. She did it. She nailed that fucker. My Viking!

The cop looked at me in shock, then disgust. 'What's so fucking funny, son?' he spat. 'There's a young man downstairs in the basement on a slab.'

'No, God, no, sorry,' I said, 'it's just the shock.'

He turned to Mum and the nurse: 'I'm not sure he's in a fit state to hear any more,' he said, pocketing his fancy notebook.

He turned back to me with a scowl: 'I'll be back to ask you more questions later.' He flicked his top coat, matador-style, off the back of the bedside chair.

My mind flailed, trying to make sense of it all. Somehow she'd fought back. But how? She must have stabbed him with the Viking prop dagger. Self-defence of course. I'd seen him attack her. I'd seen the preamble to Meehan's murder!

Or was that what I had seen? My mind recoiled at the insanity of the idea. Surely it must have been some sort of bad trip? A drug-induced nightmare out of the dark corners of my twisted, paranoid mind? Or maybe, while I was lying here out of it, I'd heard them talking about the crime. My brain had supplied pictures to what I'd unconsciously learned.

Yet I knew what I'd seen. I saw Meehan attack Eve.

But if Meehan was dead, then who had tried to kill me later, when I was already in the hospital? Surely not...

I had to ask the question.

'Sir?'

He turned, surprised.

'What time did you get the call, you know, about Tony?'

Lieutenant Dumbo looked at me, frowned and sighed. He reached back into his breast pocket.

'Ah let's see,' he said, his agricultural thumb dwarfing the notebook's inky pages.

'We got that call at ... 1.17 a.m.'

My brain flashed back to the scene, to the clock radio turning 1.13. Watching Meehan forcing himself upon Eve. Witnessing the preamble to Meehan's murder. But that made no sense. 'And when did he die?' I croaked.

The cop took a long hard look at me: 'He was pronounced dead at the scene, son. Why do you ask?'

I told myself there must be a logical explanation – must be ... must be. My head swooned. 'Donal, love, are you okay?' sounded Mum's voice as last night's blinding lights returned, slashing at my vision.

I ignored the panic because I couldn't take any more: I let myself sink down, down until all those hot white needles of hospital light went away.

Chapter 3

Clapham Junction
Tuesday, July 2, 1991; 08:15

I marched back to Sangora Road, unable to ban-
ish the squalid thought that Marion Ryan's murder represented a gilt-edged career opportunity.

My two-year probation as a beat Constable was
almost complete. In a few weeks, I'd be eligible
for promotion to Acting Detective Constable.
There were more beat officers than Acting DC
positions: competition was fierce.

Later today, I was due to make a statement to
the investigating team. By re-examining the murder scene, perhaps I could offer up a few fresh
insights or theories; make a good impression. I
needed a senior officer to spot me and think that
I was worthy of championing; to take me under
his or her wing.

I took a short cut across Wandsworth Common, ignoring the tarmac pathways. London's
green spaces seemed so orderly and controlled to
me: the opposite of nature. It's a wonder there
weren't signs saying, 'Keep Off The Grass'. As I
trod the dewy sward, I let my mind drift off-road
too. After this morning's chilling encounter, I
needed to open myself up to all possibilities. It
was time for a logic amnesty.

One fact felt indisputable: Marion's attack on

me hadn't been a dream. When she came to me in the flat, I'd been wide awake, albeit a bit pissed. I could see and hear everything around her in the streetlight orange tinge – the furniture, the traffic outside, the slamming door. I'd felt her breath on my face.

And, three years earlier, I'd felt Meehan's cold, gloved hands strangling my throat.

I didn't believe in ghosts, spirits, religion, the supernatural or any of that stuff. But the most obvious explanation for what happened last night – however crazy – was that the spirit or ghost of Marion Ryan had come to me. A few hours earlier, I'd been physically close to her recently murdered body. Three years ago, Meehan came to me at Tullamore General Hospital as I slept upstairs from the basement morgue hosting his fresh corpse. I had to ask the question: did my proximity to a body that had just met a violent death somehow open up a telepathic pathway between us? And if so, what were their spirits trying to tell me? And how could they get inside me?

The naked malevolence of Meehan's assault didn't seem to say much, apart from he wished me harm. But while Marion's attack felt every bit as threatening, there was something about the encounter that made me think she had been trying to tell me something. That slamming door. What did it mean? I had to get to Sangora Road and see if something snagged on my mind.

As the grass of the Common gave way to concrete, a rancid stench invaded my senses. I checked both soles, located the soft wet dog shit wedged between the grips of my left shoe and

59

declared the logic amnesty over.

As I rubbed my shoe against a grass verge, I tried to come up with a more believable solution. Meehan throttling me had been a graphic hallucination. After all, I'd just ingested enough tranquilliser to poleaxe a sadhu. Marion's apparition was a result of post-traumatic stress – or post-traumatic Shiraz, as Aidan put it. Seeing her wound-covered body last night had obviously affected me more than I'd realised.

Sangora Road had already recovered its leafy, anonymous poise. On one side, a road sweeper clanked along grudgingly. On the other, a couple of suits made breakneck progress towards Clapham Junction train station. Ahead of them, a racket of rotund school kids swore loudly, smoked and spat. I wondered what Tullamore's own Jesuit terrorist Father Devlin would give for ten minutes in a locked room with that lot, and how much I'd pay to watch.

Across the road from number 21, the press pack swarmed, keen as hyenas. I counted nine still camera lenses, presumably all jostling for the same shot. I couldn't help thinking: what a waste.

As I cast them my most contemptuous glare, a morose Northern voice stopped me in my tracks.

'Where do you think you're going?'

Clive 'Overtime' Hunt was one of the less offensive nicknames earned by my beat partner over the years. Colleagues would plead with me: 'Find out what he does with all the money?' He simply couldn't say no to overtime and must have worked at least seventy hours a week, every week.

'You did go home at some stage, Clive?'

'Oh yeah. I got back here at eight this morning. Easiest gig going this, standing at a door.'

'Exciting too,' I said, 'so what's been happening?'

'They removed the body about two hours ago. Forensics are still working, so don't cross the tape, obviously,' he drawled, the irritating tit.

He unlocked the internal door to the flat, then almost ceremoniously pulled it open.

'Thanks, Clive,' I said, 'but that's really not necessary.'

'Oh but it is,' he said, 'it's one of those fire doors, spring-loaded to close itself, except it's been sprung too tight.'

'Oh,' I said, putting my palm against the half-open door.

Just like last night, it pressed back hard.

PC Know-It-All's furniture-and-fittings briefing wasn't over yet: 'Clever things, these fire doors; at a certain temperature they expand and seal the gaps, blocking out flames and, even more important, smoke. Smoke inhalation is actually the biggest killer, you know.'

'Fascinating,' I said, turning on the first step, then letting the door go so it slammed behind me.

I imagined Marion coming up these stairs. She had her post, keys, handbag and jacket over her arm. Whoever killed her was either in the flat already, or had met her at the front door as she returned from work. The idea that someone was already inside felt less plausible – there were no signs of a break-in. Only she and Peter had keys. If she let her killer in, then she must have known him.

61

Ninety-eight per cent of murder victims know their killer.

He followed her up the stairs, launching his attack from behind. But if it was Peter, why would he stab her to death on the landing? He could have killed her in any of the rooms, in a variety of ways, at any time of the day or night, silently and without leaving evidence or causing a commotion. It just didn't stack up. Unless it had been a crime of passion: one of them had been having an affair, confronted the other. Peter had lashed out in a blind rage. *It's always the man, isn't it?*

My mind turned to Peter and Karen finding the body. I imagined myself as Peter coming up the stairs. I was about the same height – five ten – so I stopped at the spot where he would have seen Marion's body on the landing.

Karen wouldn't have seen the body yet. She was five foot four, tops, and must have been at least a step below Peter, if not two. He called Marion's name and went to her body.

Karen told me she'd been the one to check for signs of life. That's how she got Marion's blood on her hands. Had Peter made any sort of check first? If not, then why not? Did he already know she was dead? I couldn't be sure if this meant anything, but made a mental note just in case. I'd mention it later to the investigating officers, show them I had solid detective potential.

I walked up to the police tape and exchanged a nod with the forensics who were tweezing every inch of the landing.

There seemed to be very little blood on the carpet and walls, considering all the wounds

Marion had suffered. Either she had died quickly – blood stops flowing when you expire – or most of her wounds were superficial. I wondered if I'd get a look at the pathology report.

The window on the landing overlooked a flat roof below. Someone could have climbed onto that roof and scrabbled up the roof tiles to this window. I unfastened the latch and opened it as far as it could go: about four inches. It looked new and hadn't been forced. The killer didn't get in through here.

Cool air rushed my face, voodoo lurking in its slipstream.

After three hours, they close the window, to ensure that the spirit doesn't return.

She usually gets home before six ... we got back just after nine...

Had I been standing here as her spirit returned, hungry for vengeance?

My eyes followed the blood streaks along the wall. I wondered what would happen to the flat now. Surely Peter could never come back to live here, guilty or not. Who would paint over the blood? Would future prospective tenants be told of the horror that had taken place, here on these stairs?

The flat door below heaved open, followed by the sound of someone labouring up the stairs.

'You could probably get this for a hell of a good price now,' panted Clive, as if he'd read my mind, 'be a smashing first-time buy.'

'Could you actually live here though? Every time you'd come up these stairs, you'd be thinking someone died here, horribly.'

'I'd leave the blood and charge people for a look.'

'Jesus.'

We both stared for a moment in silence at the spattered remnants of Marion Ryan's final seconds, the red colour already browning.

'What do you think then?' said Clive.

'Well, if I've learned anything over the past two years, it's that crimes tend to be either personal or opportunistic,' I replied. 'This was definitely personal, wouldn't you say?'

'Well, if I've learned anything over the past twenty years, it's to keep an open mind.'

I could feel his look. 'Tell them what you think today, but don't be too opinionated. They won't respect that.'

I nodded.

'You're a PC, they'll see you as nothing more than a street butler; present when needed, otherwise invisible. Know your place, son.'

'Got it,' I said, the words, 'cannon fodder' drifting through my mind.

I'd be fucked if I'd know my place in Clive's class system. England, the world's only courteous tyranny.

Marion lay on the waiting room table at Clapham police station, beaming and radiant. The photo of her and Peter on a recent night out dominated the *Standard's* front page. Head tilted into Peter's chest, her smiling blue eyes oozed contentment. Her hair – big and curly à la Julia Roberts' in *Pretty Woman* – had an almost other-worldly crimson glow which seemed to drain all the blood from her milk-white skin. Her high cheekbones and freckled nose brought Eve to mind. But Marion's features – nose, chin, eyebrows, forehead – were more pronounced: she was striking, rather than pretty. Juxtaposed with her strong face was a smile so coy, kind and natural that it lit up the page, casting a sad shadow across my chest. I forced my eyes away from the photo to the accompanying report. I needed to expunge all emotion, stick to the facts.

London-born of Irish parents, twenty-three-year-old Marion O'Leary met Peter Ryan in North London's Archway Tavern when she was seventeen. Peter, from Mayo, had been her only boyfriend. They got married in Ireland last year.

I'd met lots of second-generation Irish in London, like Marion. Invariably, they held a romanticised view of 'the old country', usually based on a handful of childhood holidays, and family propaganda. Most had been indoctrinated in Irish culture since birth. I bet Marion attended the local Catholic school and church. She would have taken First Holy Communion and Irish dancing classes and celebrated Paddy's Day more than I ever did.

She would have socialised in Irish pubs and clubs, hoping to meet a dashing Irishman who'd whisk her off her feet. They'd marry and move to a bungalow in the west of Ireland, where their kids – red-haired, freckled and plentiful – would run about barefoot and gleeful, stopping only to say the Angelus together at six o'clock each evening.

We first-generation Irish had news for these 'plastic Paddies', some quite old news at that: romantic Ireland's dead and gone.

I couldn't help assuming that Marion had

bought wholesale into her parents' dream. Marrying her first proper boyfriend made me suspect she was trusting, idealistic, a little naïve – not the type to have an affair, or to let a stranger into her flat. So how then did Peter fit into all of this? Why would he kill her? Maybe he was having an affair and couldn't bring himself to tell her. After all, most Irishmen will do anything to avoid a scene. Or she confronted him about it and he flipped. But surely he didn't hack his own wife to death on the stairs with a knife, then go back to work? That didn't stack up.

I was mentally listing the most compelling reasons why this crime *had* to be domestic when I leapt at the sound of my own name. The uniformed officer led me out of the waiting room, down a long corridor, through a pair of electronic security doors, along another corridor, then left into an interview suite. I sat there in airless isolation for what seemed like an age, a hothouse mushroom incubating on stale smoke and sweat. I couldn't understand why I felt so nervous.

Two middle-aged detectives finally strolled in, coffee cups full, fags on, fresh smoke sweetening the fusty air.

'I'm DS Barratt, this is Inspector McStay,' said the taller one, letting his superior sit first.

I talked through everything that happened last night, throwing in my theories for good measure. When I wrapped up, they told me to write it all down in a statement, minus the theories. As I wrote, I repeated my assertion that Marion must have known her killer.

'Thank you, PC,' snapped McStay, emphasising my job title, 'the Big Dogs are all over it now.'

I went on, 'She clearly let her killer in. She knew him or her well enough to pick up her post.'

'Who would be your prime suspect then, Lynch?' asked Barratt, mildly amused.

'I'd have to start with the husband, Peter. Was he playing away? Did she find out? Has he got a history of violence? It doesn't usually come out of the blue, does it? I've read about a lot of other cases and it normally escalates from domestic abuse. Peter is where I'd start.'

'Good theory,' said Barratt, scanning my statement, 'we're bringing him in as we speak. He's going to talk to the press, appeal for help to find her killer.'

He looked up at me: 'Alongside Mr and Mrs O'Leary, Marion's mum and dad.'

I tried not to look confused.

McStay seized the moment: 'Peter is staying with Marion's parents. Do you think they'd have him living in their own home if they thought for one second he could have been capable of killing their daughter?'

He got up, strode to the door and flung it open: 'Better get back out there, son. Those bike thieves won't catch themselves.'

As I made my way back out of Clapham police station, I recognised the rodent-like scurrying of her majesty's press.

Amid the yapping throng surged my brother Fintan, now Deputy Crime Correspondent of the London-based *Sunday News*. If the Chief Crime Correspondent didn't have a pension plan, he needed to get one, soon.

I followed the hordes into a large conference room, taking a seat near the exit. I wanted to see Peter explain himself. I wanted to see if his in-laws exhibited any kind of suspicion.

Within seconds, my identity had become a talking point among a group of photographers. Fintan joined their chat, clocked me and scuttled over, beaming.

'I hear you found the body?' he roared, confirming he'd no shame.

'Jesus, would you not have some decorum, Fintan.'

'Maybe we can help each other.'

'I'm not talking to you.'

'Come on, Donal.'

'You know I can't tell you anything.'

'Fine. Fine. I wonder though, is a PC like you supposed to be nosing around a cordoned-off crime scene *after* the case has been taken over by a senior detective?'

A red warning light pinged on in my brain.

'Well I am a police officer, Fintan. That's pretty much what I do these days.'

'Oh okay. It's just ... ah nothing, doesn't matter.'

'What?'

'Well, you see that guy over there?' he said, pointing to a large man cradling a cannon-sized Canon camera.

'He's a snapper, from the *Standard*.'

'Bully for him.'

'He said he took your photo earlier today, as you came out of the house on Sangora Road.'

My heart set off on a gallop.

'And guess what? His editor likes it. Donal, you're going to be on the front page of the *Evening Standard*. Imagine that! You on the front page? I'll send a copy to Daddy. He'll be made up.'

'Oh Jesus,' I sighed.

Fintan guffawed: 'You, a lowly PC, sneaking around a live crime scene without DS Glenn's permission? He's a real hard ass, Donal. He'll go apeshit.'

I'd already pissed off DS Glenn – the officer in charge of the case – during our first meeting last night.

'They can't just use my picture. I have rights.'

'Afraid not, bro. It's a public place. He can snap what he likes. Would you like me to have a word with him?'

'Please,' I sighed.

Of course I'd never know if any of this was true. Fintan spent his entire life finagling leverage.

He returned in less than a minute. 'Sorted,' he said, 'you can relax. I told him you're on an undercover job at the minute, and this photo could blow your cover. He's on the phone to his picture editor now.'

He sat next to me. 'You've got to be more careful, Donal. Seriously, someone like Glenn could have you consigned to uniform for life.'

'Thanks,' I said, wondering if that's what happened to PC Clive Overtime.

'Don't mention it. You can buy me a nice pork salad for lunch.'

DS Glenn entered the room through a side door, followed by a bearded man in an ancient tweed jacket and a haunted, ashen Peter. Ten feet behind, clinging together, were a middle-aged couple who needed no introduction. Cameras whirred, clicked, and sprayed like slo-mo machine guns.

'Her people are from Kilkenny,' said Fintan, shouting over the camera cacophony.

'Who's the tweed?'

'Professor Richards, a forensic psychologist. He'll be observing Peter, you know, his body language and all that, see if he's lying.'

'He'll be able to tell?'

'Glenn swears by him.'

'How do you know that?'

'It's my job! Happily for me, you cops gossip like fishwives.'

Richards sat at the extreme right-hand chair at the top table. Glenn led Peter to the seat next to the Professor then sat Marion's parents to the left, taking centre stage himself.

He explained who he was, then introduced the Prof, Peter, and Marion's mum and dad, Mary and John.

The snappers continued to hose them down. Glenn pleaded for restraint. They eased off for fully two seconds.

As Glenn ran through the indisputable facts of the case, I took a good look at Peter, slumped, fumbling busily with his fingers, like a widow with rosary beads.

He looked impressive, handsome, if somewhat vain and self-satisfied. He had an unfortunate perma-smirk which had probably earned him more slaps in life than hugs. His slicked-back auburn hair owed much to Don Johnson and cement-grade gel. He could have been a lower-league professional footballer or a wedding DJ with a name like Dale or Barry.

My eyes drifted over to Mary and John. Mary embodied every Irish mum I'd ever known: small, tough, thick grey hair fixed fast into position, a fighter's chin. Her face puce, her body bent with grief, she clenched rosary beads in one palm and John's hand in the other. She didn't look up from the table once.

I thought about my own mum. I really needed to make that call.

Marion's dad John sat bolt upright like a guard dog, surveying the room, defending his family, defying the pain. I'd dealt with the parents of murdered people before. They usually split up in the end. The mum always blames the dad, even when she doesn't want to. It must be hard-wired deep within mothers that the father's primary role is to protect the family. Even in cases where the dad couldn't possibly have done anything to save the child – like this – that sense of blame is there. I hoped John and Mary would make it.

Glenn summarised: 'We would like to appeal to anyone who lives, works or who happened to be in the Clapham Junction area between five and seven p.m. last Monday evening to please call us with any information that may help us find this killer. It doesn't matter how minor or trivial it may seem, if you saw anything unusual or suspicious, please call us. Finally, I'd like to warn people in London, particularly lone women, to be vigilant and alert.'

It was Peter's turn to speak. He hadn't written anything down.

He looked directly at a TV camera and said: 'I'd like to ask the public to please help find Marion's killer. Whoever did this is not human ... they have to be caught...' His already high voice reached castrato pitch, before cracking. He squeezed his eyes shut, then his head fell and he sobbed. The cameras swarmed in for the kill.

No one noticed Mary sobbing too, or John squeezing her hand.

Questions rained in from the floor: 'Are there fears that a maniac is targeting women in their homes?'

Glenn: 'I've nothing to add.'

'Are you linking this to other crimes?'

Glenn: 'As part of any investigation, we look for connections to similar crimes.'

Then Fintan got to his feet: 'Is 21 Sangora Road known to police?'

John glared over. 'No,' he roared and I felt myself shrivel.

'No more questions,' shouted Glenn, summoning Peter to his feet. As Glenn led him out, Mary and John didn't look his way once.

'I'm off to find a phone,' said Fintan.

'Grand. See you in Frank's?'

'Yeah, great. Twenty minutes.'

Chapter 4

**Frank's Café, Northcote Road, Clapham
Tuesday, July 2, 1991; 11:45**

Although he could be toxic, an occasional meeting with Fintan was necessary these days, because he'd become my source of Eve Daly news.

During my first three months in London, I'd written to Eve four times. I got just one short note back, in which she apologised for not being a letter writer and asked a favour. The list of instructions suggested she wasn't taking no for an answer.

As decreed, I met Tara Molloy – a girl from home I barely knew – at Liverpool Street train station, and drove her to the job interview in Stepney Green. She didn't utter a single word, save for, 'Hi' when we first met. I sensed her nerves and tried to calm her down: 'Come on, I'm sure you'll do great.'

'I don't know,' she mumbled, staring blankly ahead. I hoped she'd think of more to say under questioning.

'What kind of job is it?' I asked.

'I'd rather not say, in case I jinx it,' she said quietly.

Almost two hours later, she emerged, looking even glummer.

I didn't say anything until we got back to Liverpool Street. 'Are you straight back to the airport then?'

'Yeah.'

'No time for a quick drink?'

I really wanted to tap her up about Eve.

'No. Sorry. I've really got to rush. Thanks so much, Donal, for the lift...'

She climbed out of the work van and marched into Liverpool Street train station without looking back. It was only after she disappeared that I noticed fresh blood on the passenger seat: enough blood to make me realise she'd just had a termination.

My next letter to Eve confirmed two things – 1: I'd taken Tara to her 'job interview'; 2: from now on, I'd prefer to communicate by phone.

Eve sent a note back containing a single quote: 'If you love something, set it free. If it comes back, it's yours. If it doesn't, it never was.' She signed it: 'All my love, Eve x.'

I couldn't quite work out which one of us had set the other 'free'. But the quote and her romantic sign-off reassured me: as soon as Eve got her life back on track, we'd give us another go.

In the meantime, I felt certain that Mum could keep me abreast of all developments in Eve's case. How wrong I was.

During my first year in London, I had been ringing home every couple of weeks from a phone box awash with stale piss, cock carvings and IRA slogans. I fed it a pound coin every three minutes while Mum ran through her news – i.e. who had died – followed by the weather – i.e. how much it had rained. She had poor news judgement, sometimes suddenly remembering the death of a friend or family member after my pound coins had run out and the beeping had started. Nothing made you feel more alone than finding out someone you knew well was already cold in the ground. We never seemed to get around to talking about how she was or how I was or the latest on Eve Daly.

On the few occasions that my dad, Martin, answered, I hung up. He couldn't be arsed to say goodbye to me before I left the country. Why would he want to chat to me on the phone? Besides, Martin was monosyllabic and opaque in the flesh; the idea that he and I could support a telephone conversation seemed laughable.

Then, about two years ago, I stopped calling home altogether. The trouble started when the Met police contacted our family GP, Dr Harnett, seeking my medical records. Unburdened by the Hippocratic oath, Harnett mentioned it to his golfing partner – one Martin Lynch – who assumed I'd got myself into some sort of trouble, and called golden son Fintan to find out what was going on. For once, my older brother didn't enjoy breaking sensational news. He had to tell Martin that his second son had joined 'the enemy' – the British police force; the same force that had framed his heroes the Birmingham Six, the Guildford Four and the Maguire Seven.

After a long silence, Martin Lynch very quietly but clearly gave Fintan the following instructions: 'Tell him never to call here again, or come home here again, as long as I breathe.'

I lost count of how many times I'd picked up a

receiver and dialled that number you never forget, only to hang up because of what he might do to her. I hoped Mum realised that those countless silent phone calls had been from me, that I was thinking of her.

So, having lost contact with Mum, I had to find another way to keep up with Eve's ongoing case and work out how our future together would pan out. Until Fintan came to London, my sole source was the Irish newspapers – especially the one that had employed my brother at the time, the *Evening Press*. Credit to Fintan's news nose, he sensed right away he had the inside track on the scoop of a lifetime. But even he could not have foreseen just how globally massive the Eve Daly case would become.

The day after Meehan's funeral, the Gardai announced that Eve had been charged with his murder and all went quiet. Two weeks later, they released a short statement announcing that they'd dropped the murder charge, pending further enquiries – a development Eve perhaps should have treated with discreet gratitude. Instead, she granted Fintan an exclusive interview, in which she revealed that she'd knifed Meehan with her Viking prop dagger as he tried to force himself upon her.

No country relishes a divisive story as much as Ireland: this one proved an ideological 'perfect storm'. There were two passionate, polarised schools of thought. The first: if a woman dresses like a slut and gets into bed with a man, then she knows what she's getting. The second: no means no, she must have acted in self-defence. I've never understood how people can get so worked up about something that doesn't remotely affect them. None of the impassioned, self-appointed pundits knew the facts behind the case, yet the entire nation engaged in an almighty gender-based ding-dong with undisguised glee.

Local knowledge and contacts gave Fintan an unassailable edge over rival reporters. It was Fintan who broke the news that Eve had been wearing a sexy Vixen Viking outfit when she stabbed Tony Meehan to death. As Fintan later explained, each great crime in history has its own Penny Dreadful moniker. The Black Dahlia. The Zodiac Killer. The Yorkshire Ripper. The Boston Strangler. Freelance Fintan coined the Vixen Viking Killer, and it stuck.

He just couldn't stop generating fresh, juicy new angles.

He broke the story that Meehan was a drug-peddling orphan with a track record for assault and bedding attached local women.

He exclusively revealed that, after Mo Daly had heartlessly abandoned her teenage daughter for a new life in New York, the family home had become notorious for wild sex and drugs parties. I found this article particularly hurtful: whoever had been having all this 'wild sex and drugs' had managed to keep it well away from me.

He announced to the world that while Meehan and the Vixen had consensual/non-consensual sex, Eve's hapless boyfriend had blacked out in the garden from a suspected drugs overdose. Fintan swore he only broke this story because the *Independent* had got hold of it, and were planning

77

to splash it on their front page the next day. He 'killed' the story by burying it on page twelve of that evening's *Press* – 'not even a facing page!' – adding, albeit in the last line, the small but significant fact that: 'Gardai confirmed at the time that Lynch, eighteen, had fallen victim to an alcoholic drink "spiked" with an unidentified substance.'

In yet another scoop, Fintan reported that the company which manufactured the Vixen Viking range were withdrawing their metal prop daggers, replacing them with reassuringly unrealistic plastic models. Sales went through the roof.

Thanks to a leaked pathology report, he scooped his rivals again with news that – in the course of her struggle with Meehan – Eve had stabbed him in the balls. This sent the story into orbit, globally. Sales of Vixen Viking costumes nosedived.

Gardai charged Eve with murder – again. She received the immediate and vocal backing of Dublin's militant feminist group, RAG (Revolutionary Anarcha-feminist Group), who announced that if she was pregnant with Meehan's rape child, they would finance her abortion in the UK.

The Society for the Protection of Unborn Children (SPUC) went apeshit. They immediately lodged a High Court injunction which banned Eve Daly from travelling outside the Irish Republic. Abortion was illegal in Ireland: if Eve couldn't travel, she couldn't terminate the pregnancy.

SPUC was backed by the Catholic church and the governing political party, Fianna Fáil. In an off-the-record chat with Fintan, Tullamore's most famous son, Tourism Minister Phil Flynn – an old pal of Dad's – accused young women of 'provoking rape by dressing like Jezebels'. He went on to describe RAG as 'a bunch of hairy lezzers who need a good root up the hole'. Fintan later admitted that Flynn had been half cut at the time, but he ran it anyway.

All hell broke loose. The opposition parties demanded Flynn's resignation: he demanded to know what he'd 'done wrong'. To this day, Flynn is credited for the election of liberal feminist Mary Robinson to the role of President of Ireland in 1990.

Pissed off by Robinson's triumph, the judiciary revoked Eve's bail. As a security van drove her through the gates of Dublin's notorious Mountjoy prison, a photographer snatched a shot of her in the back – crying, her hair in bunches, clutching a teddy bear. This secured her martyr status in the eyes of the martyr-loving Irish Left, prompting Christy Moore to write 'The Ballad of Eve Daly'.

A week or so later, Eve called Fintan and confirmed she was not – repeat, not – pregnant with a rape child. Abortion groups, pro and anti – could barely hide their disappointment at the loss of such a deliciously fleshy flashpoint. They dropped Eve faster than a smoking hornet.

Fintan too began to feel ostracised. According to his own undoubtedly self-aggrandising claims, he'd exposed too many of Ireland's gilded inner circle: politicians, the judiciary, lawyers, the Catholic church, lackey journalists. Buckling under a barrage of legal writs, personal attacks and cronyism, he fled to London.

At least *he* could escape. Three years on from Meehan's death, Eve remained locked in political and legal limbo: neither tried nor acquitted. I couldn't understand why, until Fintan helpfully put me straight a few weeks back: 'It's like all these public inquiries and judicial tribunals. They'll drag it out until people get so bored they don't give a fuck anymore.'

Two teas slid across the pink Formica just as Fintan strode through the café door, mac over his arm, fag on, pasty-faced – a film noir wannabe.

'You'll never guess who's just landed in Tullamore?' he smiled, mincing into the screwed-down plastic seat opposite mine before answering his own riddle.

'Only Larry fucking King!'

I frowned.

'Legendary CNN anchor man? Biggest name in American current affairs?'

'What's he doing in Tullamore?'

'You heard about Mike Tyson, right?'

Who hadn't? Police had arrested the self-proclaimed 'Baddest Man on the Planet' in Connecticut that week and charged him with rape.

Fintan took a violent slurp of his tea and continued: 'And you know one of the Kennedys was charged with rape earlier this year? Well, CNN has picked up on Eve's story. They're saying it's a landmark case for a woman's right to say no.'

'Will this help Eve?'

'Christ, no. Her best hope was that it would all peter out. Now it's an international news story, Ireland's politicians must be seen to be doing the right thing.'

'And that is?'

'Bush and the Republicans are in power,

Donal. They'd have fried her by now! She'll get a stretch for sure. It's just a question of how long.'

Fintan seemed delighted with this development, the twisted fuck.

'It's ridiculous,' I snapped, 'she so obviously acted in self-defence. In any civilised country she'd have been given a medal for getting rid of that menace.'

'You need to forget about her now anyway, Donal, once and for all. There's a good chance you'll never clap eyes on her again.'

I refused to believe that. My heart knew, somehow, that Eve Daly was unfinished business.

My pork-based bribe landed. Fintan tore into it ravenously.

'So what's so interesting about this case?' I asked.

Half his fry-up already savaged, Fintan turned his attention to the open-spouted sugar jar emptying the equivalent of five or six teaspoons into his muddy brew. He then lit another cigarette.

'There's two murders a week in London,' I pointed out, 'what makes Marion Ryan good copy?'

Fintan smiled and shook his head in disbelief at my obvious stupidity.

'She's white, she's pretty, she's a newlywed, she lives on a respectable street. Truth is, if Marion had been black, or Asian, or a single mum in a council block in, I dunno, Deptford, with a little brown baby, I wouldn't be here.'

'Christ, so class and social status dictate whether or not your murder merits coverage,' I sighed, suddenly feeling hot and tired.

'Don't blame me. This is who the readership identifies with, and the fact she was butchered in her own home by a crazed maniac, well, that just about ticks all our boxes.'

'Why do you say it was a crazed maniac?'

'Forty-nine stab wounds. Speak to any pathologist, they'll tell you the most stab wounds they've ever seen in a domestic is ten or twelve. And, if it's domestic, why was she killed in a frenzy like that? There are a hundred more efficient ways he could have done it. It's got to be a nutter. Hey, you're supposed to be the copper.'

I tried not to visibly bristle as Fintan pressed on. 'Maybe he charged through the door, forced her upstairs at knifepoint?'

'That's ridiculous. I'm sorry to disappoint you, Fint, but there is no Bride Ripper out there on the loose, roaming the streets in search of his next pretty ABC1 target.'

'How can you be so certain, Donal?'

'Well, she opened the door and let this *nutter* in,' I pointed out, 'we found her on the landing with her mail, her keys, her handbag all untouched. So where does that leave your ripper theory?'

He stubbed out his cigarette, leaned back and took a notebook and pen out of his inside pocket 'Post, keys and handbag,' he said, busily writing.

He stood and put on his coat: 'Breakfast and privileged crime scene information from an impeccable source, all for free. Thanks, bro. Now, I better go and rewrite some of that copy.'

Chapter 5

South London
Tuesday, July 2, 1991; 20:05

After several months on the beat together, Clive and I had hit on just one mutual interest: food. And even then we rarely saw eye-to-eye. That evening, we pounded the streets of South London discussing which confectionery fridges best, and which shouldn't be subjected to cooling at all.

As he launched a passionate defence for keeping the toffee in Rolos soft – thus, unfridged – I realised that the drama of the last twenty-four hours had made me desperate to make the jump to murder squad. I'd grown frustrated wasting time mooching about in a comedy uniform, not quite knowing what we were trying to achieve. 'Catching baddies,' I'd initially assumed, 'gangsters, rapists and people who mug old ladies.' If only it were like that...

The training at Hendon College should have given me a clue. 'I spent most of the six-week course learning about multiculturalism, hate crimes, best practices, paperwork and adopting multi-agency strategies. There was nothing about gathering evidence, hoofing down doors or bitch-slapping villains – surely the job's only real attractions.

Since then I'd spent lots of time taking statements from battered wives who later withdrew them and from gang members who didn't show up for court. I spent even more time taking statements from victims of vandalism/theft/assault whose complaints against known perpetrators never even made it to court. But I spent the vast majority of my time filling in a mountain of mandatory paperwork that accompanied every single recorded crime, no matter how petty. In other words, I was a uniformed response officer who spent eighty per cent of my time at a desk.

Occasionally, we'd be knee-jerked into an initiative on the back of media pressure. Last year's big campaign: Nike Crime. There'd been a worrying spate of young trendies getting mugged at knifepoint for their £120 Nike Air Jordan trainers. Of course, the more the media publicised Nike Crime, the worse it got, which in turn gave the media and politicians licence to grow ever more hysterical. It was a vicious cycle, or a self-fulfilling prophecy, depending on how you made your living. Before long, teenagers began to actually get knifed for their Nikes, vindicating the media frenzy and turning the spotlight directly onto the police's failure to prevent it. The Commissioner ordered every beat officer in the capital to attend a day-long seminar on how to identify Nike-wearing trendies and defend them from knife-wielding envy. The majority of cops who turned up looked too bloated to catch a pensioner wearing flippers, let alone a lithe young shoe-jacker enhanced by recently acquired air-cushioned soles.

I resented being dragged away from my soothing, pointless paperwork to protect spoiled teenagers. As far as I was concerned, anyone dumb enough to wear £120 trainers had it coming. I wanted to solve proper crimes, like who murdered Marion Ryan.

After I caught Marion's killer, I wanted to ask him: why? Why did you savagely take the life of a completely innocent woman? *Look me in the eye and explain it to me. I need to understand.*

'Well?' said Clive.

'What?' I said.

'Have you ever actually seen someone eating a Milky Way? You know, on the tube, or the bus?'

I was racking my brains when the disembodied fuzz of the radio buzzed in. It was a T call to a house on Salcott Road. A suspected intruder. I realised right away – Salcott was just a stone's throw from Sangora. Maybe Fintan was right. What if there *was* a maniac on the loose?

'Fuck, it's him,' I said.

'You what?'

'Marion's killer. I bet that's him.'

'Don't be soft. Probably some kids...'

'We're three streets away.'

Clive sagged petulantly, so I took off. But I kept it to a jog: I'd need some puff left if I was going to disarm any deranged psycho.

Images of Marion flashed through my mind: the shock in her cold, dead eyes, her partially ripped-off fingernail.

As I turned into Salcott I checked back. Good old Clive was trundling along fifty feet behind, his head bowed, nodding like a knackered pit pony.

I looked for number 16 and clenched my fists, ready for anything. I gave the brass knocker three manly raps, shouted: 'Police, open the door.'

A voice from the other side said: 'Oh, thank God.'

The bright yellow door opened quickly to a pair of big, scared, brown eyes.

'Oh thank you, thank you,' she panted, as I stepped into the hallway.

'Are you okay?'

She nodded.

'Winona Ryder,' I gasped. The resemblance was uncanny.

'Pardon?' she said.

'Where is he, er, right now?' I blurted, hoping she'd assume that's what I'd said the first time.

'He was looking through my patio door. Now he's in the alley behind the garden, looking through a gap,' she explained, shutting the door behind me.

'Oh God, he's never done anything like this before.'

'You know him?'

She nodded rapidly, scared. Just then, the knocker went again. She jumped.

'Don't worry,' I said. When I opened it, Clive nearly tumbled inside.

'I've called for back-up,' he panted.

I turned and strode through the house until I got to the patio door. I slid it open and stepped into the garden, totally calm. I'd waited three years for this.

'I'm coming, Eve,' I thought to myself, 'this time, I'm coming.' I strode to the back of the garden, focusing on the only gap in the six-foot fence.

'Wait for back-up,' protested Clive from the patio.

Why give him the chance to escape? I thought to myself, deciding there and then to leap the fence, confront the fucker head on. I took out my standard-issue wooden truncheon, ran three strides, mounted, threw one leg over and braced myself.

I looked left, right. Nothing.

I didn't need to throw my second leg over: this narrow alleyway had no hiding places. He was gone.

I jumped back into the garden and sensed Clive's shaking head.

As I walked back to the house he grabbed my upper arm, hard.

'Get one thing straight, pal, I don't want to be a hero. If I say wait for back-up, I'm waiting for back-up, whether *you* wait or not. I'm not risking my neck for you or anyone else.'

'Gotcha,' I said, yanking my arm from his surprisingly firm grip.

I marched on into the house.

Winona had backed up against a neutral sitting room wall to keep an eye on all doors. I realised she was half-expecting her tormentor to outfox us and come through the front. That's what real terror does: it bestows superpowers upon the aggressor. I loathed bullies, especially men picking on women. I'd spent years watching Dad chip away at Mum until she became what he loathed most: a timid, meek, frightened wreck.

Winona's big brown eyes seemed so embarrassed, yet grateful.

'I can't thank you enough,' she said, her soft

87

voice oozing exhausted relief.

'I'm PC Lynch by the way, that's PC Hunt. And your name is?'

'Gabby. Look, I hate calling you but he was trying to open the patio door. I'm really scared he'll do something stupid.'

'You know him?' Clive harrumphed.

She took a deep breath, clearly summoning the energy to go through it all, yet again.

'He's my ex. We split up just after Easter, and he won't accept that it's over.'

'He's still bothering you after, what, four months?' I said.

'It's getting worse.'

'Has he physically...'

'No,' she said quickly.

'Damaged any property?' added Clive.

She shook her head again: 'But this is the first time he's come into my place.'

Clive threw me a look, one that said, 'Why do we bother?'

'How many times have you called us about this?' he said.

'This is the third time. Look, I feel terrible dialling 999 but sometimes it's the only way I can be certain something bad won't happen. And it's the only way I can get him to leave.'

'The trouble is, love,' patronised Clive, 'unless he's committed an actual offence, there's nothing we can do.'

She nodded, biting her lip.

'I'm sorry,' she said again.

I could tell, right away, what she hated most about all of this: the fact that she had to ask for help at all. I'd seen it in Marion's family that morning: these dignified, fiercely independent, proud people were the ones who paid their taxes so that we could exist, but they never wanted to need us.

Cringingly, Clive wasn't done yet demeaning our non-victim of crime.

'I'm not being funny, love, but you could get done for wasting police time. We're not Relate.'

She put her hand over her face and nodded again: 'It's just ... there's no one else I can turn to.'

'Clive, a word,' I said, heading to the front door. 'Shut the door behind you,' I told him.

'Are you telling me that there is nothing we can do to help her?' I asked.

'What can we do?'

'We could go see her ex-boyfriend, have a word.'

'You know the drill with domestics, Donal. He'll say: "I was only trying to talk to her." Unless there's hard evidence of an offence, you end up going round in circles.'

'What, so we've got to wait until she's lying on her landing with forty-nine stab wounds before we get involved?'

He sighed. 'She can go to a solicitor, apply for an injunction. We could get him on that later, okay?'

'But this is our patch. We can't just abandon this woman until he hurts her. What if she ends up like Marion?'

'You've got to stop letting your emotions get in the way, Donal. You'll never survive this business if you don't. We're not here to referee relationships.'

'She's not like the other people we deal with, Clive. You know that. It's not good enough.'

He sighed and nodded: 'I know, son. I know. But we don't make the laws.'

I was growing heartily sick of our helpless appeasement of petty criminals. It felt like we were almost taunting them to go one step further, to do something that would make our dealing with them worthwhile. *Make our day, punk, stick a knife in her next time.*

'What can we do?' asked Clive plaintively.

'We can do whatever the fuck we like,' I muttered, knocking on number 16 again. I knew Clive's heart was already at the Wimpy. 'Order me a chicken burger and fries. I'll see you there in ten.' Gabby didn't open the door until he was out of sight.

Her place was classy; chic but homely. I clocked her graduation photo: she was smart too. Why then had she shacked up with a psycho?

She didn't know where her stalker, Dominic Rogan, currently lived. Mutual acquaintances had confirmed that he still worked for Bank of America in the City.

'Is there any pattern to his activities?'

'No. It's just that he seems to be getting worse. Like I said, he's never actually come into the garden before.'

'Do you think he's capable of violence?'

'I know he is,' she snapped, 'that's why I dialled 999.

'Sorry,' she added quickly, 'I know you're just doing your job.'

'What level of violence, Gabby ... are you in

fear of your life?'

'I know he's capable of ... lashing out. That's why I broke up with him.'

'What does he want?'

'I've tried talking to him, if that's what you mean. I tried for weeks. He just won't accept that I don't love him.'

'I can help you get a court order.'

'I've thought about it, but it'd probably just provoke him. I don't want to make him more angry than he already is. He'd break it, I'm certain. Then what? He gets arrested, charged, a court case? It could drag on for months. All that time, he'd still be in my life. He'd love that.'

'Look Gabby, don't listen to my colleague. If he comes again, dial 999. I'll vouch for you.'

'Thank you,' she said, biting her bottom lip again.

I took out a piece of paper and a pen. 'This is my work number, and my home number. I live half a mile away. If you feel in danger, call either.'

'I ... really? Wow, I don't know what to say. Is that...? Thank you, Officer.'

'Donal,' I said, offering my hand.

She took it and shook it hard, her tearful smile lighting up a distant galaxy.

Chapter 6

Salcott Road, South London
Tuesday, July 2, 1991; 22:31

I drove up and down Gabby's road but, of course, at that time of night there were no parking spaces. On a second pass, I spotted the entry to the street's rear alley and ignored the No Parking sign next to it.

If Dominic Rogan launched another sortie tonight, he'd get the shock of his fucking life.

During my shift, Meehan's words from three years ago had been ringing through my head: *You need to keep an eye on that one.* I couldn't just hope that Rogan wouldn't come back and attack Gabby. I'd failed to protect a woman from a violent man before. I wouldn't be taking that chance again.

Besides, Rogan had clearly slipped into a delusional cycle that only the sharpest of shocks might break. My springing out of the night could do the trick.

I also figured, somehow, that Marion's foul-tempered spirit/ghost would be less likely to find me here. And, having grown up on *The Rockford Files, Cagney and Lacey* and *Remington Steele,* I'd always fantasised about staking somebody out. I even brought doughnuts.

After midnight, the wind picked up, the last of

the house lights went off and the trees groaned.

Just a handful of people walked past, mostly carefree couples gambolling home from a night out. How I envied their playful bickering, their easy intimacy, their 'wink-and-elbow' language of delight.

It had been almost three years since I'd shared the thrill of giddy affection. Sure, there had been a few drink-fuelled end-of-night snogs and exchanges of numbers, a few awkward dates. At least, they became awkward as soon as anyone mentioned exes. I hadn't worked out yet how to talk about Eve and what happened – or how to refer to her in the past tense. Unfinished business, and all that.

I thought back to the last time we'd spoken – two days after she killed Meehan.

The lunchtime news revealed she had been released on bail. Three or four times that afternoon, I picked up the phone to call her home, only to replace the receiver. Eve wouldn't answer for sure: what was I supposed to say to Mad Mo?

'Mrs Daly, back from New York so soon?'

No doubt they'd blame me for not protecting Eve – as if her prop dagger-wielding high-jinks hadn't proven, beyond any doubt, that the one person who didn't need protecting was Eve Daly.

Dusk told me it was time to go and see her. As shadows gathered in the last corners of the golf course, I strode the ninth fairway, relieved to be 'doing' rather than 'thinking'. Barty Morris, keeper of the greens and not many secrets, spotted me and stopped dead in his tracks. It was clear, even from this distance, he couldn't quite believe what he was seeing. I gave him a wave of my white bandaged hands and turned towards the Daly back garden. To wide-eyed Barty, this represented the scoop of a lifetime. 'The Dalys are having another party!' I shouted, and he nearly toppled over.

As I hopped into Eve's backyard, I spied the press pack out front disbanding for the night. I counted six photographers and two TV cameras. To one side, an orange-faced anchor man completed an earnest piece-to-camera. Behind him, a pair of ferrety little reporters, all bustling and self-important in their flappy macs, buzzed about like bluebottles at a picnic. Fintan would feel right at home amongst that lot, I thought. Except with this story, he could scoop his rivals without leaving his flat in Dublin 4.

As I crept across the crazy paving, I was stopped dead in my tracks by bloodstains – *my* bloodstains – daubed in manic streaks on the shed's pebbledash wall. It looked like the remnants of some gruesome pagan sacrifice.

I tiptoed to the outer wall of the house. The kitchen light was off, so I took a quick squint through the window. Ghostly white shapes floated up and down the hallway. On closer inspection, they turned into forensic officers in their white boiler suits and masks. Some sort of tent blocked the doorway into Eve's bedroom. The place where we fell in love and made our promises was now a crime scene.

I knew that my only chance of seeing Eve alone was after she'd gone to bed. She wouldn't be sleeping in her own room tonight, so I gambled that Mo would give her the master bedroom. I decided to creep round the bungalow to that window and wait.

The top half of the back door was frosted glass, so I got down on all fours to crawl past. Christ, I thought, what if Mad Mo walks out now? It'd be the second death here in two days, because she'd either keel over from shock, or murder me. I had to stop crawling to laugh. I put it down to nerves.

I got to the window to find the blinds closed solid against the glass. I couldn't even tell if there was a light on inside. I waited and waited, drumming up the courage to drum upon the glass. When it turned ten p.m., I held my breath and thudded gently with my bandaged hand. Nothing. I thudded louder.

I stood back. I figured the Dalys were feeling a bit raw at the moment and I didn't want to scare the shit out of anybody. The curtain opened a fraction. The light caught Eve's fiery hair and I saw one green eye squinting through the gap. I realised I'd been holding my breath for longer than was healthy.

The gap closed, then nothing. Was someone else in the room? I crouched down and waited, and waited. Ten, fifteen minutes passed. What was going on? All I knew was: I wouldn't leave until I'd spoken to Eve – no matter how long it took. Finally, the window latch squeaked, a little reluctantly to my ears.

I reached out, put my wrapped-up hand on hers. She pulled it away. Well what did I expect?

I'd rehearsed my speech, over and over, but it was gone.

'Sorry,' was all I could think to say. 'Eve, I'm so, so sorry.'

I couldn't stop my eyes welling up. She looked at me, blankly. She was still in shock. I just had to let her know that I was here for her.

'I can't imagine how you must be feeling,' I said, re-offering a comedy mitten. She looked at it, blinked for the first time, but didn't take it. She sighed hard.

'He spiked my drink. That's why I ended up, you know...'

She looked over my head into the distance for several seconds.

'Eve, please, we need to talk.'

Finally, she snapped back from whatever far-off place she'd been inspecting, and looked at me properly.

'He attacked me,' she whispered.

'Oh God, Eve,' I said.

She leaned forward, placing her elbows on the window sill and cradling her cheeks with her open hands. With her hair in bunches, she looked so young, so fragile, so pretty. I just wanted to hold her for the rest of my life.

'Eve,' I whispered, and moved closer, 'I know this is going to sound really weird, but I think I saw what happened.'

Her hands dropped from her face. 'What?' she said, her voice suddenly hard. 'What are you on about?'

'Please, just let me explain,' I pleaded. 'When I blacked out, I had this sort of out-of-body experience. It's like my spirit came to your bedroom and saw what happened.'

'What?' she said, irritated.

'Look I know it sounds mad but I came out of my body and found myself hovering in your bedroom. I could see you on the bed. I saw ... him ... walk into the room. I saw the clock radio. It said 1.09.'

Eve stared at me, her damp eyes accusing and wounded. 'What? What do you mean *you saw?*'

'It's like my spirit got sent to your bedroom. It was as if I was in your room, watching it all happen, but when I tried to shout, when I tried to ... help you, I couldn't do anything. I couldn't move. I really don't know how to explain it.'

Eve was staring at me hard, blinking often.

'What did you see?' she demanded.

'Oh God, Eve, I don't know if I should put you through it again, I...'

'Tell me, Donal. Please. I need to know.'

'I saw him getting up, er on top of you. Then he threw his hat towards the window ... like a Frisbee...'

'Oh my God...' she murmured. 'And...?'

I rushed through the rest as fast as I could. 'You were sort of fighting back. It was all silent. He lifted up your skirt and then it went black and I woke up in hospital. It felt like I was in some sort of vacuum.'

Eve held my hand tightly.

After what seemed like several minutes, she said, 'How long were you there, in my room?'

I shook my head. 'A few minutes. The clock said 1.13 when I blacked out again.'

I decided not to mention Meehan's post-death attempt to strangle me: she'd heard enough for one night.

'That's so strange,' she said softly, her grip on my hand loosening.

'There must be a logical reason,' I said. 'Maybe I heard them talking about it, when I was unconscious. Maybe my brain formed pictures of what I'd heard.'

'Yeah but the hat thing ... no one would know that.'

We said nothing for several minutes.

'He did attack me, you know?' she said, lowering her big wet eyes towards mine, 'I had to defend myself.'

'Of course,' I said, tightening my grip. 'I – I saw.'

She gulped and looked down.

'Eve, I want you to know, whatever happens, I'll be here for you.' I had never meant anything more in my entire life.

She turned her head to the window frame. 'Just go, Donal. Don't wait for me,' she said softly.

'Okay, but I'll come back tomorrow, and every day until this has sorted itself out.'

'No, Donal, I don't want you waiting for me. It'll just make things harder. Go without me.'

'I can't do that, I...'

'Promise me you'll go to London, like we planned.'

She was eyeing me as you would a defiant child. I shook my head, trying hard not to cry.

'Promise!' she demanded sharply, pulling away from my hand and glaring at me. I could never say no to Eve.

'Promise,' I whimpered, feeling as lonely and

restless as a ghost.

'Good,' she said, 'because we're finished, Donal. It's over. I'm sorry.' She pulled the window shut – thump. The blind fell back down to earth. Thump. In one aching heartbeat, she had gone.

Three years on, my chest still twanged at the memory. I unwound the car window a few inches and gulped in some fresh night air. I decided to give Salcott Road another hour, then go home and crack open the Shiraz.

Yeah but the hat thing ... no one would know that. Three years later, Eve's words still echoed in my brain.

Three whole years. I knew I should move on from Eve Daly. Fintan had told me to move on from Eve Daly. My friends had told me to move on from Eve Daly. What no one could tell me was: *how do you stop loving somebody?*

I tried to meet girls on the North London Irish scene, but grew dispirited. They seemed immediately turned off by the fact I was a cop: no doubt their daddies wouldn't approve. Mind you, being a builder or barman hadn't exactly bowled them over either. I got the impression they wanted to be swept off their feet by a square-jawed sporty type with worldly charm, roguish self-confidence and big plans to make money and move back home. It didn't help that Fintan seemed possessed of the magic formula for instantly clicking with women. He'd get this glint in his eye that they clearly adored, and I could never make them laugh like he did. Inevitably, I got stuck with his conquest's perennially over-shadowed, unamused sidekick.

99

It irked me that girls found Fintan's blatant badness irresistible. And here was another one. Gabby had fallen for Dom Rogan, patently another bastard.

I tried to imagine her inside number 16. After what happened earlier, she wouldn't be sleeping. I pictured her in the sitting room, reading highbrow women's fiction and drinking camomile tea. Would she close the curtains, hoping Dom would stay away? Or leave them open so that she'd see him coming?

Suddenly, the back right-hand door of the car slammed shut. I jumped. My arms shot up, instinctively covering my bowed head as I braced for attack. Seconds ground past, but the blows didn't arrive. I lifted my eyes carefully to the rearview mirror: I couldn't see anyone in the back. Was he lying on the seat? Why would he wait for me to turn? To knife me? I opened my left elbow into a more attacking position and slowly turned my body around.

No one. I checked out the back window, the side windows. There was no-one there. Who the hell had opened and shut the car door?

I turned back to the windscreen.

'You're imagining things, Lynch,' I told myself, rubbing the stiff hairs on the back of my neck.

I suddenly sensed that crackle in the air: the electricity of malevolent intent. Someone wanted to do me harm, this instant. Rogan must be somewhere close by, I was certain of it.

Both back doors opened and shut this time. I tried to raise my fists and turn, but nothing would move. My entire body was frozen, paralysed. All I could feel was my heart pounding in my throat.

The back doors opened, shut, opened and shut, over and over.

I realised the only thing I could move were my eyeballs. Slowly, I raised them towards the rear-view mirror.

Marion's bloodshot eyes glared back – wet, alive, deranged. My choking throat closed down. Unable to breathe, my chest filled to bursting. Next thing, she's hammering my head against the window of the car door, over and over, thump, thump.

The banging rang in my ears, followed by a blinding flash of yellow light.

Someone was hammering the other side of the window. I tried to focus on the banger but, against the glare, could see only a gloved hand. 'Meehan?' I screamed.

'Open up, now,' came the command. I reached for the handle, slowly unwinding the window. I could move again. 'Evening, sir. Perhaps you'd like to explain what you're doing here?' said the uniformed police officer.

'Of course, Officer, yes, I can explain. I felt very tired driving home and stopped for a nap.'

'You stopped for a nap? Here? Have you been drinking, sir?'

'No. Not tonight. I'm a PC myself, Officer, based at Wandsworth.'

'Of course you are, sir. Would you kindly step out of the car?'

'Why? What have I done wrong?'

'We've received reports of a disturbance. Please, step out of the car.'

'Of course,' I said, opening the door and getting to my feet.

The first thing I saw was Gabby, cowering behind a WPC.

'Oh my God it's you,' she screamed, 'you creep.'

'Please, Gabby, I can explain,' I tried but she'd already stormed off.

'Are you this stalker she's been telling us about?' said the cop.

'No. Look, honestly,' I smiled my most reassuring smile, 'I can explain everything.'

Chapter 7

Trinity Road, South London
Tuesday, July 2, 1991; 23:00

Aidan cackled mercilessly at my noble attempts to protect Gabby from Dom Rogan. Coming from the most hapless of hopeless romantics, it confirmed that I'd irretrievably fucked up.

When the house phone rang, we both froze like spinsters. Tragically, this had never happened after eleven p.m. before. The look of mild terror on Aidan's face as I picked up reinforced my conviction that we both needed to get a life.

'Hello?'

'Hi, Donal, it's Gabby.'

By the time I recovered my composure, she must have assumed I'd hung up. Or lost consciousness.

'Donal? Donal? HELLO?'

'Hi, Gabby, hi. God, this is a surprise. A pleasant one I mean.'

Aidan's eyes sprang out on stalks as I bumbled on.

'Thanks so much for calling, I – I wasn't expecting it but I'm really glad you did because I really, really wanted to explain everything.'

'Really?'

'Yes. If that's okay? I'm amazed you called, and grateful, really grateful. And can I say sorry first, sorry for freaking you out? I can explain. Did they give you my note?'

'Oh yes, the WPC was most insistent.'

'I was so frustrated, leaving you the way we did. I had this horrible feeling he'd come back. I – I'm an insomniac anyway so I thought, well, why not pop round and keep an eye on your place? A spur of the moment thing really. Then I fell asleep in the car and had a nightmare. That must have been why I was shouting.'

Aidan cringed like a condemned Texan.

'Right. So you shout in your sleep?'

'Only at the moment.'

'Great. Soon I'll have maniacs queuing up at the front door. What were you planning to do to him?'

'I just thought I'd shake him up a bit, you know, give him a fright. Make him think twice about doing it again.'

'You don't get it, do you?' she said, her voice breaking in panicked exasperation, 'that's not going to work. That'll just make him really angry. And then he'll come back and do something awful to me.'

'I won't let that happen to you, Gabby. I promise.'

'You can't make that promise. He'll just carry on doing what he likes.'

'Like I said, Gabby, I suffer from insomnia. It's no trouble to me to drive over and keep an eye on your place. I can just sit in the car, listen to the radio, even for a few nights until you sort something out.'

'I don't ... why would you do that?'

'Look, you live on my patch. It's my duty to keep the people on my patch safe.'

I thought the next silence would never end. But I held my nerve.

'I'm not sure it's a good idea. I've got your number. If he turns up, I'll call you.'

'I hope you mean that.'

This silence lasted longer. I lost my nerve.

'Okay, well, I guess I hope I don't hear from you again then, Gabby,' I said, as brightly as I could.

'I hope not,' she said blankly, hanging up.

Chapter 8

Wandsworth Common
Sunday, July 7, 1991; 10:15

A glorious morning deserved a stroll to the Common. On the way, I picked up a copy of the *Sunday News*. In the cool shade of a gnarled old oak, I settled down to Fintan's latest journalistic handiwork.

'Cops Hunt South London Ripper', said the headline, 'by Fintan Lynch, Deputy Crime Correspondent.'

The opening paragraph: 'The maniac who slashed to death a twenty-three-year-old newlywed in her London flat earlier this week is targeting other women in the local area, police believe.'

A police source confirmed that, on the day of 'Marion's slaying' – surely not the source's phrase? – a nanny had been pestered by a stranger on the Common 'less than a mile from the scene of Marion's brutal murder'.

A day later, in nearby Clapham South, a woman had been accosted on her doorstep by a stranger. Her 'would-be attacker' tried to push her inside, only for the 'quick-thinking victim' to scream, forcing him to run away. I marvelled at the poetic licence of 'would-be attacker' and the logic that makes screaming a 'quick-thinking' response. Mind you, Marion hadn't screamed: at least not loudly enough for anyone to hear. She kept her head when screaming it off might have saved her.

I shuddered. This development changed everything.

Could the same man have bundled Marion inside her front door, then marched her upstairs at knifepoint? The mail found next to her body seemed to torpedo this scenario – unless the letters had been planted afterwards. If there was a maniac like this on the loose, how long before he strikes again?

Descriptions of the suspect in the two 'failed attacks' tallied, resulting in the usual comedy photo-fit. If we found a simian male with a face wider than was long, with no forehead, a monobrow and tiny, malevolent eyes, then that was our man. If some guy out there really did look like this, then small wonder he'd been forced to opt for non-consensual romantic encounters.

Tellingly, the impeccably connected police source for this 'exclusive' didn't explicitly say that detectives were linking Marion's murder to these two incidents. The article simply concluded that Scotland Yard had declined to comment. The entire piece was clearly sensationalist, scaremongering bollocks; opportunist skulduggery of the basest kind. Another look at that photo-fit revealed a certain likeness to Fintan. God knows that fucker would do anything to stand up a story.

I suppose the Yard didn't care, so long as the all-important Incident Room number was tagged on at the end. Sometimes, a single call from the public can save months of investigation, and other lives. But everything else in the article had to be a rip-roaring smokescreen, surely?

I was certain that the 'Big Dog' detectives would be sniffing through every aspect of Marion's life, and that soon they would work out who wanted her dead, and why.

Thankfully, Marion's vengeful spirit hadn't come to me again since her car door slamming escapades the other night. And the more I thought about it, although I had been terrified, I don't think she had actually meant me harm. She was trying to tell me something. The only thing I could think of were doors – the door she'd slammed in my flat and the car door. But what did that mean?

I doubted if the Big Dogs would entertain any of this. I doubted any sane person would entertain the notion that Marion was giving me clues to her killer from beyond the grave. So what was I to do with this information? And why had she not come to me in the last five days?

Suddenly everything around me rustled. A breeze as cold as steel snaked around my neck and shoulders, forcing them to roll together... A daytime moon winked briefly between skidding incoming clouds. Whatever Marion had in store for me would come, as sure as rain and night and death.

Chapter 9

Salcott Road, South London
Sunday, July 7, 1991; 22:00

That night, I took up my usual position at the alleyway on Salcott Road, more scared of an encounter with Gabby than Dom Rogan.

As I did so, I realised one other thing connected Marion's two visits: on both those days I had attended her murder scene. Since then, she'd been a no-show. I could have tested this theory right then – Sangora Road was just five minutes' walk away – but I had a stalker to stalk.

It had been four days since Dom's incursion into Gabby's back garden. On each of those subsequent nights, I'd waited for him here but he'd failed to show – or at least, I hadn't seen him. I was worried that he'd clocked me, and was now biding his time until I gave up. We both knew I couldn't keep coming here indefinitely.

Although he'd no previous convictions, I had been able to glean all of Dom's personal details from the police computer. I thought about turning up at Bank of America in uniform and demanding to see him. When dealing with the middle classes, embarrassment can be our most powerful weapon. But to do this, I'd have to get an official sanction and, of course, write a report.

I much preferred keeping Dom unofficial

business. With him in Gabby's back garden, face down in the dirt, my arm around his throat, I could much better explain my plans to hit him with charges of trespass, resisting arrest and assaulting a police officer if he ever showed up again. Another breach and I'd make it official: magistrates would give him two years' probation at the very least. Break that and I'd land him in jail quicker than he could say: 'I want to call my family lawyer.' I felt certain that the very real threat of prison would straighten him out, no matter how much he might squeal about his rights and his well-connected pals.

I felt uncomfortable bending the rules, but what else could I do?

As it was Sunday night, the street's houselights sparked out even earlier. If New York is the city that never sleeps, London likes an early night.

A sharp rap on the car window lifted me six inches off the seat. Gabby glared down at me, half-cross, half-amused. I unwound the window.

'We don't want him thinking he's got competition,' she deadpanned, 'you might as well come in.'

'Only if you're sure...' I started but she'd already marched off. I caught up with her at the front door.

'I've tidied and everything.'

'You knew I'd come?'

'Funnily enough, Donal, because I'm being stalked I tend to keep a bit of an eye out. I can't believe you park in the same place every night.'

My face burned.

'I'm not a weirdo, Gabby, I really want to stress

109

that point. I just want to help you get rid of this ... problem.'

'I know that now,' she said, treating me to a closed-mouth, business-like smile.

She took a quick scan of the street – almost instinctively – then gestured at me to go through first, before treble-locking the door.

I led the way down her hallway into an open-plan sitting room and kitchen. I noticed original numbered canvas artwork, a bank of photos of her world travels, an old Canon Super 8 camera, books galore – lots of Virginia Woolf and Philip Larkin.

She showed me to her kitchen table, put the kettle on. 'Tea, coffee?'

'Tea would be great.'

She opened her cupboard to reveal a rainbow of exotic brews: Darjeeling, Earl Grey, Cinnamon, Peppermint.

'What type?'

'Just normal, thanks.'

'I'm not sure I have normal.'

'Surprise me,' I demanded, pretending to be the spontaneous type.

She put a cup of what smelt like steaming rat piss in front of me and announced: 'Right, let's get this over with, shall we?'

My startled look clearly empowered her.

'You must be dying to know how I ended up with a nutty stalker boyfriend.'

How did she know?

'Well, he didn't start out like that. I suppose they never do.'

I shuffled awkwardly. I was still learning how to

listen without judgement. It didn't come naturally.

'I met him at Uni. He was shy, serious but very dry and funny when you got to know him. And clever. He's probably the only actual genius I've ever met.'

I realised I'd yet to tick a single point on her 'What I Like in a Man' list.

'Of course I was totally bowled over by this tortured and slightly depressive genius. I mean, who wouldn't be?'

'Who indeed? Do you have milk by any chance?'

She looked at me as if I'd just cracked a really lame gag, then carried on.

'After a while, he never wanted to go out or have anyone round. Looking back I can see how he isolated me from my friends and my family. They really didn't like him at all. We spent more and more time together. I didn't realise it but I'd become totally dependent on him.

'He started getting very snappy and impatient, criticising me all the time. He just chipped away at my self-esteem until I'd lost all sense of who I was and what I believed in, if that makes sense.'

The dainty china cup felt ridiculous in my meaty farmer's hand. I took a sip, careful to suppress all reaction, and apologised silently to rats.

'Then my gran got diagnosed with cancer. Dom refused to come with me to see her. She'd only met him a few times but she gave me a really stiff talking to. I was really upset by the things she said but I knew in my heart she was right. So I went home and told him.'

'And now he can't accept it's over?'

She shook her head.

'You mentioned he could be violent?'

She swallowed, inspected her hands and nodded slowly. It didn't feel right to press. I tried another tack.

'Maybe he just can't stop loving you?'

She laughed bitterly. 'He never loved me. I'm a possession to him. His ego can't accept that I finished it. Little old meek me.'

'Meek? You? Jesus.'

That got a smile.

'Look, Gabby, you need to move out of here, get a house share so you've always got people around you. Stay off the electoral roll so he can't find you...'

'But Gran left me this place. I've spent the last six months doing it up. I can't just ... leave.'

'Maybe just for a year ... you'd have no trouble renting it out. It's beautiful...'

'Thank you.'

'I promise, give it twelve months and he'll tire of trying to find you.'

'He knows where I work.'

'Where's that?'

'Hopscotch children's nursery, on Crescent Lane. I'm the manager.'

'Trust me, stalker or not, he won't hang around a nursery. He'll get lynched.'

She laughed, then groaned: 'Oh God, why do I have to move when he's the one...?'

'Look, I don't want to alarm you, Gabby, but he's escalating. You need to get away from here right away. By that, I mean tomorrow. Have you family close by?'

She sighed.

'Mum and Dad live in Maidstone. It's only an hour on the train. I suppose I could stay there for a while.'

'Otherwise you'll have to put up with me every night.'

She looked at me, eyebrow arched, quizzically amused: 'What's your story then, Donal? How does an Irishman end up in the British police force? And why do you shout in your sleep?'

'How long have you got?' I laughed.

'I'm not a great sleeper either,' she smiled, 'so you can take your time. Another tea?'

'Er no, thanks. Do you have anything stronger?'

'I've got wine.'

'Red?'

'Blimey, you get your feet under the table quick, don't you?'

'Bespoke personal protection don't come cheap.'

I skipped the stuff about Eve and Meehan: none of it showed anyone in a good light. Instead, over too much Merlot, I took her through my three-year journey from North to South London; from Irish rebel to tax-paying member of Her Majesty's Constabulary.

Put it down to gut instinct or a copper's mind but, as I poured out my story, I felt sure we were being watched, possibly listened to. I knew too that what I'd started here could end horribly. What if Dom was a disciple of that stalker's doctrine: 'if I can't have you, nobody else will'?

When I first got to Harlesden, I shared a house so crowded that only the door-less bathroom didn't have a bed. We went home to wash and sleep. We

113

ate, drank, got hired and cashed our paycheques at the Spotted Dog pub on Willesden High Road.

Standing at the bar every night were the men we'd become if we kept this up for another twenty or thirty years, the old boys who came over in the Fifties and Sixties. They had faces like elephant hide and accents even thicker; I'd never heard anyone in Ireland speak with such a strong brogue. I watched them night after night, sinking pint after pint of Guinness, failing to quench terrible thirsts while clutching white polythene bags in their non-drinking hands.

'What's in the bags?' I asked the barman quietly one night.

'That's their dinner,' he whispered. On closer inspection, beneath the polythene I could see the outline of a chop or a ball of mince, potatoes and carrots.

'Why don't they get it later? It's not like the shops round here shut.'

'Because they'll have drunk all their money later.'

You'd learn that some of them didn't go home for Christmas anymore – the lost causes. Two nights a week, a tin collecting for 'IRA prisoners' rattled under your nose. No one dared decline. You noticed that the local mini-cab firm only ever sent white drivers. No one ever asked why.

I'd landed regular work feeding cement to a trio of Connemara bricklayers. They worked like savages, as if expunging some inner volcanic rage or demon. 'Feed me,' they'd roar, but no matter how fast and hard I'd mix, I could never keep up. It sapped me of the energy I needed to change my pub-based existence. At least that was my excuse.

We spent almost the entire weekend in the Dog, drinking away our aches and gains, frittering money on horses, football and pool. We'd end up at the Gresham on Holloway Road, a vast hangar of drunken oblivion where Irish people of all ages drank, ate, danced and fought. And they always fought. The red-faced middle-aged men in ripped shirts knew they only had to land one good one to win. The police never came. You were too pissed to wonder why.

Then Fintan moved over, saw how low I'd sunk and set about breaking me out of my bad routine. But not before first establishing himself as a cut-throat tabloid hack.

Within months of his arrival in London, under the expert tutelage of the *Sunday News,* he'd sunk to the challenge of becoming one of Fleet Street's most lethal 'operators'. Both his drinking capacity and expenses account appeared bottomless, as he set about getting half of Scotland Yard well-oiled and onside. His connections didn't end there. When I'd had my fill of labouring, he told me to go see Seamus Horan, manager of the Feathers pub, near St James's Park underground station in central London. I jumped at the chance: every organ within me felt like it needed a change.

In Seamus, I found another immigrant turned to granite by hardship. He explained bluntly that he employed Irish staff because they *expected* a pub to stay open till three or four in the morning, every morning.

I quickly discovered that the Feathers had

become the favoured watering hole of officers working at nearby Scotland Yard. Boy could they drink. And, because it was patronised by the law, it was *above* the law.

We never closed before three a.m. No wonder there was a permanent vacancy. It helped that I could take a room upstairs.

The insomnia that had tormented me since I arrived in London finally proved useful. By the time I talked the last drunks down from their stools each morning, only medicated mini-cab drivers and demented birds were still up. I never heard a bird singing at night until I came to London. Those nightingales on Berkeley Square must be fucking knackered.

Gabby laughed. But I had an acute boredom sensor. It was time to wrap up.

'So I got to know a few of the officers and they persuaded me to join up,' I said, skipping the murky truth about how I became a cop. That would have to wait for another day.

'Do you have ambitions, you know, to make detective?'

'Yeah, you could say that. I'm desperate, to be honest.'

'Don't you worry that your insomnia will eventually catch up with you, make you ill?'

'Of course. I've seen specialists. I've read books. No one seems to have an answer.'

'I've got a friend about to begin her final year of a psychology degree. I remember her saying she'd like to specialise in sleep disorders. She's looking for a case right now...'

116

'Oh I don't know,' I laughed, 'it's all a bit embarrassing.'

'I tell you what,' said Gabby, 'if you agree to help Lily, I'll go stay with my parents.'

'Seriously?'

'Seriously,' she said, holding out her hand.

'Deal.' I smiled, shaking her hand and hoping I was the only one lying.

I pulled open the phone box door, sampled the air inside and nodded gratefully. It couldn't have been pissed in for at least three days.

I shovelled in three pound coins and poked those digits you never forget. On the third ring, I realised I hadn't planned what to say. I slammed the receiver down and heard the three coins clatter down to the tray.

'Hi, Mum,' I said to the stale air, 'how are you?'

Chapter 10

King's College Hospital, South London
Thursday, July 11, 1991; 09:55

The following Thursday morning – ten days after Marion's murder – I clocked the sign that read King's College's Institute of Psychiatry and winced.

Psychiatry sounded so judgemental, so incurable. But I'd come here voluntarily. They wouldn't shoot a dart in my arse and cart me off indefinitely for the good of society. Of that I felt almost certain.

Besides, Lilian Krul hadn't yet qualified. And this face-to-face with the wannabe shrink had been slated for just sixty minutes: barely enough time for her to knock the shine off my well-polished veneer of sanity, let alone scratch it.

Of course, I'd fully intended to renege on my deal with Gabby as soon as she'd moved back to her family's home in Kent. But I hadn't counted on her academic friend's tireless perseverance. I was left in no doubt that Lilian could give Dom Rogan a real run for his money in the stalking stakes. She must have left ten messages over two days to make this happen. I caved in because, if this was all it took to keep Gabby out of harm's way, then it had to be worth every second.

I told Aidan I had gone to a vinyl sale; I couldn't bring myself to admit I'd found professional help outside his place of work, the pre-eminent Maudsley. He'd been on at me for months about 'seeing someone' there. I tried to explain that every time I'd visited a specialist I wound up prescribed some sort of medieval haymaker sleeping tablet that turned me into a slack-jawed halfwit.

Aidan had even described my case in detail to a leading sleep specialist, which put me right off. For one thing, he was prone to exaggeration. God knows what he'd told them. On top of that, when confronted by shrinks, I reserved the right to edit my own symptoms and lunacy.

I would never admit to any fully qualified member of the medical establishment the true extent of my insomnia. I dreaded being labelled

118

schizophrenic or bi-polar and carted off to some screaming Gothic madhouse where – drugged, drooling and helpless – I'd get arse-fucked daily by some sick, cackling chaplain.

As an Irish male, I had a scientific right to be scared. Studies have found that four per cent of the Irish population are schizophrenic; that's four times higher than any other nation in the world.

They looked for historical reasons behind Ireland's reluctant success in producing champion nutters. In-breeding turned out not to be a factor, thankfully. After all, over the centuries all manner of imposter – Viking, Norman, Spanish, English, to name a few – had turned the Irish gene pool into alphabet soup. Our women have a proud record of welcoming exotic strangers. It felt reassuring to know that our inadequacy in the eyes of the Irish female was historical.

Another theory had been the traditional 'emigration of the strongest', but they found similarly high levels of schizophrenia in Irish emigrant groups across the US.

The experts eventually agreed that it came down to a combination of three historical reasons: maternal malnourishment during pregnancy, alcoholism and ageing sperm. In at least two of these disciplines, my auld fella Martin scored top marks.

He'd already turned fifty by the time my older brother and I came along. Like so many men in rural Ireland, that was the price he paid for inheriting the family farm a couple of decades earlier. It came equipped with his mother, May Lynch – a ringing bitch still spoken about in tones of mild terror and awe. And, like most of these narcissistic matriarchs, she wouldn't tolerate another woman in the house so he had to wait for her to die.

That was the 'ageing sperm' condition covered. As for 'the drink', Martin insisted he did so only socially. But being a local politician, auctioneer and IRA facilitator, he tended to be social every evening of the week. And he'd always wrap up the night with a few whiskies on the couch, considered so anti-social by the rest of us that we'd feel the need to hide.

So, no one could accuse Martin Lynch of not doing his bit to sire a schizo. Maybe he wanted one to join him fighting for 'the cause'. Thankfully, no matter how knackered and godawful I felt, I never heard voices. But I still felt a little paranoid about that particular prognosis, so strenuously avoided the only people who could help me. Today's 'consultation' with Lilian was an aberration, and I planned to make sure of that by telling her fuck all.

'Donal?' came a soft voice. 'Hi, I'm Lilian.'

I was expecting someone sterner, with less make-up and more gravitas.

I tried not to look too shocked: she looked surprised enough for the both of us. Her hair was scraped back into a ponytail with such severity that her eyebrows were arched, making her seem permanently startled. Gigantic, thick-rimmed black spectacles made her already large pupils look like a pair of well-polished conkers. Her pronounced cheekbones glowed pink beneath war paint.

She couldn't have been more than twenty-five, but had gone to considerable lengths to appear older. She wore a dark grey trouser suit a couple of sizes too big, as if she'd been playing in her father's clothes chest. Her shoes would've made Freud weep.

'Come with me, please,' she instructed, shutting my inspection down.

I followed her into a small room that smelt of handwash and leather.

'Let me take your coat, Donal,' she said, pronouncing it Donald but with a silent 'd' on the end. 'Please, get comfortable.'

She sat down opposite me, staring hard at her notes.

Finally, she took a deep breath and spoke: 'Okay, so Gabby told me the basics. What I'd like you to do today is run through your entire sleep history, from as far back as you can remember.'

I started, a little reluctantly. Then – like one of my dad's middle-of-the-night pisses – it just went on and on. The knowledge that this woman hadn't the authority to prescribe either drugs or indefinite incarceration seemed to liberate me.

I explained how, as a child, I used to wake in the dark, wide-eyed, unable to move, already choking on an 'I'm going to die' level of terror. The slinky black figure would soundlessly appear five or six feet from the end of my bed. Suddenly he'd be on my chest, strangling me. I'd have to fight against the swirling black liquid of his evil eyes. Then, he'd snap off, vanish ... just like that.

I'd be out of bed, gasping for breath, scared for my life. And that would be it for another night:

121

too scared to go back to sleep, too tired to do anything but loll on the sofa. Most times, I'd find Mum already there.

As far back as I could remember, Mum's eyes looked dead, as if fixed upon some distant regret. Her criss-crossed skin hung loose on sharp cheekbones, like whittled oak. She was forty-seven now; you would have guessed closer to seventy-four. A life spent almost always awake was killing her. That, and all the medication they kept prescribing.

She made light of my 'attacks', telling me it was St Giles, patron saint of bad dreams, protecting me from nightmares. Quite why this messenger of God felt the need to throttle me, we never fully explored.

The lack of sleep made me constantly ill. Dad told me not to tell the doctor about my phantom tormentor. I'm sure his primary concern was how it might sound to the local GP, a man he played golf with. Back then, men in black lying on top of defenceless little boys in the middle of the night was the sole preserve of the Holy Orders. He didn't want Dr Harnett thinking he was some sort of pervert.

I'd sometimes catch my dad looking at me with an expression that I could read, even back then, as contempt.

'What the hell is wrong with that child?' I'd hear him ask my mother. I grew up with the unshakeable certainty that, somehow, I'd ruined his life.

When I turned twelve, the visions stopped, just like that.

'But now it's started again?'

I took her through the fancy dress party and

Meehan's attack – right up to my bloodcurdling encounters with Marion Ryan outside Gabby's flat.

Lilian scribbled feverishly. She interrupted me once more, to declare that our time was up.

'I'd love to go on but the room's been booked.'

'I don't think I could, Lilian, I'm spent,' I said, getting to my feet, wobbling a little from a light head.

'Are you okay, Donal(d)?'

'I feel a bit ... giddy. It's like how I used to feel coming out of confession as a kid. That was cathartic, I suppose. Thank you.'

'I should be thanking you,' she said, 'for opening up like that. I get the feeling you've not done that before?'

I shrugged.

'I'm looking for a case study, Donal, and your condition is fascinating,' she said, tucking her notes under her arm and standing.

'Thanks,' I said, wondering why I felt flattered, 'but I'm not sure what else I can tell you. That's it, really.'

She smiled: 'You've no idea how interesting all this is to someone like me. I have a thousand questions.'

I felt myself giggling coquettishly and wondered if I had self-esteem issues.

'You said yourself you found it cathartic. Maybe we can help each other?'

My guard shot up.

'I'm not sure, Lilian, I mean I really have told you everything.'

'I need something new and original for my

dissertation. Your case would be perfect.'

'How long does a dissertation take? I'm pretty busy.'

'What if I only ask you to keep seeing me for as long as you feel you're getting something out of it?'

She'd reduced me to one last excuse.

'The thing is, Lilian, I can't have people knowing about this condition, not in my job. If any of this came out, it'd be the end of my career.'

'I don't need to use your name. You can be anonymous, even in my support notes. That's not a problem at all.'

Her giant eyes blinked into mine, pleadingly.

'No mention of my real name, at all, anywhere near it?'

'I promise, Donal,' she almost cheeped in desperation.

'Okay,' I said and her stretched face crumpled with relief, 'but I'm only committing to a few sessions, see how we go.'

'You won't regret it, Donal, honestly,' she beamed. 'Now I just need you to sign a couple of documents so that I can clear it with my tutor and apply for your medical records.'

She turned and picked up two documents from the table.

'If you could sign here ... and here,' she said, her scarlet fingernails tapping at two tiny white squares amid a torrent of text. I scrawled, both impressed and alarmed by the fact she seemed to have pre-empted my agreement.

'Great,' she said, whipping the papers away, 'Gabby was worried you wouldn't take very kindly to being my guinea pig.'

'Hey, less of the pig ... quack,' I said, strolling out and thinking: *I was pretty cool there.*

'Oh, Donal!' she called after me, 'you've forgotten your coat.'

Chapter 11

Salcott Road, South London
Friday, July 12, 1991; 20:55

It had been twelve days since Marion Ryan's murder; ten since her spirit unleashed its second assault upon me here outside Gabby's.

DS Glenn's team had still made no arrests or gone public linking Marion's murder to any other crimes. As a result, the story had all but died in the media. A contact of Fintan's inside the investigation had said that they were focusing on a 'Lone Wolf' random killer. The same source said detectives had so little to go on that they were effectively waiting for this killer to strike again.

I didn't buy their Lone Wolf theory. I couldn't believe Marion had let a deranged stranger into her home, or that a maniac had somehow forced his way in. Yet Glenn's team must have looked into all potential suspects known to Marion and Peter, and ruled them out. They seemed certain that this had been no 'domestic'.

So who did it? As mad as it seemed, I felt certain that Marion had appeared to me on both those occasions to help me catch her killer. I'd

125

just been too thick to interpret her clues. Maybe I needed to reconnect with her ghost or spirit by returning to the scene of the crime but I'd no means of getting inside 21 Salcott Road.

I felt glumly helpless and thwarted, a lowly plod forever doomed to remain lukewarm-on-the-trail of long-fled shoe muggers and evasive obsessive stalkers.

Earlier today, Gabby had left a message at work saying she was returning to her flat at about nine p.m. to pick up some clothes. She didn't ask me to meet her there. Perhaps she realised she didn't need to.

I parked up outside her place, in civvies to avoid attracting attention. A gust of wind slapped a lazy belt of rain against the windscreen: wet enough, surely, to douse the ardour of even the most fervent stalker. She'd taken my advice and was travelling each night to her parents' home outside London. She'd also acted on my recommendation to buy a can of mace and a rape alarm.

This was not a good time to spring even a pleasant surprise upon Ms Gabby Arnold, so I got out and stood in the howling wet.

A lonely streetlight ghosted on, white, dull and useless against the skimming grey cloud. The wind swatted icy rain down the back of my shirt collar and I shuddered. The streetlight warmed yellow then amber, finally kicking through the gloom. I'd never noticed how orange these lights shine. As I admired the ignited horizontal rain, I sensed someone watching me. I spun around. To my left, a footstep sounded. My pivoting eyes caught a fleeing shadow, flitting past a parked white van into the black.

I walked urgently towards what I'd seen, straining my eyes to make out more.

'Rogan,' I shouted.

I reached the back of the van and waited. My own blood hammered at my ears. After a silent count to three, I craned my face around the side.

Nothing. What had I just seen? He must be somewhere.

I crept along the side of the van. Fearing he was waiting to pounce at the front, I veered to the other side of the pavement, close to a garden wall. How I now missed my standard-issue wooden truncheon. I baby-stepped sideways until I got level with the van's front side passenger window. Again, nothing. Through the wet glass, something moved across the road, shadow settling back into shadow at the entry to the alleyway. But there was nothing there when I looked at it now: had I really seen it? Then a sound came from the same place.

I slid round the front of the van out into the road. At that very moment, a car roared round the corner into the street, engine gunned, headlights scorching like death rays. I froze like a rabbit. The car's shrill horn sliced through me. I felt myself stagger backwards into the van.

I could hear the car screaming to a halt forty feet past me. This being London, I fully expected it to reverse back so that the occupant could verbally abuse me for spoiling his joyride.

I planted a hand on each knee, took two deep breaths, ordered myself to pull the rest of me together. I straightened, stared at the alleyway entrance and strode directly towards it. The blue sporty Subaru that had almost wiped me out was turning in the road. As I got to the alley, I could hear a voice, jabbering whispers from the black.

'Fucking shit. You fucking want it. I'll fucking give it. Come on then.'

Was this Rogan? Was he armed?

Hands flat to the wall, I leaned to my right to peer cautiously around the corner. Nothing. But I could sense someone right there.

'I'm a police officer. Get out here now,' I ordered.

I suddenly realised someone was behind me.

I went to turn when the ground seemed to fly up and hit my face. Someone stood over me. Something struck at my back, thudded off an elbow. I went foetal.

Seconds passed. I scrambled to my feet. No damage done.

I sprinted out of the alleyway, checking left, then right. The car that winged me earlier roared past, in the opposite direction, no doubt carrying my assailant. Burglary? A drug deal? I'd check later for reports of crime or suspicious activity in the area.

Or had it been Dom Rogan? My gut said no. Dom was a coward who bullied women. Surely he wouldn't feel lucky enough to have a pop at me?

As I watched the Subaru scream away my eye latched onto determined movement. A blurred figure marched towards me. I still felt rattled but stepped out into the open, making my presence known. I could make out a duffle coat, a beanie hat, then a broad grin.

'Are you ever off duty, Officer?' she called.

I let the air out and mouthed a silent 'Jesus Christ.'

'You poor thing, you're soaked. Why have you got mud on your face?'

'How have you been, Gabby?' I asked, wiping my face with my drenched sleeve and following her to the front gate.

'How long has it been since you lived with your parents?' she asked.

'Ooh, about three years.'

'Six for me. I'm not sure how long I can stand it.'

'All that home cooking and free laundry? It must be horrendous.'

'Oh God, they mean so well,' she protested, to herself mostly, 'but they're so, oh I don't know, set in their ways I suppose.'

'Well it's just for a while.'

'Mum takes no interest in my job whatsoever. She talks about it as if it's a minor diversion, a stopgap until I get down to the important stuff, you know, like getting married and having babies.'

'That's just a generation thing...'

'She goes on and on about how fucking well Toby is doing. My brother. And how lovely Natalia is. His fiancée. They're always doing stuff with my parents without me. I don't know, I feel like I'm being left out.'

She attacked her fortress front door with multi-keyed gusto.

'They all say now they never thought Dom was "right" for me. Of course, no one ever thought to say anything at the time. I had to remind Mum that when I told her we'd split up, she didn't call

129

me for four weeks, she was so fucking disappointed.'

Gabby pushed her front door open and strode
purposefully over her mail. At the top of the pile,
I spied a handwritten card. My eyes snagged
upon the capital letters of 'BITCH'. I scooped
up the bundle, stuffing the hand-delivered card
into my trouser pocket.

I followed her rant trail into the kitchen and
popped the stamped post upon the stripped pine
table. She had moved on to her dad's obsession
with some Asian family that had moved into 'the
Close'.

'Sorry,' she announced suddenly, 'you must
think I'm unhinged. And thank you for doing this
for me. I'm sure it's not necessary but I really
appreciate it.'

I gave a neutral chuckle: 'Don't worry. I know
how frustrating parents can be.'

'They fuck you up, your mum and dad,' she
announced, then pointed to her heaving book-
shelves: 'Why don't you help yourself? Pick out a
Philip Larkin. I think you'd really like him. You
can keep it, as a thank you.'

'Great,' I said, sauntering over to her literary
trophy cabinet.

'There's a clean towel on the radiator. Feel free.
We don't want you catching your death.'

'Thanks,' I said, grabbing it and wiping my face.

'I'll be a few minutes,' she said, walking into her
bedroom and closing the door.

I'd heard that 'They fuck you up...' line of
Larkin's before. As I surveyed her mini library, I
wondered: just how much Martin had fucked *me*

130

up? I reminded myself that I'd never utter a single word to him again in my lifetime. I might not even get the chance to speak to Mum again, if her health was deteriorating at the rate Fintan described. I pressed Gabby's towel to my face. It smelt like spring flowers, just like home. My last hours there came flooding through me. Oh he'd fucked me up alright, good and proper.

After seeing Eve that last time at the bedroom window, I'd spent a sleepless night on the couch with Mum. We held hands and watched the giant evergreen trees dance to the single street lamp by the church. Finally, those first wisps of cloud showed, the upstairs floorboards creaked under familiar feet, the bathroom door shut and I decided to run upstairs and hide in my bedroom.

I hadn't clapped eyes on Martin since the day before Eve's party. He was swerving me, no doubt, giving me the silent treatment.

Shunning me wasn't his tactic of choice, of course – he preferred naked, unabashed violence as a rule – but he wouldn't have given me a hiding that day, not when I'd just come out of hospital. That wouldn't chime with his 'real man' moral compass at all. He'd prefer to wait until I got better, then put me back in hospital with a fresh set of injuries. But I couldn't be certain. Violent men are unpredictable: he'd caught me out before.

I was certain of one thing: perennial source of embarrassment that I was, he couldn't wait for me to fuck off to England. Tick me off the list: job done. Another tricky deal successfully negotiated.

I couldn't remember not hating everything he stood for. Councillor Lynch and his late-night muttered meetings, locked in the sitting room with the local IRA sympathisers, or the 'beardos', as Fintan called them. Earnest hirsute inadequates, who called themselves soldiers but were no more than deluded messengers and bog-hole diggers who only ever fired guns at funerals, fighting a war in which they never had to face their 'enemy' – whoever they were. Irish people with a different religion? The Brits? No mention of the fact that England was home to five of Martin's six siblings, and that all of his nieces and nephews were either English or American.

I used to sneak down and listen to their talk of 'consignments' and 'units' and 'comms' and fantasise about grassing them up to the Gardai. Or, better still, the SAS. Then see how these hardy Soldiers of Irish Destiny shaped up.

To top it all, Councillor Martin squared it in his mind to go public in the *Tullamore Tribune* as pro-IRA *AND* pro-life. The local paper loved Councillor Martin 'the Grinch' Lynch: if he wasn't a psycho, he'd be comedy gold.

I closed my bedroom door and waited. I heard the bathroom sink emptying, the latch on the door rattle, the door crash open. Footsteps, slow and deliberate, got closer, closer. Then they stopped outside my bedroom door. I shut my eyes and held my breath. What was this to be? Maybe he was going to wish me luck? Or maybe he just felt like dishing out one last battering before I headed off to live with the enemy.

Whatever was coming, I wanted it over with, so

I coughed a cough that said: 'Ready and waiting.'
I saw the handle turn. I looked up to the Heavens
and squeezed my eyes shut again. Seconds ground
past. Then – thump – I heard his feet walking
away.

His car engine gunned. The drive's gravel
crunched and I took a look out of the window
and watched him drive off without so much as a
glance up.

'Hard man Martin,' I said.

I went into the bathroom for a piss and saw his
undrained beard shavings carpeting the white
sink, infinite black stars against a blinding white
sky. I ran my finger through the veil of jet black
specks, hoping that I wasn't genetically doomed
to become a bitter, unhappy man.

Mum walked with me into town to catch the
bus. I don't know if she cried when it drove off. I
never looked back.

Reluctantly, my face parted from Gabby's towel. I
found the poem she had mentioned in a Larkin
tome and popped the handwritten note inside so I
could read it surreptitiously. For a genius, the syn-
tax of Dom's undated, unsigned message sucked.

*Dearest Gabrielle, how are you? I had a dream about
you last night. You looked beautiful. We were in our
favourite spot. Do you remember our favourite spot,
the bench at Tooting Lido?*

*I got so close to you the other day that you smelt my
aftershave. You said to your friend, 'can you smell
aftershave?' and it was mine. She smelt it too but you
have the better senses. You acted like you didn't know*

133

it was mine. But I know you knew. You seem to know when I'm watching you.

Then, in more frenzied, clearly rushed writing.

Oh you look so secure don't you?
Is this because of your PIG friend?
Why are you doing this to me, you fucking BITCH?
Do you miss me? I miss you. I need you.
I am coming for you!

He underlined the last sentence with a manic flourish. I noticed that some of the black ink had run down the damp, lower portion of the card, like a black tear. A thousand tiny cold feet scurried across my back. Dom must've watched me from somewhere outside, added this poison postscript to his love note, delivered it and ghosted off while I was dashing about chasing shadows. Maybe it was Dom who whacked me from behind in the alleyway? That'd be his style, the chicken shit.

Suddenly my back hurt where I'd been struck. I felt rattled, out-manoeuvred.

I wondered if it had been a man like Dom who stabbed Marion Ryan to death. Men like him possess that persecuted righteous rage required for sudden violence against someone they profess to love. As Gabby said, he didn't start out like that. But what if nothing halts their escalation?

I snapped the book shut, fearful now that Dom Rogan would eventually harm Gabby if I didn't do something about him. But what could I do? My only hope was to catch him in the act of breaking in here. I walked to the patio door and checked the back garden, willing him to appear.

'Is everything okay?'

Gabby stood at her bedroom door, bag in hand, as still and alert as a startled deer.

'Sorry, miles away,' I smiled, busily seeking out a positive note on which to reboot our conversation.

'I went to see Lilian yesterday. I've agreed to help with her dissertation.'

'I know! She called me. I meant to say thank you. She is so excited. And who knows, it might actually help.'

'So I've kept up my end of the bargain.'

She nodded, her closed lips resigning at the corners.

'Have you started looking for somewhere to live yet, Gabby?'

Her skin flushed.

'You haven't told your parents about Dom stalking you, have you?'

She shook her head.

'Or that you need to move out of here?'

'How can I?' she said softly, addressing the floor. 'It's so embarrassing.'

'So what excuse have you given them for staying at theirs?'

'I ... they think I'm having some floors replaced.'

I breathed a long disapproving sigh. I liked this Donal: uncompromising, direct, manly. Why could I never pull it off outside of work? I fingered Dom's deranged love note, now an unlikely bookmark. Part of me wanted to show it to her, dispense the short sharp shock she clearly needed. On the other hand, I didn't want to scythe down the green shoots of her recovering confidence. I needed to prod her in another way.

'You've got to tell them. And you've got to get on with finding a new place to live before he puts two and two together and turns up at your family's place in Maidstone.'

'He wouldn't?'

'If he finds out you're staying there, then of course he will. And what are you going to do about this?' I asked, pointing at her mail on the table.

'Oh yes, of course,' she flustered, shoving it awkwardly into her handbag.

'No I mean... Look, Gabby, because of my job, I've dealt with this kind of situation before. You shouldn't get your mail automatically forwarded to your new address.'

She looked at me, confused.

'Someone as determined and conniving as Dom could easily wheedle that information out of a Royal Mail employee.'

'Oh, gosh, I hadn't even thought of that. That's okay though, I'll pop back every couple of days to pick it up.'

'Oh no,' I blurted, 'you can't do that. I'll pick it up for you. It's no bother. I pass here every day anyway.'

She looked unsure.

'And you'll be doing me a favour. There's been a new directive at work about protecting victims of domestic abuse or stalking,' I lied. 'I really need to follow all the guidelines so it's important that you don't come back here alone.'

'Okay. Thank you,' she said uncertainly, rummaging in her handbag and producing keys.

'You really mustn't come back here alone,' I

said, way too urgently, 'and you really need to get a new place sorted, right away. When you do, I'll bring your post over to you.'

She nodded, somehow sensing that I was holding something back.

'I'll lock up,' I said brightly, 'and then I'm giving you a lift to the train station.'

As soon as her seatbelt clicked, I started the engine. I zapped on the headlights and swung the car round, part one of a tight three-pointer. As I crunched it into reverse, a figure appeared in the headlights next to that white works van I'd fallen against earlier. Clad in camo and a bear hat, Dom Rogan stared directly at me and smiled, tapping some sort of instrument against his open palm. I glanced left: thankfully Gabby was busy repacking mail into her handbag. I knocked off the headlights, completed points two, then three, wincing in expectation of some sort of attack. As I flicked on the headlights and sped off, I realised it was time I took the initiative with Dom Rogan.

Chapter 12

King's College Hospital, South London
Thursday, July 18; 09:55

The following Thursday, I turned up for my second 'consultation' with Lilian, looking forward to some answers. Her reassurances during our previous session that I'd a) retain my anonymity and

137

b) could quit at any time convinced me to really give this a go. I had nothing to lose. Ever since my encounter with Meehan, I'd been craving a clinical explanation. I had pored through all the books I could lay my hands on about the subject, but had found nothing that remotely chimed with my bizarre hyperreal encounters.

What these books did reveal is that universities have entire departments dedicated to the study of sleep and sleeping disorders. Somewhere, there was a forest of solid academic research on the subject, some of it based on people with extreme conditions. I'd little doubt Lilian had spent the week negotiating these woods, tracking down the rare condition that I suffered from. Part of me even dared to hope that the diagnosis would come with a bespoke solution, one that didn't involve secure hospitals or surgery.

'Hi Doner,' she said, this time around making my name sound like it should be followed by *kebab*.

Her hair was tied back again, but less severely. She'd even allowed herself a jaunty curl at the fringe.

'Hi Lilian,' I said, offering an awkward hand, 'I'll try to stop for breath this week, let you get a word in.'

She shook it limply, avoiding my eye. Strange, surely, for a shrink? Perhaps she was shy.

She wanted to go all the way back to my child-hood scrapes with St Johnny Giles. I regurgitated it all again, a little resentfully. How much more did she need to know?

Over the course of the hour, she kept recycling

the same stock questions:

'How did that make you feel, Doner?'
'What would you have wanted to happen?'
'What do you think this meant?'

I found myself making stuff up, rather than confess I'd never given it much thought. Even my honest answers seemed to disappoint her, as if they weren't what she'd been hoping for. By the end, her relentless probing for extra insight and meaning had worn me out. Tired answers morphed into defensive agitation.

After one more: 'What do *you* think this meant?' I snapped.

'I was rather hoping you'd be able to tell me, Lilian. That is why I'm here after all. For answers.'

'Maybe you have to find the answers within yourself?'

Oh for fuck's sake, I thought. 'What does that even mean?'

'Why are you feeling so ... defensive, Doner?'

'Look, I don't need therapy, Lilian. I'm not interested in exploring my feelings, okay?'

'What would you like to happen?'

'I'd like to know why dead people are attacking me in the middle of the night. That's why I'm here. Remember?'

'Why do you think this is happening to you?'

'You know what I think? I think that when I get close to the body of someone who's died violently, they find a way to communicate with me. I think Marion was trying to tell me something.'

'Tell you *what*, Doner?'

'I don't know. My gut reaction the first time was that she was trying to lead me to her killer. I know

139

that sounds mad, but that's the only explanation I could come up with. The second time, in the car, I just don't know. She seemed to place a lot of emphasis on slamming doors. I've been thinking, maybe this is a clue to what happened to her.'

There, I said it, out loud, I told myself. She let it hang in the air until I felt myself shrivel with embarrassment.

'That's a wonderful concept,' she said finally, treating herself to the faintest smile, 'but highly improbable.'

How fucking probable is any of this, Lilian? I felt like shouting. Dead people battering me in the middle of the night surely merited some lateral thinking? At least I'd come up with a theory, which was more than she'd managed.

'Have you been back to the scene of Marion's death, since the second attack?'

'No.'

'And she hasn't come to you since then?'

I didn't bother answering.

'So it's difficult to prove that theory, isn't it?'

Easy for her to say – I would have to be pretty desperate before I'd put myself in the way of Marion's deranged spirit again.

'Okay, well that's all we've got time for today,' she said, getting to her feet and bouncing her papers on the table, like a newsreader during the credits.

She turned back suddenly, decisively. 'Look, Doner, I'm not questioning you, or judging you. I'm just exploring the things that happened to you, so that I can make a judgement on them. Does that make sense?'

140

I'd made an arse of myself, so forced a smile: 'Look I'm sorry, Lilian. I'm just not used to talking about it.'

'Well you'll be pleased to know you won't have to for a couple of weeks now. I'm going on holiday. Can I book you in for Wednesday 7th August?'

'Of course,' I said, walking out of her office, certain that I'd never set foot in her surgery again.

Chapter 13

London, England
Monday, August 5; 15:30

August arrived, sticky, fuming and breathless, cranking up agitation on South London's seething streets and tense estates.

It had been more than a month since Marion Ryan's murder and the police had still made no arrests. The story no longer got a single mention in the media.

That afternoon, Fintan rang me with news: Shep was taking over the investigation. DS Dan Shepard. How on earth had he become involved?

Later, I found a mysterious handwritten note on my desk instructing me to meet the man himself at six p.m. that evening, at the Feathers. The site of my glittering career before joining the police, and mine and Shep's first meeting. I'd left suddenly, unannounced and under a cloud.

I'd been bartending about a week when I

noticed that Seamus, the manager, neither took nor was offered money for drinks by certain officers. I assumed this was some sort of arrangement for the nightly 'lock-in', and that these officers would expect the same from me. So whenever I handed a drink to a cop – and you can always recognise a cop – I never asked for money. Those not 'in' on the racket paid as a matter of course. The rest thought me terrific at my job.

I was about to ring the bell one night to scatter civilian drinkers when a voice behind me said: 'Do you not want paying for this?'

'Sorry, miles away,' I smiled.

'Detective Superintendent Dan Shepard,' he said, holding out a hand.

I held out mine. 'That'll be one pound forty,' I said, and he laughed.

Looks-wise, he could have been Sean Connery's tress-blessed younger brother: dark, arched eyebrows, thick white, collar-length hair, knowing blue eyes that always seemed mildly amused by something. He had the aura of someone born to power; he owned the room.

'Where are you from?' he asked.

'A small town in the Midlands,' I said, 'the flat bit you drive through to get to somewhere nice.'

'Oh I know it well,' he said, 'I spent most of my summers in the Midlands, as a kid.'

'So you know Tullamore?'

'Of course. My people come from Tipperary, Clonmel.'

'I hear it's a long way,' I teased.

'Well, my heart's still there, I can tell you. God, I used to love it. Everyone making a fuss of you, giving you cake and lemonade. The nights in the pub. Later I found out that my old man used to have to borrow the money to go, and a suit. Can you imagine?'

Another middle Irish son, I thought, having to find his own way.

'What did he do here?'

'Spent his life working on the buildings, until it killed him. His last job was in '76, digging the tunnel so the tube could get to Heathrow airport. The irony was he'd never once flown home himself. He never had the dough.'

'Do you ever go back yourself?'

He shook his head wistfully.

'Anyway, *slainte,*' he said a little sadly, raising his double scotch.

He headed to a seat in the far corner of the lounge, where he sat bolt upright and slung it back in one. Seamus came downstairs and told me he was popping out for a short while. He was always 'popping out'. I struggled to imagine where he'd be going for a quarter of an hour at this time of night.

When I next looked, Shep had gone. He only ever stayed for one, always around closing time, but he seemed on very good terms with the regulars.

Over the weeks, I got to know several of the officers by name. And soon it became routine that Shep would pop in to chat to me every day at closing time, often asking about who'd been in and at what time. This soon progressed to what they'd been gossiping about. If a titbit of news particularly pleased him, he'd stand me a pint.

He was a man you wanted to please.

I finally twigged that Seamus also 'popped out' every night around the same time Shep finished his nightcap: Seamus must have been his snout. I didn't dare confirm this by spying on them, and I never mentioned it to a soul. But I had no doubt that Seamus was passing on all he heard from pissed coppers during their late-night sessions. As was I. It was hard to refuse the man.

No doubt, the lock-ins generated little money but lots of valuable indiscretion. Because the Yard handled everything from Royal security to organised crime, the sheer scale of suppressed scandals made my eyes water. I learned about Princess Diana's apparent habit of stalking married men, the celebrity customers of major drugs dealers, the sexual peccadilloes of senior government ministers. Hardly a night passed when I didn't think: 'Imagine what Fintan would do with that information?'

Of course, I should have expected my new job to come with conditions. Four weeks in, Fintan called the pub one afternoon and instructed me to meet him at the Queen Victoria memorial, down the road near Buckingham Palace. I wondered why he couldn't just come to the Feathers.

As we walked through St James's Park, he told me how Scotland Yard had set up a secret 'Ghost Squad' to crack down on corruption. As a result, officers had grown paranoid about meeting him, or even talking to him on the phone, making his job nigh-on impossible. I was only half-listening, when he asked me if I could help him out.

'Help out how?'

'Well any cop could go into the Feathers and chat to the barman, couldn't they? That wouldn't raise an eyebrow.'

'I suppose...'

'You could pass on messages for me,' said Fintan, 'you know, act as a sort of go-between for me and my contacts.'

For several minutes, I was too shocked to speak. God knows why.

'Don't worry,' Fintan laughed, 'I'm not asking you to pass brown envelopes, just phone numbers, times and places where I can meet or talk to people, stuff like that.'

What staggered me most was Fintan's matter-of-fact tone, as if bent cops, immoral hacks and shadowy fixers was a business standard.

'Isn't that corrupt?'

'How is it corrupt? You're just passing on messages?'

'I mean you getting information from cops on the take?'

'Who said anything about them being on the take?'

'Why else would they give information to you?'

Fintan stopped walking so he could focus on putting me right: 'Some leak information to me because they can't accept a cover-up, or un-accountability. Others to boost their own careers, or to bring down a rival. The smarter ones recognise the power of the press, and use it to put pressure on their own organisation. Look, it's not my job to work out their motivation. If it's in the public interest, I print it.'

'But you pay some of them, right? Some of

them must do it just for the money?'

'There are a few who've had money troubles, and some who are plain greedy, but what's important is that they pass on vital information. This stops the people in power getting away with murder.'

'Murder?' I scoffed.

'Trust me,' said Fintan, 'Northern Ireland, Hillsborough, the miners' strike, Lockerbie, you name it, senior police and politicians have lied and lied to cover their arses. People in power don't serve the public, they serve their own agendas, which is getting more power.'

'Yeah but that doesn't justify...'

'Look what's happened to Eve. There are cops, as well as judges and politicians that would have let her hang to save their own arses, and you know it.'

'Well, yeah but, this middle man stuff, it all sounds so sleazy,' I said.

'Everything to do with power is sleazy, Donal, Jesus. I'm just asking you to pass on a phone number every now and then.'

I examined his jowly pale face, looking ten years older than his twenty-eight and racked with indignation. He'd been banished from Ireland by the gilded circle. Now he wanted to wage war against the powerful, using any means necessary. This was his unfinished business.

'How do you think we get stories, Donal?' he patronised. 'You think we just publish what Scotland Yard tells us? God they'd love that. The public has a right to know certain things that the people at the top don't want them to know. It's called democracy.'

'Call it what you like, Fintan. I can't do it. That's the end of it.'

Fintan took a deep breath.

'I think it might be too late for that,' he said, eyeing me sourly.

'What do you mean?' I said.

'No doubt you've seen Seamus giving out free drinks? Who do you think is paying for those drinks?'

I've always hated riddles.

'You've most likely seen Seamus passing envelopes,' said Fintan, 'what do you think is in those envelopes? And where do you suppose the cash comes from?'

'I've never seen any envelopes. And if I had, what would it have to do with me? Nothing,' I protested.

'Is that right?' said Fintan, challenging me with his glare. 'You think the Ghost Squad haven't been into the Feathers and seen you giving out free drinks?'

Every drop of blood in my head went south.

'You think they don't know who you are? You think they'd believe you if you said you didn't know anything about what was going on? That, as a brother of mine, you're not complicit in the whole thing?'

'I'm not complicit in anything!'

'You may as well help me, Donal. If they launch a witch hunt you'll be taking the fall anyway. At least this way you'll get some protection, from me and the officers you help. As it stands, you're totally isolated.'

147

I only became aware that my mouth was hanging open when I tried to say 'Jesus Christ', but dribbled instead.

'Have a think about it,' said Fintan, raising his collar against the biting wind, checking left and right then scurrying off.

Fintan Lynch, champion of the free press, like a rat caught out in the open.

As I saw it, I had only one option: quit the Feathers and lay low for a while.

Instead, that closing time, I asked Dan Shepard to meet me the following morning at the most obscure location I could think of, a Harlesden café so squalid that even we used to avoid it.

I figured that, after all the helpful information I passed his way, Shep owed me. As a senior officer, surely he could offer me the 'protection' Fintan seemed to think I'd need. And, although conscious that I may have been suffering either A) Stockholm Syndrome or B) some sort of unconscious craving for a father figure, I actually *liked* Shep.

Next morning, Shep's flint-sharp suit, rolled-up *Times* and flashy rainbow golf umbrella caught the eye of a few road workers sitting nearby. He had a quiet word with the boss who led us through to a closed-off back room. Shep was a man people wanted to please.

I told him everything: the non-payment for drinks, Seamus allegedly passing brown envelopes, the lock-ins. Fintan could hang. I wasn't prepared to turn a blind eye to reporters paying bent cops. Shep listened intently but showed not one flicker of surprise. When I wrapped up, he reached into his inside pocket, took out cigarettes and a gold lighter, lit up and leaned back to survey me.

Finally, he spoke. 'Of course, we knew who you were,' he smiled, and I felt myself redden. 'We were having a bit of fun with you,' he added, smirking and taking another drag.

'We assumed your brother had planted you. But there was only one way we could know for sure.'

I frowned. What is it with these people?

'The lads agreed to let slip some dynamite information your way. We sat with the *Sunday News* every week, to see if any of it appeared. When it didn't, we were a little disappointed, to be honest. Your brother's been a right pain in the arse for us. We were hoping for payback. But we realised you weren't biting.'

He took a mouthful of tea so I could catch up.

'Listen, Donal, thanks for telling me what you know. But we're all over it.'

'You are?'

'We know certain officers are selling information to newspapers, and to private investigators. But it's far more complicated than you think.'

My mind flashed back to Fintan, in the shadow of Buck Palace, railing against people in power and their secret agendas. There must be plenty in power who'd much rather avoid a scandal of this magnitude in the police force.

Shep put out his fag and swallowed the last remnants of his tea.

'I have to ask you,' he said, 'can you carry on working at the Feathers, but for us? You could really help us build a case. All you'd have to do is tell me everything you see and hear, maybe ask a few questions.'

'I don't know. It sounds risky.'

'Your role would be known only to me. I'd protect you. You have my word on that.'

'I, I don't think so...'

'Would you be willing to make a statement about what you just told me?'

'I'd rather not. He's flesh and blood, after all.'

'I had to ask,' said Shep, smiling to let me know he'd expected my answer. He got to his feet and pulled his coat from the back of the chair: 'What are your plans now?'

'I'm not even going back,' I said, 'Seamus scares the shit out of me.'

Shep laughed: 'Have you anything else lined up?'

'No.' I shrugged.

'Why don't you join the Met?' he said. 'You'd make a decent detective. I'll even put in a word.'

Now here I found myself, two years on, back at the Feathers. I walked in to find nothing had changed, except the bar staff – both bleach blonde Aussie surfer types. I recognised some of the old regulars but managed to skirt-around their half-cut eyelines to reach a low-profile table in the far corner of the lounge.

Why had Shep invited me here? Maybe he had decided to bump me up to Acting Detective Constable? By the time he strode through the door, I'd convinced myself that this had to be the case.

Like everyone in London that scorching August, he looked a little sweaty and steamed up.

I remembered how few senior officers derived so much obvious satisfaction at being called

'Guv' than Shep, or being stood a drink.

'Afternoon, Guv,' I said, getting to my feet, 'what can I get you?'

I delivered his double neat scotch and sat where he told me. 'Right, the reason I wanted to meet you is to make sure I'm not going mad.'

'Guv?'

He leaned forward, conspiratorially: 'You were the first officer on the scene of Marion Ryan's murder, correct?'

'Yes, Guv.'

'And tell me what conclusions you made please, on that night, about the crime?'

I chose my words carefully, as if being cross-examined in court: 'Well I assumed she'd let her killer in. There were no signs of a forced entry or a struggle, either at the front door or at the door into their flat. We found her at the top of the stairs on the landing, with her keys, post, coat and a handbag that hadn't been touched. I think she let her killer in.'

'Precisely,' boomed Shep, sitting bolt upright, 'she must have let the person or people who killed her into 21 Sangora Road. Marion knew this person or these people so well that she even stopped to pick up her post as they chatted. She then unlocked the door to her flat and invited them inside.'

I sensed that this clandestine rendezvous wasn't about my career after all but nodded eagerly, just in case.

'But of course DS Glenn doesn't think so. Or at least the so-called criminologists he surrounds himself with don't think so. They think that she was murdered by a maniac who barged in when she unlocked the front door. What do you think of that, Lynch?' he barked, like a Headmaster challenged by an upstart pupil.

'Well it's a possibility, of course. I assume he has other supporting evidence to pursue that line?'

'Shall I tell you what DS Glenn is, Lynch? He's a politician. And you know what politicians do?'

I shook my head.

'They jump on bandwagons, Lynch. And they try to ride them all the way to the top.'

Shep registered my confusion.

'DS Glenn has been seduced by cod science,' he spat. 'He's been bringing in these forensic criminal profilers on his investigations. Have you heard about those, Lynch?'

I'd read all about profiling in the criminology correspondence course I'd failed to finish. The results had impressed me.

'Yes, Sir, I've read a lot about it, as it happens.'

'What do you think of it, Lynch? Be honest with me now.'

I knew that I shouldn't be honest with him, now or probably ever, if I was going to get that promotion.

'Well, Sir, in the cases I read about, profiling certainly helped narrow down the list of suspects.'

'Precisely,' boomed Shep, he loved that word. 'It narrows down the list of suspects but it doesn't go out and gather evidence against them and catch them, does it?'

I shook my head, trapped as I was in the eye of his rhetorical storm.

'Most of it is plain common sense, isn't it? I

mean if there's a serial rapist out there, then of course he's going to be aged between twenty and forty-five, ugly, awkward with women, loves his old mum, lives alone, bashes off to porn, has a menial job, poor personal hygiene and no friends. I mean you don't fucking say?'

I had to laugh. Shep enjoyed being a comedian. I then realised that, at certain points in my life, I matched five if not six of the characteristics he'd just listed. I stopped laughing.

'You don't need to spend seven years studying a pile of "ologies" to tell me that, do you, Lynch? But, if you believe the Scotland Yard PR machine, profiling is the future of detective work. Have you seen the articles about DS Glenn and his "progressive, groundbreaking work" with Professor Richards? Of course the Commissioner loves it. Makes us sound like we've cracked some sort of secret code to catching baddies. There's a room full of the fuckers now at Scotland Yard, taking up desks that should belong to detectives.'

I wondered where all this was heading, and hoped it would get there soon. Lately, at any time of the day, there was a good chance I might nod off.

'DS Glenn and all these careerists have pulled off a very clever trick, Lynch. They are abdicating responsibility, by stealth. It's now up to these pro-filers to lead us to the offenders. When we arrest a suspect these days, it's up to the Crown Pro-secution Service to press charges. This used to be the responsibility of senior officers like me. But slowly they're redesigning it all so that nothing can come back on the big chiefs. If you don't have to make any decisions then you can't make any mistakes. This is the new hands-off, political world we're living in, Lynch.'

I could see Shep winding his mind back pre-rant, to what we were supposed to be talking about.

'So of course DS Glenn is now in thrall to this Professor Richards. Anything Professor Richards says is gospel. So Professor Richards has decided that Marion's murder was the work of a Lone Wolf Killer, who'd stalked her for days. They're linking it to these other attacks in South London later that week. A Swedish nanny got harassed on the Common. And a woman living about a mile away reported a down-and-out running up to her, verbally abusing her and pushing her back through her front door. Now I might not have gone to university, Lynch, but I know a crock of shit when I see one. Anyway, guess what, it's not DS Glenn's problem anymore.'

'Has he been taken off the case, Guv?'

'The Commissioner doesn't want his star pupil bogged down in a boring old murder enquiry when he could be doing something trendy and media friendly, like developing strategies to apply criminal profiling to everyday crimes. So, after three weeks investigating the insides of Dr Richards' hole, DS Glenn is taking his annual leave, then returning for his promotion.'

I was almost scared to ask: 'Promotion, Guv?'

'Oh yes, DS Glenn is being made Commander. I've been left to take over his buggered investigation.'

'Good luck with that, Guv.'

154

'I don't want it, Lynch. Whoever killed Marion has had four weeks to destroy any incriminating evidence and to copper bottom their alibis. I've got to go in there now, re-motivate his knackered team and start again, from scratch. As far as I'm concerned, today is day one of a lost cause.'

He sighed for fully six seconds, sniffed then looked at me, properly, for the first time.

'Anyway, you're probably wondering what all this has to do with you?'

I tried not to nod too eagerly.

'They've told me I can bring across three of my own. I'm a man short.'

He looked at me expectantly. 'What do you think?'

'Well you've really sold it to me, Guv,' I smiled.

He frowned: 'I've been following your progress, Lynch. You've done okay. I said you'd make a decent detective. I've pulled a few strings. If you feel you're up to it, you can start at Clapham CID Thursday, Acting Detective Constable. What do you say to that?'

I'd never been lost for words before. My first thought was Mum: how proud she'd be. I then remembered Marion Ryan's crazed nocturnal assaults on me every time I'd attended the scene of her murder, and my innards cringed. Her spirit, or whatever it was that came to me, must have known all along that I'd wind up on this investigation. That must have been why she came to me in the first place. Another point on the side of the supernatural.

'I'd love to.'

I then remembered Gabby's friend Lilian and

cursed to myself: 'There is just one thing, Guv. Thursday mornings I'm booked up for a weekly one-hour session with a specialist that I have to attend. I've got one that morning.'

'Physical?' asked Shep.

'More psychological, Guv,' I said, in a way that made it clear I didn't care to expand on the matter. Shep tilted his head sideways, either in mockery or sympathy, it was hard to tell.

'Look, son, I don't know if a priest had a fiddle with you, or your uncle or whatever, but you know you can talk to me, in confidence. You don't need to be seeing quacks.'

'It's an insomnia thing actually...'

'I mean I've had Irish colleagues, Christ, arses like colanders! They'd more sex before twelve than I've had in my entire life so, you know, don't think you're alone.'

I nodded: 'Thanks, Guv. It's good to have someone who listens.'

'So, Thursday, I've arranged for you to read all the statements, the forensics and pathology reports with a fresh eye, but I want you to assume that Marion's husband Peter is either the killer or he knows the killer. Understand? I've given the rest of the team leave until Friday to recuperate, so it'll be nice and quiet. When you've finished with the paperwork, maybe take a walk around Sangora Road, check it out. You need to know the geography inside out. I want you to call me when you finish that evening and highlight any areas you feel we should re-investigate. Here's my card with my home number. I've called a briefing for the whole team for midday Friday.'

'I really appreciate it, Guv,' I said, getting to my feet.

'Well you can thank your brother actually. He heard I'd been landed with this and gave me a call.'

'God, I'm in shock,' and truly I was. I'd no idea Fintan and Shep knew each other. I was about to say so but Shep stood and spoke first.

'There's one condition to all this, Lynch. The moment you walk out this door, you don't know me, right?'

'Guv?'

'Glenn's team know I'm bringing over a couple of people from my team. But they won't be able to make any connections between you and me. Let's keep it that way.'

He read my confusion.

'As far as everyone else on the team is concerned, you're a random recruit, drafted in by management. You don't know me. This way, you can be my eyes and ears on the ground in the incident room, okay? Tell me everything you hear, everything you see. I'll work out a way for you to meet me, regularly and in confidence.'

'Yes, Guv.' I held out my hand. He gripped it, pressed hard: 'From this point on, Lynch, your bony little arse is mine. Understood?'

That rather took the sheen off my dramatic new promotion.

Chapter 14

The Feathers, London SW1
Monday, August 5, 1991; 22:00

I paged Fintan to let him know I was in the Feathers. To ensure he turned up, I announced that I'd be standing him a towering great stack of pints.

'Congratulations on your promotion,' said Fintan, spoiling my surprise.

'How did you ... anyway, thanks. I hear you put in a good word.'

'What are older brothers for, Donal, if not to grease the ladder for those who trail behind?'

It had been preying on my mind: what was in it for Fintan this time? Did he really wield influence over a senior officer like Shep? If so, how and why? When I worked here, I'd assumed Shep was in the Ghost Squad. That's why I'd helped him.

Now I wondered if Shep was one of those cops Fintan had told me about that afternoon, outside Buckingham Palace. One of his 'sources' who used the press to get the public onside. Were he and Shep 'off-the-record' allies, running stories that suited both their agendas?

I didn't want to be a pawn in any more sleazy plays.

'I didn't know you were so tight with Shep,' I said.

'All crime reporters try to get to know Shep. He's one of those refreshing exceptions who refuse to put a positive spin on any fuck-up. He's not so much a loose cannon as a primed, one-man Armada. The Commissioner soon put a stop to him, of course. Officially, Shep's banned from talking to the media.'

'Officially?'

Fintan shrugged: 'You can't stop a grown man talking.'

'What's he like to work for?'

'From what I hear, Shep likes to see himself as one of the boys,' said Fintan, lighting up a cigarette to help him reflect, 'a trap that middle- or upper-class senior officers never fall into. And he tries hard to be funny. Nothing matters more to Shep than making his team laugh, often, which is probably quite exhausting.

'He has this distrust of anyone well-spoken or university-educated, and don't even get him started on the new breed of Oxbridge graduates or ethnic minorities being fast-tracked through the ranks,' he laughed.

Fintan suspected he secretly harboured dreams of making Commander. Maybe even Commissioner. 'Not a chance. He's a decent enough cop – in an old-school, all-guns-blazing kind of way. And he's probably the most determined senior cop in the force. When he gets a sniff of a collar, he goes proper psycho. Like a bloodhound.'

Fintan stubbed his fag out: 'You've got to be careful with him though. By giving you this break, he'll feel like he owns you. He likes to own people. All of the guys in his team owe him in

159

some way. One is a recovering alky. Another got suspended a few years back for battering someone at the Christmas party. Shep picks up waifs and strays and turns them into his bitches.'

'Great, so you've sold my ass to a man with a God complex.'

'I wouldn't go that far: dictator, definitely! Bottom line is, you have to run Shep, but make him think he's running you.'

I decided to store that away, even if I didn't entirely understand what he meant.

None of this explained Fintan's motives for recommending me, or why Shep had agreed to give me the break. Fleetingly, I indulged in the idea that maybe Shep liked me. I knew Fintan well enough not to bother with direct questions. Getting information out of him demanded a complex game of give-and-take. 'You know Shep used to come to the Feathers every night?' I said. 'He'd go off and have these secret conflabs with Seamus.'

'What, thick Seamus? The manager?'

I nodded. Fintan looked surprised, always a triumph.

'That's strange. Maybe Seamus was a snout. You know he left literally two days after you did?'

My turn to be surprised. I knew he'd left, I didn't know in such a hurry.

'Where did he go?'

'No one knows. One Monday morning, neither Seamus nor the weekend takings could be found anywhere.'

I thought back to what I'd told Shep. Had he warned Seamus off? As usual, I struggled to see the angles.

'I thought Shep was in the Ghost Squad.'

Fintan laughed hard.

'What's so funny?'

'No one knows who's in the Ghost Squad. That's why it's called the Ghost Squad. Look, stop fretting will you? You're worse than Mum. Shep likes you. He's giving you a break. You'll do fine. Life's finally working out for you, bro. Now, what's this about you owing me pints?'

Fintan was right: I should be celebrating so I bought two more and a pair of scotch chasers.

'Anyway, how's it going with Gabby?' he said as I planted four glasses on our table. 'Have you had your wicked way with her yet?'

How I wished I'd never mentioned her when we last met. 'It's not like that. I'm just helping her out.'

'Out of her knickers if you get your way. I can see it in your eye. You're like a sex-starved wolf.'

'You can't help yourself can you?'

'What?' he laughed.

'Reducing everything to a base tabloid level.'

'Your big mistake, Donal, was stopping that guy from stalking her. If Big Dom was still rampaging around her back garden every night, she'd be far more appreciative of your attentions. You'd be well in there.'

I couldn't help wondering if his rampant success with women was the root of his apparent disdain for them.

Several rounds later, drink took hold and I spilled. It began with revelations about my ghostly Marion Ryan encounters. But my drunken confessional slide took me all the way back to those

161

Tony Meehan apparitions, including how I'd witnessed him attacking Eve.

Fintan seemed particularly transfixed by the fact that these apparitions took place on the days I'd been either close to their dead bodies or the places where they'd met their violent ends.

His verdict: 'It's tempting to assume you are simply unhinged, but that's too simplistic. Obviously you don't possess any kind of supernatural gift.'

He lit a cigarette to focus.

'The only conclusion I can come to is that, in your subconscious mind, you're still trying to save Eve Daly.'

I wondered sometimes if the sole point of siblings is to remind you of past failings.

'If you only ever take one piece of advice from me,' he drawled, pissed but, for once, deadly serious, 'stop trying to save Eve Daly.'

'I'm not trying to save anyone. I've moved on.'

'Well she certainly has,' he sneered.

'What do you mean by that?'

'It doesn't matter.'

'Go on, spit it out. I can tell you're dying to.'

'I've heard that she's shagging someone else.'

'What?' I said, confused by my own sense of shock.

'You're waiting for a woman who's already moved on. I'm telling you, Donal, forget about her.'

'How can you know she's actually shagging this guy?' I protested, probably too much. Would he now work out that Eve and I had engaged in pretty much everything except full penetrative sex?

'Well maybe they're stuck at second base, I don't know all the lurid detail. The point is, she's seeing someone.'

'Who is he?'

'I don't know. Someone from her legal team, I think they said. Look, it doesn't matter who. You're stuck in a fucking time warp and you need to move on.'

I nodded. But my gut knew I hadn't seen the last of Eve Daly.

Chapter 15

**King's College Hospital, South London
Thursday, August 8, 1991; 10:10**

I sat in the waiting room of King's College's Institute of Psychiatry, blaming the clock for every lost second, occasionally aloud – which alarmed only some of my fellow outpatients.

My consultation with Lilian had been scheduled for ten a.m. The clock said ten past.

I had until, at a push, eight o'clock tonight to fillet the Marion Ryan murder file and throw a bone at Shep. It needed to be a meaty one at that. His promise to make me Acting DC had been just that, a verbal promise. If I failed to deliver a fresh clue to support his domestic theory, he could renege on my promotion. And I was short on comeback.

I thought back to our last 'consultation': Lilian's

163

endless stock questions, me galloping round in circles like an unbroken horse. Unqualified shrink meets uncooperative patient: what, realistically, were we ever going to achieve? I came to see her the first time as a favour to Gabby. I'd paid my dues. There was nothing in it for me now.

'Fuck it,' I said, standing suddenly. The waiting room recoiled as one. I bolted.

Halfway up Denmark Hill, I heard the unmistakable, *'Doner?'*

I looked up to see Lilian jogging towards me.

'Security alert! Couldn't even get on a train for an hour,' she panted, shooting down in flames any grievance I might have had. There was only one cause of security alerts in London: the Provisional IRA. Or, as senior police officers used to hilariously joke: 'One of your lot, Paddy.' With innocent English bodies piling up, it was hard to cry foul.

The ice maiden's skin looked flushed, her forehead damp.

'Are you okay?' I asked.

She blinked often and hard.

'You weren't going to come back, were you?'

'Yes ... no ... look Lilian, everything's changed.'

She looked me in the eye, properly, possibly for the first time.

'I've been brought onto a murder squad as Acting DC. Guess which case?'

Her lips parted slightly.

I nodded: 'Marion Ryan's murder.'

She looked unsettled, maybe even unnerved.

'Which means I'm bound to get back to the murder scene. If I do, and she attacks me again,

164

won't that prove something?'

She let my question bounce off her. Lilian Krul wouldn't even entertain the notion that I had some inexplicable, illogical, unscientific spiritual connection with Marion Ryan. The very thought offended her logical mind.

I worried that even hard evidence wouldn't sway her.

'Congratulations,' she said finally, politely, as if I'd just beaten her at tennis.

'My new boss wants me to go through all the statements and paperwork today. I've got to report to him tonight,' I said, checking my watch and pulling an apologetic face.

'What about our work?' she frowned, inspecting me without a blink.

'I'm not sure I'll have time ... this is a big break for me, Lilian.'

She nodded, so I kept going, 'And the last meeting felt, well, it just felt like we were going over the same old ground.'

She blinked once, slowly, almost ceremonially. The muscles in her cheeks clenched: 'You know something, Doner, I've been spending day and night researching your case, tracking down papers, reports, books, talking to experts all hours of the day and night, all over the world. I didn't even go on holiday in the end. I spent it all working. On *your* case. And you continue to act like you're doing *me* a favour. You show no faith in me or my work, or respect. I'm tired of it. You're right, let's just call it a day. I wouldn't want to waste any more of your precious time.'

That was easy, I thought. 'Really?' I said.

165

'It's just a shame, as I think I've made a break-through.'

She visibly relished my renewed eagerness.

'What have you found?'

'I've found a condition that seems to fit your experiences. I worked all week to get it ready for today but ... it doesn't matter. You've got more important...'

'What? What is it?'

I almost grabbed her by the arms in excitement. 'It has a name?'

'Yes, it has a name and there are ways to manage the condition. But look, we can't talk here.'

'My God, this is amazing news,' I said, 'all I've ever wanted was to be able to call it something. What is it?'

'I know you've got to run, *Doner*. Maybe now you'll come back next week?'

I shook my head in disbelief but laughed to hide my anger.

'I'm here, now,' I said, trying to sound calm, 'why don't you tell me now?'

I spotted a café, pointed to it: 'Come on.'

We sat at a cold metal table, face to face.

'Well?' I demanded.

She reached into her shiny, black leather bag, grabbing a chunky bale of academia.

'According to these studies, you suffer from something as old as humanity itself, yet it's only starting to get proper scientific recognition now.

'In Newfoundland, they call it the Old Hag. In China it's called *Gui Ya*, which means Ghost Pressure.'

She even did that thing of pronouncing it in a

166

Chinese accent.

'In the West Indies, he's called *Kokma*, the ghost baby that bounces on your chest and attacks your throat. The Norwegians call it *Mer* which is where we get the term "nightmare". There's a famous painting called *The Nightmare*, hanging in the Royal Academy, showing exactly this pheno-menon.

'In the last couple of years, this condition has been scientifically defined as sleep paralysis.'

'Sleep paralysis,' I repeated, 'right.'

I'd read about apnoea and narcolepsy. At least they sounded sexy. Sleep paralysis? I'd been ex-pecting something less specific, more complex, in Latin. Or named after some fearsome Germanic boffin, a Münchausen or a Heimlich. Sleep paraly-sis sounded too matter-of-fact, like glue ear or athlete's foot or irritable bowel syndrome.

'What makes you think it's sleep paralysis?'

'You exhibit all the classic signs,' she argued, seemingly bemused by my lack of enthusiasm.

'And they are?'

'Well it's a complex area.'

'Try me. But feel free to skip over the complex stuff.'

'Okay, well, you probably know what REM is? It's that dreaming period of sleep when your eyes twitch violently under your eyelids?'

She was now torturing me by going up at the end of her sentences.

'Rapid Eye Movement is when we have our most vivid dreams. You're supposed to have non-dreaming sleep first. Then you go into REM sleep six or seven times during a night's sleep.

'During REM, the brain sends your body into paralysis, so that you don't act out your dreams. It's most likely that when you doze off, REM comes to you too quickly, before you're properly asleep. Or, sometimes when you wake in the middle of the night, REM doesn't snap off.

'In either case, your body's awake, but your mind is dreaming. What you're seeing are dream images superimposed on waking images. As you can imagine, this is really common in narcoleptics.'

'No, Lilian,' I laughed, a little too desperately, 'I don't think you understand. Meehan was *real*. Marion is *real*. I can see her, I can feel her touch. I can smell her.'

'Yes, they are real to you, same as the Old Hag is real. A dream is always real while you're in it. It's only when you wake up you realise it isn't.'

I felt a surge of resentment. How dare she trivialise my real, terrifying, other-worldly episodes with such trite explanations. 'So if these are just dream images, why do I feel so terrified?' She leafed through her papers until she came across a colour-coded picture of the human brain.

'There are two things about dreams, they tend to make no sense and they tend to be negative.'

You don't say, I thought.

'Look,' she said, pointing to a part of the brain. 'When we dream, our pre-frontal cortex, this bit we use for logic and language, to make sense of things, is switched off. But the middle brain lights up. That's the part of the brain that controls emotions. See this bit?'

Her sharp, scarlet fingernail tapped what

168

looked like a crinkled testicle.

'This is the amygdala. The philosopher, René Descartes believed that the amygdala was the seat of our soul. It's actually the seat of our fear. This is on full alert when we sleep. This is why our dreams are almost always scary.'

I got up and walked around to her side of the table for a better look, if only to slow her down.

But she was on a roll: 'The amygdala is the "fight-or-flight" part of our brain. The bit that weighs up an immediate threat. Now, remember, this is in a high state of alert when you dream.'

I had remembered.

'Now, think of your condition: you are lying there, you think you're awake because you can see your room and your belongings, but your brain is in REM, so your body is in paralysis, you're finding it hard to breathe. Your amygdala is in a state of high alert, which means you're terrified. Fear is an inherent part of the experience. The feeling of terror comes, then the bogeyman. Your visual cortex has to justify the terror you feel, so it creates an image of the thing you fear most. Two thousand years ago, people saw demons. Two hundred years ago they saw witches. These days, they see aliens.'

'I don't see aliens,' I protested, 'and I can *feel* Marion! I can feel her skin. I could feel Meehan strangling me.'

'The strangling sensation is because the paralysis makes it hard for you to breathe. Your throat and chest muscles are frozen, so it feels like there's something pressing down on your chest and your throat. It's your brain that decides what that something is.'

My mind raced. I had to accept that, when Tony Meehan attacked me in hospital, he was definitely my bogeyman. After all, I'd just witnessed him attacking my girlfriend. Maybe Marion became my bogeywoman as soon as I stood between her body and the open window, making her attacks on me some sort of self-fulfilling prophecy. Her terrifying antics had come from the darkest recesses of my own twisted imagination. This was all feasible, credible. I just didn't believe it.

I returned to my side of the table, slumping in the seat.

Lilian cocked her head and studied me, as if sitting at an easel. 'You seem, I don't know ... annoyed?'

'I'm fine,' I lied, 'I'm just coming to terms with the fact that I'm seemingly incapable of distinguishing dreams from reality.'

'I sense that what I've said has upset you?'

'I mean, with respect, Lilian, sleep paralysis doesn't explain how I floated into Eve's room and saw her getting attacked that time, does it? Or why Marion only came to me after I'd attended the scene of her murder?'

'No, it doesn't,' she said softly. 'I think I've found some of the answers. There are so many things that don't make sense. You say you saw the time on the clock radio when Meehan attacked Eve. It is beyond dispute in the science of sleep that you can't read numbers or letters in your dreams. I'd like to drill down into all these elements in your case.'

'How can they even know that?' I laughed, shuffling awkwardly, ignoring her determined eyes.

'The first time we met, *Doner*, you said you wanted to know what was happening to you, and find a way to manage it.'

I nodded.

'I think I can help you manage it. But only if you let me help you. Look *Doner*, I'm making progress here. But I need you fully on board. This is it, we either go all out or we call it a day.'

I recognised the cons right away:

1: Time.

2: Opening up and all that.

I considered the pros.

Lilian was the only person who knew my entire story, albeit in a condensed format. If there was a clinical explanation for my lurid 'slasher movie' episodes – the cop in me felt convinced that there *had* to be a clinical explanation – then she was the only person equipped to find it. I didn't believe she could cure me, but I liked the idea of getting a decent night's sleep every once in a while, if only so I could live a normal life.

But there was a sweeter incentive for me to keep going with this; vindication. She'd scoffed at my theory that Marion Ryan's spirit wanted to help me nail her killer. Now I'd been brought onto the squad investigating her murder, one thing felt certain: I'd go back to 21 Sangora Road.

I'd attended the crime scene on two previous occasions. Both times Marion's ghost/spirit had launched deranged assaults upon me. What if it happened again? How would Lilian explain away a third encounter? 'Highly improbable', indeed.

I don't believe in ghosts, spirits, the afterlife or

any of that stuff. But what Lilian had singularly refused to appreciate was how *real* these encounters had been.

'You're on,' I said.

Chapter 16

Clapham Police Station, South London
Thursday, August 8, 1991; 11:45

Although deserted, the incident room hummed with subdued intent. Barely larger than an average sitting room, it was crammed with phones and fat computer terminals. Stained coffee cups jockeyed for space with full ashtrays and used sandwich wrappers.

And to think they call us pigs.

Whiteboards lined the walls, listing the names of investigating officers and the computer codes of what leads they were chasing up. Nearby, a large picture map of London was dotted with yellow Post-its.

There was no sign of anyone to set me up, so I headed to the canteen. The overwhelming stench of fried pig had the curious effect of making me both hungry and queasy. I settled for a mug of Nescafé Rough Blend coffee and a can of cola, hoping the combined hit would crank me into first.

I returned to the incident room and took a good look at that note-spattered map of London.

172

I heard a noise and turned to see a chubby man in his forties feeding disks into one of the fat computers.

'Hi,' I said walking over, 'I'm Donal Lynch, Acting DC.'

He nodded glumly without looking up.

After about ten minutes, he said: 'I trust you've done this before?'

'What, use a computer?'

'No, fly a 747,' he spat, now glaring up at me.

Was this some sort of test?

'I haven't used a computer since school,' I said flatly.

'Well it's not my job to teach you,' he said, getting to his feet and flouncing off.

I typed tentatively. Soon I found myself chewing through megabytes of Space Invader green text. Every investigative 'action' had been logged, numbered and described. Separate folders contained statements and reports. I knew exactly where I wanted to start.

During her nocturnal burglaries of my mind, Marion had repeatedly slammed doors. Her message, if I believed in her, had been clear: a door somewhere holds vital evidence to the identity of her killer. Could be a house door, could be a car door – but a door was where I'd find the smoking gun clue.

I clicked open the forensics folder, then the fingerprints file and sought out anything connected to doors at 21 Sangora Road.

I knew from my training that fingerprints are a lottery. A good print on the right surface can last for years. In one celebrated case, forensics dated a single print back forty years. Somewhat per-versely, dating fresh prints is more difficult. There are so many factors to take into consideration: the surface the print is left on, whether it has been made with sweat or other substances, the air temperature.

The report said they found fresh fingerprints belonging to Marion's husband Peter Ryan and his colleague Karen Foster on the front door and on the connecting door into the flat. All they could say with certainty was that these prints were less than twelve hours old. In other words, the impres-sions had been made sometime between ten a.m. and ten p.m. on the day of Marion's murder.

They'd found lots of other prints left within the same time frame: sixteen sets on the front door and seven on the internal door to the flat. This seemed a surprisingly large number to me. I thought about the front door to our flat: there'd be no more than three or four different fingerprints planted there on any given day. The front door to the entire block would be plastered with them: ours was one of forty-eight flats. Marion and Peter's flat was one of just two behind that front door. Yet they'd found sixteen sets of day-old prints on the communal front door. I made a note to investigate the frantic comings-and-goings at number 21 on the day of Marion's murder.

I then read that they'd cross-referenced all of these prints with police records: none of them matched a known offender.

That was that. The killer's prints could be on both doors, we just didn't know who they belonged to. Or Marion's husband Peter was the killer. Maybe that's what Marion had been telling me during her ghostly visitations: look no further than him. But unless a witness saw Peter at 21 Sangora Road at around six p.m. on the day of the murder, his prints on the doors were evidentially useless.

I felt flat and a little foolish. Naïvely, I thought Marion had been leading me directly to her killer. But I refused to give up on the idea that a door somehow held the key. I just needed to work out which door, and how.

An overview report in the forensic folder directed me to a filing cabinet containing the scene of crime photos.

These included a close-up of Marion's torn, dangling fingernail. I couldn't understand why this single image flooded my body with such leaden sadness. I thought of Marion as a baby; how her mum and dad would have marvelled at this hand and treasured it. And as she grew up, they would have grasped it tightly to cross the road. Her dad held this hand when he gave her away to Peter, probably thinking he'd done his job, that she was safe now.

I got back to the computer to track down the pathology report. I felt under real pressure to find something – *anything* – that pointed to Peter Ryan. Shep had given me this golden opportunity: I didn't want to let him down.

Bruising showed that Marion had received a karate-style chop between her upper lip and nose which may have momentarily stunned her. The forty-nine stab wounds were delivered in rapid succession; seven to her chest, nine to her throat,

175

the rest to her lower stomach, back and bottom. One wound pierced her right hand as she tried to ward off the blows. Some were delivered with great force – suggesting a male attacker – but others were mere pinpricks. Could it have been a two-hander? Peter and his secret lover? What about Karen, the colleague who'd been with Peter when he found the body?

The two 'significant wounds' were one to her throat which slashed her windpipe and one to the left side of her back which pierced her lung. According to the pathologist, the force of these blows suggested they had been delivered by a man. She died through a combination of loss of blood and asphyxiation as it flowed into her lungs.

The pathologist estimated that the attack would have lasted between two and three minutes. The murder weapon appeared to be a five-inch blade. There had been no sexual assault or wounds to her genitalia. I felt these last facts warranted attention. Presumably, the Lone Wolf Killer had to be some sort of sexual deviant. Didn't the lack of sexual assault or genital injury point more towards a domestic? The pathologist didn't say so.

He put her time of death at six p.m., with an hour window each side. A handwritten note said: 'CCTV provides more precise timing.' The pathologist noted that he'd never come across a domestic murder victim with more than nine stab wounds. One nil to the Lone Wolf Killer theory.

I took the pathologist's cue and tracked down the CCTV tapes. I hunted and found a VHS player in a tiny room, closed the blinds and watched with horrible fascination as Marion Ryan strode purposefully to her death.

She left her place of work – Reuters news agency on Fleet Street, where she'd been employed as a copy taker – at 17.06 p.m.

'God, what are you wearing, love?' I couldn't help myself saying. In her big flowery dress, thick tights and heavy shoes, she could have been heading to the Ballroom of Romance.

She turned left onto Waterloo Bridge. The next camera captured her on the bridge, from above, the murky old Thames flowing lazily beneath. The song 'Waterloo Sunset' drifted into my mind. I banished it out of respect.

She walked efficiently, without fear – never once checking behind her. This wasn't a woman worried about her wellbeing.

No one appeared to be tracking her. Time-lapsed stills recorded her ghost-like progress across the ants' nest concourse of Waterloo station. Again, she didn't check behind her and had no obvious pursuer.

She must have caught an overground train because the next tape came from Clapham Junction train station. The time read 17.32 as she turned right at the main exit, setting off up St John's Hill. The fuzzy frames revealed no potential   stalker/killer. She looked oblivious to what lay ahead. She crossed at the traffic lights, just yards from the entry to Strathblaine Road, turned left – and that was the last frame we had of her.

The empty screen flickered and shuddered, as if aware somehow of the grave magnitude of what happened next. I thwarted all emotions by fixing upon cold, hard facts and ordering them in my mind: *Whoever murdered Marion had waited for her on Sangora Road. The question is, was it someone she knew or an opportunist maniac? At that time of day – rush hour – someone must have seen something.*

Back at the computer, I clicked open the door-to-door enquiries file. The team had asked neighbours on Sangora Road if they'd seen anything suspicious on the afternoon/evening of Marion's murder. What a stupid question, I thought. I mean, what's suspicious? You might as well ask if they'd seen any maniacs running about brandishing blood-soaked, five-inch knives. Surely they should just ask people what they saw that day. It's up to us to decide if any of it points to a suspect. I made a note of this. It was something to toss Shep's way if I failed to come up with anything better.

Unsurprisingly, the officers' limited questionnaire yielded nothing. I was running out of time, and decided that the most likely place to find anything incriminating against Peter would be in his supposedly rock-solid alibi.

He and Karen had made brief statements on the night of Marion's murder, then detailed statements two days later. The devil is always in the detail, so I focused on the latter.

I laid their longer statements out side-by-side. By switching between the two, I could check more easily if and when their stories didn't tally.

Peter described how he first met Marion at the Archway Tavern when she was seventeen: he was twenty-three. No doubt she was swept off her feet by this square-jawed Irishman with worldly charm, roguish self-confidence and big plans to make money and move back home. They married last year in her parents' home town in Kilkenny.

Peter worked as an assistant purchasing manager and gardener at the Pines, a private home for the elderly in Lambeth, South London. Karen Foster was also employed at the home as a trainee nurse and resided on-site in staff accommodation. I found this a little odd. She'd told me herself that her family live in Lee, just a few miles down the road. I knew from Aidan, my flatmate, how little trainee nurses earn: why didn't she save money by staying at home? Then I thought about the anti-social shifts they have to work and moved on.

On the morning of the murder, Peter took the overground train from Clapham Junction to Waterloo with Marion, which was their usual routine. He arrived at the Pines just before nine a.m. He always put the keys to the flat in his briefcase, which he kept next to his desk in the shed/office in the grounds of the Pines: they were too big to carry about in his trousers. He left work just once during the day.

At about 15.45, he took a ten-minute walk to the street known as The Cut where, each fortnight, he bought fifty pounds' worth of feed, tank cleaner and water treatment granules for the home's fish tanks.

He went on to explain that every second Monday evening, he did a couple of hours' overtime for extra money, cleaning and replenishing the home's fish tanks. He was helped by his colleague and friend, Karen Foster.

I turned over 'colleague and friend' in my mind. It struck me as oddly formal, a little defensive.

179

On the evening of Marion's murder – Monday, July 1st – he met Karen as usual at around six p.m., just outside the main ward at the home. They finished just before eight p.m. when Karen gave him a lift to Sangora Road. He didn't own a car and Karen often dropped him home when they'd worked late.

An appendix showed that Peter's movements during the day had been verified by the manager of Pet Fish, London SE1 and a work colleague at the home. The man from Pet Fish recalled the day particularly well because Peter had forgotten his chequebook. The manager accepted a signed IOU which he was able to produce later. This sounded to me like an alibi being created before the crime had even been committed. A colleague at the home claimed he chatted to Peter as he came back in with the fish supplies, at about 16.45. This left a window of one hour unaccounted for in Peter's afternoon. I felt sure Shep would have picked up on this already, but made a note of it anyway. At least it showed that I was thinking the way he'd instructed me to.

I flicked over to Karen's statement.

I finished work at about 17.15 when my younger sister Laura called to say she was arriving at the home. We'd arranged to watch a soap on TV with Bethan in her room at 17.30. Bethan Trott is a colleague at the clinic and we watch this show together most days because I don't have a TV in my room. She lives in the room four doors down from mine in the staff halls of residence. I met Laura at reception. As we came upstairs, we saw Bethan in the communal kitchen and went with her to her room. We had a cup of tea and

180

watched TV until six when the show ended. I went to the main ward and met Peter. Every second Monday we clean and re-stock the fish tanks in the wards. He pays me ten pounds in cash. It's extra money and I've always liked fish.

I thought it odd that Peter hadn't mentioned paying her. Karen went on to say she had an upset stomach and, before leaving the home, went to the toilet.

The journey to Sangora Road took fifteen minutes at the most. I couldn't park on Sangora Road because it was already full. I had to park on the side road. I don't know what it is called.

She and Peter walked to the flat. Because of her upset stomach, she wanted to use the toilet again before returning to the Pines. Classy girl, I thought. She also intended having a quick chat with Marion, who was a friend. On top of that, Peter wanted her to take two flower pots from his flat to the home. They were too heavy for him to take on the train. When Peter put his key in the communal front door, he found that the mortise lock was not on. This was so unusual that he remarked upon it – Marion always kept it double-locked. He then unlocked the door to the flat and walked upstairs.

Karen described coming up the stairs directly behind Peter. At this point, she broke down. Glenn's officers felt sorry for her and let her take a break.

Next, they jumped forward to the nature of Karen's friendship with Peter. I couldn't understand why they hadn't pressed Karen about discovering Marion's body. Clearly, Glenn's team had already concluded Karen couldn't have had anything to do with this murder. I made a note to check out how they'd made this seismic leap.

Karen said she first met Peter at work and they became friends. When Peter and Marion moved into the clinic's staff accommodation after their marriage, she became friends with Marion. They visited each other's rooms. She and Marion sometimes went to the pub. She visited them in January after they rented the flat on Sangora Road.

I've always been suspicious of men and women claiming to be friends. In my experience, one of them always has some sort of romantic designs on the other. But none of this was proof. None of this provided the fresh plot twist Shep craved. I'd seen the bloodlust in his eyes. I dreaded having nothing juicy to throw his way. He might devour me instead. I had to find something – anything – to impress him.

I asked my frosty new colleague if I could take a look at the exhibits recovered from the murder scene. Wordlessly, he handed me a numbered list, led me to a cupboard, unlocked the door and stomped off. I pulled the door open, my eyes fixing instantly upon the grisly familiarity of Marion's handbag, jacket, keys and post. A shiver fizzed across my neck, making my shoulderblades rattle.

I reminded myself that these were inanimate objects, nothing macabre, and got stuck in. Soon, all that remained unsearched was the very first thing I'd clapped eyes on in the chaos – Marion's flowery plastic handbag. It was the usual dumping ground for receipts, make-up, a brush, some loose change. She smiled out at me from a Reuters security pass: demure, poised, gentle – a far cry from the crazed harridan who had been attacking me. I pulled out a tissue with a bright pink impression of her lips. I held it reverentially, this last remnant of her living body, and let a fresh band of melancholy pass through me. Marion's Turin Shroud. I thought about how much an item like this would mean to her family, yet here it is, stuck in a sterile cupboard, destined for the skip. I knew it would never be evidence in the case, so I folded it carefully and pocketed it: one day I'd send it to her mum Mary.

A small gold zip on the back of the bag revealed a thin compartment. I could barely slide my fingers in. Right at the bottom, I felt something long and thin. More prodding revealed that this object was trapped within the inner lining. I looked inside the handbag again. I noticed for the first time a barely-visible little compartment – lining on lining and stitched in the middle. I tried the small opening on one side and could only get two fingers in. I pulled out the object: a tampon. I realised this was Marion's secret compartment. There was nothing else on this side of the stitching, so I slid my fingers into the small gap on the other side. I felt a thin scrap of paper. I dragged it up and out.

It was a folded page ripped out of a small notebook. I opened it.

'*Dear Andrea,*' began the undated, unfinished letter, clearly from Marion to a close friend. My eyes popped: the contents of this note changed everything.

Chapter 17

Church Road, London SW19
Thursday, August 8, 1991; 21:01

I hadn't seen Gabby since intercepting Dom's deranged love note a couple of weeks back and packing her off to Kent. Earlier today, she left a message on my home answerphone.

Hi Donal, Gabby here, from Salcott Road, you know the woman men can't stay away from. Anyway just to say I moved into a house share in Wimbledon on the first of the month with some old friends from Uni. They happened to have a room free so it felt like it was meant to be really. Anyway, thanks for all your help these past couple of weeks. If you could drop my post around some evening this week, that'd be great. If you'd like to call me at work to let me know when you're coming, that'd be even better because then I can thank you personally and maybe introduce you to everyone. I've told them all about you! But don't worry if you can't do an evening. Hopefully see you soon.

By the time I got to Church Road SW19 it was already after nine p.m. I couldn't wait to see Gabby and tell her about my breakthrough today. On the downside, I felt knackered and wasn't sure I could handle her no doubt highly educated and very chatty friends. These days, I seemed to have about ten per cent of everyone else's puff.

But her bundle of post included a couple of large

184

packages – books of course – that wouldn't fit through her post box. I buzzed and reassured myself that I could hold my own with these people if I had to. I'd discovered that my accent acted as an impenetrable shield against what certain English people wanted to do most: pigeonhole you by class and education. It was impossible for them to judge whether I was educated or thick, rich or poor. So long as I avoided the subject, they might not even be able to tell that I'd never been to university.

The door was flung open by a lady with spiky blonde hair who asked me what I wanted. I held up the bundle and explained I was dropping round Gabby's post. She turned, shouted, 'Gabby, someone for you', and disappeared. So much for the hero's welcome.

Gabby bounced down the stairs in denim shorts over black tights and a tight white vest, all indie rock and beaming. Sharing with Uni friends had clearly made her regress.

'Evening, Officer. Do please, come in.'

She got to the bottom of the stairs and strode confidently towards me, a new woman. I couldn't understand why her familiarity made me uneasy: maybe I found it easier to empathise with victims.

'Well, what do you think of the place?' she said, arms outstretched. Before I had time to answer, she ordered me to follow. I got the grand tour of a grand old sprawling Victorian family home, complete with wonky chandeliers, oriental rugs, vanity watercolour portraits, a grand piano, vast leather couches, school corridor radiators and a mossy-glassed, off-kilter conservatory.

185

Robert Johnson played on an old-school record player stained with candle wax.

Her flatmates lounged about with music magazines, red wine, rolling tobacco and Rizlas, clearly determined to test my law enforcement convictions.

'Hi everyone, this is Donal,' Gabby announced, and I felt like I'd gatecrashed cool.

The goth girl squeaked: 'Hello, Donal' and I couldn't tell if she was taking the piss.

'Hi,' smiled spiky blonde, as if she'd just met me for the first time.

The man – skinny, blonde and more feminine than either of the girls – cut straight to the quick: 'How would you feel, Officer, about me engaging in some doobie, here in my own home?'

'That's Ricky,' said Gabby, in a manner that suggested everyone else in the world would have known already, 'he's a session player.'

'Rick, is that short for prick?' I thought better of saying, opting for the more convivial: 'Yeah you go for it, man. I'm only a bastard on duty.'

That seemed to calm everyone down no end. Before long, I was red-wining them under the table while enduring their stories. I foolhardily took several tokes on several joints – declining to tell them the one about the last time I sampled drugs, you know, when one person died and another ended up in prison.

They were all completing Masters' degrees or PhDs, had jobs they felt beneath them and no real idea what they wanted to do with their lives. I resisted the temptation to say: 'Find something you like and just go for it.'

At some point in the night, one of them mentioned Sylvia Plath. When I asked if she was the woman who sang 'Je Ne Regrette Rien' they nearly died laughing.

Just as they recovered, I said, a little bitterly: 'I guess not then.'

They slid like capsized Alps into balls of hysterics: Gabby's convulsions the most pronounced and cutting of all.

Not wanting to appear petulant, I waited fully five minutes before making my excuses to leave. As Gabby went to grab my coat, friendly goth said: 'We haven't seen her laugh like that in years. You're really helping her come out of herself.' The others concurred and insisted I come back soon.

'Any time you like, dude,' drawled Ricky.

At the front door, Gabby inspected my tatty old coat and asked when it had last been to the cleaners.

'No gumshoe worth his salt sports a dry-cleaned coat. Look at Marlowe, Sam Spade, Columbo?'

I slipped it on. Before I knew it, she was buttoning me up like a schoolboy.

She fastened the top button and gazed up at me, well inside my personal no-fly-zone. Her eyes glazed, mischievous, sexy, her scent netting me like a helpless mackerel. 'Get in there,' I ordered myself. Instead, inexplicably, I spouted a line of Larkin poetry.

'But they were fucked up in their turn. By fools in old-style hats and coats.'

'You read it!' She smiled, her eyes ignited, loving. A seal formed, somewhere, inexplicably. Everything had changed.'

She leaned in and kissed me, hard. She pulled away only after several seconds, smiling coyly. The earth tilted.

'Well he's like Morrissey aged seventy, isn't he? What's not to love?' I laughed.

'Friday night, would you like to come round for dinner?'

'I'd love to,' I said, but the moment had fled. 'Now I really must go. I can't drive like this. I've got to find a bus. Good night.'

I clung onto various parts of the door until it opened, bundled my body out and focused hard on putting one foot in front of the other.

My car looked so inviting. I put the key in the lock, then told myself not to be stupid and walked on. I slowed before crossing the road. Behind me, footsteps stopped suddenly. I pretended not to notice. Halfway across the road I stopped dead. A single footfall echoed behind. I spun around.

No one. I sniggered. The pot had made me paranoid.

I turned and walked on, my ears on high alert. Feet click-clacked in time with mine, but on the other side of the road. I stopped. They stopped. My chest froze. I was being followed.

I walked on, heart pumping like a thresher. How the fuck had Rogan found her? Had he followed me here? Had I put Gabby in danger? I badly wanted to teach Rogan a lesson. The cowardly fucker had floored me once, from behind. It was time for payback. I came to a skip. Walking on the spot, I peered in and grabbed hold of a brick. I rounded the front of the skip then launched three giant strides across the street.

188

'Hope you like the taste of masonry, fucker,' I roared.

A high-pitched scream stopped me dead in my tracks.

I spun around to where it had come from. A woman stood next to a bin holding a rubbish bag, jaw hanging.

I scanned the pavement. Empty.

'Fuck,' I said, jogging back the way he'd come, checking left and right. That scream had given him the second he needed to duck in somewhere.

Now I had a decision to make: should I tell Gabby that Rogan may have tracked her down, or should I just hope the weed had been playing tricks on me?

Chapter 18

Clapham Police Station, South London
Friday, August 9, 1991; 12:00

At noon on the dot, Shep strode into the incident room.

'Morning Guv,' we all bleated.

That simple tribute turned his stride to swagger. He looked scalpel-sharp in a gunmetal-grey woollen suit, Italian for sure, a sky-blue tie, pressed white shirt and shiny black brogues. You could tell he was a man worshipped and served by his dear wife.

Earlier, Mick and Colin – the detective sergeants seconded from Shep's team – introduced themselves. Stout, with a bushy moustache and side-parted mousy hair, Mick could only be a cop. Balding, tall Colin looked more like an accountant or a tax inspector.

Officers of varying rank slunk in like wounded strays. I recognised the Big Dogs, Barratt and McStay, who took my statement, and the piss, the day after Marion's murder. They didn't even recognise me. The grunting psycho who did so little to help yesterday pointedly blanked me. I recognised a couple more from the Feathers. They acknowledged me with the faintest of hostile nods. I understood. They were hurting. Our arrival had endorsed their failure to catch Marion's killer. We were a rubber stamp stain on their proud record.

'Sorry I couldn't get in first thing,' Shep addressed the room. 'Detective Sergeants Mick Mulroney and Colin Gibson have come across with me on this. Stand up and say hello, gentlemen.'

They stood up and grunted

'And we've a newcomer. Where are you, Acting DC Donal Lynch?'

I stood up.

'Welcome aboard, Lynch, probably not the best name for a cop in some of our rougher estates.'

The laughter – thin and forced – spelt tough crowd.

Shep dipped another comedy toe in the freezing water: 'I met an American cop once called Lou Tennant. Can you believe that?'

Silence.

Quicksilver Shep changed tack.

'Okay, so we don't have a weapon. We don't have a witness who heard the incident or saw any suspects on Sangora Road.

'We've run all the prints found at the scene: none matches anyone with previous convictions or any potential suspects.

'The lab has come up with nothing else from the crime scene.

'CCTV shows nothing.

'We don't have a motive: according to colleagues, friends and family, Peter and Marion were blissfully happy. Neither has any enemies or buried skeletons. Peter has no history of violence and a watertight alibi for the day.

'In short, we've got no witnesses, no forensics, no weapon, no motive, no suspects.'

His new underlings shuffled awkwardly and murmured. The hectic chaos of the incident room told me they'd been living, eating, smoking and drinking Marion's murder for over four weeks now, without a result. Shep was gambling that they'd respond to a good old-fashioned half-time rollicking. He was smashing metaphorical teacups against dressing room walls.

'All this points to an opportunist, says Professor Richards, a maniac on the loose with a knife and a hatred for women, a Lone Wolf Killer who has escalated to this level of violence ... unhindered by us blundering cops.'

Nice touch, I thought, driving a wedge between Professor Richards and 'us blundering cops'.

'The Prof's Lone Wolf Killer is a curious chap. He will have stalked Marion for a few days, maybe even weeks, learned her movements. But on the day he decided to kill her, he didn't stalk her. He waited with his trusty murder kit on Sangora Road, for her to come home from work. Somehow, he talked his way or barged his way into her flat. Ever the gentleman, he let her pick up her post first, before following her up the stairs and stabbing her forty-nine times.'

'DS Shepard, with respect, that is a rank over-simplification of the stranger killer theory,' barked McStay, the Scottish terrier.

'That may be so, but you see I didn't study psychology or forensics or any of that stuff. I didn't even go to university. I'm an old-fashioned cop. As you all know, before the computers and the psychologists, we were taught to look for two things: probability and motive. And we all have a pretty good record at this, let's not forget. So let's deal with probability first. We all know the stat – virtually all murder victims know their killer. Random attacks are extremely rare. That's a fact.

'That leaves motive...'

Shep was playing every card he had. *I'm just a workaday cop like you, I don't understand all that high-falutin' psychology stuff, I just catch baddies like we used to in the good old days, before computers and mandatory solicitors and taped interviews and internal disciplinary procedures.*

Shep made a big play of producing the piece of notepaper from his pocket.

'This was found hidden in Marion's handbag yesterday. I've confirmed that it's a match for her handwriting and I've spoken to the intended recipient.'

192

The room leaned forward as one.

'This is a letter Marion was writing to an old school friend who now lives in Glasgow. Allow me to read you the content.

'Dear Andrea, I'm so thrilled that you're coming down to London and staying with us. I really need to offload to someone about Karen. I could write pages but I would rather wait till I see you.

Obviously don't mention it to any of the girls. Last time we got together of course she was there and everyone was saying how nice she seemed. I felt like shouting 'no she isn't! You don't know her!'

I will fill you in on the whole story when I see you. Peter tells me Karen's off to Ireland in a couple of weeks for a weekend. I'm saying nothing until she's gone. I hope I don't sound bitter and twisted.'

Shep let it hang and slowly folded up the paper. McStay asked to see it.

'Now, who can say that Marion didn't have an enemy?'

No one breathed.

'I rang Andrea last night. She told me that Marion felt that Karen was obsessed with Peter, and constantly trying to involve herself in their lives.

'This letter suggests to me that Karen was the third person in their marriage. Marion was "saying nothing" until Karen went to Ireland for the weekend. What did she mean by this? Was she about to confront Peter about his affair with Karen? This has to be our focus now.'

Murmured agreement: he was winning them

193

over, some at least.

'Tomorrow, I want you to split into four new teams – I'm breaking up your partnerships just for a few days, freshen things up a bit – and I want you to focus on Peter and Karen. Were they once an item? Was he sleeping with her? Was Karen, as Marion's closest friend Andrea has expressly stated, obsessed with Peter Ryan?

'I want one team to go back to the Pines old people's home where Peter and Karen worked. If anything was going on between them, at least one colleague will know.

'Karen's people must know if she has a thing with Peter, either now or in the past. I want a team to talk to her family, friends, ex-boyfriends.

'Another team can do the same with Peter: talk to everyone he's ever known in London. Was he or is he a player?

'And finally,' he said, looking at McStay, 'I need you to take on the toughest job of all. Go back to Marion's family and find out what they know. Marion must have talked to someone about why she disliked Karen. She wasn't the disliking kind. Something was up.'

McStay wasn't buying it.

'Are you telling us, DS Shepard, that we're now focusing solely on Peter and Karen? Based on one undated, half-written page of girlie gossip?'

Shep looked at him, confused. McStay held up the note and decided to spell it out.

'She doesn't actually state here that she suspected Peter and Karen of having an affair. She says nothing of the sort. There's no anger or suspicion, just irritation. I've heard worse in the

194

staff canteen. And I trust you've read the pathology report. No woman could have carried out this crime.'

'No, but a woman and a man could have,' said Shep.

McStay refused to budge: 'They have solid alibis. Both of them. You clearly have some sort of personal grudge against Professor Richards. I think that's why you're ruling out the stranger theory. Well, what if her killer strikes again while we're looking the other way? The wrong way?'

I had to agree with McStay: Shep wanted to prove Richards wrong so badly that he'd donned blinkers. I'd seen Peter and Karen the night they found Marion. Both had been deeply traumatised and clearly in shock. You can't act emotions like that.

Shep changed key: 'I'm not ruling out the Lone Wolf Killer theory, McStay. I just think it's about time we eliminated the most obvious suspects in this case once and for all. That's Peter, her new husband and Karen, her husband's work colleague and friend whom Marion clearly disliked. As for the stranger theory, I happen to think that needs a fresh pair of eyes. That's why I'm putting DC Lynch on it.'

'What?' I stopped myself from saying.

McStay turned and looked at me: 'You're giving this to the new kid?'

'He'll liaise with Mulroney and Gibson. That's why I've brought them in. Sometimes fresh eyes see new things.'

McStay turned back, still shaking his head.

'Guv, you said you want us to get on with this

tomorrow. What about today?' asked one of the younger DCs.

'Ah, yes, this afternoon we're going on a team-building exercise.'

Groans all round.

'To the pub,' Shep smiled. Everyone looked around in confusion.

'I'm serious,' said Shep, 'you've all been through the wringer. I think we need to finish our chat over a few pints.'

An hour later, among the cut mirrors, etched glass and faded Victorian grandeur of the Falcon near Clapham Junction, opinions and gossip vied for air supremacy with thick cigarette smoke. I wondered if policing was the unhealthiest profession in the world, maybe even elbowing out journalism in the wheezy sprint to early death.

Privately, some of the officers told me about the 'Big Dog' culture of DS Glenn's team. They all felt that Peter Ryan hadn't been properly investigated. But the pack leaders – DS Glenn, the Professor, Barratt and McStay – had ruled out Peter and Karen from day two. I'd pass this on to Shep later, though he probably guessed as much already.

Shep got stuck into McStay, Barratt and a real ale chaser. He tirelessly reassured them that the Lone Wolf Killer line of enquiry remained open and live. Within a couple of hours, he had them rolling on their backs.

As drink took hold, more damning claims emerged about Peter. Officers said he 'loved himself'. The only woman on the investigation team

196

– a brunette who looked capable of taking any one of us in a fist fight – swore he'd flirted with her.

'I mean, his wife's barely cold. What a slime ball,' she gasped. Within a week of Marion's murder, Peter had emptied both her personal bank accounts and got a refund on her annual rail ticket.

'Disgusting,' said Shep.

'Shows what a ruthless bastard he is,' said someone else.

I decided to join in: 'Well, I suppose it'll tide him over until her life insurance pays up.'

That got a good laugh.

'Actually that's a good point,' said Shep, 'have we checked whether he gets anything for her death?'

The silence told us no one had bothered. I couldn't believe it: life insurance, one of the oldest motives in the book. Shep and I exchanged a fleeting look of disbelief. But we needed to win the team over today, so said nothing.

I was taking a leak when Shep came crashing in. He checked the cubicles, then stood at the latrine next to me: 'Did you see that Scottish git's face when I read out Marion's letter? Can you believe he demanded to see it?'

'He just can't accept that they messed up, Guv.'

'Well done on finding it, Donal. Otherwise we'd never have persuaded them to target Peter and Karen.'

'No problem, Guv. You've definitely got them onside now, most of them at least. The junior officers are saying they never felt Peter had been properly looked into. But they were overruled.'

'That's good to hear. Honestly, the day you stop listening to other opinions and ideas, you're no longer a manager but a tyrant.' I recalled Fintan's description of Shep as a dictator. He seemed the opposite to me.

'Of course he's right in one way,' said Shep, shaking his cock vigorously, 'the letter tells us nothing on its own. We still don't have one solid piece of evidence. Someone will have to cough tomorrow.'

I waited so that he could wash his hands first.

'Guv, about me looking for connections to other stranger attacks,' I started, 'I do worry that maybe I lack the experience...'

'Nonsense Lynch, it's common sense. If anything catches your attention, flag it up to Mick and Colin,' he said, shaking his hands and ignoring the dryer. He looked at me and read my anxiety.

'Come on, these fuckers spent four weeks looking for a Lone Wolf Killer. I'm not expecting you to find one because there isn't one. I just have to keep McStay onside. You can be sure he's reporting back to Glenn who's reporting back to the Commissioner. You'll do fine, Lynch.'

He left me drying my hands and hoping to God he was right. If not, some maniac slasher was roaming London unchecked, seeking out his next victim.

Chapter 19

The Falcon pub, Clapham Junction
Friday, August 9, 1991; 19:00

I left the pub with a mouth like Gandhi's flip-flop and a head like Christmas afternoon. The sweltering, petrol-drenched early evening air didn't help.

Shep had united the team but I still felt odd man out. I'd no experience. No allies. I needed to pass this test to become a fully-fledged member of a murder squad. My career hinged on making a good impression.

I let the booze unfetter my mind so that I could once again run with the illogical idea that Marion was trying to steer me to her killer from beyond the grave. What if Marion's spirit somehow knew that I'd end up working on her case? What if that's why she came to me on both those occasions? But why had I failed to crack the clues she'd given me? This seemed to let the whole concept down.

I began to wonder: if I returned to the murder scene, would she come to me again with a fresh clue? Once again in my life, booze galvanised me. I decided to give it a go.

Sangora Road was ten minutes' walk. I'd get as close as possible to number 21, then see what happened.

No matter how slowly I took it in the screaming low sun, I got there breathless, a little delirious. Heat to an insomniac must be like thick-crust pizza to an anorexic: it knocks you out.

At the bottom of the road, I stumbled into the Roundhouse pub, craving its cool inner gloom just for a few minutes. I took my pint to a window seat out of the sun. My eyes – still scored by the glare – struggled to adjust to the darkness. I tried to focus on something midway between shine and shade, and settled on the people sitting outside enjoying their evening meals. Couples, friends, families chatted, gossiped, laughed. Beyond them, a grandstand view of the steps to number 21, just a half dozen doors up the road. The carefree revelry seemed disrespectful and shallow. Didn't these people know what happened here a few weeks ago? Didn't they care?

As I drained the glass, a flash of auburn hair on the sunny street caught my eye. I put the glass down and stared hard through the alfresco diners. She stood on the pavement, side-on to me, just staring towards 21. I knew that thick, curly, blood-red hair. I knew that dowdy, flowery dress. I blinked hard and fast to make sure she wasn't a hallucination.

'Marion?' I mumbled.

'Marion!' I called, loud enough for the drinkers inside to look my way. Someone on the outside table stood, blocking my view. I jumped to my feet.

Still she stood there, motionless, oblivious.

'Marion!' I shouted. Now everyone on the outside tables stared.

200

'Fuck it,' I thought, and made for the door.

I got outside and scanned the pavement: there was no sign of her. I jogged up to where she'd stood and looked around. She'd vanished.

As I walked on towards 21, I noticed the To Let sign in the front garden. I wondered who'd cleared out Marion's stuff. Who had painted over the bloodstains on the wall and scrubbed them out of the carpet? Knowing estate agents, they'd probably raced here with buckets and J-cloths. I was certain they wouldn't be mentioning the grisly murder to any would-be tenants.

I didn't want anyone thinking I was some sort of crime scene deviant, so as soon as I reached the steps to Marion's house I wheeled left, back past the pub towards the Common. I looked left to cross the road and saw her: Marion, motionless on the pavement of Strathblaine Road. Again, she was staring towards 21. Her hair blazed scarlet along with the raging low sun. This time I didn't panic. I walked steadily up towards her.

'Marion?' I called out gently. She didn't respond.

'Marion!' I cried loudly.

Next thing, I found myself walking past the pub again. I turned to look where I thought I'd just been. She was gone. Had that actually happened? I felt rattled, disorientated, scared. What was happening to me? I aimed for the shade of the nearest tree on the Common.

I felt in no doubt now: Marion was breaking through to me from the other side. She was hijacking my subconscious, I presumed to help me find her killer. It was illogical, supernatural, an affront to logic. But it was the truth.

I lay down to better cling onto the tree and the wildly spinning world.

Chapter 20

Clapham Police Station, South London
Saturday, August 10, 1991; 10:00

While the rest of the squad were out focusing on Peter Ryan's relationship with Karen Foster, I was office-bound on the paper trail of Marion's Lone Wolf Killer.

DS Glenn's team had made strenuous efforts to get their hands on the case files for every unsolved stranger attack on a woman in London over the past four years. Some were on the computer system, the rest were in box files strewn across an empty office floor.

The Met police was in the throes of ditching its old manual 'card' system for computers, so records were a mess. By now, a few stations had everything on computer. Some had part of their records on computer. More still hadn't even started the process. As a result, lots of paperwork was in transit. And we all know what happens when paperwork gets moved about.

Not that getting hold of case files from other murder squads proved simple at the best of times. Bitter rivalries simmered between many senior officers and, as a result, their CD teams.

Most Detective Chief Supers ran their 'manors' like personal fiefdoms. They resented other teams snooping around and cracking their outstanding cases. It was petty, small-minded and dangerous – nobody dared stock-check the number of deaths caused by police teams who had failed to cooperate or communicate. The Met hoped technology would tear down these walls of ego and secrecy, and that computers would one day crack crimes all on their own.

I clicked open the folder named Unsolved, then the file named Overview and congratulated myself on my initiative. It was a painstakingly prepared report of the records that had been requested, but not received from stations still converting to the chip. Someone had optimistically dubbed these files: 'Currently Misplaced'.

A second file contained a comprehensive list of sexual offenders recently released from prison. None of their prints matched those found at Marion's murder scene. Each had been interviewed and eliminated from the investigation. I had to hand it to Glenn's team: they were thorough, dogged, methodical – eager hounds chasing the wrong scent.

The third file was a report penned by forensic psychologist professor Laurence C. Richards BSc, MSc, FRSA; criminal behavioural analyst.

Despite Shep's cynicism, if there was a Lone Wolf Killer (LWK) lurking somewhere in these files, I wanted to know how to identify him. Before I waded through hundreds of offences, I needed some sort of criteria to narrow down the suspects: a sort of *LWK Modus Operandi* tick list.

I was terrified of missing a vital clue, leaving the killer free to strike again.

I quickly realised that Professor Richards' chief skill was to deliver lots of general, common sense observations with absolute certainty. Whoever killed Marion must have escalated to that level of extreme violence. He will have forced his way into homes before and attacked women at knifepoint. This was 'his thing'.

The report went on: 'Although the victim had not been raped or sexually assaulted, the attacker will have gained sexual gratification from the attack. He may well have shortcomings that prevent him having sexual relations with women. As a result, he may despise women. However, we shouldn't rule out that he's raped women in the past.'

In short then, we were looking for a violent misogynist who was once a rapist but now can't get it up so he takes it out on random women with a knife. Or possibly not. I couldn't help thinking that the Prof was covering all the bases.

I decided to start on the 'unsolved stranger crimes' already in the computer system: it looked less daunting than the scatter of dusty binders.

I scrolled down through countless unsolved attacks on women, mostly sexual.

London's rape statistics were one of the few things that stayed with me from my training. Every day, the Metropolitan police force received six reports of rape and twenty-one reports of sexual assault. About ten per cent of these attacks were carried out by someone unknown to the victim: that's about four stranger rapes per week. Judging by these cases, most 'stranger' rapists tried to force anal intercourse on their victim too.

The sheer scale of random, seemingly arbitrary violence scared me: the city is full of men who despise women. Every time I concluded that an unsolved rape/attack on a woman couldn't be linked to Marion's murder, I wrestled with more guilt. It felt like I was walking away from their cries for help, leaving them lying in the dirt where they'd been violated.

Yet I knew I had to be brutally selective, or we'd wind up with more suspects than police officers.

Of course, detectives all over London had already been busy making connections. The first serial attacker to catch my eye was the so-called Night Stalker, who operated in South East London. Described as black and in his thirties, this man expertly broke into the homes of old women living alone in the middle of the night. He raped them at knifepoint and stole anything valuable to hand.

Marion was twenty-three. She hadn't been sexually assaulted. As far as we could tell, her killer hadn't broken in. Nothing had been stolen from the scene. I ruled him out.

Links had been made between four attacks near train stations in West London. The attacker threatened his victims with a knife, led them to covered wasteland then raped them. Marion's flat was five minutes' walk from Clapham Junction train station. Had he been casing out that station, only to discover a complete lack of deserted areas to strike? He noticed Marion. He came back to wait for her again, and again. One day he followed her, found out where she lived, did nothing. He bided his time, confirmed her daily routine over days and weeks, like an assassin. Then one day he waited near her home. Somehow he distracted her as she opened the front door, forcing her at knifepoint to unlock the flat and walk up the stairs. She fought back. He lost it and went berserk, then fled the scene.

I realised that the same case could be made against every stranger rapist in any file. I had to find something more tangible, a connection more damning and evidential. I trawled and trawled that eye-bleeding green text until the end, failing to settle on a single connection.

I printed out the list of 'Currently Misplaced' paper case files and cross-referenced it with the folders sprawled across the empty office floor. I realised that one new file had turned up since this stock take. I spotted it immediately – the one not caked in dust. The courier's packaging confirmed it had been delivered from Plumstead police station in East London that weekend.

As I opened the box file, I felt an icy frisson of fearful anticipation: no one else had seen this 'unsolved stranger attack' paperwork. What if he was in here? What if I found him? I told myself to be extra-vigilant. I reminded myself that he liked to use a knife and attack women in their homes. I thought of the messages Marion's spirit had communicated to me: banging the door, appearing to me on two streets near the crime scene. I pushed it all to the front of my mind, ready to snag on any link or connection in these files.

The first case to catch my eye, because of its name, was the Green Chain Attacks. To my relief, the Green Chain turned out not to be some soothingly-coloured yet gruesome martial arts weapon but a series of connected parkland walks near Plumstead. Over the past four years, a lone male had attacked over seventy women on the Green Chain. His crimes had escalated from beatings, to sexual assaults to rape. He sometimes used a ligature, more often a knife.

Descriptions of the suspect were vague because he always wore a balaclava or a mask. As I'd discovered in most other linked sex attacks, witness estimations of weight and height varied wildly. He'd been described as five foot six and broad, six foot two and slim, and just about everything in between. But DNA evidence proved it was the same man.

I looked at the other odds and ends in the box file. An intelligence report from two months ago caught my attention. A couple with an address at Winn Common – part of the Green Chain expanse – had phoned police describing a man 'hanging about' in their neighbour's back garden, apparently spying on a young blonde woman 'who often walks around her flat semi-naked'. The husband went out and kept an eye on the suspect until a police patrol arrived.

'I bet he did,' I thought.

When police quizzed the loiterer, he insisted he was merely taking a walk and had stopped for a piss. He gave his name and address: Robert Napper, 126 Plumstead High Street. The officer wrote: 'Subject strange, abnormal. Should be considered a possible rapist, indecency-type suspect.'

I took a deep breath and stopped my mind skidding off in too many directions. Had this man progressed from attacking women on the Common to breaking into their homes? Surely we should at least cross-reference his DNA with the Green Chain victims?

I rifled through the file's remaining contents. Intelligence reports identified other local weirdos skulking around parks and commons, spying on sunbathers, flashing and wanking behind bushes. Other notes identified couples and gay men and their repeated attempts to initiate 'stranger sex' in public. I was beginning to realise that London's green spaces gave a whole new meaning to the term, 'Parks and Recreation'.

Then I found a handwritten note. It was dated almost two years ago – October 1989 – but someone clearly believed it deserved attention. 'At 9.10 a.m., Mrs Maureen Napper of 19 Raglan Road SE18 rang to say that her son, Robert, 26, of basement flat, 126 Plumstead High Street, told her he'd raped a woman "on the Common" two months earlier, in August. The police sergeant on duty checked the records and found no report of an attack or rape on Plumstead Common, or any connected green spaces, during August or the previous two months.'

My hands trembled. It was that man Robert Napper again, who they'd recently found in the garden of a woman's flat. Allied to this rape confession, his MO surely made him a suspect for the Green Chain attacks, if not Marion's. I asked Mick what the procedure was for pursuing leads like this: 'Just ring 'em up,' he said. Soon I was on the phone to a duty officer at Plumstead. He agreed to check the log book of all recorded crimes for August 1989. He confirmed there had been no reported rapes or sexual assaults on any Commons on their patch that month. He checked July and September: same result.

...*on the Common*. Did Napper even mean Plumstead Common? He could have struck at another Common: Clapham Common? I checked the A to Z: there are Commons all over London, dozens of them.

It was already after six. As Mick got up to leave, I asked him to run Napper through the police computer. 'Robert Clive Napper born February 25, 1966, one criminal conviction: possession of an airgun in a public place, 1986.'

'Sounds like a menace, at least to the local rabbit population,' he laughed.

I had a feeling about Napper. But I didn't want to present it half-cocked at Monday morning's briefing. I needed to connect Napper to the rape he'd boasted about. If I pinpointed that rape – the rape he'd confessed to his own mum – we could cross-reference it forensically with any DNA and prints found at 21 Sangora Road. This new twist made me realise I had to go through all of the remaining paperwork – and back again through the cases on the computer – to cross-reference all rapes on London Commons between June and September '89.

Before getting stuck in, I called Gabby to say I couldn't make it over tonight.

'What a shame,' she said, 'it's so unusual for the

house to be empty. And I've bought all this lovely food.'

My body groaned.

'Were there going to be candles?'

'I can confirm there were going to be candles,' she giggled, 'and Shiraz.'

'I'm truly sorry,' I said, 'mostly for me.'

'You're missing out, I can assure you of that, Donal,' she teased, 'I'd even tidied my room.'

'Wow, I've seen your room. That's commitment. You must be exhausted?'

'I've got more stamina than that,' she giggled.

'Okay, I think under some UN guideline this actually constitutes torture. I can't take another second.'

'Wimp!'

'We'll see about that, madam,' I said, realising at that point that I could only fuck this up now, so I added a swift: 'I'll call you tomorrow.'

'Look forward to it.'

'Bye,' I managed, before slamming the handset and my forehead down against the desktop, over and over.

Chapter 21

Archway Tavern, London N19
Sunday, August 11, 1991; 14:00

Next day was one of those glorious mid-summer Saturdays when English people clog coast-bound motorways and Irish folk head to the pub.

The Archway Tavern's back bar heaved, the big screen boomed and the blinds failed to block out the searing afternoon sunshine. I found Fintan leaning against a ledge nursing two stools and two pints. I took a quick scan: we had a perfect view of a screen and a short, clear path to both the bar and the gents. I marvelled at his attention to detail. He wouldn't relax until he got exactly what he wanted.

I completed our traditional pre-match preparations by popping two more pints onto the ledge. Today was the most anticipated game of Gaelic football in our lifetimes. This was no longer just a game. This extraordinary encounter between two giants – Dublin and Meath – had come to represent the titanic struggle between Ireland, new and old.

Dublin had a young team on the rise. They were slick, fast, smart, progressive: the future. Ageing Meath had been All-Ireland winners in '87 and '88. They were talented but cynical, dogged, pugnacious. Old Ireland. At least that's how we read it.

These teams had already played three times and drawn three times – twice after extra time. Dublin had thrown away commanding leads in two of those games. Like New Ireland, the Dubs didn't quite believe in themselves: not yet.

Before throw-in, Ireland's trendy new liberal President Mary Robinson (Bright New Ireland) shook hands with both teams. A week earlier, she shook hands with the Dalai Lama against the express orders of the Prime Minister, Charles Haughey (Corrupt Old Ireland). Apparently Haughey – former IRA gunrunner, bribe-taker and friend to Mugabe, Castro, Gaddafi – took a dim view of Mr Lama and his hippie, spread-the-love ways.

Fintan and I were rooting for Dublin and a bright, new Ireland. To our dismay, most of the neutrals wanted the warriors of Meath to put these cocky young Dubs firmly in their place.

The Game not only lived up to the hype but eclipsed the Rocky-style pantomime drama of all that had gone before it. We all got totally sucked in. Dublin led all the way. Mulish Meath launched a typical comeback and, with seconds remaining, sealed a last-gasp, single-point victory. The white flags went up. The pub went up. Mayhem spilled out onto the busy Archway roundabout.

'Another failed Irish revolution,' spat Fintan.

The sombre opening notes of U2's 'One' rose from the jukebox, offering succour. The window blinds and big screens rolled up. Thick smoky shafts of sunshine sought us out, grim reality's merciless searchlights. I felt washed out, dried out, post-cinema depressed.

I looked around. A low evening sun burned hard, silhouetting everyone near the large windows and open doors. Everything else in the pub looked sepia and somehow suspended in time.

A rim-lit figure came striding through the main door, purposeful, confident, entitled. I recognised that gait. I turned to see Fintan's tired eyes darken. As the silhouette got closer, it slowly morphed into a woman with a dark brown bob, smiling so hard that she couldn't seem to blink. I felt sure I knew her, but I couldn't quite place the face.

'I thought I'd find ye here,' she said.

I would have walked past her on the street.

'Jesus, Donal, you look like you've seen a ghost,' laughed Eve Daly, coming in for a hug.

She didn't hug Fintan, who just stood there bloodless and open-mouthed, like a dead fish.

'You were right, Fintan,' she said, 'suspended sentence. We got the verdict at the High Court yesterday, in camera. The media doesn't even know.'

'That's great, really great,' Fintan said, but he seemed rattled.

'Are you not going to buy me a drink then, after all the exclusives I gave you?'

That snapped him out of it.

'Of course. Your usual?'

She nodded and I frowned in confusion as he scuttled off. How did he know her 'usual'? What did she mean: 'you were right'? What the hell was going on?

'He's been my rock,' said Eve, her cat green eyes glazing slightly, 'I wouldn't be standing here

213

now if it wasn't for him.'

'What do you think?' she said, palming her new brown bob in disbelieving hands. 'No one's recognised me yet,' she added, turning to the bar to double check.

I hadn't the heart to say it sucked the prettiness right out of her. I was too busy trying to work out what had been going on between her and Fintan.

'I wrote to you, four times...'

'I know, I'm sorry, Donal, it was just crazy. I didn't know what was going to happen to me. I wanted you to get on with your own life. And now I hear you're a copper. Jesus.'

'Detective Constable, actually,' I smiled.

'Oh my God,' she laughed, shaking her head at the good of it, 'why?'

I stopped myself saying: 'Because of what happened to you.' Too corny. Too soon.

Fintan almost ran back with drinks. I'd never seen him shaken before. I liked it.

'Eve here has been telling me how you've been her rock,' I spat bitterly, emboldened by the drink.

He ignored me. So did Eve.

'I told my legal team to do what you said, Fintan, and it worked a treat.'

Pennies were starting to bounce off my thick skull. Fintan had been pulling the strings for her all along, even from London. No wonder he looked uncomfortable.

'I wish we'd pushed it further now,' she went on, 'I reckon we could have negotiated an acquittal.'

'I'd no idea you two were still in touch,' I said, glaring at him. He kept his focus firmly on Eve.

I turned to her: 'Pushed what?'

She looked at Fintan, who finally spoke: 'Haven't you heard? We're the poster boys of Europe. We've agreed to sign the Maastricht Treaty without a referendum. That means single currency for Europe, grants galore for Ireland.'

Eve took up the slack, Bonnie to Fintan's Clyde: 'So we threatened to take my case to the European Court. They shat themselves!'

They shared a conspiratorial grin.

'Another masterstroke,' she said, raising a glass which he met almost instinctively. Another quiverful of flaming arrows sliced through me.

'Where are you staying?' I demanded.

'Hammersmith, a bail hostel.'

'Sounds grim.'

'Are you kidding me? After Mountjoy, a single room in Hammersmith is heaven.'

'And what brings you over here, Eve?'

'My barrister thrashed out a deal, me coming over here and lying low was part of it, at least until the vote goes through parliament and the treaty is signed. When it all blows over, well, let's see...

She smiled at me and my skin ignited. Fintan asked if we fancied another. We looked at each other and nodded, smiling.

'G and Ts please,' we said as one and laughed. 'Lime not lemon!' demanded Eve.

'No problem,' said Fintan, gathering up some empties which I'd never seen him do before, 'you two must have so much to talk about.'

The next round seemed to calm us all down as Eve and Fintan regaled me with every stage of their three-year joint operation to beat her murder rap.

As I learned more about their hilarious law-bending japes, I felt alternating twinges of resentment and confusion. Why had he kept this secret from me? How close had my brother got to the love of my life? Surely they hadn't...?

As soon as she set off to the loo, finally, I launched into him.

'Why didn't you tell me you were still in touch?'

'She asked me not to. She wanted you to get on with your life.'

'So you've been helping her, all along?'

'She gave me so many stories. I owed her.'

'Even after you came over here? There were no scoops in it for you then, Fintan. Why did you stay in touch? What was in it for you?'

'Like I said, I felt like I owed her. And you know what she's like. She wouldn't stop calling. Look, she didn't have a friend in the world, Donal. Her own family fucked off back to New York. Someone had to try and help her.'

'Why do you always have to hold secrets over people? Is it the only way you can function?'

'Look, she's here now isn't she? If you want to rekindle your relationship, then now's your chance. She's nothing to do with me. Go for it.'

I took that as a clear signal: Fintan had no hold over her.

She got back to our silent scowls: 'Talking about me, were ye?'

I felt a jolt of rage. 'You know something, Eve, we weren't fucking talking about you actually, because we've all moved on. You're not the centre of our universe anymore,' I stopped myself from yelling.

216

The horrible truth was: we *had* been talking about her. I hadn't moved on at all. My ego was even hoping she'd come to London to rekindle our relationship.

At some point later, I realised I was badly out of training for drinking, Irish-style. Everything became a blur, save for fragmentary moments of lucidity that seemed to last forever. Like when I got back from the loo at one point, to find Eve clearly agitated.

'I was just telling Eve here about your gift,' Fintan sniggered, 'you get visited by the dead, isn't that right, Donal?'

She looked at me, almost accusingly: 'What's all this about?'

She refused to let me laugh it off, so I found myself running her through my entire history with Marion Ryan: how she attacked me at home and in my car, before appearing to me twice near Sangora Road in broad daylight. She hung on every word, a rapt audience of one, while Fintan took the piss.

'He tells me Meehan came to him too,' he sneered.

The night stopped dead at the mere mention of his name. A sickening angst took root in my core.

'Oh my God,' Eve mouthed, her face blanching, 'I feel sick.' She got to her feet and dashed to the ladies. The next fragment: Eve murdering an Irish folk song: Fintan and I sneering at how so many Irish women think they're Aretha Franklin after a skinful. Amid the aural bloodletting, I was struck by a verse:

217

So soon may I follow,
When friendships decay,
And from Love's shining circle,
The gems drop away.
When true hearts lie withered,
And fond ones are flown.
Oh! Who would inhabit
This bleak world alone?

Fintan, self-styled music guru, told me it was an ancient ballad called 'The Last Rose of Summer'.

Then Eve launched into 'Summertime', Fintan explaining how that song had been ripped off from an old Negro classic, 'Sometimes I Feel Like a Motherless Child'. As Eve demanded and got the attention of the entire bar, I wondered if her subconscious mind somehow knew this.

At some stage, one of those generic Irish country bands that specialises in sedating pissed immigrants spurted into life. They duly churned out the bog-standard repertoire of corny ditties and misery-milking ballads we'd all heard a thousand times before.

When lost love and the joys of hole-digging failed to rouse the rabble, they belted out a good old IRA song. I watched the crowd whooping and howling in delight, their pockets bulging with Sterling.

I bid the place 'an Irish farewell', slipping unnoticed out of a side door, leaving my homicidal ex in the sole care of my morally bankrupt brother. I couldn't help thinking what a perfect couple they'd make.

218

Chapter 22

Clapham Police Station, South London
Monday, August 12, 1991: 10:00

Next morning, the incident room crackled. Teams yapped like excited hounds, the scent of prey tickling their impatient noses. Shep's bold decision to get everyone pissed and onside Friday had been his first masterstroke. Judging by the atmosphere, the weekend's four-pronged assault on Peter Ryan and Karen Foster had been his second.

At the centre of it, Shep darted about, desk-to-desk, like some deranged orchestra conductor. He'd bark a brief question, place his hands to his lips, prayer-like, then listen hard, head bowed, to the long and winding replies. Occasionally his hands would fall, he'd lean forward professorially and squint at whatever he was being shown on a computer screen or a map.

After an hour, he looked set to burst with excitement and called an impromptu briefing.

'Now, I'd like each team to enlighten us about what they found out over the past two days. But please, give me the baby, not the birth.'

He pointed first to DC Young, the female officer who'd been so clearly unoffended by Peter Ryan's flirting.

'A couple of colleagues at the Pines revealed that Peter and Karen had been an item some

219

years back, perhaps three or four years ago.'

'Why did no one mention this before?' asked Shep. 'And why haven't Peter or Karen mentioned it at all? If only to prove it's over between them? Or that it was just a fleeting thing?'

'Their colleagues said the same thing; it had been so brief and it was finished by the time he met Marion. In fact, they were under the impression that Karen had grown close to Marion. They talked about them going to the pub together, quite often.'

'But one colleague has a different story to tell. Isn't that right, DC Young?'

She failed to completely suppress a smile.

'I spoke to Bethan Trott. She's the nurse who watched TV with Karen and her sister Laura between five thirty and six p.m. on the day of Marion's murder. When I asked her about the nature of Peter's relationship with Karen, she became a little uncomfortable.

'I pressed her and she finally started to open up. She told me that after Peter and Marion got married last June, they moved into a room in the staff accommodation quarters at the home which happened to be next door to hers. Around the same time, Karen asked Bethan for a spare key to her room so she could go there to watch TV when it was quiet. Bethan agreed. Bethan now claims that she returned to her room on several occasions to find her eavesdropping on Peter and Marion.

'On one occasion, Karen had written a list of the presents Peter had bought Marion for her birthday and had added the words "sick, sick, sick" at the bottom of the page. When Bethan asked her why, she said something along the lines of "if only she knew what he was up to behind her back". Bethan said she'd forgotten about this incident until a few days ago, when she found the piece of paper under her bed. Karen must have dropped it as she listened to them next door.'

Shep interjected: 'I've got that piece of paper here, if anyone wants to see it. She's scrawled the words "sick, sick, sick" in manic writing across the bottom.' He nodded for WPC Young to continue.

'On another occasion, Bethan found Karen in her room in tears. When she asked what was wrong, Karen said that Peter was taking Marion away for a weekend, adding words to the effect of "he won't even spend the night with me". When Bethan asked her what she meant by this, Karen clammed up. So Bethan decided to do some investigating of her own.'

The air in the incident room fizzed, charged, electric.

'Last November, she saw Karen and Peter enter a shed in the grounds of the home where Peter has a desk. Fifteen minutes later, Karen emerged, as Bethan put it, "dishevelled". She's convinced that they'd had sex in the shed.

'A few days later, she confronted Karen, who denied having any sort of sexual relations with Peter Ryan, insisting that they were just good friends. Bethan claims she believed her, which is why she hasn't mentioned any of this before.'

Shep swelled with almost unbearable self-satisfaction, a raging blush igniting both cheeks.

'So, Peter Ryan and Karen Foster were having sex late last year, just months after Peter had married Marion. The challenge now,' he declared, all-conquering, Churchillian, 'is to prove that Karen Foster acted upon her obsession with Peter Ryan, by killing Marion.'

'Obsession?' scoffed McStay, holding up a VHS tape. 'If Karen had some sort of homicidal hatred for Marion, then why did she attend their wedding in Ireland last summer? Karen is on this video, having a great time. Certainly looking nothing like the woman scorned.'

'I'm sure she presented well to camera,' sniffed Shep.

McStay wasn't done: 'It's worth noting that Peter Ryan is still staying with Marion's family up in Enfield. They don't suspect him of any wrong-doing whatsoever. They'll be shattered by this accusation.'

That punctured the euphoria. The O'Learys had been almost saintly in their dignity and patience. They really didn't deserve a sordid sub-plot.

Shep set about resurrecting the mood: 'DS Barratt. Tell us please what you discovered from Peter's best friend?'

'Not his best friend, Guv, his best man, who comes from his home town in Ireland but lives in North London.'

Shep blinked impatiently.

'He told us that Peter and Marion were planning to move to Ireland in the autumn to start a family. They hadn't told their families yet: they were waiting until Marion was pregnant.'

Shep decided to editorialise for anyone failing to keep up: 'Karen got wind of these plans. Time was running out for her and Peter, the man she loved.'

I wondered if, on the sly, he read his wife's Mills and Boon books.

Barratt remained deadpan: 'Well we need to find out if Karen actually knew about these plans first, Guv.'

Shep ignored him and turned to the last of the four teams. Maurice, the younger of the pair, spoke up: 'We found out something from Pam Foster, Karen's mother. She attended Clapham police station on the night of the murder while Karen and Peter were making their initial statements. When they were finished, she offered to drive Peter to Marion's parents' home. He told her that he couldn't face them, and stayed the night at the Foster family home in South London, on the couch apparently.'

Shep raged: 'So we let the two prime suspects spend a night together, to get their stories straight. And we didn't even know about it? Christ almighty.'

Shep wasn't as rattled as me. I realised I'd forgotten to read those initial statements made by Peter and Karen on the night of the murder. They'd given these statements raw – before their all-night, post-murder conference. If they were going to slip up, it would be in there.

I scolded myself for making such a basic error. As soon as this briefing ended, I'd gut those initial statements. But at that moment, I faced a more immediate dilemma. I realised that if I flagged up my stranger suspect, Robert Napper, Shep would probably destroy me.

He was coming to me next, soft soaping the old guard in the meantime: 'Of course, we still have to keep an open mind about other potential suspects. Peter and/or Karen could have roped in an accomplice. And, of course, the Lone Wolf Killer line of enquiry remains open. Lynch, did you come across anything we need to check out?'

My face burned. I had to flag up Napper. *I had to*. If I chickened out and Napper struck again, I'd never forgive myself.

'Yes, actually I think there is someone we need to check out, Guv,' I said, my voice shaking slightly. I felt like a noise pollution officer shutting down a banging party.

'Did a Lone Wolf jump out of the paperwork and bite you?' he laughed.

The sniggers sucked the last drop of moisture from my throat.

I told them about the Green Chain Attacks. I pointed out the obvious connections to Marion's murder: the suspect had escalated, he'd used a knife, he'd targeted women both in public spaces and in their homes.

So far, so plausible. I then hit them with the notes that put Napper in the frame: the first written by the patrol officer who caught him hanging around a woman's back garden ('abnormal, rapist, indecency type'), then the note which described the rape claims he'd made to his mother.

That last revelation shocked even these gore-hardened hounds.

'Christ, what sort of pervert would boast about a rape to his own mum?' said Shep to murmured agreement.

'So what sex attacks on local Commons did you find to match his confession?' asked Shep.

224

'Well, none, Guv, but I think it's worth checking him out.'

'What's his form?' asked Shep, irritably.

'Er, not much,' I mumbled, my cheeks sizzling like fried rashers, 'possession of an air rifle in '86.'

I sounded half-hearted, it sounded half-arsed.

'And?' said Shep, chewing his lip.

I shrugged: 'That's it,' I said, trying not to swallow my own voice box. Nobody moved a muscle.

Shep spoke patiently, as if to a child: 'So he's got no form for a crime like this, and the note from his mother is from nearly two years ago and doesn't match any reported crime?'

'That's correct, Guv, but it's not every day a mother shops her son for rape. She must know more. He must be some sort of deviant.'

'I think you're clutching at straws, Lynch. I mean none of the Green Chain Attacker's victims were stabbed, correct? As far as I know, the attacks all took place in public places. I just don't see the connection.'

'He may have struck in someone's home. We just don't know yet. But in conscience, Guv, I had to bring this guy to your attention. This nutter is the only person I could find who's on the loose and capable of this level of violence. He's escalated to this. He's worth checking out. That's all I'm saying.'

Shep shook his head: 'This is a weirdo who lurks in the bushes at night and jumps on random women. You think he suddenly took a bus to Clapham, saw Marion and decided to stab her up?'

Childhood humiliations flooded through me. *Can someone else go in goal now?*

'He might have been stalking her?' I heard my feeble voice plead.

Shep smiled: 'Do you think he brought his air-gun with him, on the bus?'

That got a laugh.

'Lynch, get the officers at Plumstead to check him out. Can you stick to solving this case for now?' he said with a mixture of disgust and pity. I hoped to God he'd let it go.

Shep surveyed his flock slowly, dramatically. He leaned forward and spoke quietly, conspiratorially: 'Let's be bold and run with the idea that Karen Foster murdered Marion.'

Hang on, my mind protested, *the pathologist said it had to be a man.* My memory flashed back to Karen that night, convulsing as I questioned her. That can't have been an act.

But Shep had the blinkers back on: 'Okay, so based on what we've got, Karen takes the afternoon off work. She meets her accomplice. She either brought the weapon with her, the accomplice brought it or they went somewhere to pick it up. They drive to Marion's home at Sangora Road. She and the accomplice park where they can see the far end of the street and the front door. Marion turns into Sangora on foot just after five forty p.m. Karen and the accomplice meet her at the bottom of the steps to 21. One of them is carrying a bag containing the weapon and a change of clothes.

'They explain that Peter has asked them to bring some pots from the house to the Pines –

226

they're too big for him to carry on the train. Remember, according to Peter and Karen, that's the reason she drove him back to the house that night. Peter may have mentioned this to Marion that morning, to prime her. Marion lets them in. She picks up her post and leads them up the stairs to the flat. On the landing, one of them stuns her with a blow. She falls. They go to work.

'According to the pathologist, the attack took two to three minutes. They change out of their bloody clothes, leave the house, get back to the car and return to the Pines old people's home where Karen is seen just after six.'

I wondered if I was the only one not buying it. Either way, Shep kept selling.

'Was Peter involved? I think that's the toughest nut to crack right now.

'Check out Karen and Peter's bank and phone records. Get back to the Pines. We need to look at their precise movements on the day of the murder again. Who saw them and at what times exactly? Check out if anyone working at the Pines or anyone employed there in the past twelve months has form for violence. Also find out if any of them has a martial arts belt. Remember, Marion was knocked out by a karate-style chop.

'The first thing I was told when I joined this investigation was that both Karen and Peter have watertight alibis. But do they? Have we really challenged those alibis rigorously? I don't think we have,' said Shep, resisting the temptation to leer at McStay and Barratt.

'I want them both brought in for interview. Get Karen in first. With Bethan's revelations, we can

227

really shake her up. I think she's our prime suspect. Mulroney and Gibson, oil the thumbscrews. Lynch, help them prepare for the interviews. I want nothing short of a full confession from her about the affair with Peter, then a full confession to the murder of Marion. It's her time to bleed, understood?'

Chapter 23

Clapham Police Station, South London
Monday, August 12, 1991; 11:00

Before I did anything else I had to look through Peter and Karen's first statements. What if I'd missed something?

I printed out both, along with the lengthier versions they gave later, laying them side-by-side for inspection.

Peter didn't appear to make any factual contradictions in either. However, I noted a few potential banana skins. How convenient that he'd forgotten his chequebook when buying the fish feed and water cleaner that day. A dated, timed and signed IOU seemed almost too good an alibi to be true.

He'd made other claims that sounded distinctly like arse-covering exercises – or attempts to direct detectives down the 'stranger killer' route. He thought Marion had been wearing a bracelet on the morning of her murder that he hadn't been able to find since. She phoned him at work that afternoon to say she had to run an errand and would be a little late home. He couldn't remember what that errand was.

Firstly, if Peter wasn't getting home until nine p.m. – three hours after Marion – why would she bother telling him this? Secondly, while I was no sugar-hearted sentimentalist, I'd have recalled, stored and treasured every single word of the last conversation I'd ever held with my murdered wife, even the details of her trivial errand.

Of course, in neither statement did Peter mention that he and Karen had once been lovers. Mind you, DS Glenn's blinkered and mis-directed team hadn't asked him.

None of this was proof, though.

As I read through Karen's statement from the night of the murder, my eyes seized upon a para-graph.

The journey to Sangora Road took no more than fifteen minutes. We drove into Sangora Road and I parked up next to the pub at the bottom of the road.

I grabbed her later statement and located the paragraph I was looking for:

The journey to Sangora Road took fifteen minutes at the most. I couldn't park on Sangora Road because it was already full. I had to park on the side road. I don't know what it is called.

My mind flashed back to Friday night: the blazing heat, those visions of Marion, first near the pub on Sangora, then on Strathblaine Road. My guts knotted tight.

Was Strathblaine Road the side road Karen had been referring to in her second statement? And

229

why had she changed her story? I checked an A to Z. Strathblaine Road is the *only* road off Sangora that you can park on. So that part must be true. So why did she say she'd parked near the pub on Sangora in her first statement?

And then it struck me: what if Karen Foster hadn't made a mistake? What if she'd been to Sangora Road twice that day? When she first came to kill Marion, she parked near the Roundhouse pub on Sangora Road. This location offered her a grandstand view of Marion's front door and the top of the road. I'd been near that pub at about five thirty p.m. on two occasions: there were free parking spaces both times. When Karen returned later, at nine p.m. with Peter, there were no spaces left on Sangora. Strathblaine Road has houses on one side of the street only – the other side falls away to railway tracks leading to Clapham Junction station. But it has parking on both sides of the street. There were always parking spaces available on Strathblaine Road.

My shaking finger dialled Shep's number. I haltingly told him about the differing statements.

'So? She forgot where she parked. I mean that's an innocent enough mistake, isn't it?'

'Maybe it's not a mistake, Guv.'

'I don't follow,' said Shep.

'Maybe Karen parked her car in that area twice that day.'

Shep was silent, then: 'My God, you're right. You're right!'

'It's not evidential and, of course, she'll say she just made a mistake.'

'Yes but we know better. And this puts her and

her car in two very specific places at two very specific times. There have to be witnesses who saw her getting in and out of the car between five thirty and six, especially if she parked near the pub.'

He sounded stoked. 'Make sure you tell Mick and Colin. Good work, Lynch,' he said. I basked in those final three words long after he'd slammed down the phone.

But as the glory faded, an eerie chill sent spiders scuttling up my spine: Marion had appeared to me on both those streets. Had she been making sure I picked up on this discrepancy?

'Sleep paralysis, my arse,' I said, dialling a phone number.

Chapter 24

Falcon Pub, Clapham Junction
Monday, August 12, 1991; 19:00

That evening at the Falcon I leafed impatiently through a copy of the *Evening Standard,* but none of it could distract me from the news I was about to impart.

'Wonderful concept, but highly improbable,' was how Lilian had laughed off the idea that Marion was coming to me from beyond the grave with clues. Well, how could she explain my twin daylight visions of her, and the fact that it had proven critical to the case?

231

I'd never bought her sleep paralysis theory. Even though I craved a diagnosis, I resented her desperation to hammer square peg clinical conditions into the uniquely shaped hole of my experiences.

I'd hatched a plan to tell her about the dual-hallucination first, without mentioning its relevance. I'd let her explain it away clinically; then hit her with the fact that Marion's spirit had directed me to a critical clue. I couldn't wait to see how she'd go about applying pragmatic science to this inexplicable development.

Lilian crept tentatively through the door: clearly not at home in a pub. After much deliberation, she settled on a white wine spritzer. Thankfully, the barmaid knew what this was.

'How have you been Donal(d)?' she asked, back to her original mispronunciation. 'Look, I know you weren't entirely convinced by my prognosis, so I got hold of two books, both written by eminent professors who specialise in sleep paralysis research.'

'Thanks,' I said, wondering how they managed to fill two hefty tomes on the subject, and why they'd bother. The back sleeves revealed that, apart from sporting obligatory professorial beards, both men suffered from the condition.

'In Dr Cheyne's book, I think I may even have found the answer to your out-of-body experience when you entered Eve's house that night and saw her ... you know...'

'Being attacked by Meehan,' I finished helpfully.

'Professor Cheyne has evidence that if sleep paralysis is prolonged, it can become an out-of-body experience. I've been thinking, the absinthe you consumed, that had been spiked with cannabis and tranquilliser, could have slowed down your brain's reactions. You may have stayed asleep for longer than usual.'

I nodded, trying not to look thick.

'If the cannabis prolonged your sleep paralysis episode, then it would have developed into an out-of-body experience.'

I scoffed: 'Oh right, so I floated into Eve's bed-room, for real?'

Lilian's eyes flashed steel.

'You really shouldn't sneer,' she snapped, 'out-of-body experiences are scientifically-proven phenomena, even if we don't fully understand what causes them. In one experiment, a woman came out of her body and memorised a five-digit number positioned in the corner of the room by the scientist, which she couldn't possibly have seen from the bed. They're also more common than you might think. One in ten of us has had one. Some people have them regularly. I could induce one in you right now. Look up the God Helmet in the library. Electrical impulses to certain parts of the brain can induce an out-of-body experience.'

'So you're saying I left my body, went through the wall of the house and witnessed what hap-pened, in real time?'

'Cheyne talks about flying over Toronto at night when he's out of his body. He can see the streets below him, the traffic and the people. It's called lucid dreaming. It's a very exciting new field. Look, Donal, all I'm asking you to do is read the

233

books and then we can start breaking down your experiences based on what's already out there in the field.'

'Do either of these men know how to stop it happening?'

'That's the fascinating thing about Cheyne. He says that as soon as he comes out of his body, he no longer feels fear. Sometimes he can watch himself having a nightmare from above, while feeling totally calm.'

I couldn't believe what I was hearing: these academic claims were even wilder than mine.

'The bottom line is: there is no cure. The best you can do is manage it, and the only way to manage it is to prolong the experience so that you come out of your body. You have to train yourself not to freak out and wake up.'

'You make that sound so easy, Lilian,' I smiled, 'I don't think you quite appreciate how terrifying it feels when I'm having these encounters. Can you imagine waking up in the middle of the night to an imposter who then attacks you?'

'I'm just saying you could look at this as an amazing opportunity.'

'Oh I am, Lilian. Some night I'll fly past your place, maybe tap on the window.'

It bounced off her. She wasn't one for playful banter. She took a sip of her drink as I poured out my story about Marion's twin apparition the previous Friday evening. I didn't mention that I'd been drinking all afternoon, or that I'd wound up in the foetal position next to a tree that had been pissed on that day by two thousand dogs.

I wrapped up: 'I'm thinking maybe this isn't

connected to the night-time stuff. It didn't feel as ... real.'

I couldn't wait to drop the punchline: how these appearances had helped me find a key contradiction in Karen's alibi. Explain that away, *Sigmund Fraud...*

'This is almost certainly connected to your other visions of Marion,' she announced, planting her drink firmly on the table. 'There's a phenomenon called *daytime para-hypnagogia* or DPH,' she began and I stared at her in disbelief. At least it had a good name this time.

She was off: 'DPH is when a dream-like image or thought intrudes into your waking consciousness. It's this threshold consciousness thing, between sleep and wakefulness, like sleep paralysis. DPH happens to people suffering from extreme tiredness, or extreme boredom. For example, it's been described by prisoners who've spent a long spell in solitary confinement. The brain normally doesn't bother remembering the image, unless it's been influenced by some form of autosuggestion.'

'Autosuggestion?'

'Autosuggestion is like, oh I don't know, "I must I must increase my bust?"'

I managed, somehow, not to look at her tits. It was a miracle.

'The man who coined the term autosuggestion, Emile Coué, believed that anyone can change themselves by continually feeding their subconscious an idea. For example, he had a group of patients with all sorts of physical ailments say to themselves several times a day: "Every day, in every way, I am getting better and better." He

235

proved that the patients who did this recovered better than the ones who didn't.

'The same man came up with the placebo effect. He found he could prescribe a tablet that was just powder, but if he told the patient it was the best thing ever, their health would improve.'

What the fuck has this got to do with anything? my expression must have said.

'Okay, so let's start with DPH. You were exhausted on Friday, from your usual lack of sleep. You'd been walking in extreme heat. The auto-suggestion could be that you'd been thinking about Marion over and over. Your subconscious had been slaving over her case. So when your poor dazed brain slipped into REM, it's only natural that Marion should appear.'

'Okay but the thing is, since this happened, I've found out that the two places where she appeared to me are connected and could be critical to the case.'

She sat forward.

'It turns out that one of the suspects in the case said in her first statement that she parked her car near the pub on Sangora Road before discovering Marion's body with Peter.'

Lilian was nodding lots, blinking little.

'Then in her second statement, which she gave two days later, she said there were no parking spaces available on Sangora, so instead she parked on the only road off it, Strathblaine Road...'

'So if she wasn't lying, she must've parked near Marion's home twice that day,' Lilian finished for me.

'Exactly. The thing is, I never would have

spotted this contradiction had she not appeared to me on both streets a few days earlier.'

Explain that, doc? I almost cried.

Her eyes drifted to a distant horizon. I imagined her scientific mind rampaging away behind that frown, pulling up trees until logic found a course through this bewildering wood.

'Science accepts that the hypnagogic state can provide the answers to problems. There's the famous case of a scientist who was trying to figure out the atomic structure of benzene. He was half-asleep in front of the fire. In the flames he could see molecules forming into snakes. Suddenly, one of the snakes grabbed its tail in its mouth. Bingo, he realised that the structure of benzene is a closed ring.'

Her brain was hurtling like a dead star. Mine ached.

'Edison, Newton, Tesla all credit hypnagogic states for some of their best discoveries. Beethoven, Wagner, Edgar Allan Poe all used it for inspiration.'

I couldn't stop my head wobbling with pride. But I thought I'd better bring up one key difference between me and my genius hypnagogic brethren.

'The only thing is, I didn't make the connection between the roads while I was in that hypno state you describe. I made the connection much later, when I read Karen's statements.'

'Yes, but you were most likely in a hypnagogic state when you saw Marion.'

'Which means?'

'Supposing you made the connection, and your

subconscious stored it until you needed to call upon it. Let's run with the theory that your subconscious mind has found a way to use sleep paralysis and the hypnagogic state to identify clues in a live case. What if your sleeping disorder actively helps you find contradictions or mistakes – clues – that have got past everyone else? Now that's a paper I could get published.'

'I'm telling you, Lilian, it's more than that. It feels ... I hate to say it ... supernatural.'

'Hold on to your horses there, Donal,' she smiled, 'let's keep this in perspective. What's happened here is that a hallucination may or may not have helped you spot a contradiction in a statement. Looking at it in a cold scientific light, Karen had made that mistake irrespective of your visions. At our most optimistic, what you're exhibiting here is an ability to use your disorder to make you better at your job. I think that's potentially really interesting. We don't need to cheapen it with second-rate science fiction.'

I couldn't let that go: 'Yes, God forbid something comes up that doesn't fit neatly into one of your approved little scientific boxes.'

She threw me that look of hers, the one that said, *This guy is a weirdo.*

'What we need to show now is a consistent pattern of this happening to you. To use police parlance, we need to build a case.'

'And that would be enough for your dissertation?'

She nodded and smiled: 'I think the fact we're even having this conversation is amazing, Donal.'

'Great,' I said, but I couldn't help feeling that

her cold scientific light was failing to illuminate the bigger picture.

By the time I rang Gabby it was after ten p.m. and she sounded knackered. I promised to call her much earlier tomorrow and take her out for dinner.

'A proper date?' she asked.

'There'll even be candles,' I assured her.

Chapter 25

Clapham Police Station, South London
Tuesday, August 13, 1991; 10:00

Next morning, I clicked open the forensic report and began re-reading intently.

Now that Marion's daytime appearances had proven relevant to the case, I felt convinced that her night-time attacks also held clues to her killer. To crack this case, all I needed to do was decipher her macabre nocturnal charades.

The theme of both her visits had been slamming doors. I concluded that she must have been leading me to the front door of her flat. The key to finding her killer must somehow be connected to that door. I just needed to figure out in what way.

We knew already that the fingerprints of Peter Ryan and Karen Foster had been found on both the front door of 21 Sangora Road and the door to Marion's flat. This fact in isolation was evidentially useless. But what if Karen had carried out the crime with another, unidentified male accomplice? The violence of the attack meant it had to be carried out by a man. Was that what Marion had been trying to lead me to? Was there a third person we hadn't identified?

Forensics had found sixteen unidentified prints on the front door, seven on the flat door. None of them matched known offenders. But did one of these prints belong to the muscle; the knifeman? This *had* to be what she'd been trying to tell me. I needed to identify the owners of those twenty-three unknown fingerprints. But how?

Marion was clearly security-conscious, cautious. I figured that she wouldn't have let Karen into her flat with a stranger; Karen probably knew better than to even try. Whoever she recruited, Marion must have known at least by sight or by first name. The common denominator could only be the Pines care home. Peter and Karen worked there. Peter and Marion lived there in staff accommodation for seven months after their marriage. I decided to ask Shep if we could take the fingerprints of every employee at the home, including contractors and any workers who'd left within the past year. If we cross-referenced their prints with those found at the scene, I felt sure we'd find the missing link in this case. Well, it was the best I could come up with.

Shep said he'd only sanction this expensive and time-consuming operation if they got nothing out of today's interview with Karen. He seemed more ratty and irritable than usual.

240

'You okay, Guv?'

'No I'm not fucking okay,' he spat.

He looked at my startled face and softened: 'I'm just back from Marion's family. I had to tell her mum and dad that Peter used to go out with Karen Foster, and that they may have resumed their affair. I might have known he wouldn't have had the balls to tell them himself. They took it badly. I had to call an ambulance for Mary.'

'Christ,' was all I could think to say, then: 'Surely he can't carry on staying with them now?'

'My worry is, if Peter moves out, his family or friends might convince him to do a midnight flit to Ireland. You know what the extradition situation is like right now. It could drag out for years. And we haven't got enough to charge him.

'So I had to ask her dad John – would you mind keeping him a bit longer. While I'm asking him I'm thinking, "if he'd done that to either of my daughters, I'd have thrown him out the fucking top floor window." But John agreed, right away. "If it helps catch Marion's killer, we'll do it," he said. Can you imagine? They're living fucking saints, that family.'

Shep's voice cracked and eyes moistened: something I hadn't seen before.

'Anyway,' he coughed, instantly regaining control, 'Mick and Colin are limbering up for Karen's interview. Why don't you come and watch with me? I could use a spare set of eyes and ears.'

I remembered those dank, fusty interview suites from when I'd made my statement the day after Marion's murder. As we walked along that single long corridor to the adjoining block, Shep

241

explained that Karen Foster had been formally cautioned and brought in first thing. Peter Ryan had agreed to come in voluntarily at ten a.m. tomorrow.

When we came to the security doors, Shep dialled in the code and invited me to go through first. I pulled down the handle and pushed.

'Put your shoulder into it, man,' he said. It was another one of those tightly-sprung, self-closing fire doors. My mind shot back to Marion's flat: what the hell was I missing on that door?

I pushed it open, held it for Shep, then followed him along more corridors and left into a small kitchenette. Like two prize fighters pre-bout, Mick and Colin stalked about, psyching themselves up, mentally ordering their verbal combinations.

Shep brought them up to speed on the loose ends from last weekend's purge of Peter's workplace, the Pines care home. 'As we know, Karen took a few hours off work. She told colleagues she was going shopping in Blackheath with her younger sister, Laura. One of the nurses there, Sharon Healy, finished work at four p.m. and saw Karen driving her purple estate car out of the clinic car park. She was alone, with her hair tied up, wearing shades and a red top. Colleagues report her wearing a red top and jeans throughout that day and evening.

'Another employee, Valerie Donald, left the clinic at six p.m. on the dot. She knows this because she has to pick up her kid from childcare. She saw Karen's purple estate car stationary at the end of the driveway, facing towards the home. Sitting inside it was Karen still wearing her shades and, she thought, a dark top. She remembers Karen waving back at her.

'The question is, of course, what had Karen been up to in those intervening two hours? And with whom? What's your strategy, gents?'

'We don't want her clamming up, so we're going to take it nice and gently,' said Colin.

'We've got all we need to peel her open like a can of sardines,' added Mick, calm but focused, 'there'll be no need for bawling and shouting.'

'Follow me, Lynch,' said Shep, careering up the corridor and through a door.

'Ringside,' he said, taking the furthest of four seats facing a window. On the other side of the glass, Karen sat nearside of her duty solicitor, her arms folded, chewing a piece of gum. She might have been waiting for a bus.

'She can't see us, right?' I whispered.

'Or hear us,' boomed Shep.

I was grateful for the chance to have a good ogle at Karen. As *femmes fatales* go, she was something of a let-down. Her best feature: long, glistening brown hair. Her face was several cheap tanning booths too teak, resembling a glazed bagel. Her tight black jeans and t-shirt served only to high-light her excess flesh, forcing it to spill out in the places she probably least wanted it to.

'She reminds me of a busted bin bag,' said Shep.

Her lifeless blue eyes conveyed a sullen insolence. When she spoke to her solicitor, she ended most sentences with a questioning, 'you know?' that implicitly granted her victim status. 'This is the third time I've had to take time off work, you know? I can't believe I have to go through it all again. It's quite traumatic for me, you know?'

'If the Foster family ever fall on hard times,' piped up Shep, 'they could charge people to slap her.'

The boys started on the afternoon of the murder: nothing too taxing. Karen parroted her original alibi: afternoon shopping in Blackheath with her sister Laura; she wore the same thing all day – jeans and her red Levi's t-shirt; back to the Pines just after five p.m.; meeting Bethan Trott in the communal kitchen and heading to her room for tea and a soap opera; fish feeding with 'Pete' at six.

Problems verifying these events cropped up early. Karen and Laura didn't buy anything in Blackheath, and she couldn't remember any of the shops they'd visited.

Shep shook his head: 'I mean, really, are you telling me a woman wouldn't remember *every* shop she went into, on any shopping trip?'

Karen couldn't recall being in her car outside the home at six p.m.: 'I may have popped out to get cigarettes which I sometimes leave in the car, or a bottle of water.'

While helping to clean out the fish tanks, Karen developed an upset stomach. At about 7.45 p.m. she went to use the toilet and agreed to meet Peter by her car at eight p.m. She went back to her room to pick up her car keys and car park pass.

Almost inaudibly, she took up the story: 'There weren't any parking spaces on Sangora Road at that time of the night. So I parked on a street around the corner. I don't know what it's called.

When we got to the house, Peter was surprised that the front door wasn't double-locked. Marion always locked the mortise lock.'

'And why did you go into the flat, Karen?'

'My stomach still wasn't right. I needed to use the toilet. I also wanted to say hello to Marion. We were good friends, you know?'

'So you're in the hallway of the house...' prompted Colin.

'He unlocked the door to the flat and went ahead of me up the stairs. When I heard him call out "Marion! Marion!" I ran upstairs. Pete felt Marion's hand for a pulse and put his hand on her forehead. He said she was still lukewarm.

'I felt for a pulse in Marion's neck. I put my hand underneath her head and tried to lift her up. I told Pete that she was all stiff. I noticed Marion's eyes were bloodshot and I saw cuts all over her dress. I saw blood around her mouth and ears. I started to scream. I must have gone into shock.'

She stopped, bowed her head and pushed her hair back with a trembling hand: rattled by grief or guilt, I couldn't tell.

'What was Pete doing?'

'Pete didn't touch her again. He said he was going downstairs to the neighbour's flat to ring the police. I remembered seeing a police officer on the street as we were looking for a parking space. I ran outside to try to find him.'

'That's bullshit,' I interjected, 'we were the nearest cops. That's why we got there first.'

Karen carried on: 'I looked around but I couldn't see him so I ran into the pub and told them to call the police because someone was dead. A few of the guys at the bar tried to calm me down and were asking me what had happened. I was hysterical.

'Three or four people from the pub came with me back to the flat. They went upstairs to see what had happened and I followed them up. They looked at Marion, then went back downstairs.'

My heart sank; this explained all the prints on the doors.

I could barely hear Karen now. 'Her skirt had risen up around her waist. I didn't like people seeing her like that so I pulled it down and pushed her hair away from her face. I realised I had blood on my hands, so I went to the bathroom to wash them.'

Karen stopped for a quivering sob as Shep bucked in his seat.

'I tell you what really troubles me here, Lynch,' he ranted, 'most people are instinctively wary of touching a dead body. It's just not something civilians in that situation do. I mean, take Peter. He touched Marion's hand and forehead. Once he knew she was dead, he didn't touch her again. And he's her husband. That might sound cold, but that's the natural response.

'What isn't natural is Karen touching every part of the body, getting people in to trample the crime scene, washing her hands in the sink. The one place that she wouldn't have been able to explain away her fingerprints would have been in the bathroom sink. She'd even thought of that, the crafty bitch. I'll tell you what she was doing, Lynch. She was systematically contaminating the

246

crime scene.'

Karen regained her composure. 'Pete came back upstairs. He wanted to see if they'd been burgled. I followed him into the sitting room to check.'

Shep tutted: 'Good old Pete. Wife dead on the landing, better check no one's made off with the telly.'

'Everything seemed normal and undisturbed. On my way back downstairs, I opened the window on the landing because I felt sick and wanted some fresh air. I remember the clasp on the window seemed loose.'

Shep shook his head: 'While everyone else was in shock, she was busy destroying evidence and creating fake suspects.'

'Okay, Karen, we want to move on to another area of interest now,' said Mick.

Colin began. 'What was the nature of your relationship with Peter Ryan?'

Karen bristled, 'As I've said before, we've been working together for five years. We became friends. Then he met Marion and I became friends with both of them, you know?'

Colin went hunting through his papers, settled on one sheet and laid it carefully before him.

In a deadpan voice, he said: 'On October 23rd, 1990, you listed the presents Pete had bought Marion for her birthday. At the bottom of the list, you wrote the words "sick, sick, sick". Do you remember this, Karen? Would you like to see the piece of paper to confirm this is your writing?'

Karen's bottom lip dropped slightly. I could

sense her insides collapsing like cliffs into a raging sea.

'What I want to know, Karen, is how you managed to listen to them in their room? Your room was four doors down the corridor.'

'I had a key to Bethan's room, which was next to theirs. I went in there to watch telly sometimes. I overheard them next door.'

'You went in there to eavesdrop, to spy on them, didn't you, Karen? You were obsessed with Peter Ryan. You wanted him all to yourself.'

She shook her head.

Colin raised his voice: 'You told a witness that Peter was up to something behind Marion's back. What was Peter up to, Karen?'

'I don't know what you're talking about.'

'Peter took Marion away for the weekend, but he wouldn't even spend a night with you. Isn't that what you said?'

'I never said anything of the sort.'

'Sex in a shed, Karen. That can't be very comfortable.'

She remained stoically inscrutable.

'We have a witness who saw you and Peter going at it in a shed at work last November. Must have been chilly too.'

Karen folded her arms, looked to one side and sighed petulantly.

'You're not denying it then, Karen? You admit having sex in the shed at work with Peter Ryan, last November?'

Karen's gaze remained locked onto the side wall.

Good cop Mick interjected calmly.

'Karen, we know you and Peter were having sex

last year and that you used to go out together. There's no point wasting our time here. So, why don't you tell us, when did your sexual relationship with Pete begin?'

She turned to Mick, blinked and took a deep, resigned breath: 'We started going out three years ago, in 1988. I used to meet him in his room at the home. He lived in staff accommodation at the time. He came to my twenty-second birthday party at my house and met my family. We went for drinks. We took up classes together, weight training and aerobics.'

'Christ,' chuckled Shep, 'I'd have thought he got enough weight training and aerobics humping that lump.'

'How would you describe your relationship at that time?'

'We was girlfriend and boyfriend, you know? That's how I introduced him to my family. That's how he introduced me at the classes, as his girlfriend.'

'Did you not find it strange that he was never available at weekends?'

Karen shrugged.

'And when did you learn that he was in a relationship with Marion?'

'They threw an engagement party for them at the home.'

'That would have been, let me see, almost two years ago, in June 1989? How did you react?'

'I was furious. I didn't speak to him for months.'

'Did you resume your relationship with Pete after this?'

249

'After the wedding in June last year, he told me that he'd made a mistake, and that he didn't love Marion. He loved me.'

'So you resumed your affair with Pete?'

She nodded.

'I need you to answer the question for the tape recorder,' said Colin, gently.

'Yes,' she said, 'but I realised he was lying to me and using me. The night of his birthday, in December last year, he tried it on with me and I refused. I ended it.'

'So when was the last time you had sex with Pete?'

'November last year. Nine months ago. By then I'd got to know Marion and I liked her. We became good mates. We went to the pub. I baked a cake for her birthday. I helped them move out of the home. By the end of last year I hated Pete and thought Marion deserved better.'

Colin laughed: 'It was Marion you hated really, wasn't it, for standing in the way of you and the man you loved?'

'I didn't love him. I was angry and hurt. But that was last year. Like I said, I became friends with Marion and stopped seeing Pete.'

'It can't have been easy, Karen, especially when Marion moved into Pete's room after the wedding, seeing them together, happy. The man of your dreams married and in love with someone else.'

Karen darkened.

'You went to the room next to theirs to eavesdrop. This sounds to me like you were obsessed with Pete. I think that you remained obsessed with Pete. I think this obsession turned into a murderous hatred. Of Marion.'

Karen muttered something to her brief and folded her arms. 'My client does not want to make any further comment at this time,' he announced.

Mick told the tape recorder they were stopping for a break. We reassembled in the kitchen.

'I tell you what, for a fat bird, she's lively on her feet,' said Shep, 'she gambled that we only knew about them having sex last year. I bet he carried on screwing her, right up until the murder.'

'The trouble is we have no evidence that the affair continued after November last year,' said Mick.

'And she's clamming up,' added Colin, 'she's probably guessed that her best bet now is to keep her trap shut.'

Shep checked his watch: 'I'll make sure we get a twenty-four-hour custody extension, let the bitch stew for a day. By the time we finish with Lover Boy tomorrow, we'll have enough to charge her with perverting the course of justice. That should open her up a treat.'

Chapter 26

Trinity Road, South London
Tuesday, August 13, 1991; 19:00

'I'm at the Wheatsheaf, Eve x' read the Post-it note on my flat door that evening. I wondered how she got inside the building's front door.

I studied that 'x' for clues. It looked very neat, very formal. I wondered what it meant, if it meant anything at all. What did she really want? Me? Fintan? Neither of us? The other evening at the Archway had been a disaster. The whole night felt as if the three of us had regressed to 1988, or before.

I walked into the pub and scanned the tables. I met her smile in the very far corner: had she been watching the door? Butterflies that had been dead for years rose for a fluttery circuit of my chest.

She looked pretty, if a little formal: skirt, blouse and suit jacket, ready for business. I walked to the bar, gesturing if she'd like another. She nodded, toasting me with another smile. God knows how many gin and tonics (lime not lemon) I'd bank-rolled the other night.

As our drinks were being poured, I glanced over and caught her looking at me. We shared bashful smiles and I wondered why your first love remains special after you'd forgotten all others. I suppose aged sixteen or seventeen, you don't

252

believe *anyone* could really actually love *you*. Not in a sexual way. Maybe your first love helps you learn to love yourself.

I wanted to tell her all of this, but said instead: 'Well, how's the head?'

'Still fragile,' she husked in a voice that made Lauren Bacall sound like Mammy Two Shoes out of *Tom and Jerry*.

'Listen, I meant to say the other night, it's great to see you.' And I meant it. 'I was just a bit shocked, and half cut...'

I scolded myself for the unwitting knife pun. She didn't seem to notice.

'I did try to let Fintan know I was coming to London. I left God knows how many messages but he never got back. Do you think he's okay with me? He seemed very ... cold would you say?'

'I didn't think so,' I lied.

'Now I'm not newsworthy I don't think he gives a shit,' Eve spat.

I was shocked by her sudden change of tone. Underneath that sombre brown bob still lurked a volatile redhead.

She saw the alarm in my face and quickly changed tack: 'Well, Detective Constable, have you cracked that case yet?'

We weren't supposed to discuss live cases with anyone, but I couldn't help myself. Especially the part about me unearthing Marion's damning letter to her friend.

'Wow, you're quite the Columbo aren't you?' she teased. I laughed it off, wondering why no one ever compared me to a sexy detective.

For the rest of the night, I sat back and let Eve

253

take me on a languorous, drink-fuelled trawl through the lives and times of our contemporaries.

Some sort of unspecified Catholic guilt prevented us getting straight down to the sweet *schadenfreude* of other people's misfortunes. Instead, Eve kicked off with a few success stories: someone's brother scouted by United; Fidelma Daly landing a role in a daytime soap; a guy we barely knew inheriting a fortune from some great uncle in Canada. But the really interesting news invariably involved downfall and ruin: babies popping out, students dropping out and people coming out.

I was surprised by the number of girls back home who'd fallen pregnant, clearly without planning to. I wondered how many more had undergone secret abortions in England, like Tara Molloy, the girl I'd unwittingly chaperoned to a clinic in Stepney. Mind you, in late Eighties Tullamore, it was easier to get hold of Semtex than a pack of Jonnies. Women had to beg their inevitably God-fearing, pro-life GP to go on the pill. So Eve and I went without. We did everything but. Why play the Russian roulette of unprotected sex? Yet I couldn't help thinking now: were they all at it, all along, hammer and tongs, except us?

Some of the pregnancies resulted in shotgun weddings, usually in Rome. One couple compounded their degenerate behaviour by 'living in sin', forcing their hard-line religious families to disown them. As Fintan says: 'He sure moves in mysterious ways.' But most of the 'fallen' young mums were staying with their families. I was amazed to hear that none of the dads had scarpered, at least not yet. I couldn't help thinking what a life these young parents faced now, trapped in a town with few job opportunities, playing second fiddle to a child they didn't want, beholden for the rest of their lives to some man/woman they'd shagged a few times, unable to meet someone else because they were 'damaged goods with baggage', forever under the thumb of the child's maternal grandparents. But that was the Irish way. You didn't run away. You made your bed. Pain was your penance.

A couple of guys hadn't so much come out as been flushed out by local gossip, mostly spread by Tullamore's only openly gay man. Maybe he resented the competition because, once outed, none of them hung around for long.

As for those who made it to third-level education, most were already abroad. Every year, Ireland dished out 120,000 degrees/diplomas to people who then had to emigrate to get a job. We were the leading supplier of over-educated barmen, waitresses, labourers and cab drivers to the world.

I couldn't begrudge Eve the merciless relish with which she imparted these grim allegories. As far as she was concerned, there was only one difference between her and the rest of us: her life went off the rails first, and very publicly.

'Fintan tells me you're sharing with Aidan Walker.'

I nodded.

'Jesus, Aidan "Stalker" Walker. Is he still falling in love every week?'

'Three times a week now, what with all the

random women he encounters in London.'

'How does he find time to write all those bad ballads? He still writes bad ballads, I presume?'

'I can confirm that he still writes bad ballads. Though he's been seeing the same girl for over three weeks now, so he's got a double album of new material all about Ruth. Or is it Rachel?'

'Rachel's hard to rhyme. It must be Ruth. He could knock out a song a day with a name like that. Just think of the possibilities: truth, forsooth, youth...'

'Phone booth. Bucktooth. Uncouth.'

'He should call the album *Now That's What I Call Moothic*.'

We both laughed again, hard. We used to laugh so much.

We recovered to find ourselves in that awkward post-joke void. I sensed Eve's green eyes molesting me. She had something to ask.

'Listen, Donal, I need a favour,' she said sadly.

I stopped myself from saying, *Name it*.

'There's a photographer sniffing around the hostel, someone must have tipped off one of the papers that I'm staying there. They've agreed to move me to another hostel but there aren't any free spaces at the minute. Could I stay at yours? Just for a few nights, until I get myself sorted?'

'Of course,' I smiled. Surely this meant she still had feelings for me?

'Thanks, Donal. When I get back on my feet, I'll buy you all the beer you can drink,' she said, pointedly planting her empty glass on the table.

It felt good drinking with a woman who could keep up, even if it was costing me a fortune. But

I needed to know what she had in mind for us. How would we move on from here?

I slung her the gin and cut to the chase: 'What are your longer term plans, Eve?'

'I don't really know,' she said quietly.

'But you're staying in London?'

'I can't go back,' she said, slightly panicked. 'I'm like the scarlet bloody woman over there. I could never live in Ireland again, not after all that's happened.'

'What about the bungalow?'

'We tried to sell it but no one can afford to buy such a monstrosity. Some of the neighbours put in offers way below the asking price, because they knew we were desperate. Can you believe that? That's why Mum and the boys had to go back to New York, to pay the mortgage.'

I wondered why she hadn't followed them; then remembered that the Land of the Free doesn't admit people with criminal records.

'We've got a company that hires it out to tourists but we don't get a lot of takers. I mean, who in their right mind would want to spend a week in a big damp bungalow in the middle of the bog?'

'What about your dad? Maybe he could help...'

'Do you honestly think I could bear to set eyes on that home-wrecking bitch Sandra Kelly? I'd rather sleep on the streets. She broke my mother's heart.'

I felt confused: she had seemed happy enough to accept a favour from Frank three years ago, when we were planning our move here.

'Don't worry, Donal, I won't be a burden on

257

you for too long,' she spat, her red fuse fizzing.

'That's not what I mean, Eve...'

'I signed on today, and I'm seeing the probation people Thursday, so it might just be for two nights. Hopefully you can stand me for that long.'

'Stay as long as you like, Eve,' I said, 'honestly. We've got so much to catch up on. And so much we didn't get a chance to talk about before I left.'

I thought to myself: 'Where could we even start with that?'

But Eve seemed to know exactly where she wanted to kick off our darker reminiscences. 'You know the other night, when you mentioned Meehan?'

I nodded.

'Tell me again, Donal. Everything you saw that night.'

'God, Eve, are you sure you can handle...'

'Tell me,' she demanded.

She listened intently as I ran her through the sequence of events in graphic detail: scored as it was inexorably on my memory.

When I wrapped up, I asked, 'What I saw, Eve, is that actually what happened?'

She nodded gravely.

'Did he...?'

She kept nodding.

'God, I'm so sorry.'

Eve looked at me with those big watery eyes: 'You said you couldn't hear anything?'

'No, it was all in total silence.'

'But you can hear everything when Marion comes to you?'

I nodded, surprised she could remember minutiae like this from our booze-fuelled night at the Archway Tavern.

'The way you talked about it, you sounded really convinced that she is actually coming to you with clues?'

'Even more so now.'

'Why?'

I explained how my dual sighting of Marion on Sangora and Strathblaine Roads the previous Friday turned out to be pivotal to the case, exaggerating the impact, but not wildly. I next reiterated my absolute certainty that the identity of Marion's killer lay on a door somewhere at number 21.

'My God,' she said, troubled, uncomfortable, 'that's so specific.'

Meehan flashed into my mind suddenly; the way he came for me as I lay in Tullamore General Hospital, hours after Eve had killed him. I couldn't remember if I'd told her about this the other night. I decided it would do no good telling her now.

'Will you ever go back?' she asked suddenly.

'Only to see Mum, probably after Dad croaks it.'

'I heard what he said,' she took my hand and squeezed it, 'I don't blame you.'

I explained that I felt no loss for Martin, just regret that we'd failed to find a way to tolerate each other, if only for Mum's sake.

As we left the Wheatsheaf, Eve sensed my gloom and resurrected a running joke from the old days. No vocabulary on the planet has more words for

259

being drunk than Ireland's: *clattered, flootered, ossified, mangled, locked, stocious, scuttered, manky* to name just a few. As we staggered into the night, we traded them just like we used to, until one of us could think of no more.

I felt this connection to Eve that I doubted I'd ever develop with Gabby. We'd grown up together, in a way. She knew me inside out. Because of what happened to her that night, we had a bond that would never be broken.

She dozed off on the couch as I sank a Shiraz. The crook of my shoulder felt as if her head had never left it. When she stirred, I raised her gently to her feet and walked her to my bed.

'So soft,' she slurred as I laid her out. I pulled off her shoes and sandwiched her in duvet.

She rolled over and giggled. 'Soft,' she whispered again.

I watched her grind her face into the pillow and thought about lying down behind her, throwing my arm over her slender shoulder like the old days.

Retreating to the door, my mind raced: what did this all mean? Could we pick up where we left off? Why not? But what were we to do about the missing three years? Maybe we could start again, from scratch?

I didn't know the answers, but decided that if Eve wanted to give our relationship another go, then I owed it to her – to us – to try. After all, external forces split us up last time. By getting back together, we'd find out ourselves, once and for all, whether we were meant to be. If it didn't work out, then at least we'd know, for certain.

Chapter 27

Clapham Police Station, South London
Wednesday, August 14, 1991; 10:00

Next morning, Mick and Colin joined us in the bleachers, pre-interview, to take a good one-way look at Peter through the two-way mirror. He sat slumped and unmoved, still fumbling with his fingers, still wearing his wedding ring.

He'd made an effort, wearing a freshly pressed blue striped shirt tucked into a pair of beige chinos. I wondered if Mother-in-Law Mary had ironed them for him this morning. On his belt sat a bright blue pager, standard-issue in any hospital or care home. They would have seized his cash, keys, belt, any potential makeshift weapon. Why hadn't they seized his pager?

'Who the fuck let him in with that?' barked Shep, his contemptuous squint peeled on Peter.

'It's work-issue,' sighed Mick, 'the rule is they have to be contactable at all times.'

Shep growled. 'Look at that narcissistic prick,' he sneered through an upturned punk lip, 'I want you boys to give this fucker a real good going over. Let's face it, his pursuit of a bit on the side is the reason Marion is in the morgue. No matter who wielded the knife, it's Peter who killed her. Since day one, he's lied through his teeth. We've had to drag every last piece of information out of him. Today he finally tells us the truth.'

Peter's face shot up as the door burst open. Mick and Colin strutted in, chests out, fists clenched, flexing their clamped-shut jaws. If Karen had been a sardine can that needed peeling, Peter was a coconut begging for a hammer.

There was no ceremonial organising of papers, no, 'so Peter, tell us about...'

Colin read the tape recorder its rights. Mick read the most damning revelations from Karen's interview. Peter looked on, wide-eyed and bewildered. By the end, his face had twisted into the grotesque grimace of a hooked fish.

'Karen has told us all about your sexual relationship. We'd now like to hear all about it from you. And don't leave anything out,' said Mick.

Peter took his time, obviously treading carefully. He'd got to know Karen soon after he started working at the Pines.

'I didn't consider her any more than a work colleague,' he said.

The boys made it clear they weren't here for an am-dram production of *Brief Encounter*.

'Did you fancy her, Pete? Did you want to sleep with her?'

'I found her to be pleasant, outgoing, friendly, but not pretty. Not like Marion, who was beautiful.'

Peter started to crack, which earned him no respite.

'How did your sexual relationship develop?'

'I became responsible for stocking the nurses' quarters and that brought me into more contact with Karen. We spoke about twice a day.'

'Don't stop,' barked Colin.

Peter winced and carried on. 'Around the end of 1988, Karen had to have an operation on her knee and was recovering in her room. I went to visit her a couple of times a day. Then I attended her twenty-second birthday party at her family home in Lee, in the spring of 1989. I met her mum, dad, her sisters Laura and Stacey.'

'Did you bring Marion along?'

'No.'

'Karen tells us she introduced you as her boyfriend.'

'I don't remember her ever calling me her boyfriend, to anyone.'

'She said that at weightlifting and aerobics classes, you told everyone she was your girlfriend.'

'That's not true. Go and ask them yourselves. I never introduced Karen as my girlfriend. She never was my girlfriend. She was just ... casual.'

'Your bit on the side. Yes we understand, Peter. When did you start having sex with Karen?'

'It was around that time.'

'So you'd been going out with Marion for over two years by now. You started sleeping with Karen in the spring of '89, a few months before you got engaged to Marion.'

Peter nodded, shame rising through him like red sap.

'And how did it happen with Karen, that first time?'

'I can't remember the details.'

'What do you mean, you can't remember the details? You can't remember the first time you gave one to your mistress?'

Peter's eyes flinched.

'Did it mean that little to you? I bet Karen remembers every detail.'

'We did it in my room at the Pines one evening. I honestly can't remember how it came about.'

'So you don't remember who initiated it?'

He shook his head.

'You have to speak,' screamed Colin, making everyone jump.

'No,' whined Peter.

'And what were your feelings for Karen?'

'I thought it was just casual. Nothing serious.'

'And did you tell Karen the news, that you saw her as a piece of meat? That in the meantime you'd got engaged to Marion?'

'I didn't tell her,' said Peter.

'But she must have found out?'

Peter nodded, too quickly, too often, flushing, cracking under the pressure again.

'How did she find out?'

'The matron threw an engagement party for us. Karen was there.'

'How did she react?'

'She didn't make a scene or anything. She cooled it for a while.'

'When did you resume your sexual relations with Karen?'

'She moved into a room in the home around May of last year. We started sleeping together again.'

'Let me get this straight: a month before your wedding to Marion in June of last year, Karen moved into the staff accommodation at the Pines residential care home?'

Peter nodded. 'I advised her to move.'

'Oh I bet you did, Peter. You could have sex on tap then, couldn't you, with your unsuspecting fiancée and your 24/7 fuck buddy.'

'It wasn't like that,' groaned Peter, 'she needed to get away from her family.'

'And why was that, Peter?'

He blinked twice, then let his head drop, resigned to giving away a confidence: 'Her dad, Terry, when he gets drunk he picks fights with them. He was hitting her, hitting all of them. He's been doing it for years. She stayed to protect her sisters, but I told her they were old enough to look after themselves now.'

'So while she was looking for a shoulder to cry on, you provided a bed for her to lie on. What a gentleman you are, Peter. How many days did it take you to get your end away with poor old vulnerable Karen in her new accommodation?'

'I ... we ... look, she wouldn't leave me alone. I told her to meet someone else, but she was always there.'

'And did Marion know Karen during this time?'

'I thought they were quite friendly, but after a while Marion started to make certain comments like "we know what she's after". But as the wedding got closer they seemed to get friendly again. It was Marion's idea to invite her over for it.'

'Tell me about that, Peter,' said Mick, 'I can't imagine what it must have been like having your mistress at your wedding.'

'She came over to Ireland with us, in the hire car.'

He broke down and sobbed.

'Gives a whole new meaning to Hertz,' cackled Shep to me behind the one-way mirror, 'and Budget rental. That's all Karen was to him, a Budget rental fuck. And what a masochist she is. Karen kept taking this punishment until she snapped. He's spilling his guts because it's all clicking together in his thick fucking skull, at last. Karen was obsessed with him. He's finally realising that he drove Karen to it. What I want to know is: did he know she was going to kill Marion?'

I couldn't believe that for one second. He'd been crushed on the night he found her. He was broken now.

'Did you spend any time alone with Karen on your wedding weekend?' asked Mick.

'The night before the wedding, she came into my hotel room. There were two single beds. She lay on one and fell asleep. She woke up and went back to her room. We didn't have sex.'

'Denying yourself pre-marital sex until the bitter end, Peter, wow, how very Catholic,' chirped Colin.

Peter was now on a confessional slide.

'After the wedding, we got back to my room at the Pines to find that Karen had cleaned it and put up balloons and good-luck messages. She invited Marion and me to dinner at her family's home. I really thought that she'd finally accepted that we couldn't carry on. But we still did the fish tanks together every fortnight and one Monday, a few months after the wedding, we had sex again.'

'Is it true that you told her you'd made a mistake in marrying Marion? That you really loved Karen?'

'No, God no,' said Peter, 'I would never say anything of the sort.'

'She said you told her that you loved her.'

'I did one night when I was drunk, but I never loved her. I loved Marion. She knew that. She knew I would never leave Marion.'

'So what were your feelings for Karen?'

'I cared for her. But that's all. Like I say, it was a casual thing. She wanted it as much as I did.'

'So every second Monday, she invited you to her room at the Pines for sex?'

'Not her room. It's next door to the matron's and we didn't want to get caught. She had the key to Bethan's room. We preferred to do it in there.'

Shep leapt to his feet: 'Bethan's room was next to Marion and Peter's. He must be talking about after they moved out. After January this year. Karen said they finished two months earlier, in November.'

Colin and Mick had already homed in on this anomaly. 'Karen says that by the end of last year she hated you, and that she and Marion had become friends.'

'You could say they were close around the time of the wedding. They maybe went out for a drink together twice late last summer. But by October last year, it was cooling between them. The three of us didn't get together very often. When we did it was awkward. There was an atmosphere. They knew they didn't like each other.'

Shep appealed to his inquisitors through the soundproof glass. 'Bring it round to this year, boys.'

'Did Marion realise you were sleeping with Karen? Did she catch on? Is that why she's dead?'

'She had no idea. She never knew. To be honest, I was thinking about telling her and getting it off my chest, because it was winding down.'

Shep leaned forward: 'Winding down?' he said.

'What do you mean, winding down?' asked Mick.

'This year, we only had sex when we did the fish tanks, every second Monday. I told her I was finishing doing the overtime. That Monday was to be the last time.'

Peter started breaking down again.

'Keep going, keep going,' roared Shep.

'When did you tell Karen that you were going to stop cleaning the fish tanks with her?'

'The previous time we did them. Two weeks earlier.'

'Right, so on Monday, 17 June – two weeks before Marion's murder – you told Karen that you would be cleaning the fish tanks with her just one more time,' said Mick, 'so when did you last have sex with Karen Foster?'

'That same evening. But I told her this was to be the last time.'

'Did you tell Karen about your plans to move to Ireland?'

Through heaving sobs, Peter gasped: 'Karen heard the rumours. I told her they were true, that we were moving to Ireland.'

'When did you tell her?'

'That night again, two weeks before, you know ... Marion got killed.'

'What did you tell her, exactly?' shouted Colin.

'I told her that Marion was pregnant. It was the only way I could put an end to it for good.'

'You told your secret lover that Marion was pregnant, so that you could dump her?'

'Yes. Oh God forgive me...'

Peter barely got the last word out before collapsing onto the table.

'Bloody hell,' said Shep, mouth agape, 'I can't fucking believe he held all this back for six weeks with his wife on a slab.'

Back in the kitchenette, Shep congratulated Mick and Colin for breaking Peter. Now, they needed to go for his jugular. 'This is our last chance to find out if he was involved in any way,' he said.

'He seemed genuinely shocked about Karen spying on them,' said Mick, 'I think it only started dawning on him during the interview that Karen is twisted enough to have killed Marion.'

'Could he be saving his own arse though?' asked Shep.

Colin shook his head: 'I think he never considered Karen capable of doing something like this before now. He's one of those "God's gift to women" types – too thick, selfish and vain to ever think about the consequences of his actions.'

'Oh he's the classic Golden Boy Irishman,' said Shep. 'He only cares about himself because he's never had to care about anyone else. I bet he's adored by his dear old mum. He'll use and abuse women until he finds one who'll adore him the same. How can we be certain he didn't goad Karen into doing it?'

'If we can work out for certain that he genuinely loved Marion, then I think he's innocent,' said Mick, 'but how do we do that?'

'Come on fellas,' urged Shep, 'he's Irish Catholic for Christ's sake, there's a reservoir of guilt in there. Tap it. Ask him if he went to see Marion's body in the morgue. That'll open him up.' He was interrupted mid-flow by the sound of his pager. 'Shit,' he said inspecting the message, 'we've got to go.'

'What?' we all asked.

'The Commissioner's PA just paged me. He's in a right flap. They've found a woman stabbed to death in her home in Woolwich.'

My heart plummeted through my arse.

'We've got to get there before the press. He wants to know if Marion's killer has struck again.'

Then he turned to me: 'You better not have fucked up, Lynch.'

Chapter 28

Woolwich, South East London
Wednesday, August 14, 1991; 12:30

Shep drove fast while I raged silently.

Until now, he'd refused to even consider possible links between Marion's murder and other crimes. When I brought up Napper, he had humiliated me in front of the team. Now suddenly, if I'd missed a clue or a connection in the 'unsolved stranger attack' paperwork, it would all

270

be on my shoulders.

I should have been thinking about the victim. I should have been hoping and praying that this poor innocent woman didn't die on account of my failings. But I was too overwhelmed by the fear of exposure, humiliation, punishment to think about anyone but myself.

The injustice of it all! I'd been Acting Detective Constable for six days. Maybe that was the problem: I'd been just acting. I didn't really know what I was doing.

I had ground through all of the 'unsolved stranger attack' paperwork with painstaking zeal. But did I really know what I was looking for? Of course I didn't fucking know! That's why Shep picked me for the task. As a rookie, he could dismiss any of my findings, leaving him free to focus the team on Peter and Karen.

He pulled up abruptly outside a four-storey block of flats on Heathfield Terrace. A crowd of people stood on one side of the billowing police tape, gaping and gossiping while two paramedics leaned against their ambulance, awaiting instruction. We lifted the tape and strolled right through, just like they do in the movies. I hated myself for enjoying the moment.

'What's the score?' Shep asked the officer at the front door of the basement flat.

The officer stood to one side: 'Hope you haven't eaten in a while.'

The walls of the hallway were spattered bright red.

'Oh great,' said an older officer, eyeing us bitterly.

'It wasn't my idea, Kenneth,' drawled Shep, 'we've both got enough to do.'

Kenneth was shaking his head: 'Why do we constantly have to dance to the media's tune? We should tell them the truth: we can't link cases until we've got all the reports in.'

'You know how it goes, Ken. The Commissioner's primary concern is that we don't get another savaging in the Sunday papers.'

'Okay,' said Ken, snapping into senior cop mode, 'the killer stabbed the woman, Samantha Bisset, twenty-eight, to death here in the hallway. You'd better come into the bedroom.'

We followed him into a typical box room with crayoned drawings on the wall. A little girl lay sleeping, face up, on the bed.

'He came in here, sexually assaulted the child, Jazmine, aged four, and smothered her. We can't be sure in which order yet.'

A spasm reversed my swallowing mechanism. I stopped the gag reflex just in time.

'But that's not the worst of it,' said Kenneth in his jovial, sing-song Welsh accent, leading us into the sitting room.

'What in the name of God?' said Shep.

I peered round his shoulder.

My mind felt like a misfiring one-armed bandit, reels spinning in different directions. I simply couldn't absorb what I was seeing.

I heard Ken say: 'He sliced her torso open from the pubic bone up to her throat and pulled her ribcage back to expose her organs.'

'Like some sick work of art, said Shep.

'He's taken part of her stomach, we presume as

272

a trophy. The sick fuck covered her in tea towels so that whoever came on the scene first – which turned out to be Samantha's partner – had to unwrap his masterpiece.'

Just like that, every bone in my body turned to liquid. Fully conscious, my knees buckled and I keeled slowly, head-first, into the carpet, sliding down in front of Samantha's lovingly butchered corpse.

'Oh for fuck's sake,' said Shep as I lay there, helpless but still lucid, a beached whale.

'Get him outside,' ordered Ken.

Two uniformed officers yanked me to my feet and carried me out of the house. As they hauled me through the hallway, I could feel my helpless feet skidding along the ground, bouncing off the thresholds.

'Fuckin' poof,' muttered one of my bearers.

'Should think about another line of work,' said the other.

I could see the crowd pointing, laughing.

'Fucking hyenas,' said the first officer.

'What would you expect in East London?' said the second.

The two paramedics took over. One of them looked into my eyes. 'You can hear me, can't you?' he said. All I could do was nod and blink twice. 'He's fully conscious,' he told his partner, 'this is weird.'

They bundled me skilfully under the police tape and hauled me to a patch of grass on the other side of the road where they laid me out in the recovery position. Within seconds, I felt my-self recharge from the feet up. Finally, I hoisted

273

myself into a sitting position and helped myself to a few greedy lungfuls of air.

I was a frequent fainter as a kid, nutting more carpet than a devout Muslim. I knew what it felt like to pass out. This had been different. I had remained fully cogent throughout. I hadn't even felt queasy. My body simply gave way. I could see and hear everything.

'Are you narcoleptic mate?' asked the kinder-faced paramedic.

'Not that I'm aware of. I am being treated for insomnia.'

'You need to tell them about this. It could be cataplexy.'

'What's cataplexy?'

'It's when an extreme emotional experience causes your muscles to seize up. It can be triggered by anything really, shock, love, even finding something funny. I've only ever seen it in narcoleptics though.'

'Should I be worried?'

'There's no long-term damage and it usually only lasts a few minutes. But lying about helplessly on the streets of London is never a good idea. Definitely mention it to your specialist.'

Despite what everyone had assumed, it wasn't the gore that had knocked me over. It was the shock of confronting the unthinkable: had I let Marion's killer remain free to do what I'd just seen, to slaughter a mother and her four-year-old daughter? If Samantha and Jazmine died horribly because of my mistake, how was I supposed to live with myself? How could I ever atone for that?

The sound of a car braking hard snapped me

274

back to the here and now. Out jumped Fintan, his fat panting snapper in tow. I crawled behind the tree trunk but the fucker had better radar than a bat.

'So they *are* linking it?' Fintan gasped shamelessly. 'Christ, I told you, didn't I? Forty-nine stab wounds in a domestic? It's unheard of. So, he's done a mother and child this time?'

A pair of violated corpses suddenly felt like better company. I scrambled to my feet and headed back to the crime scene, meeting Shep on his way out.

'Didn't know you were the squeamish sort, Lynch,' he said.

'Neither did I, Guv. Fintan's turned up.'

'Let's get the fuck out of here,' said Shep, setting off at his usual lightning pace.

It was too late: Fintan's baboon hosed us down all the way back to the car. 'How many photos of us do you need?' Shep shouted.

We hopped in like fleeing bank robbers. Shep gunned the engine, tried to run down the snapper then took me through what I'd missed.

'I hate to tell you, but that murder has a lot in common with Marion's.'

My stomach swapped places with my mouth.

'There's no sign of a forced entry. She was attacked with a knife near her front door. It was frenzied.'

I closed my eyes as hard as I could and rubbed my face.

'So what are you going to tell the Commissioner?' I finally managed to ask.

'I have to tell him that they could be linked,

because they could be.'

The world fell silent.

'Of course, Ken was right. We won't know for certain until the reports are in. But the media will link the attacks right away. They won't be able to resist it, climbing onto their high horses and demanding to know why we haven't caught this maniac targeting vulnerable young women in their homes. For them, it's a Godsend.'

'What if I've fucked up?'

Shep sighed hard: 'There's only one way to fix this, Lynch. We've got to gather enough evidence to charge Karen Foster. And we've got to do it quickly. As soon as she's charged, you're out of the woods.'

I wondered when and how I'd found myself in 'the woods', but patently I was in them alone. But at that moment, Shep was the only person who could save me. He must have smelled my desperation. 'Fuck it,' he said, performing a joyrider's emergency stop. 'Run over to that phone box. Ring the incident room. Tell whoever answers that the team needs to call their families. They won't be home tonight.'

Chapter 29

Shep called a wildcat briefing. He told the assembled team that, as yet, there were no definite links between the murder of Marion Ryan and the Bissets in East London – and that we should ignore any media reports saying otherwise. McStay sniffed and gave Barratt the eye. He wanted so badly for us to be wrong. I decided to watch his smug face as Shep delivered the rest of today's news, starting with the interview suite revelations.

'Peter Ryan admitted today that he slept with Karen Foster two weeks before Marion's murder.'

He gave that statement plenty of air for dramatic effect.

'That same night, Peter told Karen that he was giving up their twice-monthly Monday night trysts, thereby ending their affair. He also told her that he and Marion were moving to Ireland. Because Marion was pregnant.'

Even my neck hairs stood to attention: and I already knew about it.

'By telling Karen this news, Peter effectively signed his wife's death warrant.'

McStay's nose turned the colour of a scalded bellend.

'Marion wasn't pregnant, but Karen Foster

277

didn't know that. She and an accomplice murdered Marion and, as far as she was concerned, their unborn baby because she wanted Peter Ryan all for herself. The challenge now lies in proving it. We have no weapon, no witnesses, we still haven't found a hole in her alibi and, as for forensics, we need a fucking miracle.'

He took a deep breath.

'I'm asking each of you to give it one last push. Not for me, but for Marion and her family.

'The murder weapon: I want a team to carry out a search of Karen's parents' home in Lee. Maybe Karen and her accomplice went there to pick up the murder weapon before driving to Marion's flat.

'Witnesses: get back to Sangora Road, conduct another door-to-door. Karen and her accomplice parked near the pub at around five thirty p.m. There would have been drinkers in at that time, some possibly sitting outside. Someone must have seen them. The last door-to-door team asked locals if they'd seen anything suspicious. This time, just ask people what they saw.'

Barratt piped up: 'It's almost seven weeks ago now, Sir.'

'Yes but it's not that usual to have a murder on your street, is it Barratt? Even in South London. I call it the JFK Syndrome. Neighbours will remember exactly what they were doing before and after they heard the news. All we need is one person to place Karen at the scene at the right time.'

Shep drove on: 'Alibi: we have to prove that Karen and her accomplice could have murdered Marion, changed their clothes and made it back to the Pines by six p.m., when she was seen in the car park. I need a team to make that journey at the same time of the evening, several times. Record it in real time on video. We will need to prove that this is possible.

'Also, get Karen's main alibi providers in. That's her sister Laura and the woman they watched TV with between five thirty and six p.m. that day, Bethan Trott.

'Forensics: I want the fingerprints of everyone employed at the Pines, and anyone who's worked there in the past twelve months, temporary, agency, contractors, everyone. Cross-reference them against the prints found at the murder scene.'

I felt my head shake. I'd suggested this yesterday morning. We knew that Karen couldn't have carried out this killing without a male accomplice. Why had we wasted two days before looking for him?

'I can keep Karen in custody until nine a.m. tomorrow. I've already applied for a twelve-hour extension. We'll only get it if we come up with something new. We need to attack this with all we've got.'

Shep walked over to where I sat. 'We'll nail her, don't worry about that.'

'Thanks, Guv,' I said, and I meant it.

'Now I want you to draw up a comprehensive list of why we shouldn't link Marion's murder to the Bisset case. I'll have the Commissioner on the blower first thing tomorrow, as soon as he's read the papers. Make sure I've got enough ammo to buy us a couple of days.'

279

Before convincing the Commissioner, I had to satisfy myself that Marion's killer hadn't struck again and murdered the Bissets.

As I sat down at the computer to compile my list, the warnings I'd fended off rang through my mind.

If it's domestic, why did he attack her on the stairs?

Speak to any pathologist, they'll tell you the most stab wounds they've ever seen in a domestic is ten or twelve.

Perhaps Fintan and the Big Dogs had been right all along: there's no way Peter and/or Karen would have stabbed Marion forty-nine times – even with an accomplice.

On top of that, the odds that there were two knife-wielding maniacs on the loose in South London capable of butchering female strangers in their own homes seemed remote.

If, somehow, I'd missed Marion's Lone Wolf Killer in the 'unsolved stranger attack' paperwork, and he'd gone on to kill Samantha and Jazmine, I'd quit the force right away. I saved for another day the imponderable matter of how I'd live with the guilt.

Before that, I'd have to deal with the shame. The media – no doubt exhaustively briefed by McStay and Barratt – would hammer the team and annihilate me. I'd read enough of Fintan's toxic, hysterical prose to know how he'd garner maximum public outrage.

Blundering cops left a maniac knifeman free to slay a mother and her four-year-old daughter when they missed vital clues from his previous attacks...

...Despite warnings from an eminent forensic

psychologist that a Lone Wolf Killer was on the loose, the investigating team tried to frame a twenty-five-year-old trainee nurse with no criminal record...

...An insider today revealed that a junior officer – Acting DC Donal Lynch – missed several clues that pointed to the triple killer...

I had to hope Shep was right. And I needed to provide as many compelling reasons as possible to make the Commissioner believe us. If I could show him significant differences in the modus operandi of each crime, he'd realise that there had to be two killers, however improbable.

Soon I had scraped the barrel and come up with a list, which I wrote out in large hand on a clean sheet of paper.

• *Samantha Bisset's killer(s) attacked her as soon as she opened the front door. Marion Ryan had let her killer(s) inside her flat, which suggests she knew her killer(s).*
• *Samantha Bisset's killer(s) spent a considerable amount of time fastidiously dismembering her body before leaving the scene. Marion Ryan's killer(s) carried out a frenzied attack which lasted between two and three minutes, then fled.*
• *Jazmine Bisset had been sexually assaulted. Samantha Bisset had been genitally violated with a knife. Marion Ryan had not been sexually assaulted or genitally violated.*

That was the best I could come up with. I might as well have written: 'He didn't rush so much the second time.' I placed my handy, bite-sized, exaggerated bullet points on Shep's desk: I would have felt less grubby squatting over it and taking a dump. Guilt and doubt gnawed away at me, eroding what little bottle I had left.

I exited the station into the hum of a warm summer night. As I turned into Lavender Hill, a sudden guttural grunt startled me.

'Cheer up pal, it might never happen,' said a drunk in a doorway.

'It happens all the fucking time, pal,' I said wearily, flicking him a pound coin and wondering why they always seemed to be Scottish or Irish.

'Yer still here though, aren't ya?'

I had to smile: today's events had pretty much stripped me down to that level of existential optimism.

As I turned onto Trinity Road, it hit me like a brick in the face. Today I'd attended a double murder scene. The spirits of Samantha and Jazmine Bisset would come to me tonight, for sure. At that precise moment, I wanted to be dead. I'd never felt like that before.

Chapter 30

Trinity Road, South London
Wednesday, August 14, 1991; 21:00

I got back to the flat, forced the front door open over the junk mail we never picked up, and smelled cleaning products. Confused by the gloom, I crept cagily into the shadowy sitting room, sensing someone inside. The irrational part of me feared that the Bissets were already waiting.

Slowly, my eyes adjusted to register a pair of candles glowing above a table set for two. The romantic mood failed to soothe my gnawed nerves.

'Is that you, Donal?' Eve called from the kitchen.

'Yeah, wow, what's all this?' I said, feeling unsettled, wrong-footed.

She walked in with a bottle of wine and two gleaming glasses.

'I've cooked you dinner, just to say thanks for letting me stay.

'Here,' she handed me the uncorked bottle, 'it's one of your favourites. I made a note when I threw out all your empties.'

I wondered what else she'd made a note of. I couldn't figure out why her efforts had set me on edge: I said she could stay for a few nights, not assume the role of Woman of the House. I hoped to Christ that Aidan hadn't planned to come home tonight.

She returned to the kitchen as I filled a glass to the brim, downing half of it. 'Shall we pretend it's 1988?' I said, to no one in particular.

I sat at the table as she carried in two steaming oval plates. As she placed one in front of me, I registered her low buttoned white blouse and scarlet lips. She teetered back to her side, giving me an eyeful of her short, tight black skirt and strappy heels. Had she remembered my thing about waitresses?

'Wow,' I said, as she sat down, 'and the food looks tasty too.'

'Stop it,' she giggled. 'Now, tell me all about your day.'

I looked down at the plate, registered the ribs and managed, somehow, not to spew.

'Are you okay?' she demanded.

In a bid to distract myself from recalling the Bisset horror show, I focused on Peter's interview and the bunny boiler antics of Karen Foster. Once we'd exhausted that subject, our unplanned date began to feel a little awkward. I realised that we'd already wrung dry all our news from the last three years. The only subject that remained unresolved was our future. Did we have one? We had hit an impasse. I had to find out how she felt.

'So, what are you planning for the rest of the summer?' I tried.

Somehow, she wriggled free of this and steered the conversation back to Marion and her post-death visits. I'd found her initial interest in the topic flattering, but now it was all we – she – wanted to talk about. It reminded me of the time she became obsessed with the murder of Choker Meehan's mother; how she hassled me for months to get Fintan to pull all the newspaper cuttings for her.

I was growing jealous of my dubious 'gift' – it was getting more attention than me.

She seemed particularly fascinated now by my daylight visions of Marion at both Sangora and Strathblaine Roads.

'You need to stop going to that road, never mind the murder scene. It'll drive you spare,' she said, and I had to smile. 'Drive you spare' already seemed such an outmoded-teenage expression. I

284

realised that the trauma of her ordeal had stunted Eve emotionally so that, in effect, she was still seventeen – suspended in 1988 like an ant in amber. I suddenly felt overcome with pity.

'And what did your psychologist say about it?'

'Oh well, that's another story. It's the most excited I've seen her. She wants to try to prove that my subconscious is using dream imagery to crack the case. In the scientific world, this could be quite a big deal, apparently.'

'You never mentioned it was a she,' said Eve, eyeing me suspiciously. Another realisation: she was now a professional victim, always seeing and interpreting things in ways that made her the wounded party – deceived, wronged, cheated. What an effective distraction from looking within.

'Didn't I? She's about forty. Nice old dear.'

I wasn't sure why I'd said that.

'What's her name?'

'Lilian. Lilian Smith. Why do you need to know?'

'I'm only asking. Jesus, why are you so defensive?'

I was trying to think of an answer when the doorbell's electroconvulsive buzz shook my bones.

'Shall we ignore that?' I said.

'It could be important,' she frowned.

I went to the door, booting the post to one side to open it.

'Hi,' said Gabby, reading my startled face.

'Hi,' I said, wondering if she could see inside.

'Are you not going to ask me in?' she smiled. I noticed she was wearing more make-up than usual. And a dress.

'Yeah, erm, of course,' I said, taking a step out

into the hallway, half closing the door behind me.

'Just to let you know, I've got someone staying at the moment. An old friend from home,' I said quietly.

'Aren't you going to introduce us?' she said, her smile now quizzical, curious. I had two choices: run inside and slam the door or let her in. I stood to one side.

As Gabby tiptoed over the mail into the sitting room, I added quickly: 'She's made dinner actually, just to say thanks.'

As we entered the room, I saw it through Gabby's eyes and knew I should have slammed that front door.

'Hi,' smiled Eve, a little triumphantly, I thought, not bothering to get up.

Gabby spent what seemed an age taking it all in.

'Candles,' she said, finally.

'Oh God it's not how it looks...' I said, each word shrivelling faster than the last, 'Eve's staying for a few nights until she gets herself sorted, isn't that right, Eve?'

Eve didn't say a word.

'Perhaps you could give me a call some time,' said Gabby, 'when you're not busy.'

She turned to Eve: 'It was nice meeting you, Eve.'

Eve pulled a 'yeah, whatever' shrug. Gabby turned, marched out and gave the front door fittings their sternest test yet.

'Well thanks a lot,' I said, 'you could have said something there to help me out.'

'I didn't know who she was. You didn't introduce us.'

'Oh and I suppose Fintan didn't tell you all about her. He tells you everything else.'

'*You* didn't tell me though, did you Donal?' she spat, slamming her cutlery on the table, storming into my bedroom and creating another Force 10 door quake.

'Don't worry, I'll take the couch,' I shouted after her.

As I scraped our aborted rib dinner into the bin bag, I spotted a pink overturned Post-it note deep in the mulch. I managed to fish it out. 'Gabby called, coming over at 9' it said, in Eve's unmistakably neat print.

What the hell was she playing at? Did she really want us – me – that badly?

As I blew out the candles, my brain suddenly bit on a thought and refused to let go. Was I as bad as Peter Ryan? The *same* as Peter Ryan? Shep's words boomed between my ears:

Oh he's the classic Golden Boy Irishman, adored by his dear old mum.

I would have slept with Eve last night, had she let me.

He'll use and abuse women until he finds one who'll adore him the same.

Could I look in the mirror and say I was any better than Peter Ryan?

I dismissed the idea, flopped onto the couch, opened a Shiraz and wallowed in grape-based guilt. The Bissets were coming tonight: fuck it, bring them on. I could take the terror of another ghostly encounter, if it got me any closer to the truth behind their murders.

Chapter 31

Trinity Road, South London
Thursday, August 15, 1991; 08:00

Samantha and Jazmine didn't show.

I spent the night wondering why I wasn't being accosted by their tormented spirits. I came up with two possible explanations:

A: I'd been deluding myself about having some sort of 'gift': I was simply a borderline alcoholic insomniac with a history of inexplicable mental and physical collapses.

B: They didn't need to come to me because I was already on the trail of their killer.

I favoured A, dreaded B. Did their no-show confirm what I feared most: that they'd been murdered by the same person who killed Marion?

As I walked to work, Samantha and Jazmine winked at me from every window. They were blonde, pretty, murdered in their own home – all ingredients guaranteed to secure them blanket newspaper and TV coverage.

The red-tops screamed 'serial killer' with undisguised glee. The young, pretty women of London were not safe in their own homes, and this 'monster' would come for their 'tots' too.

The incident room seemed strangely deserted. Mick warned me that Shep had been summoned to the Yard for a 'crisis meeting'. 'I'd make myself scarce if I were you.'

Before I left last night, Shep had flushed some judge out of his Mayfair drinking club to sign a search warrant. At daybreak, the Foster family home in Lee, South East London got the knock.

A forensics team was busy taking fingerprints from all current and recent employees of the Pines residential care home. How I craved a result there.

Two teams had spent the evening going door-to-door on Sangora Road. Mick told me to get stuck into their reports.

I quickly realised that London must be the best place in the world to get away with murder. The citizens of this city simply don't look at other people, let alone observe their behaviour. We avoid eye contact because that eye might belong to a psychopath actively seeking someone to batter. Having read the blood-curdling contents of London's unsolved crime files, I couldn't blame them.

I found one single reference to a woman on the street at the relevant time. The statement read: 'At about five forty p.m., Charles Crosby, of 74 Vardens Road was cycling home from work along Sangora Road when he saw two women coming down the steps of either 21 or 23. The second woman carried a black gym bag and may have been black.'

I dug out testimony from the residents of number 23 – the house next door to the murder scene. Angela Adeyemi, an IC3, or African female, said she left the house with a friend at about five thirty-five that evening to attend a gym on Clapham

High Street. This surely torpedoed any hopes that Crosby had seen Karen and her accomplice fleeing the scene.

Just after eleven, Shep almost ran into the office. 'I've just had my nuts blowtorched for two hours,' he said, 'we've got to make this collar happen.'

I handed him the note detailing what Crosby saw. Then, with an apologetic grimace, I passed over the statement from Ms Adeyemi.

Shep read both, gave them back and said: 'Get Crosby in, as soon as possible.'

As he walked off, I gave Mick a quizzical look.

'Desperate times...' he said.

I rang Crosby's home phone number. His haughty wife delighted in informing me that he couldn't possibly make it to the station until after four p.m.

Just before lunchtime, DS Barratt returned with his forensic ferrets, fresh from their forage of the Foster family home. He sported the smug gait of a man with sterling news.

First, he produced half a dozen true crime books, retrieved from Karen's old bedroom: these included the bestselling *Murder Scene Secrets*, by Professor Laurence C. Richards BSc, MSc, FRSA.

'This is how Karen learned to thoroughly and comprehensively trash our crime scene,' said Barratt.

'Can you believe Richards is allowed to make money giving away our techniques?' barked Shep.

Barratt said they were wrapping up their search when he spied a mop in the garage.

'And look what I found buried in the mop's handle,' he said, pulling out a metal ruler which had been pared down to a point at one end. 'This end is potentially lethal,' he said, 'and it measures five inches. As we know, that's about the length of the blade used to kill Marion. Karen's dad, Terry, is a window cleaner, she and her sisters often help him at the weekends. He told us he uses this ruler to scrape dirt out of awkward corners.'

I couldn't help thinking a ruler as a murder weapon looked a little desperate.

'When I asked him about the day of the murder, well, that seemed to be his most awkward corner yet.

'He told us that he got home at his usual time, three p.m. He said he left the mop in its usual place, standing in the corner of the garage. We asked him if he remembered this metal ruler being there the day after the murder. He got really agitated and, get this, said he couldn't remember. I pressed him and he said it again, he couldn't remember.'

Shep decided to do our thinking for us: 'Karen wouldn't have had access to potential murder weapons. She could have popped home on the afternoon of the murder, when she was supposedly shopping in Blackheath, picked that up before driving to Marion's.

'After killing her, Karen had to get straight back to the Pines, because Bethan Trott and her sister Laura were her alibis. She must have brought the weapon back with her and stashed it somewhere before going to see Peter to do the fish. Then, at a later date, she would have slipped the weapon back into the mop.'

It was plausible, if a little stretched. Without forensic evidence, I felt a jury would never buy it.

Shep went on: 'I trust you took it to the lab?'

'Got it checked out, right away. Of course it's clean,' said Barratt, 'but at least you can wave it in front of Karen, see how she reacts. Judging by Terry's response, this is our murder weapon and they know it.'

Shep told him to take the blade to the pathologist: 'See if he'll confirm that it could have been the murder weapon, in terms of shape, size, sharpness.'

'There's something else,' said Barratt, relishing his moment in the sun and wringing it out for all it was worth. 'Karen still gets some of her post sent to her family home. When I looked on top of the fridge, I found her bank statement from July. It seems that when she was shopping in Blackheath with her sister Laura on the afternoon of 1st July, at four ten p.m. her cash card was withdrawing ten pounds from Lambeth High Street – just up the road from the Pines.'

Shep grabbed and scoured the statement: 'So much for Karen's rock-solid alibi. The only people backing her story now are her sister Laura and the woman they watched TV with from five thirty to six that day. What's her name?'

'Bethan Trott,' someone said.

'Get her in, Barratt, as soon as you can.'

Charles Crosby turned up bang on four, bang on stereotype. Late forties, cowlick fair hair, square face, strong chin, pinched pink cheeks, chunky knitted pullover, big tits, big arse, mustard cor-

292

duroys: 'A good cove,' was how any judge would view him. I'd always found it fascinating how the two most pronounced social stereotypes in Britain are the richest and the poorest: the Toffs and the Chavs. Maybe they're not as different from each other as they think.

Unlike my colleagues, I held no inferiority-based grudge against posh English people. To me, they seemed very polite and very sexually repressed – characteristics I could readily relate to.

As instructed by Shep, I took Crosby into his office and left them to chat. About fifteen minutes later, Shep called me in.

'Mr Crosby has kindly agreed to give us his statement. Can you write it down for him please?' The media studies lecturer wasted no time getting to the important bit: 'At about five forty-five p.m., I was cycling down Sangora Road on my way home from work when I saw a man and a woman coming down the steps of number 21. I didn't get a close look but the woman was aged between twenty and thirty, had long dark hair and wore a red top. Both she and the man were white Europeans. The woman carried a black gym bag.'

'Thank you, Mr Crosby,' Shep cut in abruptly, 'we really have taken up enough of your very valuable time.'

'Thank *you*, Superintendent,' said Crosby, 'I really do appreciate you putting me forward for the remuneration.'

'Think nothing of it,' laughed Shep, shaking his hand, 'that's what it's there for.'

As soon as Crosby was out of earshot, I asked: 'What was that about?'

'He'd heard that Marion's family have put up a £20,000 reward for information leading to her killer. I was just assuring him that his evidence may well put him in the running for it. Anything to keep a key witness happy.'

I struggled to understand how anyone with key information about a tragic murder could even think about money. Maybe it was a class thing.

'Didn't he originally say that he saw two women, and that one of them may have been black?'

'Well, he seems to have cleared it up in his own mind,' said Shep, as a knock sounded on his office door.

'Come in,' he called.

I wanted Karen Foster banged up, not fitted up.

I reminded Shep: 'What about the black woman who lives at 23? Shouldn't we check if it could have been her and her friend heading to the gym?'

'Mr Crosby has made his statement,' said Shep, absently, signing for two packages. I noticed that one of the parcels came from Woolwich CID, the second from the Agfa video transfer company.

As the courier shut the office door behind him, Shep turned to me and said: 'If we can turn over Bethan Trott, we've got a case.'

I remember Fintan's words that afternoon at the Feathers: *When he gets a sniff of a collar, he goes proper psycho. Like a bloodhound.*

He handed me the first package: 'This is a preliminary case report into the Bisset murders. Take a very thorough read. See if you can find more reasons why the nutter who did this didn't kill Marion. Report to me by lunchtime tomorrow.'

My hand shook as I took it and headed to the door. Half of me dreaded what might be in here. What if they'd found proof that Marion's killer also murdered the Bissets?

'Lynch,' Shep's command made me jump. I turned around: 'Your arse is mine, son. Don't forget that.'

Chapter 32

Trinity Road, South London
Thursday, August 15, 1991; 22:00

That evening, I walked into my spick-and-span sitting room, called Eve's name and saw a note on the table.

Dear Donal, I've already ruined your life once. I don't want to ruin it again. Thank you for everything. I've gone to stay with a friend. I'll be in touch. All my love, whatever that is worth to you or anyone, Eve x

She hadn't added a number. I screwed up the paper and lobbed it over the back of the couch. The two barely burnt, lopsided candles on the table caught my eye. That was us now, I thought. We'd burned once, and brightly. But no longer.

I rang Gabby. Her spiky blonde flatmate answered.

'Hi,' I said brightly.

'Hi,' she said flatly, her tone confirming that

Gabby had been talking. I couldn't help feeling slightly pleased: at least she obviously gave a shit.

'Can I speak to Gabby?'

'Er, no, she's out actually.'

'Out?' I said, but it sounded more like, 'yeah right'.

'Yes, out. And I don't think she'd want to talk to you if she were in.'

'If she were in?' I repeated back, sarcastically.

'Look, Donal,' said Spiky coldly, 'she doesn't want you calling here again. Ever. Understood?'

'But...' I protested to the dead line.

I poured a monstrous Shiraz and suddenly thought about all those Masses of my childhood. Those words you heard, Sunday after Sunday, never leave you.

I raised the glass and addressed the wall: 'Take this, all of you and drink from it: for this is the cup of my blood, the blood of the new and everlasting covenant, it will be shed for you and for all men so that sins may be forgiven.'

For the first time in my entire life, I felt free. Truly properly free. Bar Fintan, I had severed all personal ties. Even the ones I'd pursued. Emotionally, I had no duty or responsibility, no debt or investment, no plan or fear, no guilt or blame.

The wine tasted sweeter than anything I'd ever drunk.

Chapter 33

Clapham Police Station, South London
Friday, August 16, 1991; 10:00

I speed-read the Bisset file. The killer's fastidious handiwork made it plain that it wasn't a domestic. However, as a matter of course, detectives checked out Samantha's partner and an ex, immediate family, neighbours and everyone on her phone call records. They found nothing of interest. Yet again, neighbours didn't see or hear anything unusual, and I marvelled at London's collective determination to mind its own business.

Samantha's family revealed that, until four years ago, she had been a new age traveller living on the road with a commune. Then she settled down to be a full-time mum to Jazmine. Her daughter didn't know her father, who had continued living the nomadic life. Detectives were trying to contact him.

Conrad, Samantha's boyfriend of nine months and the poor bastard who found her, revealed that she rarely locked her doors or windows, sunbathed topless on her balcony and never shut her front room blinds. 'She was a free spirit,' said Conrad. I hoped her spirit had finally found the freedom it craved during her physical life.

Normally, you'd guess that some local Peeping Tom loser had spotted this hot blonde sunbathing with it all on show, grown obsessed and turned stalker. But the clinical, methodical, ritualistic butchering of her body and the removal of a trophy suggested that her killer had mutilated bodies before. His craftsmanship made the frenzied attack on Marion Ryan look amateur. But my mind kept getting pulled back to one indisputable connection between the cases – both Marion and Samantha had been frenziedly stabbed to death just inside their front doors. I felt convinced that it had to be the same killer. Maybe he'd planned to ceremoniously carve Marion open but got spooked or disturbed somehow.

After lunchtime, Shep bounced out of his office: 'Bethan Trott's in. I'm taking this one myself, Lynch. Come and watch a master inquisitor at work.'

I struggled to match Shep's breakneck pace down the corridor. Once again, he punched in his secret code to release the security door, then stood back to let me do the work. As I pulled down the handle and shouldered hard, my thoughts turned again to that flat door at number 21, spring-loaded to cut off your fingers.

We walked into suite two, past Bethan, to the far end of the table. She sat alone, her right hand playing nervously with a large crucifix around her neck, her brown eyes darting between us. Everything about her looked meek, timid: her mousy hair, scared, tired eyes, thin busy lips, nervous fingers.

Shep didn't turn on the tape recorder.

'Now, Beth Ann,' he mispronounced, probably deliberately, 'reading your second statement, you suddenly felt a moral compulsion to mention the small fact you caught Karen and Peter fucking in the shed at work last November?'

Bethan reddened.

'And that Karen had been using your room to spy on Peter and Marion? Then, like a magician, you produce Karen's handwritten list of the presents Peter had bought Marion for her birthday with the words "sick" scrawled across the bottom. You know what I think, Beth Ann?'

Bethan's eyes shot up to Shep's for a nanosecond, the target taking one last chance to read her assassin's bullet.

'You *know* Karen killed Marion Ryan, don't you, Beth Ann? But you don't want to be the grass who puts her away, do you? I understand this, Beth Ann. After all, no one likes a squealer.'

Her eyes didn't know where to look.

'Do you know what perverting the course of justice means, Beth Ann?'

She dropped her crucifix and shook her head.

'It's when someone misleads the police or the justice system and wastes our time. It's a criminal offence. Do you know what you can get for perverting the course of justice, Beth Ann?'

'I've done nothing wrong,' whispered Bethan.

'A life sentence. Imagine that, Beth Ann? Locked up in Holloway prison for eight or ten years? Big old jack-booted, tobacco-chewing dyke screws making you lick 'em out every night? I bet you'd love that, wouldn't you, Beth Ann?'

She looked at me, shocked, pleading. I enjoyed giving her nothing back.

'I want a solicitor,' she said, her eyes narrowing, determined.

'I offered you a duty solicitor when you first came in, Beth Ann, and you said no. Have you forgotten already? Why would you need a solicitor anyway? You've got nothing to hide, have you?'

She opened her mouth to speak, then thought better of it.

Shep read out her original statement: '"I had been in the communal kitchen in the Pines staff residence preparing food when Karen and Laura Foster arrived between five fifteen and five twenty p.m. There was no one else in the kitchen. I can be sure of the time, because we'd planned to watch a TV soap together, in my room which started at five thirty."

'Tell me about Marion Ryan. Did you like her, Beth Ann?'

She nodded, uncertainly: 'I was close to Marion. She was lovely.'

'If you had to choose between Marion and Karen Foster, who would you say was your closer friend, Beth Ann?'

'I've known Karen for a lot longer than I knew Marion, so I was closer to her.'

'I see,' said Shep, 'but you don't have to choose, do you?'

Bethan frowned. I didn't understand what he was getting at either.

'I don't have that luxury,' said Shep. 'I like you and I like Karen, but which of you am I going to charge with perverting the course of justice?'

Bethan's jaw dropped and she blinked three

times, very quickly.

'Because either Karen Foster is lying to us, or you're lying to us. One of you is not telling the truth. Now, Beth Ann, this is your last chance to save your arse. Do you understand me?'

She nodded rapidly, making it abundantly clear that she'd grasped precisely what he meant only too well.

Shep leaned forward, switched on the tape recorder, told it the time and attendees. He then asked Bethan to tell us everything she did and saw from lunchtime onwards on Monday 1st July, 1991.

She sounded desperate, hunted: 'I was with my mother that afternoon and got back to the Pines at about five past six. I saw Laura Foster waiting for me on the balcony of my room which is on the first floor. Karen had a key to my room and they sometimes watched TV when I wasn't there. When I got to the door to the building on the ground floor, Laura opened it for me. We walked upstairs together. Laura said she and Karen had been in my room since five p.m and that Karen had left at six to do the flowers with Peter.'

'What was Laura Foster wearing?'

'Jeans and a black t-shirt.'

'Just remind me briefly of the times again.'

'I went to my mum's in Tooting at about two, stayed until five thirty and got back to the Pines at about five past six. I didn't see Karen until later.'

'Okay, stick to 6.05; when you got back, how did her sister, Laura Foster seem?'

'Well... She didn't seem to be her usual self. She

301

was fidgety and kept pacing around the room, whereas normally she just sat down and chatted.'

'Did she say anything that struck you as odd?'

'Not that I remember,' said Bethan.

'Did you see Karen again that evening?'

'Karen came to the room at about eight. She said she couldn't stay long as she had to drive Peter home. She had a cigarette and some water and then left.'

'I didn't know she smoked,' said Shep.

'She doesn't, usually.'

'Did she say anything unusual?'

'She mentioned in passing that her and Laura had been in my room earlier, from about five to six.'

'What was Karen wearing?'

'Jeans and a red t-shirt.'

'Did she use your bathroom?'

'No.'

'Did she mention anything about an upset stomach?'

'No.'

'So she left and Laura stayed. What next?'

'At about nine, the phone in my room rang. Karen asked for Laura. She took the receiver from me, went white and said something like: "Marion's been killed" or "Marion's dead". She seemed very shaken.

'During their conversation, Laura started crying. She put the phone down and said Marion had been stabbed and that Karen and Peter had found her body.'

'You say she was crying, can you describe how?'

'She was hysterical. She was in a really bad way,

302

even though she didn't really know Marion. I phoned a cab, gave her ten pounds and sent her home.'

'Did Karen or Laura have any items with them?'

'I noticed after Laura had gone home that she'd left a black gym bag under a seat in my room.'

'Did you look inside?'

'I had a quick look inside and saw a red t-shirt and a make-up bag on top, but I didn't go through the rest of it.'

'Oh come on, what was in the bag?'

'I told you, I felt bad prying into her personal stuff. I just glanced in the top, saw the red t-shirt and a make-up bag, then closed it again.'

Shep sighed, letting Bethan know that she hadn't earned her freedom yet.

'Next morning, when did you next see or hear from Karen or Laura Foster?'

'I went into work at about eight a.m. I told my boss that Marion had been murdered and that Karen and Peter had found the body. Later that morning, at about ten a.m., I got a call from Karen. She sounded annoyed. She said to me "Bethan, who have you told?" It turned out that Karen had been speaking to one of the hospital bosses and had been surprised to discover he already knew about the murder.

'Around midday, the porter rang me to say Karen was at the home and wanted to pick up something from my room. I went down to meet her in the foyer. Laura was there too. They said they wanted to pick up the gym bag they'd left behind.

'We all walked up to my room. Karen looked

upset and tired. She said to me again: "We were here just after five yesterday." They picked up the bag and left.'

Like Peter a day earlier, the more Bethan spoke the more she came to realise that Karen Foster could have murdered Marion, and that her sister Laura may have been somehow complicit in the crime.

'Had you any dealings with either sister over the next few days?'

'Laura rang me a few days later to tell me that the police would be calling to see me. She wanted me to call her as soon as they'd been.'

'Didn't that strike you as suspicious?'

'I just thought she was being supportive, as a friend.'

Shep took another loud, deep, disappointed breath.

'Go on,' he said, a headmaster tolerating a tall tale.

'The Sunday after Marion's murder, the police came to my room at the clinic. DC Young told me that they required a statement from me but, in the meantime could I write down everything I'd done on the day of the murder. I was also asked to recall how long Karen and Laura had been with me and at what times. I was frightened. I didn't know what to say. If Karen and Laura said they were in my room from five p.m., why should I doubt them? After they left, I phoned Laura and told her about it.'

'Did you express your reservations to Laura about lying to the police?' said Shep.

'I didn't lie. I believed them. She could tell I

was worried but she kept assuring me: "We really were at your room just after five. We were not lying. Just tell the police you were with us at that time." Why would I doubt the word of a close friend?'

'Did you not start to wonder why Karen and Laura were so anxious for you to give them this alibi?'

'I don't think they had anything to do with Marion's death.'

'Marion's murder,' Shep corrected her, 'she was stabbed to death, remember?'

She nodded quickly, obediently, close to breaking.

'When did you next speak to either Karen or Laura?'

'I called Karen after I'd made my written statement, to tell her what I'd said.'

'And how did she react?'

'She just said "okay".'

'Did you speak to her again?'

'She phoned me a couple of days later and asked me if anyone else at the Pines had been interviewed. She told me again that she and Laura had been in my room from five.'

'What did you think of this behaviour? Surely you must have wondered why she was so insistent that you stick to your story?'

'I was beginning to think maybe something wasn't right.'

'Oh come on, Bethan,' shouted Shep, his gag of mispronouncing her name lost in rage, 'enough is enough. You knew Karen murdered Marion. You agreed to provide her with an alibi. You're an accessory to the murder of Marion Ryan.'

'No! I never for one minute thought that. Never. Everyone knows it must have been a man. I think you're fitting them up.'

'Are you scared of her, Bethan?' sneered Shep. 'Were you frightened of what she'd do to you if you told the truth? Were you frightened you'd end up stabbed to death, like Marion?'

'No, no,' she cried, her face screwing up into a hideous ball, 'I want a solicitor.'

'You'll need a solicitor,' said Shep, 'because I've got a good mind to charge you. Interview terminated at sixteen thirty-two.'

Shep bolted upright, knocking his chair back with an almighty crack. 'May God forgive you,' he spat at her bowed, shaking head: her crucifix rattling the table top.

I followed Shep outside and back along the corridor: 'My God, Lynch, Karen Foster did it. It's the only explanation. Jesus Christ, they plotted it down to the last detail. That gym bag they left in Bethan's room held the murder weapon and Karen's change of clothes. That was a smart move, leaving it there. Even if we suspected them at the very start, we never would have searched Bethan's room. What Bethan saw in that bag had to be the red t-shirt Karen wore when she helped carry out the murder. Of course it's all probably in the bottom of the Thames now.'

I nodded. 'And if you're going to look inside a bag, you take a good bloody look, don't you, Guv? Why is she protecting them?'

'She was trying to save her own arse while not dropping them completely in it. She knows enough not to make herself the star prosecution witness. The Fosters would make her life a misery. So she's playing dumb. Bethan Trott's a hell of a lot smarter than she comes across,' said Shep.

I was struck by a new twist. 'Neither Karen nor Laura have an alibi now for that afternoon. We've got to get Laura in. Why the hell would she back her sister to the hilt when she knows she's murdered someone?'

I thought back to Marion, all those banging doors. 'My God, Guv.'

Shep looked at me, expectantly.

'Have we got Laura's fingerprints? We need to check the doors at the scene for her prints. She might be an accomplice.'

'We've had no reason to take her prints, until now. Get it sorted, Lynch, you could be onto something there.'

'Laura's prints at the scene would make it watertight, against both of them, wouldn't it? We could definitely charge them. Then it's just a case of working out who they used as muscle.'

This must have been what Marion had been leading me to, from her very first visit: Laura's prints on a door at the murder scene. Relief coursed through me so violently that it caused me to giggle. Within seconds, laughter infested every fibre of my being until tears streamed down my cheeks and I had to bend over to breathe.

Shep looked at me, bewildered: 'Jesus, you're not having another one of your funny turns, are you?'

Chapter 34

Church Road, London SW19
Friday, August 16, 1991; 19:00

I tried calling Gabby again, but her house phone was constantly engaged – probably off the hook. I reminded myself that I'd done nothing wrong, galvanised my pluck with three humongous Shirazs and made a pilgrimage to Church Road.

On the way, I realised I'd learned quite a few lessons since my last visit to SW19, about me, about Eve. The erstwhile love of my life now seemed self-obsessed, devious, a little unhinged – small wonder, after all she'd been through. I realised that I'd wasted the last three years of my life refusing to move on from her, from us. I'd been waiting for some sort of closure that would never come. As Fintan put it, I was still trying to save Eve Daly. Now I realised that the only person I could save was Donal Lynch, and there was work to be done.

I could put Eve behind me now, once and for all, move on with my life. That left me free to give Gabby one more go. After all, she seemed like everything I'd ever wanted in a companion: kind, smart, independent. She deserved better. I had to be a better man for her now.

I gave myself one last talking to and rang her doorbell. I couldn't believe nobody was in, so pounded the knocker. After another minute, I tried the bell again. Finally a shape appeared behind the stained-glass panels.

Reluctantly, the door opened four inches to the face of an elderly man. I felt pissed suddenly, and confused.

'What do you want?' he barked.

'Good evening. I was hoping to see Gabby.'

'I'm afraid that's not possible,' he said, stiffening and taking a baby step forward. I felt like I was being faced down by Sophia out of the *Golden Girls*.

'What's the problem?' I said.

He turned inside: 'Richard, are you ready to dial the number?'

'Ready, John,' grunted Gabby's rock'n'reefing flatmate Rick the Prick.

'What number? Sorry, I really don't understand what's going on.'

'Gabby no longer lives here. You have no reason to come round here. Do you understand?'

'I'm not Dom Rogan,' I laughed, 'I'm Gabby's policeman friend, Donal. Just ask her housemates.'

'We know exactly who you are. Now ... f – f-fuck off.'

I couldn't help but laugh 'Sir, I don't want to make any trouble. But I won't leave until someone explains what's going on. Please.'

Gabby materialised in the hallway. 'It's okay, Dad,' she said, 'I'll talk to him.'

They shared a solemn nod, then Gabby stepped outside.

'Just say the word, darling,' said her dad, stepping inside the door.

She stood an unnatural distance from me, retaining that front door as an escape option. She looked at me with a mixture of confusion and betrayal, like a child I'd just slapped for no reason.

'Gabby, what's going on?'

She took a deep breath and eyed me with mild contempt: 'When we got up yesterday, we found all our clothes cut up on the clothesline.'

'Oh, Christ,' I said, thinking: *Dom's back.*

'I called the police. Of course they couldn't help. But they gave me a number to call if they turned up again.'

'Why didn't you call me?'

'I did. I left a message on your home answerphone. I left a message at your work.'

'I didn't get those messages, Gabby. I'm sorry. I'll get Dom charged for you this time, I promise.'

'You promise?' she smiled, turning her contempt on full beam. 'That's not all. Someone left a package this morning,' she said, looking at me accusingly, 'newspaper clippings about your friend stabbing some guy to death.'

Finally her tears burst through: 'It was addressed to me. It totally freaked me out.'

She cried at the ground as I tried to figure out what the hell was going on.

'I meant to tell you about Eve, I really did. But I thought I was never going to see her again. She turned up out of the blue.'

'So now I'm going to be stalked by your ex as well, a demented murderer that you never even bothered telling me about. She could be watching us right now. I can't stay here. I'm too scared to go to work. Everything's fucked. Because of you.'

She glared at me through tears.

'Gabby honestly, I don't think any of this has anything to do with her. She's not deranged. It's got to be Dom.'

'She's *not* deranged? She stabbed a man in the balls during sex! I mean for God's sake, Donal, how would Dom even know about her? How would he have got cuttings about her case? She sent them, to warn me off you.'

'Gabby, it wasn't her. I'll prove to you that Dom's behind the cuttings and the slashed clothes and, this time, I'll get him out of your life once and for all.'

She stared at me now, her head shaking in disbelief.

'You – let – me – down.' Gabby enunciated every word with all the bile she could muster, turned and stormed back into the house.

This had to be the work of Dom Rogan. He'd followed me here last week. Or he'd found her new address another way. Dom worked for a bank so could pull anyone's personal information at a stroke. He'd most likely checked me out too, discovered my connection to Eve Daly and sent the cuttings to Gabby to drive a fatal wedge between us. I couldn't let him win. It was time for me and Dom to have it out.

I took the tube to Barbican near the city of London, stopped off at the Old Red Cow for a couple of sharpeners, then stomped to the brutalist block

311

containing Dom's swanky apartment, determined to scare the living shit out of him.

I pressed his number on the chrome intercom system violently and repeatedly, an avenging angel with no plans to pass. After the fifth or sixth thumb-grind, a shrill voice finally sounded.

'What do you want?' demanded the posh female.

'I'm here to see Dom Rogan,' I demanded, teeth clenched, pumped, 'I need to speak to him right away.'

'Who is this?'

'A friend.'

'If you're a friend, then you'd know he's not here anymore.'

'Let's just say I'm here to dispense some friendly advice.'

'Well you'll need to contact him at his new home.'

'And where's that?'

'Cape Town.'

Chapter 35

Clapham Police Station, South London
Saturday, August 17, 1991; 10:00

Next morning, Laura Foster had her fingerprints inked at Lee police station. Forensics bumped her up to the top of their list of suspects to be eliminated from the crime scene.

I was certain they'd find her prints somewhere

on or near a door. Marion's spirit had been telling me this since day one. I'd failed to make the connection because Laura had only just drifted onto our radar. This had to be the breakthrough we craved. We'd have to work out later Laura's motivations for helping her sister murder an innocent woman, and who had provided the muscle. The bottom line was, if we could place Laura at the scene, we could take both deadly sisters off our streets.

Most crucially of all, if we found irrefutable evidence that the Foster sisters murdered Marion, then I wasn't to blame for the deaths of Samantha and Jazmine Bisset. My insides still ached with the dread that I'd missed a Lone Wolf Killer in the 'unsolved cases' paperwork, leaving him free to butcher the Bissets.

It still troubled me that Samantha and Jazmine hadn't appeared to me after I attended their murder scene. I'd have to figure out why later... Nailing the Foster sisters would have to be enough for now.

As we waited for news from forensics, Shep outlined our case against Karen and Laura. He couldn't have looked more supremely all-knowing had he just lugged a pair of freshly inscribed tablets down Mount Sinai.

'Bethan Trott now says she didn't see Laura Foster on the day of Marion Ryan's murder until six o-five p.m. The Foster sisters merely *told* her that they'd been together in her room at the Churchill Clinic between five and six p.m. Nobody actually saw them in her room. As for the phantom shopping trip to Blackheath, Karen

313

Foster's cash card had been used near the Pines residential care home – six miles away – at four ten that afternoon. They have no record of buying anything in Blackheath. No one saw them in Blackheath. In short, we've obliterated the sisters' alibis.

'We believe that Karen left the Pines at four p.m., got some cash out, drove home to pick up the murder weapon, Laura and a set of fresh clothes which she placed in a black gym bag, then drove to Sangora Road to wait for Marion.

'We have a witness who saw a woman aged twenty-five to thirty and a white man coming out of 21 Sangora Road – at the time of the murder. This witness says that the woman was carrying a black gym bag.

'We have video evidence showing that the journey from the murder scene to the Pines residential care home at that time of day takes, on average, just under twelve minutes. The Fosters and an accomplice murdered Marion between five forty-two and five forty-five – remember, the pathologist estimated that the attack took two to three minutes – changed their clothes and drove back to the Pines where they were seen separately by employees at about six p.m. Bethan Trott says that Laura left a black gym bag overnight in her room. She looked inside the top of the bag and saw a red t-shirt. She claims she didn't inspect the rest of the bag's contents but we will argue that it contained the murder weapon and their blood-soaked clothes. They collected this bag the day after the murder, presumably to destroy the incriminating clothes and to clean the murder weapon.

'We believe that the weapon used was the steel blade found in the Fosters' garage yesterday. Remember, the girls' father, Terry, was unable to confirm that the blade had been there on the day after the murder. The pathologist has confirmed that this blade is consistent with Marion's injuries.

'Most convincing of all, we've got motive. Peter was sleeping with Karen until two weeks before Marion's murder, when he ended their affair and announced that Marion was pregnant. Karen is the classic woman scorned. Laura ... well, sibling loyalty? Maybe she thought they were just going to scare Marion, rough her up a bit? Who knows? We'll have to figure out her motivations once we prove that she was at the murder scene.'

Almost on cue, a records clerk walked in and handed him a piece of paper. The room sat forward as one and held its breath. This was one of life's penalty shoot-out moments: everything I cared about in the universe had now been reduced to that single piece of quivering paper. If it confirmed Laura's fingerprints at the scene, my life would never be the same again. It would be proof – surely – that I had some inexplicable hot-line to those funsters, the recently-murdered.

'They've found no matches,' mumbled Shep, blankly. My heart landed in lumps on the floor, like shot birds.

'Are you sure they checked both sides of both doors?' I said, a little desperately.

'And the handrail, and the interior walls. They checked everywhere. There isn't anything there.'

I didn't believe in much anymore: religion,

politics, policing – even romance – seemed corrupt, self-serving, narcissistic exercises, fuelled by human failure rather than strength. But I had allowed myself to believe in this 'gift', hoping, somehow, that it would help me believe again: in the afterlife, in policing, in saving people. In love itself. The only other verse I ever remembered from Gabby's book of bitter Philip Larkin poetry sprang to mind:

But superstition, like belief, must die.
And what remains when disbelief has gone?
Grass, weedy pavement, brambles, buttress, sky.

Shep refused to let this setback upstage his moment: 'Listen, I'm confident we've got enough to charge Karen Foster. Even if we can't place Laura at the scene, she must know what happened that afternoon. Let's get her in for a grilling. If we apply enough pressure, she'll make a mistake or break down and confess. Then we'll have them both, bang to rights.

'I'm going to present our case against Karen to the CPS lawyer now. He's up the corridor waiting, so let's see what he says. Regardless of what he decides, well done, team. Go and spend the rest of your Saturday with your loved ones. Keep your pagers on, in case the lawyer has questions or wants anything triple-checked. See you in the morning.'

A ticking bomb wouldn't have cleared the room quicker. I sat alone, empty, idiotic.

We didn't have a case. I didn't have a gift.

I realised I couldn't carry on like this. I needed

316

to quit therapy, quit drinking, quit the job: quit consorting with dead bodies.

Shep reappeared and started packing up his briefcase.

'Well?' I said.

'He's a lawyer, Lynch, they charge by the hour. He's going to take his time.'

'Will we know today?'

'If he's the first honest one I've ever come across, then maybe. It's a fucking miracle we got hold of him at all on a weekend. Listen, there's nothing more you can do now. Go home, get some rest, spend some time with your girlfriend. Come back fighting fit tomorrow.'

'I wouldn't mind waiting around, Guv, in case the lawyer does come back. And they're still checking the prints from the Pines' staff. That might throw up something.'

'Well page me if there's any developments,' he said, grabbing his briefcase and coat, 'I'm off to win hearts and minds.'

I watched him bustling towards the stairs, all business. Fintan popped into my mind – another Riddler, constantly hinting at bigger, mysterious, behind-the-scenes plays. At that precise moment, I wanted to know what Shep was up to more than anything else in the world.

I sprinted to the window overlooking the station's front entrance. Shep came out and turned right – away from the car park. Wherever he was going, it was on foot. He took another sharp right onto Lavender Hill.

I vaulted down the stairs three at a time, strode outside and turned onto Lavender. In the distance I could see Shep stomping down the hill towards Clapham Junction station with the stilted urgency of a fleeing assassin. He walked past the station on his right, then crossed the road. The first time he looked around, I was behind a gaggle of people two traffic lights back. I couldn't tell if he'd seen me. I had to run now to have any chance of catching him. I turned into Strathblaine Road and saw him fifty yards ahead. It's a quiet residential street with no cover. If Shep looked around, he'd see me for sure. I stopped and willed him towards a gentle bend in the road: 'Don't look back, don't look back.'

He disappeared round the corner. I assumed he was on his way to the murder scene. I couldn't for the life of me imagine why. I peeked around the corner and saw him stride into the Round-house pub.

I didn't know what to do next. If I walked past the pub, he might spot me through the window. Whoever he was meeting could pass this way. How suspicious would I look hanging about here? I had a sudden brainwave and speed-walked, Shep-style, back to Clapham Junction. I had remembered the short taxi rank at the traffic lights, opposite the entrance. Luckily, a single black cab sat there, light on. I jumped in, flashed my badge and told him to drive towards the Roundhouse pub. I explained that I needed him to park further up Sangora Road, facing the pub so that I could see who was coming in and out. And that I needed him to be quick.

He didn't move.

'What are you waiting for?' I muttered.

'I usually set the meter to night-time rates for surveillance operations,' he announced cheerfully. I was scarcely in a position to negotiate.

'Fine,' I said, and he hauled his wheezing black beast into thick traffic.

The nagging voice in my head wondered why Shep was so confident that the CPS lawyer would back his decision to charge Karen. We didn't have a firm sighting of her at the scene. The steel ruler's modified blade may or may not have been the murder weapon: it was impossible to prove. There was no forensic evidence at the scene. Her affair with Peter was winding down. She hadn't expressed a desire to kill Marion to anyone. And what about the male accomplice? No one had any idea who that could be.

Yes, Karen and Laura had lied about their whereabouts on the afternoon of the murder. Yes, Karen had lied about ending her affair with Peter in November last year. But none of this proved they killed Marion Ryan. Since day one, Shep's obsession with Karen Foster had been all-consuming. What if McStay and Barratt and the Big Dogs were right all along? What if she was innocent?

As the black cab pulled up on Sangora, I ducked down. I didn't have to wait long. Fintan emerged from the pub, blinking like Barabbas against the light. He raised his collar and set off up Strathblaine, battered leather satchel tucked firmly under his arm. Ten minutes later, Shep stepped out. He looked right, then left, directly at the taxi. He raised his arm to hail it, then registered that the light was off and started walking our way. I got down on all fours and told the driver to step on it to Clapham police station.

As I stared at the stippled grey plastic flooring, Fintan's words outside Buckingham Palace that day pealed through my mind.

People in power want more power. They don't serve the public, they serve their own agendas.

'I'm off to win hearts and minds,' Shep had said. What had he told Fintan?

The smarter ones recognise the power of the press, and use it to put pressure on their own organisation.

I jumped out at the police station, overpaid my overweight getaway driver and took a look at my beeping pager.

'Lawyer says we haven't got enough,' read the group message from Shep.

As I'd suspected, the CPS brief felt we still lacked that single piece of irrefutable evidence – that elusive smoking gun – to charge Karen.

I marched back into the incident room, my mind made up. I was going to find out who killed Marion myself, once and for all. I had just scooped up the keys to 21 Sangora Road, when the receptionist walked in.

'Donal Lynch?'

I nodded.

'I've got a message for you to call Fintan.'

As I dialled his direct office number, I thought about mentioning that I'd just seen him in Clapham. That'd rattle the smug fucker.

'Yeah?'

'Fintan?'

'Donal, I'm being arse-fucked by a deadline. Can it wait?'

320

'I just got a message to call you.'

'News to me.'

'Oh. Okay. What time do you knock off?'

'I've got, let's see, twenty-six minutes to write the splash.'

'Meet me after,' I said, 'I'll be at the Round-house pub, near Sangora Road in Clapham. You know it?'

'I don't think so,' he lied, 'but I'm sure I'll find it.'

I took the overground train to Brixton, bought what I needed on Electric Avenue and headed back to Clapham Junction. By the time I got to the Roundhouse pub, Fintan was waiting.

'Didn't even know this place was here,' he smiled, confirming that you shouldn't even believe his 'hello'.

As the barman approached, I remembered one of my dad Martin's favourite expressions – 'Beer isn't drinking' – and ordered two large scotches. Lame liquor had no place in this enterprise.

'As delightful as it is to see you, Donal, what are you after?'

I opened the palm of my hand, revealing a set of house keys.

'Let me guess,' said Fintan, 'we've been invited to a swingers' party?'

'Try again,' I said, 'and think about where we are.'

'They're not... Holy shit. Isn't it still a crime scene?'

'No, they're all done. And I've brought along a little something to help me prolong the experi-ence,' I said, opening my other hand to reveal an eighth of cannabis.

It must have been about nine when we walked out of the pub into the snug, muffled dusk. At the doorway, Fintan furtively removed the batteries from his pager.

'What are you doing?'

'Making sure no one can place me at the scene.'

'What?'

'These things send and receive messages via the nearest transmitter, which means they can work out your location. But not if you take the batteries out.'

I dreaded how paranoid he'd get after a joint.

We popped into an off-licence for a bottle of scotch, tobacco, a lighter and extra-long papers.

As we walked up the steps to 21, I felt giddy, high, fairground-scared. I suddenly understood the buzz that breeds serial burglars. The key clicked sweetly in the lock. An icy chill wafted my neck. I thought of Marion that evening, turning this key, Karen Foster fingering her blade in the gym bag, poised to strike.

I opened the door and stood aside for Fintan. He looked shaken, lost.

'This is too weird,' he said, his eyes restless, unsure.

'Get in for fuck's sake, before someone sees us.'

As we stood facing the flat door, I felt his helpless stare.

'Just pretend it's my place,' I urged, stepping forward and sliding the key into the lock.

I pulled the heavy door open, leaned against its weight and nodded at Fintan to enter.

'Why do I have to go first?'

'Jesus just get in the fucking door!'

He faltered, then crept inside. I took the key out of the lock and followed him.

Something cracked me in the back.

'Jesus,' I cried out.

'What?' squealed Fintan.

'That fucking door just tried to knock me out.'

I followed him up the stairs and turned on the landing light. The zap of familiar yellow instantly banished my nerves. Sure enough, Marion's bloodstains had been painted over. I talked him through the crime scene, hoping my breezy tone would normalise this morbid tour.

'So what now?' he said when I'd finished.

I led him into the sitting room. He sat on the couch, bolt upright, tense. I plucked two glasses from the kitchen and poured large ones.

As he glugged greedily, I hoped one bottle of Glenmorangie would be enough. As I knew only too well, numb don't come cheap.

We sat there in tortuously stilted silence. But that's murder scene parties for you. Then I remembered the pot and set to work on a six-sheet Clapham Courgette, as they call them in that neck of the woods. Fintan took an almighty toke: we were both craving levity of any kind. Soon I was entertaining him with imitations of Peter Ryan, Karen Foster and Shep, and had him slapping his knees in helpless hilarity.

I got back from the loo to find Fintan comatose. I dipped the light and checked the time: 1.12 a.m. My mind shot back to that night in Tullamore, watching Meehan on top of Eve, the clock radio flipping to 1.13. The boffins say you can't read the time in your dreams: I hadn't been dreaming.

Just then, my head jolted back. Pain rang through my face like it was a tuning fork. A starburst of colour cleared to reveal Marion inches from me, her raging bloodshot eyes locked onto mine. I screamed but the vacuum devoured the sound whole. My senses twitched and flinched, sensing that, this time, she'd come to do me real harm.

I felt her cool flesh against mine as she clasped my right hand. Slowly, she brought it up towards her. She then pressed it, palm-down, on the arm of the sofa. She leaned on it with all her might. My hand tried to fight back, shaking and quivering against her domination.

Her free left hand pinched my little finger and pulled it apart from the other restrained digits. Something glinted in the palm of her hand. I realised what it was, winced and swooned.

As the sharpened metal object– a steel ruler, if I wasn't mistaken – bore down on that lonely little finger on my right hand, my brain clicked into survival mode. I diverted every ounce of my being into that hand to fight her grip. But it felt limp, useless, dead.

I wanted to look away, but I couldn't move at all. My eyes fixed upon that descending metal. Without even a nanosecond's hesitation, the blade pierced the skin, just below the top knuckle. My insides convulsed.

I felt an instant circuit of scalding white heat from that finger to my brain. She struggled to contain my stricken hand's sudden, frenzied twitching. Then calmly, efficiently, she sliced through my finger's soft exterior flesh, sending nails of fire bolting through me.

Now the ruler was bending, under pressure, scraping up against the bone and tendons. I wasn't expecting it to bend. It slipped, slicing the skin down the front of the finger. The digit disappeared in blood: not spurting blood like in the movies, just endless, welling blood. My head lolled, bloodless.

'Why are you doing this?' my mind pleaded.

The blade tried again. Real pressure this time. It bent. It slipped under the weight, this time up into the knuckle. I was burning alive now. I wanted my brain to shut down, to cease feeling.

My finger was minced: a small hunk of gristle with threads of blue running through it. Just bone and red mulch, all puddling blood. The ruler's sharp tip came in again. Glinting. Determined. It was forced down, full-pelt, on the digit's bone.

Now she set about sawing at the bloody lump. My vision rapidly flickered, as if struggling to comprehend the full horror. Finally, my brain went into shutdown.

My eyes snapped on again, seeing a tiny red lump, wretched, alone, on the arm of that sofa. Everything spun, lurched through black. White exploded, filling my vision, firing me at supersonic speed through more white.

Then I was looking down at myself asleep on the couch, jabbering in tongues, Fintan perched on the edge of the sofa, taking snaps with a tiny stills camera. I could hear the shutter. I could smell the weed. I felt no terror, no pain: just high, ecstatic, free.

'Whatcha doing, Donal?' I asked myself, inspecting my floating, unbutchered hand.

'Just hanging,' I replied.

I realised I could tilt side-to-side. I willed myself forward through the air and floated on cue, in control, my brain now a jet pack. I thought about performing a Red Arrows-style full roll, when I got distracted by a loud bang downstairs, followed by another, and another.

I laughed in the face of the door and glided through the wall to the landing. Marion's body lay there, lifeless, just as I had seen her that night. The rhythmic banging continued – boom, boom, boom – as a chill rustled my face. I turned to see the open landing window.

I looked towards the banging at the bottom of the stairs. The flat door crashed shut, over and over. What was I not getting about that fucking door? I floated down, determined to stop the banging, to close that door once and for all.

At the foot of the stairs I reached out, but the door passed straight through my arm, again and again, boom, boom. I turned and looked up the stairs. Marion's eyes stared directly into mine: bloodshot, betrayed, accusing. I floated up towards those eyes and made my vow: whatever it was on that door, I'd find it.

I snapped back inside my body to find myself sitting cold, calm and sweat-soaked on the couch. Mercifully, my little finger appeared to be intact and the banging had stopped. All I could hear were the crunching metal clicks of Fintan's camera.

'Tell me what just happened?' he demanded

I looked around at the closed sitting room door, wild spatters of whisky all over my shirt and jeans, the couch, the carpet.

I told him everything, from the impromptu finger amputation to the flat door's ghosting back and forth through my outstretched arm.

'What is she trying to say?'

'Well she's clearly telling me that the pared-down ruler we found in the Foster family's garage is the murder weapon.'

'Why did she cut off your finger?'

'When she first came to me, she kept slamming my sitting room door, over and over. I thought she must be leading me to a clue to do with the door.'

'What could that be?'

'I haven't got the foggiest. Hey, you didn't say you were bringing a camera?'

'Are you kidding? I take this with me everywhere. You never know, do you? I'll get them developed tomorrow, should give us a right laugh.'

'What was I doing?'

'You were growling and sort of gurning with your teeth clamped together, like a horse on a motorbike.'

I desperately needed to pee and got to my feet. My head sprung stars as I stumbled into the bathroom.

My water-splashed pale face inspected itself in the mirror. Spidery red cracks had turned the white of my eyes into low-grade marble. They looked lifeless, jaundiced: two decades older than me. When I blinked, my mother's eyes stared back.

I shivered, then batted the image away and

returned to the couch.

'Lilian was right about one thing. Once I came out of my body, I felt sensational.'

'Did you consciously decide to come out or go back into your body?'

'No to both. And I won't sleep at all now unless I get another drink. There's that all-night off-licence near Clapham Junction. I'm starving too.'

'Thing is, Donal, I'm not actually an insomniac or an alky. I'm going to grab a taxi home. You should go home too,' he said.

'Okay.'

We strolled silently through the sultry night, London's buried hum soothing our frazzled nerves.

'Safe home,' Fintan said, hopping into a cab. I watched until the car turned the comer, then walked back towards Sangora.

Chapter 36

Sangora Road, South London
Sunday, August 18, 1991; 09:00

A slamming door jolted my eyes open to dazzling sunlight. I sat up, recognised the sitting room of 21 Sangora Road and my own naked body.

I could hear people coming up the stairs, chatting. I jumped up to grab my clothes but could see only fried chicken-themed carnage: greasy cardboard boxes, half-eaten drummers, a cornon-the-cob. Beyond that: joint butts, beer, can ashtrays, splattered whisky and red wines but no fucking clothes. The chatting got to the door just as I spotted my boxers near the window. I hurdled the puddles of filth to reach them, then realised I wasn't going to make it.

The door opened slowly, almost ceremoniously. I stood in the middle of the room, both hands over my knackers.

'It's surprisingly spacious...' said a voice. The estate agent saw me, dropped her clipboard and emitted a horror movie scream. Her two would-be tenants stared for an age, frozen in shock, then wordlessly ran away.

The estate agent bent down slowly to pick up her clipboard without taking her eyes off me.

'Is this leasehold?' I asked, trying to suppress my reawakened pot-based euphoria.

She shook her head.

'Oh, so it's freehold,' I said, 'a bit like this.'

I lifted my hands and wiggled. She screwed up her face in utter disgust, then bolted.

I popped into a corner shop for a diabetic fizz fix but failed to get as far as the fridge.

Blaring out from today's *Sunday News*: 'Judas Kiss' by Fintan Lynch, over a photo of Karen Foster kissing Peter Ryan fully on the lips. Peter's wearing a morning suit because the grainy image is a still from his wedding video.

Tender embrace ... the lovers share a kiss just a few feet from Marion, Peter's new wife. Now Peter's mistress Karen is prime suspect in the hunt for Marion's killer...

My hands shook as I read a couple of the more damning revelations from Karen Foster's police interview. I couldn't believe it: Shep had leaked her statement and the wedding video to Fintan. A scene replayed in my mind from Thursday night: Shep signing for two packages, one from Woolwich CD, the other from a data transfer company. He must have got a copy of Marion and Peter's wedding video made to give to Fintan.

Clever Shep. How could the CPS lawyer not charge Karen Foster, now that the world knew the truth?

Another realisation abruptly stopped me applauding Shep's ingenuity. The team – and the Met Commissioner – would want to know how Fintan Lynch of the *Sunday News* got his hands on not one, but two pieces of evidence critical to an ongoing murder enquiry. Well, Commissioner, guess who works on the team? Step forward Donal Lynch, younger brother of the journalist who broke the story.

My mind was spinning. Shep knew everyone would suspect me of supplying this material to Fintan. He leaked it anyway.

Fintan knew everyone would assume that I was his snout. He ran it anyway. Judas Kiss indeed.

By the time I got to Fintan's street in North London, I'd convinced myself that he and Shep had plotted this from the very start. My very invitation to join the investigating team had been a ploy cooked up in their Machiavellian imaginations. Both were chess players: they knew they'd find a way to prosper while letting me take the fall. What they couldn't have anticipated was that

I knew the identity of the real leaker.

I couldn't wait to deliver this little checkmate.

I rang Fintan's doorbell over and over. Finally he appeared, dishevelled in shorts and my Sonic Youth 'Goo' t-shirt. Fucker.

'What do you want?' he squawked.

'You've really fucking done it this time,' I muttered through gritted teeth, barging past him into his barely-furnished bachelor pad.

'Hey,' Fintan called after me as I stormed into the tiny nightclub that passed for his kitchen.

'Who's that?'

Instantly I recognised her voice, coming from his trendy mezzanine bedroom. Fintan stopped dead in his tracks, opening his arms in a pleading gesture.

'Look, we were going to tell you,' he began.

Eve appeared at the top of the metal staircase, wearing my best white linen shirt. I almost expected a serpent and an apple tree. By the time I managed to close my mouth, I'd forgotten why I came here.

'You've been ... all along,' I said, my voice shaking.

'We never planned it,' said Eve, quietly.

The sheer scale of their deceit, their betrayal, was too much to take in.

'Jesus,' was all I could say.

'You,' I said, pointing up at Eve, 'get the fuck out of my sight, right now.'

'You,' I said, pointing at Fintan, 'outside.'

He led the way, shoulders slumped, head down.

I pinned him against the outside wall, shouted into his wincing face.

'I'll have the truth about you and Eve later. Right now, I want the truth about you and Shep, starting at the Feathers.'

Chapter 37

Clapham Police Station, South London
Sunday, August 18, 1991; 11:00

My entrance silenced the incident room. Being last in didn't help. Trust me to have my first good sleep in years at a murder scene. And Fintan had a lot to tell me.

'Glad you could join us, Lynch,' Shep said drily.

'Sorry Guv, domestic thing.'

I sought somewhere to perch and felt all eyes on me.

He'd turn the team against me now, for sure – if he hadn't already done so. I'd served my purpose. He was ready to dish me up. I told myself to box clever for once. If I threw my one big shot too early, he could evade it and destroy me. I had to bide my time.

'I've already told the team that the Commissioner has announced a full investigation into how the Sunday News and more specifically, *your brother*, got hold of Karen's latest statement and the wedding video,' he announced.

I hated myself for reddening. I wanted to tell everyone it was anger, not shame.

Shep eyed me coldly.

'Just to reiterate, we will find out who did this, and that person or those people will never work for the Met police again. As I'm sure you can appreciate, Lynch, this is the last thing we need right now.'

I stood up. Shep squinted, Dirty Harry-style, at the punk not making his day.

'I am not the source of this story,' I said clearly. 'I've never passed information to my brother about any case. Think about it. Everyone knows he's a crime reporter. It would be career suicide.'

Had I got photographs of Shep and Fintan coming out of the Roundhouse pub yesterday, I would have produced them, there and then. As it stood, the only person who could corroborate what I saw was that taxi driver. I scolded myself for not making a note of his driver ID number. All I knew about him was that he was fat, bald, Cockney, objectionable and grasping which, when it came to black cab drivers in London, didn't exactly narrow it down. I'd pop over to the rank later today, try to trace him. If I was to be the fall guy, I'd do all I could to take Shep down with me.

Shep now adopted a lighter tone: 'On the plus side, the story has made our lawyer have a re-think. That, and a call from the Commissioner. So our legal eagles are re-examining our evidence against Karen Foster this morning. In the mean-time, Laura Foster is in suite three, waiting to be interviewed. Let's see what we can squeeze out of her.'

As the prime suspect in Leakgate, I didn't bother asking permission to observe Laura Foster's interview. Rather than give Shep the pleasure of saying no, I tracked him at distance down that long corridor to the interview suites. As he punched in the secret code to the security door and heaved it open himself, I realised I wouldn't beat the slam unless I ran. If Shep caught me, he'd send me back – but I'd nothing left to lose.

I launched into a Penelope Pitstop-style series of silent, high-speed, extra-long paces. I felt ridiculous but I caught the door an inch shy of shutting. I expected Shep to turn round at any moment, but he didn't. Blinkered Olympian speed-walking had proven his downfall again, just as it had when I'd followed him to the Roundhouse pub yesterday.

I followed him into the observation room, took a seat and ignored his lighthouse glare.

The beauty of a two-way mirror is you can stare all you like. Laura Foster was worth a good look. Slim, with lightning blue eyes, she had a pretty, sculpted face and a lithe body – a real beauty. How Karen must have resented her sister's outrageous good fortune in the genetics lottery.

She wore textbook South London clothing – faded jeans torn at the knees, tight white t-shirt, a chunky gold necklace and a pair of trendy, box-fresh trainers.

The only let down was her voice: like Karen, she spoke in a nasal and whiney monotone.

She sat alongside a podgy man in a tight suit who busied himself with stationery and kept telling her that everything was going to be okay. He looked far more nervous than she did. Just like Karen – and Peter Ryan, for that matter – Laura seemed oblivious to the gravity of the situation. You'd think they got quizzed about a murder every few weeks. I didn't know whether to put their collective ambivalence down to arrogance, guilt or just plain ignorance.

Mick and Colin burst in, all-business. They sat down and began reading material without saying a word. I saw Laura – glancing sideways at her solicitor. He raised his eyebrows as if to say: 'Fucked if I know.'

This was it: our one-and-only chance to nail Laura. She had lied consistently to protect Karen, and possibly to avoid incriminating herself. One thing was certain: Laura knew a lot more than she was saying about Marion Ryan's murder. But we had nothing on her. Unless she slipped up now, or broke down and confessed, she'd walk out of here for the last time. She could even get her sister off the hook, if she put on a good show.

After what seemed an age, Mick put his papers down and whistled lightly, as if to say: 'I've got all I need now.' Without signal, Colin turned on the tape recorder, announcing the time and guests.

Mick opened with the afternoon of the murder. Just like her older sister, Laura couldn't remember any of the boutiques they'd browsed in Blackheath. They'd clearly thought it through: shops have CCTV.

Laura repeated her alibi as if by rote: returned to the Pines after five, met Bethan Trott in the communal kitchen, watched TV until six when Karen left to service the home's fish tanks with Peter. They let her regurgitate the entire story, confidently and at length, without mentioning that it had now been completely discredited by the only independent witness – Bethan Trott. I hoped that, sometime soon, a jury would get to decide which of these young women was telling the truth.

Mick tried a fresh tack: 'Have you ever been to Marion's flat, Laura?'

She shook her head.

'The client has shaken her head to indicate a negative to the question. It's better if you speak Laura, so that we can get it on tape.'

'No,' she said, sullenly.

'No what, Laura,' sighed Mick.

'No, I've never been to Marion's flat.'

'Do you know where it is, Laura?'

'It's in Clapham somewhere.'

'And how do you know that?'

'How do you think I know?' she sneered, then screwed up her face in disbelief at the question. 'Karen used to go there all the time, to see Marion and Peter.'

Colin sprang to his feet, spun away and prowled the top of the room. He composed himself, sat back down and took over.

'Karen's obsessed with Peter Ryan, isn't she, Laura?'

'No, she isn't.'

'She moved out of your family home and into staff accommodation at the Pines a month before his wedding to Marion, didn't she, Laura?'

'Yes but...'

'In a last-ditch attempt to win Peter Ryan, wasn't it?'

'No.'

'To stalk Peter, spy on Peter, tempt Peter.'

Laura's face reddened.

'No.'

'So that Peter could have her any time he felt like it.'

'No,' shouted Laura, 'she moved out because of my dad.'

'Oh come along now, Laura. You don't expect us to believe that.'

'My dad, when he gets drunk, he can get ... aggressive.'

'Really? The police haven't been called to your home. Doesn't sound like the violent type to me?'

'He's different when he's drunk. He's attacked us all, loads of times.'

'Attacked?' sneered Colin.

'Karen used to stand up to him, to protect me and Stacey. That's when he turns into an animal and beats the hell out of her, smashing her head into the wall and all sorts. When she got a chance to move into a room she could afford, we persuaded her to go for it. By then, me and Stacey were old enough to look after ourselves. Sometimes, when Dad's drinking, I go and stay with Karen. I've got a spare key.'

Shep got to his feet and walked to the glass. 'I wonder what else Karen had to protect her pretty little sister from? Their dad, Terry, probably wasn't attracted to Karen, so moved straight on to Laura. I've seen it before. That'd partly explain Karen's crippling insecurity, and Laura's blind loyalty. Lynch, as soon as we're finished here, call up Terry Foster's previous, and find out if social services have taken an interest.'

As usual, Colin and Mick seemed to be thinking along the same lines.

'So, you'd describe yourself as a loyal sister?' asked Colin.

'Yeah, of course,' she said, frowning in disdain at the question.

'She took a few beatings for you, did she, Laura?'

'Yeah, quite a few actually.'

'It's fair to say you feel a sense of debt to Karen for this?'

Laura nodded.

'Can you please speak?'

'Yes I do.'

'So when she asked you to come with her, to confront Marion, you weren't really in a position to say no, were you, Laura?'

'Like I said, I've never been to Marion's home.'

'You thought she was only going to tell Marion about the affair, maybe scare her a little. But then it all got out of hand, didn't it, Laura?'

'No comment,' said Laura. I noticed she wasn't looking at Colin or Mick now. She'd picked a spot on the far side of the room and was focusing on that. I'd read about this in one of my correspondence classes: a classic anti-interrogation technique, used by IRA suspects and the like. It made her look as guilty as sin. But no jury would ever see this – only sound was being recorded.

'And now you're going to get done for murder as well, Laura, as an accessory. You know why, because you're not taking this chance to tell us the truth? What do you say to that, Laura?'

'No comment,' she said, unblinking, spectral.

They needed to get her talking again, or all was lost.

'Well guess what, we know the truth. We've got evidence putting you at the scene.'

Laura's stare faltered for just a nanosecond, then refroze.

'You'll go down for life, Laura, don't you understand? Twelve years in Holloway prison. That's what you're facing. Is that what you want?'

'No comment,' said Laura.

Colin sat back and took a deep breath. Shep pressed his forehead against the two-way. 'This is it,' he said to the glass, 'last throw of the dice.'

Colin began gently: 'You know what they hate most in prison, Laura? Nonces. You know, paedophiles, child molesters, perverts who target children. Did you know that?'

'No comment.'

'Do you know what they hate most after nonces, Laura? They hate child killers. Especially people who kill really young kids.'

Laura just glared at that spot, her brain in autofocus.

'You did know Marion was pregnant, Laura?'

She stiffened, then shivered, losing her focus spot on the wall. This was it: if she was ever going to break, it would be now.

After a series of sharp breaths, Laura turned to her solicitor and whispered something.

He spoke up. 'My client is feeling unwell and would like some fresh air. And I really must object to this tone of questioning.'

Mick told the tape recorder the news and shut

339

it down.

'Fuck,' screamed Shep, butting the glass, 'that's all our ammo gone. She's never gonna break now.'

A uniformed WPC walked into the suite and signalled to Laura and the solicitor to come with her. The solicitor ushered Laura to the door first. It was then that I spotted just how garish her trainers were. They had a quirky blue and green, cross-strap design on the side that reached above the ankle and bright green soles. I'd only been off the streets a few weeks but I'd never seen a pair like it, even at our Nike trainer identification seminar last year. I couldn't help thinking: what delicious irony if she got stabbed for them.

I walked out to the corridor just as Laura was being led past. I took a closer look at her shoes: they were Nike, but not the much-stabbed-for Air Jordans. The WPC led them to the security door that divided the interview suites from the main block. Laura's idea of fresh air clearly meant a Superking in the car park. The WPC hit the green release button, pulled the tightly-sprung door open towards her and walked through, making just a token effort to hold it for Laura.

Feeling the weight of the door, Laura instinctively turned her back against it to keep it open and signalled for her solicitor to walk through next. But he was lumpen, meaning that Laura needed to push the door back further so that he could get past. She achieved this by planting the sole of her trainer against the door and pushing her foot back. While doing this, she turned and looked directly at me.

The case rewound before my eyes, to a soundtrack of the door of 21 Sangora Road slamming shut, over and over. 'Oh my God,' I said out loud.

I turned and chased Shep, already galloping towards the kitchenette.

'We've got to ask her about her trainers, Guv,' I said. He looked at me with withering contempt.

'Look, Lynch, our case is falling apart in there...'

'Please, Guv, I'm serious. Just get them to ask her where she got them. Please, you've got to trust me on this.'

'Jesus, Lynch,' sighed Shep, shaking his head, 'this better be good.'

Back in the interview suite, before switching on the tape recorder, Good cop Mick cracked a bashful smile and said: 'Laura, can I ask you something before we start, though it's a little embarrassing?'

She looked sideways at her solicitor, then back to Mick.

'It's just that we've got a very fashion-conscious WPC in the team who's really taken a shine to your trainers. She just wanted to know where you got them from.'

Laura turned again to her solicitor, her frown flipped, clearly dying to elaborate. Her solicitor shrugged as if to say: 'No harm in it, I suppose.'

'They're Nike Air Huaraches,' she announced loftily. 'My uncle sent them over from the States for my birthday last month. They're not even on sale in the UK yet.'

I told Shep I'd be back in a few minutes and ran

into a nearby office. I called Fintan for one reason: he had an extensive cuttings library at his behest. He didn't answer, so I paged him. He knew I'd only do this in an emergency. He called back right away. I told him to find out all he could about Nike Huarache shoes and to let me know as soon as possible. He didn't dare ask why or object.

He got back to me in record time.

I learned that the Nike Huarache trainer was the brainchild of Tinker Hatfield, also the designer of Air Jordans and the Air Max. It was inspired by his water-skiing boots, and has a sock-like lining which they called Dynamic Fit.

'Is any of this relevant?' asked Fintan.

'Just keep talking.'

Because of their unusual design, sales of the Huarache shoe hadn't taken off. Last year, Nike didn't get enough pre-orders to go into production. But then, a few months ago in April, some marketing guru decided to sell them, guerrilla-style, at the New York Marathon. Suddenly demand soared. Last month, Nike had re-launched the Huarache in the US, but they weren't scheduled to be sold in the UK until October.

I raced back to Shep and told him the news.

'There can't be more than a handful of Huarache shoes in the whole of the UK,' I said.

'But forensics combed the scene for footprints. If they found prints from a shoe that rare, they would have flagged it up,' said Shep.

'Yes but I want them to check the doors.'

'For shoeprints?'

'Yes. You'll see why, next time they take a

break,' I said, my growing conviction somehow eclipsing my inner terror at making a total arse of myself, yet again.

By now, Laura had reverted to her 'no comment' wall stare. Good cop Mick tried reason. Bad cop Colin attempted terror. He managed to scare the shit out of everyone, except Laura.

I stood and walked to the corner of the two-way to get a good look at those trainers. Beside the solicitor's brogues, they looked tiny.

'Get them to ask her what size shoe she is,' I said.

Shep shuffled in his seat, irritated and reluctant. 'Please, Guv, it's just one more question.'

He paged Mick and met him at the door to the suite. I could see Shep having to work really hard to convince him. As Mick shut the door, he turned to the two-way, shook his head and mouthed, 'wanker'.

After a time, Laura's solicitor asked Mick if his client could take a bathroom break.

'Of course,' said Mick, terminating the interview and switching off the tape recorder.

As they all got to their feet, Mick smiled at Laura and said: 'Before you go, our foot fetishist was wondering what size shoe you take.'

'These are a size three,' she smiled, 'and even that's a bit big for me. I have to wear thick socks.'

I ushered Shep to the corridor: 'I want you to watch them go through the security door, Guv, really closely.'

After ten seconds, I almost had to shove his sceptical arse out to the corridor ahead of me. I hoped to God Laura would do the same as she

343

did before. Otherwise, my theory would never fly and my career might crash land before it even had the chance to take off.

We watched the trio of WPC, Laura and lawyer walk towards that security door. As before, the WPC pressed the green release button, pulled the security door towards her and walked through first. Laura took the weight of the door with her arm, then turned her back against it, once again inviting her solicitor through next. As he waddled closer, I willed her to use her foot again.

'Use your foot, Laura,' I mouthed at her head, 'use your foot.'

As the solicitor got within touching distance, her foot went up, her trendy green sole planting itself on the door and pushing it back, right up against the wall.

'You see that, Guv?' I said.

'See what?' he said.

'What she did with her foot.'

He nodded.

'The door to Marion's flat is spring-loaded, like that one.'

'Shit!' He was with me.

'The evening of the murder, when they waited for Marion at the bottom of the steps of number 21, Karen would have held the gym bag containing the change of clothes and the weapon. After all, she was the older sister and the one with the beef. To ensure Marion didn't notice or question the bag, she stood behind Laura.'

Shep nodded, happy for once to ride pillion.

'Marion would have led the way up the garden steps and through the front door, followed by

Laura, then Karen. Marion picked up her post. She already had a handbag and a coat over her arm. When she pulled open that spring-loaded door to the flat, she had no spare hand to hold it open for Laura, who wouldn't have been expecting the weight of the door.'

I could almost see celestial light passing across Shep's rapt face.

'Marion unlocked and opened the flat door towards her, walked through. Laura came next. She felt the weight of the door, turned her back against it to let Karen through ahead of her. But to open it wide enough to let fatso past, she needed to use her foot.'

I headed off Shep's next question before he had the chance to ask it.

'We know they probably destroyed their blood-soaked clothes, but there's no way Laura would get rid of a pair of two-hundred-quid designer trainers.'

'Two hundred quid? You're joking.'

Shep flew up the corridor, me in hot pursuit.

He explained the scenario to the forensics officer.

'What are the chances that a shoe print could still be on that door, after seven weeks?'

'Well, it's a flat surface. It's not like a door handle that gets touched every two minutes. I'd say if she left a shoe print on that door, part of it should still be there.'

'If the print is there, can we prove that it belongs specifically to her shoe?' I asked.

'They're better than fingerprints actually, because they usually leave a more specific pattern.

345

We can match it for design, size, even how worn the sole is. If we find a trace, then you've hit the jackpot.'

Chapter 38

Clapham Police Station, South London
Sunday, August 18, 1991; 13:00

Shep sent a team to formally arrest Karen Foster and bring her back to the station. We stood together at the custody desk as Laura was led out of her cell, minus the trendy trainers that had sealed her fate. She looked composed, impenetrable. As she was being processed, I heard the security door beep. I peered around the corner to see two officers leading Karen in. She looked flustered, scared, a busted flush.

As she turned the corner and came face-to-face with her younger sister, she crumpled. Laura's malignant glare said: 'Pull yourself together.' Karen swiftly recovered her sullen insolence. I couldn't help wondering if Laura had thrown her a similar look that July evening as Marion turned into Sangora Road. Perhaps Laura Foster had been much more than bystander in this murderous escapade.

Shep charged Karen and Laura Foster with the murder of Marion Ryan. As they were escorted to separate cells, they didn't look at each other, or utter a single word.

Shep summoned the team for a newsflash. He looked strained, thwarted.

'The good news is, we can now prove beyond doubt that Laura Foster was at the scene of the crime,' he said.

'We have established major flaws in both the Foster sisters' alibis. We can show that Karen had motive: she was sleeping with Marion's husband Peter until two weeks before her murder. According to her work colleague, Bethan Trott, she'd shown signs of being obsessed with him.

'Why did they act together? I spoke to our old friend Professor Richards, and he mentioned a condition known as *folie à deux*. This is a psychiatric term for a shared psychosis or delusional belief between two people who are very close, often twins. He showed me a few examples and the best way I can describe it is "psychosis by osmosis". Did Karen's obsession with Peter Ryan somehow rub off on Laura? Did her devotion to Karen suck her into a state of mind where she would kill for her sister? We can get a judge to order psychiatric reports and investigate this right away.

'Normally, we'd now try to turn the suspects against each other. But as the Prof has pointed out, these girls are too close for that. Both stopped talking to us some time ago.

'I've just come from the lawyer who advises me that we still haven't got enough to swing a jury. So where do we go from here? According to the pathologist, only a man could have inflicted several of the knife wounds suffered by Marion because of the strength required. Who was it? We're still matching prints from employees and ex-employees of the Pines care home with those found at the scene, but so far we're drawing a blank.

'The bottom line is, until we find the man and can place both him and Karen at the scene, we haven't got a case. And, to be blunt, I'm clean out of ideas.'

Marion's butchering of my little finger flashed through my mind so I piped up. 'The weapon, Guv.'

His tired eyes located me and squinted.

'What about the weapon, Lynch?'

'Nothing concrete, Guv. But let's suppose that the murder weapon was the metal ruler that DS Barratt found in their dad's mop this week. He told us how nervous Terry got when he was asked about the ruler and whether he'd found it in the mop the next day. We now know that Laura left a gym bag in Bethan Trott's room. We know she came from the scene of the crime so the ruler would have been in that bag until they picked it up at midday the next day. It definitely wasn't in the mop the day after the murder and Terry knows this. Also, I checked out Terry Foster like you asked. He's got form for burglary. It's twenty years ago, but he did a stretch. Eighteen months.'

'Get him in,' barked Shep, 'and get that fucker Peter Ryan back in. Something's not adding up about his story.'

Chapter 39

Clapham Police Station, South London
Sunday, August 18, 1991; 16:00

Shep and I sat in the interrogation suite's viewing gallery, watching Peter Ryan fumble with his wedding ring.

'We're letting Terry Foster stew in the other suite,' said Shep, 'Barratt told him we've got some news about the weapon. By all accounts he's rattling away in there like a garden gate in a hurricane!'

Yet again, they let Peter bring in his work pager. I couldn't understand how this object could be considered any less dangerous than his cash, belt or keys. My mind flashed back to the night of Marion's murder on Sangora Road, Peter fumbling in his pocket for the flat keys, when my mind snagged on a tiny detail.

'You know, in his statement, Peter said he always kept his keys in his briefcase at work, otherwise he'd lose them. Karen would have known that.'

Shep blinked repeatedly. 'What are you saying, Lynch?'

'What if Karen or Laura took the keys out of his briefcase, let themselves into 21 Sangora and waited for Marion?'

Shep nodded slowly.

The sight of Peter's pager transported me back

to last night. Fintan removed the batteries from his so that no one could triangulate his location. I couldn't fail to suppress a guffaw.

'What's so funny, Lynch?'

'Fintan often takes the batteries out of his pager. He claims that otherwise spooks could work out his location, because the messages are re-directed from local transmitters.'

Shep smiled: 'He's got a vivid imagination, that boy.'

We both looked at each other suddenly, thinking the same thing. Karen was a trainee nurse at the Pines. She too would have been issued a work pager as standard. I followed his march to the kitchenette.

'We need to find out if Karen Foster has a pager. We need to get hold of it and get it to our tech people,' he gabbled, 'that way we can place her at Sangora Road on the day of the murder.'

'Better still, why don't I just tell lover boy that we already have?' said Mick.

Shep nodded.

I chased him back to the viewing gallery. He got on the phone to Barratt, told him to track down Karen's work pager as a priority. He hung up and said: 'I wouldn't be surprised if the crafty bitch has already destroyed it. She's done her homework, that girl.'

Mick and Colin strolled into the suite, smiling and relaxed. Peter frowned in confusion. Mick switched on the tape recorder and Colin took up the slack.

'We're having a very good day, Peter,' he said brightly. 'We now have evidence that Laura was at the scene of Marion's murder.'

'And we now know where you and Karen were at the time Marion died,' added Mick, planting his pager on the table, 'thanks to the marvels of modern technology.'

Peter frowned.

'DS Mulroney has just placed his staff pager on the table,' Mick told the tape recorder.

'May I see yours?' Colin asked.

Peter visibly sagged, unclipped it and slid it across the table.

'We got hold of Karen's work pager a few days ago and let the tech boys do their work. Did you know that every pager message is relayed via the nearest transmitter? That means we can work out exactly where a pager has been. I must say, we were a little surprised to see where Karen spent her afternoon.'

Peter's hideous, hooked-fish face returned.

'Is there anything you'd like to tell us, Peter?'

Chapter 40

Clapham Police Station, South London
Sunday, August 18, 1991; 17:00

When Shep declared he'd be taking the interview with Terry Foster, neither Mick nor Colin looked remotely surprised.

'Don't you mind?' I asked Mick as we settled in the viewing gallery.

'Shep's like the cavalry,' he quipped, 'he loves riding in when all the hard work's been done.'

Terry sat bolt upright, rigid, defensive. Karen had clearly inherited his talent for sullenness. He was a short, slight man, which he compensated for by growing a scrubby beard and holding himself like a bantam cock – chest out, head wobbling, objectionable. His gaunt face radiated ill-health – a heavy smoker for sure. He wore black tracksuit bottoms, white trainers and a skin-tight grey Puma t-shirt which showed off his muscular arms, vein-green from faded tattoos.

'Shouldn't we get him a duty solicitor, even if he doesn't want one?' I asked. 'At least then he can't complain later?'

'Maybe he's ready to spill,' said Colin.

To me, Terry just looked ready to kill.

Shep strode in with his suit jacket on, tie Windsor-knotted, carrying his briefcase, all business. He sat down: 'How are you, Terry?'

'Fine,' snapped Terry.

'My name is Detective Superintendent Dan Shepard. You've elected to conduct this interview without a solicitor. Is that correct?'

'Correct,' said Terry.

'Fine. Just so you know, Terry, before we start, Karen's been talking, Laura's been talking and Peter's been talking. Do you understand?'

Terry shrugged.

'We now know, thanks to Peter Ryan, that Karen spent the afternoon of the murder in Bethan Trott's room at the Pines, as she's said all along. Except she wasn't watching telly with Bethan. She was having sex with Peter Ryan. She's what you people in South London would call a slag, isn't she, Terry?'

Terry's cheek clenched.

'Your Laura's a pretty girl, isn't she, Terry?'

'Fuck off,' spat Terry.

'Is she a slag too, Terry?'

'You're brave aren't you, copper? I bet you wouldn't talk to me like this outside.'

'I just ask because my colleagues at the Historic Sex Abuse team would love to get hold of the statement your Laura's just made.'

Terry shuffled uncomfortably.

'Imagine that, Terry? The South London press reporting that you've been charged with kiddie fiddling? Wouldn't be very good for business, would it, Terry? No one wants a paedo rinsing their kiddies' bedroom windows, do they? But that's what'll happen if you don't tell me the truth today. Do you understand?'

Terry glared at Shep, who now changed tack.

'The best thing you can do, Terry, is seek the mercy of a jury. Tell us how it all went wrong that day, how you'd no idea it would end the way it did. How you too are a victim.'

Before Terry had a chance to punch his lights out, Shep leaned over, switched on the tape recorder and announced who was in the room.

'Terry, please tell us all your movements from lunchtime on Monday July 1, 1991. And please, don't leave anything out.'

Terry coughed. 'I get home from work at about three, as usual, and leave my cleaning kit in the garage. At about quarter past, I'm watching the horse racing on telly when Laura comes in.'

353

Terry started breathing heavily through his nose.

'Where were your wife Pam and youngest daughter Stacey at this time?'

'Stace's at school, Pam's at her mum's.'

'Can you describe Laura's appearance?'

'Blue jeans and a black top with her hair tied up.'

'And how did she seem?'

'She's very agitated. She tells me Karen's being bullied at work by a woman. Laura wants to go to the Pines and have a word with this woman. I tell her I don't want anything to do with it.'

Terry's short breaths cranked up another notch.

'Please, Terry, go on.'

He shuffled in his seat again, his restless eyes looking everywhere but at Shep.

'She keeps going on and on. About what a shit dad I am, not even standing up for his own daughters. She winds me right up.'

Terry's heaving breaths now bordered on snorts.

'And?'

'I agreed to go with her. As far as I'm concerned, she's just gonna shake this woman up a bit. Give her a fright. Nothing like what happened.'

'Please, Terry, try to stick with the order of events if you can. I don't understand why you went with her at all?'

'Like I say, she says if I was a proper dad, I'd back her and Karen up.'

'*Have* you been a proper dad to your three daughters, Terry?'

'What do you mean by that?'

'Why would Laura accuse you of being a shit dad?'

'It's not easy is it? If you have kids then you'll know. They can be … trying.'

'I've got two daughters, Terry. But I don't get pissed and hit them like you do.'

Terry's eyes darted towards Shep, his head wobbling in rage. Shep lifted his chin defiantly: 'Or worse.'

'Oh, fuck off,' shouted Terry.

'Is this how you get, Terry? And now you're sober. Imagine that temper after a skinful.'

Terry grimaced, turned his head away from Shep and folded his arms: 'I don't have to listen to this shit.'

'Look, I know you're not a killer, Terry,' said Shep softly, 'I believe you when you say you didn't want to go with Laura that day. How did she make you go, Terry? What did she have on you?'

Terry's hog-like snorting returned.

'Maybe your lovely wife Pam could enlighten us? Or Lee social services?'

'They make things up, don't they?' Terry spat, 'and you can't prove a negative. You can't prove you never done the things they accuse you of.'

'What was Laura going to accuse you of, Terry? Who did she threaten to tell?'

'I never did any of the stuff she says. But people like to choose who to believe, don't they? And Laura's good at playing the victim, when it suits her.'

'I bet she is,' nodded Shep, 'so Laura blackmails you into going with her. What happens then?'

'I agree to drive her to the Pines. I go outside and get in the van. She comes out about five minutes later, carrying Karen's black gym bag.

'I drive her over to Lambeth. We get to the Pines about four. Laura tells me to park on the street outside and wait for her. She walks in past the car park barrier.'

'Where's the gym bag at this point?'

'Still in the van.'

'Go on, Terry.'

'Next thing Laura pulls up alongside the van in Karen's car. 'Get in and bring the bag,' she says. I get in and ask her what's going on. She tells me Karen's not well and the woman's gone home so we're gonna go talk to her there.

'She parks up to use a cash machine, then drives on to Clapham. At about five twenty, she pulls up near a pub and tells me this woman should be getting home any minute. She says she doesn't want a scene on the street. We're gonna go inside and wait for her.'

Terry grimaced and bent forward. He clamped his hands together and stared at them.

'I says to her "we're just gonna tell her to leave Karen alone, right? No rough stuff." She says "yeah, yeah, just a word. That's all it'll take." We go up the steps. Laura unlocks both doors and we go in. Laura leads me up the stairs. I follow her into a bedroom at the front of the flat. We stand there a few feet from the window, waiting for this woman to get home.'

He shivered, looked up at Shep then back down at his interlocked hands, now shaking wildly.

'Where was the gym bag?'

356

'I...' he faltered, 'she told me to bring it in with me.'

'Go on,' ordered Shep, sensing that Terry was at the top of a confessional drop.

Terry started breathing hard again, in short, greedy bursts.

'As Marion unlocks the front door, Laura tells me to get behind the bedroom door and wait until she calls me. As I'm stood there, I hear the bag unzip and her footsteps walking out onto the landing.'

Terry started blinking a lot, as if trying to bat away the images of these dreadful recollections.

'I hear the flat door open, Marion's feet coming up the stairs. I can see Laura through the crack in the door, crouching at the top of the stairs. Next thing, I hear a commotion...'

He squeezed his eyes shut and buried his face into his hands.

'Go on,' ordered Shep.

'I hear squealing, like cats fighting. I step out and see my steel ruler in Laura's hand, Marion crawling about on the landing, blood splashes on her face, her eyes wild, staring.'

Terry's eyes weren't focusing at all anymore. He was right back there.

'Laura's stalking her about the landing, saying: "That'll fucking teach you. That'll fucking teach you" over and over. I recognise the girl as Peter's wife. She came to ours for dinner once. I cry out: "Jesus, what have you done?"'

Each breath Terry now drew sounded more primeval, guttural, strangled than the last.

'Laura turns, glares at me, holding the ruler up

between us. I'm thinking: "She's gonna do me now." Then she focuses on the ruler and recoils, as if she's no idea what she's just done. Marion gets back on her feet. She's stumbling about. "Terry," she says, "Terry, please?" She's seen us both now.'

A bestial grunt formed deep in his guts, like a trapped soul. 'The girl, Marion, she's deranged. She lunges at me, scratches my eyes so hard she leaves a piece of her fingernail in my cheek. I lash out. Instinct, you know? That's when I realise I'd taken the knife off Laura. I've stabbed the girl in her hand. She's seen me now. She knows who I am. I can't go back inside. I have to finish her off.'

His face planted itself into the table and slid about helplessly on slobs of phlegm and snot and tears.

'Interview terminated, 18.08,' said Shep. He turned off the tape recorder, stood and inspected his stricken quarry.

'Shit,' said Mick, bolting to his feet and dashing to the door just ahead of Colin.

They reached the table just as Shep smashed Terry Foster's face into the table. Mick and Colin swallowed Shep in a bear hug and led him out of there, rage convulsing his whole frame like bolts of lightning.

Chapter 41

Clapham Police Station, South London
Sunday, August 18, 1991; 19:00

Terry and Laura Foster were charged with the murder of Marion Ryan. Karen Foster was charged with perverting the course of justice. All three were denied bail.

Shep disappeared into his office for forty minutes, then summoned a briefing. As he outlined the case against the Fosters, he seemed flat, sickened, as if soiled by the words he was delivering.

'Peter Ryan finally admitted today that both he and Karen Foster have a watertight alibi for the afternoon of Marion's murder after all: from about four fifteen until six p.m. on July 1st, they were shagging in Bethan Trott's room at the Pines care home. Of course neither of them wanted to admit it, right until the bitter end. It was only when we told Peter that we'd seized Karen's pager and worked out all her movements from the transmitters on the day that he finally coughed. That's not all he coughed to, but we'll come to that later.

'I have to be man enough at this point to say I became too focused on Karen Foster and it cost us valuable time and resources. McStay, Barratt, you were right. She didn't murder Marion Ryan. But there was a reason why Karen kept popping up in the frame. Her own sister was trying to frame her.

'A couple of days before the murder, Bethan Trott told Laura Foster that she was going to her mother's after lunch that Monday, July 1st, and planned to be back by six p.m. Laura told Karen this news because Laura knew what Karen would do next: invite Peter to the room for sex that afternoon. Remember, Peter himself has said that, once he and Marion moved out of the halls in January, he and Karen preferred using Bethan's room for their secret trysts as it was at the end of the corridor and out of sight. Karen's room was next door to the matron's.

'Laura knew that Peter Ryan kept the keys to his flat in his briefcase, which was usually in the shed on the care home grounds. So, let me run through Laura Foster's actions on the day.

'She got home at three p.m. and told her dad Terry that Karen was being bullied at work by a woman who she wanted to "sort out". When Terry refused to get involved, Laura threatened to tell her mum about something Terry had done to either her or one of her sisters. We might never get to the bottom of that, but it must have been pretty damning to give her that kind of leverage.

'Terry agreed to drive Laura to the Pines in his work van, he thought to confront this woman who'd been bullying Karen. Before they left, Laura grabbed a black gym bag. When they reached the Pines, Laura told Terry to park up on the street outside and wait for her. Laura got out of the van and went inside the home. Ten to fifteen minutes later, she pulled up alongside Terry's van in Karen's car, wearing shades and a red top, told

360

him to grab the gym bag and get in.

'I will argue that Laura Foster went to the shed to retrieve the keys to Peter and Marion's flat, then went to Karen's room – remember, she had a key and her sister was with Peter in Bethan's room – changed into her sister's clothes, got hold of her sister's car keys, car park pass and ATM card.

'She used Karen's pass to get out of the car park, pulled up next to Terry and told him that Karen wasn't feeling very well. She said that the bully had already gone home and that Karen had asked them to go speak to her there. Terry got into the car with the gym bag.

'Here's where Laura decided to gamble. She parked just up the road from the Pines and used her sister's bank card to withdraw ten pounds. She knew this would demolish both their alibis but had already decided that both Karen and Marion had to be taken out of the equation, and this was the only way.

'Laura pulled up outside the Roundhouse pub. She and Terry unlocked both doors into the Ryan flat and waited for Marion, Terry behind a bedroom door, Laura up front on the landing. They must have both been wearing gloves.

'When Terry heard Laura attack Marion he came out of his hiding place and realised Laura had stabbed her with the metal ruler he used for work. But she was still alive and she knew them both. Fearing a return to prison, he flipped and finished Marion off.

'Laura had already packed a change of clothes for them both. She changed back into the black

361

top she'd worn earlier, then drove them back to the clinic, dropped Terry off on the street and entered the car park. Right at the entrance, she spotted a woman emerging from reception who knew her and Karen. She stopped the car so that this woman couldn't get a good look at her. It worked; that witness later assumed she'd seen Karen.

'After Peter set off to clean the fish tanks, Laura got Karen out of Bethan's room, greeted Bethan from the balcony and let her in. Laura told Bethan both she and Karen had been in her room since five. She left the gym bag in Bethan's room because she knew she could bully and control Bethan. She had a two-hour window at that point to get the bank card, car keys, car park pass and shades back to Karen's room, so that her sister wouldn't suspect a thing.

'Laura knew how crucial Bethan's testimony would be. That's why she put on such a show of grief when she heard the news about Marion in Bethan's room. That's why, the next day, she made sure Karen came with her when she retrieved the bag from Bethan's room.

'Laura must have been gutted when Glenn and his team ruled Karen out as a suspect. Five weeks later, when we started sniffing around, asking about Peter and Karen's relationship, Laura saw her chance. She'd been controlling Bethan all along. Remember, she made Bethan provide the original alibi for both of them. It's at this point it becomes clear now just how well Laura Foster has played us.

'On the evening of the murder, Laura made

sure she got Karen out of Bethan's room before Bethan got back. By making sure Bethan didn't see Karen, she could later prime Bethan about her "suspicions" about Karen's involvement in the murder. Laura told Bethan about the times she'd caught Karen in her room eavesdropping on Peter and Marion. She told Bethan the hints Karen had dropped about what Peter was up to behind his wife's back. She told Bethan about the time she saw Peter and Karen going into the shed together to have sex. She told Bethan she couldn't shop her own sister to the police. Bethan had to pretend to be the one who'd seen and heard these things.

'Remember the list?'

Shep produced a piece of paper from his inside pocket.

'Bethan said she found this under her bed. It is a handwritten list of all the presents Peter bought Marion for her birthday in October last year, with the words "sick sick sick" scrawled at the bottom. Remember, this single sheet of paper set us on the trail of Karen and led to us finding out about the affair with Peter and Marion's plans to move to Ireland. Well, guess what? I've had this examined. The list was written by Laura Foster.

'I've just spoken to Bethan Trott. It took me ten minutes to convince her Laura was in custody before she'd open up. She admitted providing the sisters with the original alibi because she was scared of Laura. Once she'd told that lie, Laura had the power to make her tell more. It seems like Laura was especially proficient at playing "good cop, bad cop". On one hand, she told Bethan that she was doing the right thing by leading the police to Marion's killer, Karen. On the other hand, she threatened to expose her original lie if she didn't go along with everything Laura said. Bethan was so scared of being charged with perverting the course of justice, and so scared of Laura, that she did exactly as she was told.'

I thought back to Shep's bullying of Bethan during her interview: we'd played right into Laura's hands.

Shep took a breather, pacing about to reflect on the course of events.

'So why did Karen keep lying? Did Karen know that Laura and Terry were going to Marion's home to "sort her out" that afternoon? I will argue that she didn't. Terry only made the decision that day on the spur of the moment. It all comes back to Laura. She wanted Karen out of the way so she could frame her for the murder.

'Did Laura tell Karen what happened afterwards? How it had all got out of hand? Of course not. She was too busy framing her. Did Karen or Peter suspect that her sister and dad had murdered Marion? Again, I don't think it's a line worth pursuing.

'One thing is certain. Karen never suspected that her own sister was trying to set her up. All Karen feared was the exposure of her affair with Peter and how it might look. That's why she stuck to the alibi that she and Laura had been shopping that day. Laura would have assured her, over and over: they can't get you for this because you didn't do it. But she also drummed into Karen what she'd already used to brainwash

Bethan: "All they can get us for now is lying, so we must stick to our stories." So they did.'

Shep stopped walking, frowned and turned: 'You know something, if we hadn't found Laura's trainer print on the flat door at 21, we never would have cracked this case. When I asked Peter Ryan how Laura's shoe print might have got there he exhibited, for the first time in this whole sorry episode, a tinsy slither of shame. After six weeks pissing us about, he suddenly came clean: the day before the murder, while Marion was visiting her folks in Enfield, he fucked Laura Foster in their bedroom, in their sitting room, in their kitchen, in their bathroom and, on her way out, against the flat door.'

Chapter 42

The Roundhouse Pub, South London
Sunday, August 18, 1991; 20:00

I called Lilian from the Roundhouse pub and told her I had big news. She told me she'd be there in fifteen minutes.

The rest of the team were in the Falcon. I'd join them later, after I tied up my life's loose ends.

I ordered another pint and thought about everything that had happened over the past seven weeks. I was in no doubt that Marion's spirit had directed me to two key clues in the case. The first had been Karen's unwitting admission that she'd parked twice near Marion's home on the day of the murder. From that point on, I knew Marion had been steering me towards her killers, I'd simply guessed the wrong one.

Had she not persisted in pointing me towards the door to her flat, we never would have made the breakthrough with Laura's trainer. It was illogical, an affront to science. But it was true.

I thought about poor Samantha and Jazmine Bisset. Why hadn't they come to me? I resolved to do all I could to help them, even if it meant returning to the scene of their murders and risking the wrath of their restless souls. Whatever I'd suffer would pale in comparison to the warped depravity of their wretched deaths.

My thoughts then turned to Meehan, three long years ago. What the hell had he wanted with me? Would I ever get to the bottom of the event that started this whole thing? Had he somehow opened up this channel to me from the other side?

Lilian turned up, humanised by free-flowing hair and a yellow summer dress. She smiled and threw me a little hand wave, both catching me by surprise.

We got straight down to business. I felt empowered relaying my extraordinary story as she wrote feverishly, obediently recording every detail. When I finished milking the udders of my undoubtedly unique gift, I asked her what she thought.

'I've already written most of the paper,' she announced breathlessly, 'the only thing missing is you uncovering hard evidence as a direct result of a sleep paralysis episode. This is the missing link, but I can finish it now. I really think I might be able to get it published.'

'Can I read it, when you're done?'

'Of course,' she said.

'And just so we're straight on this, you're definitely not revealing my identity.'

'I promised,' she sighed. 'I call you The Empathist, because you clearly identify with these victims. It's like you feel their agony.'

'The Empathist,' I said, giving it a good roll around my mouth, 'I like it.'

Then, adopting film trailer gravitas, I announced: 'In a world where tormented souls seek justice, one man offers hope.'

Lilian laughed, properly. It felt like my biggest breakthrough yet, so I ploughed on, genetically compelled to spoil a good gag: 'Paramount pictures presents: The Empathist.'

Cue dead-joke awkward silence. I should have bailed out when I was on top.

'So what now, Doc?'

She took a deep breath: 'Well, I've done all I can do for you, clinically speaking.'

'So I am no longer your patient?'

'I am no longer your psychologist,' she announced, holding out her hand. I smiled and shook it.

'My God,' I thought to myself, 'this woman knows the real me and doesn't seem to hate me or find me terrifying. And now, just like that, our relationship is over. I've confided in her, spilled my guts. I can't just let her slip away.'

'So, you've done all you can for me clinically,' I

teased, 'but I think there's still work to be done, emotionally. I'm not at all well in that department.'

This silence felt less awkward, more cringing. Finally, Lilian reached for her drink, then changed her mind.

'I'd really like to get to know you better, Donal,' she said, choosing her words carefully, 'I think you're a really nice guy.'

I stopped myself saying *but?* She'd clearly figured this all out already.

'There are strict rules about this sort of thing. The Association expressly forbids us from starting any kind of relationship with a patient until at least two years after we've finished treating them. Even a friendship.'

My brain recoiled: two years? Two. Whole. Years. 'But you weren't treating me. I was helping you,' I argued, a little too pleadingly.

'But if my paper gets published, and they find out I'm involved with the patient, no one would take my research seriously. There's a good chance I'd get struck off before I even qualify. I can't risk that.'

'Fine, then. I'm withdrawing my permission.'

That felt good.

'What?'

'Listen, Lilian, I've made up my mind, I don't want you to publish anything about me or my condition.'

'What? Oh my God. So this is the real you, is it, Donal? You try it on with me and when I turn you down you ... fuck me over?'

She wanted me to say no. I couldn't.

368

'Well I'm glad I got to see the real you before anything more developed.'

'Yeah well, you give yourself a big slap on the back for working that much out, Doctor. What a brilliant reader of minds you are. Like I said, I'm expressly forbidding you from publishing anything about me and my condition.'

'It's too late for that, Donal,' she said, quietly but firmly, holding my glare.

'What?'

'That day you first came to me, you signed a waiver which permits me to publish anything about your treatment, providing I don't identify you.'

My mind rewound to that first appointment, those papers. 'You can't do that ... I have rights.'

'Oh I can, Donal,' she said, getting to her feet, 'and I will. Here.'

She snatched a file out of her bag, slung it on the table and stomped off.

'Hang on, Lilian,' I called, leaping to my feet and scaring the shit out of the Roundhouse regulars.

'Lilian?' I roared, as the final person who cared about me left the building.

I opened the file and found her cover note. In psychotically neat handwriting, Lilian explained how she'd failed to get hold of my medical records but, remembering that Mum is insomniac, applied and received hers from Tullamore General Hospital. She warned that the file contains a lot of information about my traumatic birth. Her conclusion: 'I really think you should get a CT scan on your skull AT ONCE, to check for intracranial pressure which is a common cause of severe insomnia.'

She'd added pink Post-it notes in the relevant areas, helpfully explaining the content. This exercise must have taken her at least a couple of hours. I started to feel bad.

The headlines: I came out of my mother too quickly, too early. She'd suffered perineum and rectal tearing (no explanation given, nor sought) and life-threatening blood loss. She was found unconscious on the kitchen floor and required intensive care treatment. A surgeon had to re-open her cervix by hand to release the placenta.

Had I finally found the root of my dad's contempt for me? I'd almost killed his wife, probably killed their love life and killed stone dead the chance of more children. In all likelihood, Martin had to explain himself to the local priest, who'd be wondering why there wasn't a conveyor belt of Lynches.

Because of the speed of my exit, I suffered a suspected diastatic fracture to my lambdoid suture. Lilian's microscopic, precise notes explained that the skull is made up of eight cranial bones, separated by fibrous joints called sutures that fully close at different stages of your life. The lambdoid suture is the one that runs horizontally around the back of your skull – about halfway – and should fully close by the time you reach forty. Lilian explained that a diastatic fracture may have caused a widening of the lambdoid suture, and that I should get this checked out.

Through the pub chatter wafted those words from my youth.

If you stand between the window and the body during this time, then God help you.

Had this spider-web fault line in my skull acted as some sort of spirit catcher for restless souls seeking peace? Was my brain a living purgatory for the pilgrim spirits of the recent dead?

Another Post-it explained that I'd suffered craniosynostosis, caused when other sutures close too quickly. This causes pressure in the skull, which can lead to extreme headaches and sleeping problems.

Another typed column showed that Mum was first prescribed benzodiazepine sleeping tablets four months after my birth. And since then she'd been prescribed a Latin phrasebook of pharmaceuticals – which she still took to this day. I'd read how over-prescription of these pills in the Seventies and Eighties led to thousands of middle-aged addicts suffering depression, painful withdrawal and, ironically, insomnia.

The horror sank in quickly. I had been the root cause of Mum's insomnia and need for drugs, drugs that exacerbated her insomnia so that it was now killing her. No wonder Dad hated me.

Poor Mum had never told me any of this, or ever blamed me. I managed not to burst out crying until I got to the loo.

I paged Shep and told him to meet me at the Roundhouse, right now.

I leaned forward and felt the reassuring weight of the bar pushing back, my hands enjoying its cool smoothness. I was ready.

'That was a masterstroke about the trainers,

371

Lynch. How did you even think of that?' said Shep, clambering upon a stool beside me.

For once, I didn't feel myself redden.

'I've been really impressed with your work, son. Stick with me and you could go far.'

My drained, streaked-white Guinness glass needed no cue. He ordered another and a double Glenfiddich for himself. Again, he eschewed anything that might give his drink a leisurely twist. Water, say, or a cube of ice. I doubted that Shep ever did anything simply for pleasure: every action had to somehow reinforce his image of himself. Shep was basically a socially-adjusted psychopath, like Fintan.

He raised his drink: 'Here's to a very important pair of collars,' he said, and I clinked.

He took a sip. I took a long draw, relishing the burnt-barley taste, toasting my burnt ties.

As we sat there side-by-side, Shep intertwined his fingers and started twirling his thumbs. I imagined the cogs in his brain grinding hard, working out his next play.

'We have a problem,' Shep finally said, glancing over to me.

'If this is about Fintan's story,' I started, but Shep put his hand on my arm, indicating that I should shut up.

He reached inside his suit jacket and pulled out a piece of paper. He laid it out on the bar in front of me. 'What's this?' I asked.

'Phone records,' said Shep, 'from the incident room. The records show you rang the *Sunday News* at 4.23 p.m. yesterday.'

My mind flashed back: getting the note to call

Fintan, his insistence that he hadn't left any such message.

'How do you know it was me?'

'Because the receptionist has confirmed that you were the only member of the team who stayed behind. She watched you making the call. She heard you say Fintan's name.'

Round one to Shep.

I suppressed my swelling rage. I had to box clever here, play Shep at his own game. I picked up the records and scoured them. There it was, in black and white, the record of my call to Fintan's direct line.

I stuck to the facts: 'It says the call lasted less than a minute, hardly enough time for me to pass on a thoroughly detailed story. Not to mention copies of her statement and a wedding video.'

Shep had already thought of this, of course: 'But enough time to arrange a meeting. Did you meet Fintan on Saturday evening?'

I said nothing, but realised he'd trapped me.

'If you did, then it doesn't look very good for you, does it, Lynch?'

Shep was now doing to me what he'd done to the Fosters. He was building a case piecemeal, skilfully creating a comprehensive picture out of fragments of truth and supposition. Jigsaw Justice.

He likes to own people. All of the guys in his team owe him in some way.

'I got a message to call him, Guv. I didn't speak to him about this case. I've never spoken to him about any case. And I didn't leak him Karen's statement or the wedding video. I've never had access to the exhibits cupboard.'

'Everyone knows where the key to that cupboard is,' spat Shep.

Shep scooped up the phone record sheet and presented it to me: 'There is only one other copy, which I've put in a very safe place. Feel free to destroy this.'

'Why would you do this for me, Guv?'

'Let's just say you owe me a favour,' he said.

Shep picks up waifs and strays and turns them into his bitches.

I had two choices. I could take the phone record sheet, keep the peace and learn a vital lesson about how Shep operated. Or I could show him that I wasn't prepared to be anybody's bitch. I had plenty of dirt on him now. When I had pinned Fintan against his bachelor pad earlier today, he finally coughed about how the racket at the Feathers worked. How he and Shep worked.

Fintan admitted that Seamus – the pub manager – had been acting as a middle man between him and his police sources for about four months, passing messages and money. It soon transpired that Seamus was a double agent, also working for Shep, who knew about every single officer on Fintan's payroll.

Fintan had expected Shep to put an end to the racket, maybe even press charges. Instead, Shep approached each officer on the take and let them know he could destroy their careers. Before long, Shep was in control of the whole racket, deciding what these officers would and wouldn't leak. Shep never made a penny out of it. But he took down a few rivals and ducked a few scandals.

Shep owned their arses. Now he thought he

could own mine.

'I know you leaked the story to Fintan,' I said.

Shep's reflex turn gave him away.

'I'd be very careful, making unsubstantiated claims like that, Lynch,' Shep said slowly, menacingly.

'I followed you yesterday. I saw you meeting Fintan, here.'

'Lynch, I'd strongly advise you to stop right there. That is an outrageous allegation.'

'Do you remember when you walked out of here? You saw a taxi over there, to your left? You started to hail it, then stopped when you realised he didn't have his light on. I was in the back of that taxi.'

Shep picked up his glass, took a swig, then planted it back on the table, hard.

'You can't prove a thing,' he spat.

'I've made friends with that taxi driver,' I lied, 'he's the smart, observant type. He's confident he could pick you both out of a line-up.'

'So I happened to be in a pub at the same time as your brother. What does that prove? Nothing. I didn't even know he was here.'

'It wouldn't look good for you though, would it, Guv?'

'Don't cross me, Lynch. I could destroy you like that.' His finger snapped like a bone.

'Of course, I'd probably only raise the matter if I was directly accused of leaking a story to my brother.'

Shep placed his hands to his lips as if in prayer. He stared hard into his scotch.

'You know something, Donal,' he said, 'you're

not that different from your brother.'

'I'm beginning to learn to see the angles,' I said, sounding and feeling grubby.

He stood, drained his glass and slammed it down hard on the shiny counter.

'People are now saying McStay is the leaker,' he said, and strode off.

Chapter 43

Trinity Road, South London
Sunday, August 18, 1991; 22:30

Had Laura and Terry Foster greeted me at my front door that evening wielding pared-down steel rulers, I would have felt more hospitable.

'I'm not in the mood, Eve,' I snapped.

'Donal, please, I just want to explain a few things.'

I decided to hear her out. My ego badly needed some contrition, and my inner martyr demanded to know how and why my ex-girlfriend had started shagging my older brother, in her own words.

'I'll let you in on one condition, Eve,' I said, 'I want total honesty. No more lies. Do you understand?'

She nodded, her eyes damp, her bottom lip quivering like a scolded toddler. Here was a woman unused to begging.

After all that had happened today, I felt cold, hard, untouchable. No more Mister Nice Guy.

Let's get ready to rumble.

We stood in the kitchen, face-to-face. She was dressed for housekeeping: jeans, green jumper, hair tied up. I wheeled round to make sure I was closer to the cutlery drawer, and did a quick scan of the sink for any potentially homicidal objects: thankfully all clear.

'The thing is, Donal, Fintan really was my only friend in the world, you know, when things got really bad. You wanted to help but you weren't even in the country. I felt so ... alone. We started a relationship, by accident really. We kept it secret. We had to, even from you. We knew if anyone found out, it would totally compromise Fintan, and me. They'd have used it to destroy me.'

'I don't understand.'

'Think about it. I couldn't be the rape victim and be having a relationship, especially with a reporter who got all the exclusives. I had to play the victim all the way, until I saw it through. I still have to play the victim now, or they'll find a way to send me back to prison. I'm on a suspended sentence. They could dream up any reason to send me back.'

I felt disorientated, in need of an emotional standing count. I was struggling to keep up with the political intrigue and Machiavellian shenanigans, which now seemed the very lifeblood of her and Fintan's existence.

I watched her look through my eyes into some dark, buried memory. 'I promise you, no matter what it takes, I am never going back there.'

Then she snapped back to now: 'But someone did find out about us. Fintan didn't tell me who,

377

but they threatened to expose our relationship. Fintan gambled that they knew about us, but couldn't prove it. That's why Fintan left so suddenly and came to London.

'He didn't even call me, for months. I understood he had to protect himself, but I started to get paranoid. Did he want to make a clean break? Was I too much hassle? When I turned up last week at the Archway, he seemed so ... put out. I thought to myself: "Eve, you've been a fool." He'd gotten his stories out of me; I was no use to him anymore. He didn't want this burden, because that's what I am now to everyone, a burden.'

She blinked fast but that failed to stop a tear breaking through, carving a wet scar down her left cheek. All of me wanted to go to her. Instead, I held firm, inviting my newfound hard-nosed cynicism to take a sniff, see if it could detect the real story flitting between her words.

I felt certain Fintan had been shagging Eve just to get her exclusives. He recognised her as his meal ticket to Fleet Street. When there was nothing left to milk, he invented some know-all nemesis bent on exposing them just so he could scarper. He never expected her to beat the rap and follow him over; he'd said so himself. Then, when she turned up at the Archway, he realised a shocking truth: he could be saddled with her for good. He was all she had in the world, for fuck's sake.

My frown told Eve that I'd caught up, so she carried on.

'One morning last week, I had it out with him. He said he wasn't ready for anything "too heavy". After all the promises he'd made to me, I couldn't believe it. I stormed out. I then realised you were the only person in the world who gives a shit about me. So I found out where you lived and came to see you.'

I suddenly felt a step or two behind the action.

'Then, when you and me spent time together this week...' She broke into a full-on sob, burying her face into a hand. 'You're so kind and funny. I remembered why I fell in love with you,' came her muffled tribute. 'I began to think that the only reason I ended up with Fintan was because he reminded me of you.'

I couldn't stop my ego climbing off its stretcher and performing a series of somersaults around the kitchen. *Yes that's right,* it boomed, *in a straight shoot-out with my older bro, I was the better man.*

Eve sniffed back her composure. Finally she looked up, her wet eyes seeking out mine.

'Then when your friend Gabby came around, I realised that I couldn't just expect to pick up where we'd left off. She obviously has strong feelings for you. You didn't want me anymore. I'd nowhere else to go but back to Fintan.'

This was the cue I needed to ask another critical question: in between shagging my older brother, had she been terrorising my fledgling girlfriend? You know, sending her newspaper cuttings to underline her murderous credentials, slashing her clothes. My film noir alter-ego wanted to ask her out straight. The rest of me settled for gentle probing.

'Speaking of Gabby, some weird stuff's been happening to her.'

379

'What do you mean, weird stuff?'

'Someone's been sending her newspaper cuttings, about you. Old articles about the trial.'

Her eyes and mouth fell open.

'Who the fuck would do something like that?' she snapped. I could see the red mist swirling. 'Jesus, you don't think it was me do you?'

I knew Eve well enough to recognise genuine indignation and felt strangely vindicated: of course it hadn't been Eve.

'She has this ex-boyfriend,' I reasoned, 'a bit of a stalker. He's obviously tracked down her new address. He must be doing this from abroad. Speaking of which, how did you find out where I lived?'

Eve searched my face, weighing up how I'd cope with bad news.

'I rang your mum,' she said quickly.

My defences sprang up: 'You did what?' I felt like screaming.

'You don't mind do you, Donal? I've always really liked her and I didn't know who else to ask.'

'What did she say?'

Eve grimaced. I braced myself.

'She sounded in a bad way. She really needs to see you, Donal. She didn't say as much, but I could tell...'

The flimsy dam I'd hastily constructed to block Mum out gave way, sending guilt gushing through me like a mountain stream.

'Why don't you go see her?' said Eve, mirroring my desperation. 'There must be a way.'

I couldn't think how: not with Martin still capable of whisky-fuelled fisticuffs.

'She sounded so lonely,' Eve said quietly.

How could I have done this? I'd cut Mum out, my only ally. I didn't need Martin's permission to see my own mother. Fuck him. Eve seemed to be reading my mind.

'Your dad doesn't even have to know. You can stay at the bungalow, meet your mum in town?'

This sounded too weird, even for me, but Eve had already made up her mind. 'I'll call the rental people. Just let me know the dates. It's no problem at all.'

Her voice softened. She moved closer, her hand touching mine: 'You need to reconnect with your mum. It'll be good for you.'

'You're right,' I said, squeezing it and realising no one else knew me like Eve.

She leaned into me, her cool skin still smelling of fresh pines. 'You do know that today was the day three years ago we were supposed to move to London? August 18th.'

I couldn't believe she'd remembered. After all she'd been through.

'The 18th of the 8th, '88,' I whispered.

'If you want to try, again,' she breathed, 'I know we can make it work.'

I knew already. Deep down, part of me realised that I could never move on with my life until I gave it one more go with Eve Daly. Nor could she move on with hers. My brain just couldn't fathom how my gut felt so certain of this.

I turned my lips to hers. Both our mouths opened, ready to kiss. As I leaned in, she turned away.

'I'm sorry, Donal,' she said, 'but I have to finish with Fintan first, properly. I want to tell him we're

381

back together. If we're going to make this work, we've got to do everything the right way, by the book, right from the start. I'm done with lying and sneaking around. Let's do it right this time.'

Chapter 44

Dublin Airport
One Week Later

I had arranged a secret rendezvous with Mum tomorrow afternoon at Tullamore's Bridge House Hotel. I couldn't wait for a proper face-to-face. I now knew the debt I owed her, one which I would spend forever trying to repay.

Tonight's plans were altogether less straight-forward. As promised, Eve had put me in touch with the rental company, and I'd managed to get the old Daly bungalow for the weekend. I then paid a week's wages for a tiny hire car and headed West. Soon, a low, grey Tupperware sky levelled the land. The air thickened, dampened. I wound down the windows: all that yawning was wearing me out.

I stopped off in Kinnegad and bought four bottles of the only red plonk I could find. As I loaded them into the boot, I unzipped my travel bag to check that the Grade A skunk I'd rolled inside a pair of socks had come through un-scathed. I now had all the tools I needed for tonight's mission.

When forensics had found Laura Foster's unique footprint on the flat door of 21 Sangora Road, I had felt certain that Marion had directed me to the clue from the other side. This seemed confirmed to me when, a few days ago, I returned to the murder scene. I didn't tell the unwitting new tenants why I needed to examine their landing. I just flashed my badge and hung about for ten minutes. Every time I'd attended that address in the past, Marion's raging spirit had appeared to me later. But that night, she didn't come. I'd done it. I'd caught her killers.

But there was one ghost I still needed to exorcise. My personal bogeyman. If I didn't, I was scared that he'd always be there, waiting in the corners of my dreams.

I turned left off the Dublin–Galway road for the last leg. Now I'd learned how to prolong the sleep paralysis experience – lots of red wine and weed – I no longer felt scared. I was ready. Tonight felt make-or-break: *come to me, Tony Meehan.*

As I approached Tullamore, a soft rain made the windscreen squint. I welcomed the watery cover. It would take just one sighting for my arrival to become known to all. I wasn't here on a homecoming tour. I was here to make peace with Mum and, in a weird way, Tony Meehan.

I turned right into the tiny lane that led to Frank Daly's vanity project. More spanking-new, splayed-out bungalows leered at me from both sides of the boreen. I turned into Daly's driveway: the house looked smaller than I'd remembered it, dwarfed now by the sparkling white mini-mansions all round it.

I parked up. The house keys swung gently in the back door. Just five hours ago, I'd been in South London: this was another world. I saw my distorted face in the back door's window and remembered that night, cooling my raging skin on this glass. I turned to look at the crazy paving and the pebbledashed shed. The blood from my scrabbling, minced hands had long since been soaked up by the interminable damp air.

I stepped inside. It looked the same but it didn't feel the same. The family furniture had been replaced by processed, generic Ikea products. It felt cold, empty, unloved, making us perfect holiday companions. Eve's old bedroom now contained a single bed and a cot. My eye snagged on a single familiar item: the clock radio. I picked it up and cradled it in disbelief. How many times had I visualised this clock, my fellow witness to the events of that fateful night?

It was just gone seven p.m., a good time to light the fire, hit the couch and uncork bottle one.

By nine thirty, the sun had fallen behind the Slieve Bloom mountains and bottle number two had dropped below the label: surely the signal to roll a big fat Tullamore Torpedo.

At about midnight, the national anthem heralded TV closedown. I stood and clutched my chest. Just as *Amhran na bhFiann* reached its vainglorious climax, I zapped the TV off and laughed: in the Irish pubs of North London, that type of behaviour would get you murdered.

I basked then in the vast, suffocating quiet. A tree branch creaked. A dog barked into the void. Something rattled in the roof. The lamp went

384

out, causing my heart to race.

'Fuck,' I said, just to break the silence. I walked over to the light switch, flicked once, then twice – nothing.

'A power cut, great. Just perfect,' I told the house.

I reminded myself how much I was being charged per night and rang the rental company's emergency number. No one answered, so I left a rambling message. I'd have to wait until morning. Now I had just the light of the fire to work with, so I threw on two more logs.

'Could be worse,' I told myself, uncorking bottle number three and rekindling the Torpedo. I decided to lie back on the couch so that I faced the door. Say what you like about these psychopathic spirits, but they've got manners: they always come through the door.

The room felt thick with smoke so I stabbed out the joint. I laid back, willing the chemical swimmers through.

Out of nowhere, a slamming sound jolted me upright. My heart broke into a jog. Not so calm now hey, Donal? I could hear footsteps in the hallway, slow but deliberate, getting closer and closer. My ribcage seemed to shrink until it strangled my thrashing heart. The fire hissed like a snake. This was no fucking dream.

I looked up to see him standing at the doorway. Terror riveted my guts like a nail gun. My brain screamed: 'Get up. Run.' But I was rooted to the couch. Frozen.

I couldn't see his eyes: just his silhouette creeping closer, closer. Now I felt myself backing up

385

against the arm of the couch. I could move. Had I come out of my body?

I screamed with all my might and scrambled over the back of the seat, knocking over the bottle of wine.

The figure kept coming, steady, relentless, determined. It was then that I saw the knife glinting in his hand. I palmed the floor, scooped up an empty bottle in my right hand.

'Come on then,' I roared but the fucker kept coming, zombie-like.

Suddenly, swirling bright lights illuminated the room for a split second.

'What the fuck?' I cried, recognising those eyes.

I lurched forward, incensed, then found myself free-falling through cold, streaking lights into dark, darker black. I hoped to Christ it was the cataplexy.

Chapter 45

Tullamore, County Offaly, Ireland
Tuesday, August 27, 1991; 00:06

My eyelids opened, fighting against blinding yellow light. They swooned and rolled, trying to fix on a shape or a colour.

Slowly, a face came into focus. Eve's face.

'What the fuck?' I mouthed.

'It's okay, Donal,' said Eve, 'you'll be fine. Just take it easy, I'm here now.'

These should have been the sweetest words I'd ever heard. But not after what I'd just realised.

'Lie back, Donal,' she ordered, bossy now.

I defied her, sitting up to survey my body. A cough spluttered out from deep inside. A twinge twisted my gut and sharpened my mind.

'What the hell happened?' I asked, coherent now.

A balding, friendly-faced guy trotted in merrily from the hallway, screwdriver in hand. 'Ah good man, you've come to.'

I looked at him, then looked at Eve.

'I can't mix the blow and the booze at all,' he said. 'I'm like Woody Allen, I spend the rest of the night trying to take my trousers off over my head!'

'Who are you?' I asked.

'I'm Pete,' he said, coming over and shaking my hand, 'from Irish Getaway. I missed your call earlier. I tried to call you back but the phone seemed to be dead. I thought I'd better come over and make sure you're okay. Eve here explained that you've, er, overdone it a bit.'

I sat up and took another deep breath. I realised that this handyman had proved very handy indeed. He didn't know it, but he'd just saved my life.

'The power went out... Pete, listen to me, please don't leave me here, with her,' I said. Pete looked at me strangely. He then looked at Eve as if to say: 'This guy is mashed.'

He looked back at me: 'Ah now, listen my friend, I think you're maybe a bit paranoid from the hash. Take it easy, alright?'

He had no idea what he'd interrupted. Pre-vented.

'Is the phone working?' I asked, getting up.

'That's the funny thing,' said Pete, raising an eyebrow as if I was taking the piss, 'someone cut the line just outside the house.'

'And why did the power go off?'

'Er, someone pulled a fuse out,' he said, still looking at me like I might be yanking his chain. Then he turned to Eve: 'Are you sure you're gonna be okay, love?'

'Yeah, fine Pete, thanks,' said Eve, giving him her most reassuring smile.

'Right so, as long as you're sure, because I could really do with getting off. I'll get the phone people out tomorrow.'

He looked at me again, with a mixture of pity and concern. My eyes pleaded with him not to leave.

'Please don't go, Pete – I think she's trying to kill me.'

'Go, Pete, for the love of God,' laughed Eve, 'he'll be alright when he gets some sleep.'

'Grand then. Okay, you two have a good night now,' said Pete, backing out of the door hesitantly.

'Thanks, Pete,' I said, not taking my eyes off Eve. I reached down behind the couch for a fallen wine bottle and tried to work out where she'd stashed the knife.

As soon as the front door shut, she ran. I set off after her, my mind trying to process what had happened. My first thought: she's got rid of the knife and is racing to the kitchen to get another. My second: she's trying to escape. As she got close to the kitchen door, I launched myself.

We slid against the back door as one. I yanked her over, face-up, gripped her throat and held the bottle over her face like a primed axe.

'What the fuck, Eve?' I roared into her face.

'Why are you doing this to me?' she demanded.

'You were going to stab me!'

'I don't know what you're talking about. You're scaring me now, Donal. Get off me.'

My mind raced. I knew what I'd seen: Eve coming for me, with a knife. Only the headlights of Pete's van had saved me. Had he not swung into the driveway at that very moment, I'd be lying on that couch now, bleeding to death with no way of phoning for help. That hadn't been any sort of sleep paralysis episode. Eve had set me up to be here, so she could kill me.

'You know I can't just let you walk away from this, Eve, as if nothing happened? I have to arrest you for attempted murder.'

'No one will ever believe you,' she hissed.

'What?'

'I've known Pete for years. I told him you'd been smoking weed and drinking and started hallucinating. I told him you got so paranoid that you cut the phone line and shut off the power. He was worried sick about me. He refused to leave until you came to. He wanted to make sure you weren't going to do something stupid.'

Fireworks exploded in my head.

'Go on, hit me with the bottle,' she gloated, 'strangle me. They'll put you away.'

'Hang on a second, you just tried to...'

'Go on,' she said, 'call the Guards. Tell them

what you think you saw. I'll say you were tripping because you were high. Look at the state of the place. Look at the state of you! I've got your thumbprints on my neck. I could tell a very different story, far more believable than yours. Pete will back me up. You haven't got a prayer.'

'Don't be ridiculous,' I spat, 'I'm a police officer. And let's not forget, you have form for this.'

'You invited me for the weekend, got pissed and stoned, confronted me about my affair with your brother and flipped out. Pete will back me up and he's the only witness.'

My grip weakened on her throat, my mind feeling like a bank of footlights all panning in different directions. She was right. How would any of this sound to a Guard? To a judge and jury? Fair play, she'd set me up beautifully.

'Okay, let's say we don't call the Guards,' I said, removing my hand from her throat but keeping the bottle poised, 'just tell me why, Eve. Why were you going to do that to me?'

'I knew you wouldn't just leave it alone,' she rasped bitterly, rubbing her throat. 'Tony's visits. I knew your prying copper's mind would have to work it all out...'

'What were you scared I'd find out, Eve?'

'I'm not going back to prison. Ever. No matter what it takes,' she almost recited.

'What is it Meehan's been trying to tell me?'

Her cold hateful eyes held back, but her sneering mouth couldn't wait to deliver the lacerations her knife had failed to.

'I was never going to go to London with you. Did you really think I could face Daddy after

390

what he did to us? And have to look at that slut Sandra Kelly? I was going to New York. They'd even sent me the ticket. I just didn't know how to tell you. God, you just wouldn't fucking listen.'

The universe flipped over like a coin. Strength gushed out of me until I heard my wine bottle weapon shatter on the wooden floor.

'I was going to announce it at the party, get it off my chest. But then of course you got wasted and carted off to hospital.'

I dismounted, unable to feel the floor beneath my feet. She sat up, coughed hard.

'Come on, Eve, get to the point. What's he trying to tell me?'

'Fine. I'd been seeing Tony since Easter. He was coming with me, to New York.'

She searched my eyes for pain, rage – anything. I just felt blank. A hologram.

'Then he told me he wasn't coming with me. He was seeing someone else and he couldn't leave her because she was pregnant. Tara fucking Molloy. The slut.'

'Tara Molloy? The girl you sent over to me, for the abortion?'

'It's a very long story,' she smiled bitterly, her eyes peering into the past.

'How could he do that to me? I gave him everything. Everything.'

'But you said he tried to rape you. You lashed out in self-defence.'

'Jesus, Donal, don't make me spell it out.'

'But what I saw ... he forced himself on you.'

'You still haven't fucked anyone, have you, Donal? Well when you do, don't be afraid to get rough. Most women like being fucked properly.'

My head felt like it was no longer attached to my body.

'So you had sex with him. He told you that he wasn't coming with you, that he'd knocked up Tara Molloy. And you stabbed him. That's what he's been trying to tell me.'

She got to her feet, glaring at me all the while, her face puce with hatred.

'And you thought there was a chance I'd find out tonight, if I connected with Meehan. You couldn't risk it so you waited until I was stoned, pissed, asleep...'

'I've got nearly three years left on my tariff. I'm not going back to prison. No matter what it takes,' came her demented mantra.

I saw the knife shaking down by her side, in her clenched right fist, pointing behind her. I wheeled towards the kitchen door. She stepped in to cut me off, raising the knife above her shoulder so that it now pointed at my face.

'They taught me how to do this in prison,' she said, in autopilot now, all her energy focused on the knife scoping out my heart.

I stumbled backwards but her lunge was greater. As she flew towards me, the world stopped turning. Everything went into slow motion. Total soundless calm.

She flew past me, face down into the hard wooden floor. A figure followed through with a drop kick to the back of her head that sent a sickening thud ringing through the cold hallway.

'Is that rough enough for you?' screamed Fintan as her knife skidded along the fake wooden floor, all the way to the sitting room door.

He rolled her limp body over.

'I think I may even have out-scooped myself this time,' he congratulated himself.

I heard myself gurgle helplessly like a contented baby. My head felt insanely calm. My brain must have dosed me in preparation for traumatic death.

Fintan walked over and handed me a hipflask. He *was* film noir, after all.

I took a long draw, letting the liquor pinch me back to reality.

'How did you... What...?'

Fintan started pacing the hallway; all-knowing, buzzing on adrenaline.

'I spent the past week working on getting you both here,' he announced, 'I made sure Eve believed you have this gift. I figured it was the only way I could flush her out about what really happened here that night.

'But things kept getting in the way, like Gabby. I couldn't risk you falling for her, Donal. That would have stopped Eve from being able to talk you into coming back here.'

'What, so you...?'

Fintan nodded: 'The clothes slasher, the cut-tings.'

'You wanker,' I snapped.

'That's the thanks I get for saving your arse?'

I took a double draw on the single malt.

'The more Eve told me about it, the less I believed her story. But it made great copy. That's all she ever was to me. Great fucking copy.

'Come on! Let's get the fuck out of here.'

He offered me an arm. I let it hang. Too many questions squirmed like maggots in my brain.

'I don't understand. You helped Eve escape prison?'

'No, I didn't! I got everything I wanted from her and then I told her to plead guilty. Told her it would get her a lighter sentence. I couldn't believe it when they fell for that treaty shit. Come on.'

I ignored his demanding arm, and looked over at Eve's limp body. As blood trickled from her mouth, my mind flashed back to Marion Ryan sprawled across that landing. A horrific realisation hit home: if Eve died here tonight, the bitch's crazed spirit would torment me for all eternity.

'We better check that she's ... you know?'

Fintal walked over, leaned down and gave her face a couple of sharp slaps. Eve groaned.

'Don't bother getting up, love,' he sang to her.

'We should call an ambulance,' I said, 'and the Guards.'

Fintan laughed bitterly: 'You're kidding, right? Who would believe any of what went on here? It'd destroy all of us. Come on, I've rooms booked at the Bridge House.'

I didn't get up.

'Come on, Donal, for fuck's sake. She'll be alright.'

I refused to budge.

'Alright, we'll call an ambulance from a phone box. Now can we go?'

I ignored his arm and hauled myself up, feeling spent and idiotic.

Fintan opened the front door and stood aside.

'You're not going to write a story about this are you?'

'No, Donal. I think I'll save this one for the memoir.'

Chapter 46

New Scotland Yard, London
Monday, March 16, 1992; 10:00

'Commander Glenn?' I said, holding out my hand. 'DC Lynch. Please call me Donal.'

Glenn shook my hand lamely, glanced at me but thought better of taking a good look. He'd already made up his mind. I was a goner.

The convictions of Laura and Terry Foster for murder this week had triggered a media Blitzkrieg. Quite simply, the story had all the best elements – sex, lies, videotape and biblical comeuppance.

When they ran out of ways to re-interpret the avaricious sexual mores of Karen and Laura Foster and Peter Ryan, they began to look for other angles. A hungry, eagle-eyed agency reporter spotted a piece in medical bible *The Lancet* and deciphered that it could only have come from contact with an officer working on the reigning crime story of the year.

And so, on pages four and five of the up-and-coming *Sunday Herald* newspaper, the banner headline read: 'How Psychic Detective Brought Down Twisted Sisters.'

Of course, Lilian never sent me a copy for approval. She honoured her promise not to use my name but revealed my age, nationality and details about the case that anyone vaguely connected to it would have recognised right away.

Before I'd even seen the article, a curt pager message instructed me to attend a meeting with Commander John Glenn at Scotland Yard, nine a.m. tomorrow. I marvelled at the irony. My fate lay in the hands of Glenn, the senior cop whose devotion to Professor Richards' hocus-pocus forensic psychology derailed the Marion Ryan murder probe in the first place. I knew that Mc-Stay would have briefed him to the hilt, relishing the chance to bring down one of Shep's bitches.

'Please sit,' he said, scanning his psychotically well-ordered desk.

Glenn had the wavy brown hair, thick set, pinched pink cheeks and impenetrable inner confidence of a Tory Toff. He looked at some papers as I took in the view from his eighth floor office window at New Scotland Yard. I wondered what had happened to Old Scotland Yard.

Finally, in his own time, he spoke.

'Can I be frank with you, Donal?' he said, pronouncing it like Donald with a silent second 'd', just as Lilian had done.

'You've got a simple choice, Donal. You can do the decent thing and resign. Or you can hang on for an internal inquiry. I dare say though, we'll find enough grounds to get shot of you.'

'Get shot of me, Sir?' I said.

'This revelation is a total embarrassment to the Met. The only consolation is that you're so junior.

Otherwise it could have bankrupted us. The Fosters could appeal and sue. The family of Marion Ryan could sue. You do understand this, I trust?'

'I'd like there to be an inquiry. I want to give my side of the story, Sir,' I said flatly.

'Thought as much,' sighed Glenn, 'the Police Federation no doubt advised you to hang on for as long as possible so that you can keep bleeding us of your salary.'

'I've never spoken to the Police Federation, Sir,' I said.

He shifted in his seat, agitated, desperate to get something off his chest.

'*Your side of the story?*' he snorted with contempt. 'What's that then, that you have some psychic connection to murder victims?'

'Sir, that was Dr Krul's theory, not mine. My name isn't on the article.'

'So what do you have to say for yourself about this, er ... gift of yours then?'

'I just think my subconscious sometimes influences my dreams, and that helps me piece things together, Sir.'

His mouth contorted as if he'd just bitten into a dog-shit sandwich.

'Look Donal, the days of building a case against a suspect are gone. I thought you of all people would know that. Haven't you read about your compatriots, the Guildford Four and the Birmingham Six and what not?'

'And what not?' I said, surveying his over-privileged, jowly, smug chops.

A bomb went off in my head. Before I knew it, I had Glenn by the throat, pinning his flabby face

397

on the green leather surface of his ridiculous antique desk.

'Now I want you to listen to me, Commander Glenn,' I spat in his hairy ear. 'I want you to do something for me. I want you to repeat some words after me, understand?'

He mumbled incoherently, reddening until the port-induced, cracked-vein bundles in his face looked set to explode. I saw his free hand reach under the desk for a panic button and grabbed it, twisting it back until he yelped like a kicked puppy.

'What's the panic, Commander? Now, I want you to say the word *doughnut.*'

'What the blazes?' he began, so I pulled his arm to breaking.

'Doughnut,' whimpered Commander Glenn.

'Very good, Commander. Now I want you to say another word for me.'

He nodded desperately.

'Commander, I want you to say "Anal".'

'Anal,' squawked Commander Glenn.

'I bet you had plenty of that at the posh school, didn't you, Commander? Now, I want you to put them together. Can you do that for me, Commander?'

'Doughnut. Anal. What in God's name...?'

'Now I want you to drop the nut from doughnut and the A from anal. And put those words together. Do you think you could do that for me, Commander?'

'Dough Nal,' he wheezed.

'Again?' I barked.

'Dough Nal,' he repeated.

'One more time now, Commander. Both words together please?'

'DoughNal,' he said.

'Now that wasn't so hard, was it?' I said, letting go of him and, quite possibly, my career.

Chapter 47

Frank's Café, Clapham-Junction
October 1995

It always troubled me why Samantha and Jazmine Bisset – the mother and daughter so savagely butchered in East London – hadn't come to me for help. I'd stood next to their recently murdered bodies, just as I had with Tony Meehan and Marion Ryan. Tony and Marion led me to their killers. Why hadn't the Bissets?

When they didn't show, I put it down to two reasons:

A: I'd been deluding myself about having some sort of 'gift'.

B: They didn't need to come to me because I was already on the trail of their killer.

But I soon learned that my gift was real, whether you believed the scientific explanation or the metaphysical one. More dead people came to me in my dreams, and directed me to their killers. This just added to the torment: what the hell had I missed in the Bisset case?

Gradually, though, I let it go. Until one day,

and a chance sighting of a newspaper article.

The Met Police was criticised by an Old Bailey Judge today for missing 'countless' opportunities to catch a notorious serial killer and rapist. Robert Clive Napper, 29, of Plumstead, East London, was convicted of the murder of Samantha Bisset and her four-year-old daughter, Jazmine and detained indefinitely at Broadmoor Hospital.

Napper: the man who boasted about raping a woman on a common to his own mother. I'd flagged him up as a suspect in the Marion Ryan murder case.

I remembered Shep's patronising putdown:

Lynch, get the officers at Plumstead to check him out. Can you stick to solving this case for now?

Except I hadn't got the officers at Plumstead to check him out. I never raised the subject of Napper again, to anyone. I let my stupid male pride get in the way of doing the right thing. Again.

Of course, I couldn't have saved the Bissets. This 'gift' didn't bestow upon me the powers of a guardian angel to swoop down and rescue the doomed. I wished it had.

But, sitting in Tony's sun-drenched café that morning, I told Samantha and Jazmine Bisset that I'd learned to trust my gift, and promised them that I'd never miss a clue like that again.

The publishers hope that this book has given you enjoyable reading. Large Print Books are especially designed to be as easy to see and hold as possible. If you wish a complete list of our books please ask at your local library or write directly to:

Magna Large Print Books
Magna House, Long Preston,
Skipton, North Yorkshire.
BD23 4ND

This Large Print Book for the partially sighted, who cannot read normal print, is published under the auspices of

THE ULVERSCROFT FOUNDATION

THE ULVERSCROFT FOUNDATION

… we hope that you have enjoyed this Large Print Book. Please think for a moment about those people who have worse eyesight problems than you … and are unable to even read or enjoy Large Print, without great difficulty.

You can help them by sending a donation, large or small to:

**The Ulverscroft Foundation,
1, The Green, Bradgate Road,
Anstey, Leicestershire, LE7 7FU,
England.**
or request a copy of our brochure for more details.

The Foundation will use all your help to assist those people who are handicapped by various sight problems and need special attention.

Thank you very much for your help.